FAITHFUL

Also by Michelle Hauck

Birth of Saints Trilogy
Grudging
Steadfast

Kindar's Cure

Also by Michelle Hauck

Birth of Saints Trilogy
Grudging
Faithful

Kindar's Cure

FAITHFUL

Birth of Saints Book Two

MICHELLE HAUCK

An Imprint of HarperCollinsPublishers

This is a work of fiction. Names, characters, places, and incidents are products of the author's imagination or are used fictitiously and are not to be construed as real. Any resemblance to actual events, locales, organizations, or persons, living or dead, is entirely coincidental.

FAITHFUL. Copyright © 2016 by Michelle Hauck. All rights reserved. Printed in the United States of America. No part of this book may be used or reproduced in any manner whatsoever without written permission except in the case of brief quotations embodied in critical articles and reviews. For information, address HarperCollins Publishers, 195 Broadway, New York, NY 10007.

Digital Edition NOVEMBER 2016 ISBN: 9780062447173

Print Edition ISBN: 9780062447180

Harper Voyager, the Harper Voyager logo, and Harper Voyager Impulse are trademarks of HarperCollins Publishers.
HarperCollins is a registered trademark of HarperCollins Publishers in the United States of America and other countries.

FIRST EDITION

17 18 19 20 21   OPM   10 9 8 7 6 5 4 3 2 1

For everyone who finds they have a hero hiding inside.

FAITHFUL

CHAPTER 1

Ramiro held the reins loosely in his left hand and combed through Sancha's mane with his right. There hadn't been time to give his horse a proper grooming since the walls fell at Colina Hermosa two days ago, and guilt for neglecting the mare added to the burdens on his shoulders. Sancha would forgive him.

He was not so sure others would.

A patrol through the desert, looking for lost evacuees in the middle of the afternoon, was pure duty. No one would do so for fun. Yet, the missing people had to be found, and his brother, Salvador, had beat the precepts into his head: *Always see first to Colina Hermosa and its citizens, then fellow* pelotón *members, other military brothers, and last self.* Ramiro had always tried to do his brother proud.

Now that he was gone, Ramiro worked even harder to prove himself to Salvador.

Hot sunshine beat down on the back of his breastplate, turning the metal into an oven, and making sweat run freely. Heat waves shimmered off the packed sand of the hill ahead, and the air smelled of salty sweat, summer, and distant smoke. As he rode, his naked sword lay ready across his lap—the balancing act natural after years of practice. Not all the Northerners had thrown down their weapons or leapt to their death on the orders of an illusion of their god. It paid to be vigilant.

But no matter how hot or unpleasant, he'd much rather be on patrol, broiling in full armor and saving lives, than lugging corpses from the bottom of the quarry to the burn pile. And it was a thousand times better than sitting around with too much time to think.

It's way too hot to think . . .

Sancha's ears twitched, and Ramiro darted sharp glances to the men riding spread out on either side. A search-and-rescue party worked better with distance between them to cover more ground, but that meant most of his patrol was out of eyesight. He relied more on Sancha's senses than his own. Yet after hours of riding, even the nearest men rode on without a word, discovering nothing.

A pang of what could only be termed homesickness washed over Ramiro and a knot formed in his throat. Riding a patrol without his friends Alvito and Gomez created a hole in his gut. Orders given to him from a captain other than his brother stung, a painful reminder.

It had been over a week, but he felt their loss more keenly in the silence out here, only broken by the desert wind and calls of cactus wrens.

He unclenched his fist from Sancha's mane and forced himself to resume freeing an embedded sandbur from her hair. The new captain of the *pelotón*, Muño, was a good man. Ramiro had known him forever, and he'd been a loyal and capable lieutenant for years. The sergeant from the gate guards they'd brought in to replace Gomez seemed competent, too. But nothing was the same. Not the fact that he could never see his brother, Salvador, again, or that he could never return home to a city burnt by the Northern army.

He didn't even have Claire for company, having left the witch girl behind with his mother at the camp outside Colina Hermosa's shell as he attended to duty. His mother might not be a warrior—or approve of Claire—but she would do the best she could for his sake to guard the girl from the harassment sure to befall a witch. He just wished he felt right about leaving Claire with *anyone*. He also wished he could understand why he thought of her at all, considering he hadn't always worried for her safety.

"Hi-ya!" came distantly from his left.

Ramiro dropped the burr and scrambled to don his helmet and pick up his sword. To his relief the men closest to him did the same, proving just as unready. That call could mean anything from a party of aggressive Northerners, to a group of lost refugees, or simply a break to eat. Sancha picked up her feet and pranced as Ramiro used his knees to guide her toward the call.

"Steady, girl, steady," he told her. No matter what it was, there was time enough to assess the situation. He was no longer the naïve *bisoño*, striving to earn his beard and be considered a man. Those days of eagerly throwing himself forward were, like his brother and friends, also gone.

Ever watchful, his eyes tracked a bit of bright yellow peeking above an outcropping of rock. He dismissed it as a prickly pear flower, not important compared to the call, before his eyes jerked him back. The yellow was too large and too flat to be a flower. Considering the Northerners wore black-and-yellow uniforms, the color alone demanded he investigate as he passed. Ramiro edged Sancha in that direction and saw a piece of bright shirt. Cornering around the rock revealed a plump woman clutching two children to her breast, all three crouched small against the stone. They had the same brown hair and brown skin as himself, proclaiming they could not be the pale Northerners.

Eyes clenched shut, one boy had his hands clamped over his ears. The other boy had burrowed his face into the woman, as if her presence alone could save him. They trembled and shook in the grip of great terror, though all around them was calm.

A shiver ran up Ramiro's back. He glanced hastily around, but saw only sunshine, rocks, and cacti. What had happened here to instill so much fear?

"San Andrés protect us," the woman was chanting in a dry whisper. "Santiago shield us. San Andrés protect us. Santiago shield us. San Andrés . . ." When she lifted her head, eyes squeezed shut, he was shocked.

He knew her.

"Hi-ya!" Ramiro called out before sheathing his sword and swinging down from Sancha. "Over here! Survivors!" He stepped forward and grasped the woman's shoulder. "Lupaa, you're safe now." Even without the woman's apron, he recognized the motherly face of the citadel's head cook. The woman always ready to sneak him bread slathered in her special honey. What were the odds that of all the people of Colina Hermosa he should rescue someone he knew?

"What happened here?" he asked. "Lupaa!" He shook her.

Only then did her eyes open, slowly as if doing so pained her after clenching them too tight. But instead of greeting him, her gaze darted in all directions, passing over him.

One of the boys moaned and actually folded himself smaller, pressing into the rock. The new sergeant, Jorge, and a second soldier arrived and dismounted from their *caballos de guerra*. The horses had the same dapple-gray coloring as Sancha, and every *pelotón* member had their own bond with one of these intelligent animals.

"Report," Sergeant Jorge said. Everything about the sergeant spoke of precision and exactness to detail, from the crease in his uniform, to the careful placement of his equipment on his saddle. His beard, simple and cut close, reminded Ramiro painfully of his brother's.

No time for that now. Ramiro drew himself up. "Refugees, sir. This one is Lupaa from the citadel kitchen. One of my mother's cooks."

"It's not every *bisoño* who has his own chef," the other soldier teased. Gray tinted Arias's hair and spread liberally through his thick beard. The man had been a member of the *pelotón* for longer than Ramiro had been alive, but he remained lean and fit.

Ramiro bristled, but bit back a sharp retort lest he look childish in front of Sergeant Jorge. "I'm a rookie no longer."

Arias held out his hands. "Old habits. No offense meant."

Sergeant Jorge cleared his throat. "The matter at hand, *caballeros*."

Ramiro bent over Lupaa and met the woman's brown eyes, but found no recognition in them. "Lupaa." He snapped his fingers close to her face. "*Lupaa.*"

"Santiago shield us. San Andrés . . ." She started and recognition flooded back. "Ramiro? Thank the saints! Is it over? Tell me it's over."

"Over? What happened here? Why . . . this?" He waved a hand at her and the boys. "How did you get here?"

"I . . . we assembled at the Santa Teresa section of the city. Ran with the other evacuees when Colina

Hermosa's wall fell to let us out. I couldn't keep up." She gave the boys a squeeze, and one lifted his head. "My grandsons stayed with me. We ended up with a smaller group, going in what we hoped was the right direction."

"You are south of the swamp," Ramiro said. The evacuees from the city had been meant to head west for the swamp of the witches to hide, or to Crueses, the closest safe city. It was his father's plan to save the people of the city from the Northern army, and it had worked well . . . for the most part. But many of the people were too slow to stay with the soldiers guarding them, too old or weak, and had been left behind. "Off course. And then? Why this hiding?"

"Northerners found us. We took what shelter we could and prayed."

"Then the screaming started," the boy added.

Ramiro looked around again. There was no sign of Northerners or of other evacuees from his city. He turned to Sergeant Jorge and shrugged. Perhaps fear had caused Lupaa to imagine things. Maybe she mistook the normal sounds of the desert for the enemy.

"I told my grandsons not to look, never to look, and we prayed," Lupaa said. She struggled to set her legs under her, and Ramiro took her arms, levering her to her feet. "We prayed so hard." The taller boy, probably twelve winters old, stood under his own power. The smaller child still clung to his grandmother.

Sergeant Jorge waved Arias to go on ahead toward where the first call had originated. "You're safe now, ma'am. In our custody. Soldier, bring her and catch up with us." The sergeant followed after Arias, pulling his *caballo de guerra* after him.

"Hi-ya," Ramiro acknowledged, though the man had already forgotten about him. It shouldn't sting that the sergeant didn't remember his name. The man had barely time to learn all the officers, let alone every ordinary soldier under his command—though maybe he pretended not to remember in order to avoid showing favoritism toward the *Alcalde's* son.

Sancha sidled up against him, and Ramiro plucked a water skin from his saddle, offering it to Lupaa. "Drink." By the time they had all taken a turn, color was coming back to their faces and the younger child had his eyes open.

"You hid from the Northerners," Ramiro said. "How many were there? When did this happen?"

"Many," Lupaa said. "I could not count them all. They seemed to be everywhere, and we were few. Unarmed. We had just finished a noon meal. I ducked against the rock with my boys and prayed for the evil to stop. Thank you. Thank you a thousand times for saving us. My kitchen is always open to you. We owe you our lives."

"You are most welcome, but the danger was long gone." Ramiro glanced at the sun. If her story was true, they'd been against the outcropping for at least three hours. No wonder they looked to be in shock. But he couldn't quite figure out something: *Why had they stayed like that once the Northerners passed them by*? Something she had said bothered him. "You said screaming?"

The youngest put his hands back over his ears, eyes wide. "Horrible," the older said. "For hours." He shook, and Lupaa drew them close again.

Something didn't add up. The Northerners would have done their killing and moved on. Unless they'd spent time on some elaborate torture. That sounded like the enemy's way, but it made no sense. Claire had routed them, her magic sending them running like devils were in pursuit. Most believed the Northerners would not stop until they reached their distant homeland. Indeed, none of the patrols over the last day had met with sizable resistance, if any at all.

That *had* been a day ago, though, and things during war could change fast. What if the Northerners managed to regroup? His own people were far from recovered. Still in smaller groups and spread over distances, they reeled from the loss of their city and from the death around them. The people of Colina Hermosa were not up to fighting an organized enemy.

The feeling of unease along his spine grew, urging him forward to investigate. His mother's stories of the Sight in his family came to mind again, but this felt more like a suggestion than an outright warning of danger. "Which direction did the screaming come from?"

The boy pointed after the sergeant, and Ramiro gripped Lupaa's hand. He fixed a relaxed smile on his face to reassure her. "Wait here for me. Then I'll take you to the camps. Sancha, stay," he ordered. The warhorse would keep them safe for the few minutes it would take to scout around and discover what had happened here.

He pushed through a cluster of tall ocotillo, its thorny branches spreading out six feet in all directions. He could see that most of the fifteen members of his small patrol gathered in a spot ahead. The needles of a barrel cactus scraped against the steel of the greave below his knee. Too many flies filled the air. A rust-colored stain spotted the flat leaf of a prickly pear. He bent closer. *Blood.* Dried by the sun.

He soon spotted another splotch on a rock, and then larger discolorations in the dirt. Puddles he would have walked right past if not for the tingling along his spine, something he attributed to his share of the family Sight and his heightened awareness after Lupaa's strange behavior.

The first clump of what could only be flesh showed a few steps later, a torn and unidentifiable bit the size of his thumb. It could be from an animal.

He hoped it was from an animal.

Ahead, one of the soldiers vomited into the sand. Ramiro stopped, heart racing.

Saints.

An arm hung from the crook of a tall saguaro cactus, the skin intact and too pale to be from one of his countrymen. It ended near the elbow in a jagged tear. The hand was missing.

Ramiro's stomach rolled, the hair at the back of

his neck standing up. As Santiago had taught centuries ago, he touched mind, heart, liver, and spleen in quick succession to clear his body centers of negative emotion.

It almost helped.

That wasn't done with a sword or ax, he thought. *Nothing sharp.* None of the vegetation nearby looked hacked or disturbed as if a battle had taken place. He quickly spotted more body parts and pieces of flesh. Here a torso missing its head and wearing the bright colors of an evacuee. There, under a pincushion cactus, an ear. A scrap of fabric in the black-and-yellow of a Northern uniform. An eyeball under a buzz of flies. Blood covered everything, as if thrown from buckets. Too much blood even from the number of bodies he could see. The smell, sharp and metallic, filled the air. Some of it in the shade still looked wet.

He'd seen death many times in the last few days, but this wasn't death. These people had been torn apart.

This is savagery.

He scrubbed his hands on his breastplate and forced himself to join his fellow soldiers.

"A wildcat?" Arias was saying. "The Northerners didn't do all of this. There are more of them dead than civilians."

Sergeant Jorge shook his head. "Bears perhaps." It was clear, though, he didn't believe that either. Bears would kill for food, but this wasn't hunting. This was a massacre.

Ramiro remembered the white-robed priests of the Northerners and the rod they carried that could kill a man with one touch. His fellow soldiers hadn't seen the fanatical light in their eyes or witnessed their depraved cruelty. They killed from more than necessity. They *enjoyed* it. This must be a new devilry of the Northern priests. He could picture the fanatics killing their own soldiers for running from Claire's magic.

Claire.

Ramiro's heart leaped, and his hand darted to his sword hilt. If the Northern priests sought revenge, she would be their prime target. Claire was alone, except for his mother. The girl might have magic, but she was immature in so many ways. He had to return to the camp. "Sergeant, I'll escort the civilians we found back to safety."

Sergeant Jorge gave him an absent nod, waving off the flies. "Arias, go with him. The rest of you spread out and look for more survivors. Try and figure a count on the dead. See if anyone can find any signs of what happened here. Animal prints. Anything. Otherwise all we've got is a group of Northerners killed some refugees, then turned on each other. Insane devils."

The sergeant's voice fell behind as Ramiro returned to Sancha, only to be brought up short. He'd ridden double on Sancha before with Claire, but the girl was small and he'd been without most of his armor when it was left behind and stolen by that blackguard Suero. Now he wore borrowed armor . . . and Lupaa was no slip of a girl.

Arias arrived, and they traded glances, both aware of the difficulty. "I'll take the boys and you the woman," Arias said. "It's going to be a long walk back."

Ramiro turned to help Lupaa mount. The prickle along his spine demanded he hurry. Ramiro closed his eyes for calm as he realized his volunteering had actually harmed his cause. Camp was only a few hours away, but leading Sancha while the civilians rode meant they'd be lucky to be back by nightfall. The rest of the patrol would beat them there.

He just hoped his mistake didn't cost Claire.

CHAPTER 2

Claire concentrated on rolling the strip of cloth into the tightest bandage possible. Hard to do when the air in the large tent was stifling. Even with the flaps folded up to catch the nonexistent breeze and the sun setting, the heat pressed down inside like being trapped in a fiery forge instead of a pavilion of ladies working and chatting. Claire closed her eyes and held them for a count of three, but it did no good. Worse than the heat was the incredible dryness, mixed with the persistent smoke that even infiltrated their food and robbed it of taste. Her eyes ached, so tired from the lack of moisture in the air. And the inside of her nose . . . well, she was afraid to touch it for fear it would start bleeding. Fronilde said she'd grow accustom to it. That time couldn't come soon enough.

The tent, like so much else, was an unintended present of the Northern army. When that army had burned Colina Hermosa, no one had wanted to rescue tents over people. Very few even brought food with them out of the city. Thankfully, the Northern army had made a run for it and abandoned all their supplies, including many tents of all sizes. Even the cloth Claire rolled had once been a yellow uniform shirt of some Northern soldier.

Claire let her mind skirt away from why the army had thrown down their weapons and run like children with the boogeyman after them. Somehow it was entirely her doing, and she hadn't a clue how it came about. Two days ago, Ramiro suggested she Sing about the Northern god, Dal, just to save their own skins, and the result had reached beyond her wildest dreams, sending the entire army running instead of just the mob of thirty or so surrounding them. Now the people of Ramiro's city didn't know whether to treat her as savior or monster.

She wasn't sure herself.

With the cloth rolled as tight as she could manage, Claire attempted to tuck the end inside in the mysterious manner demonstrated by the other women. The roll should be solid as a brick if done correctly. She gave the final product a shake to be sure, and it unspooled in her hands. Anger flared over minutes wasted. She wadded the material up and shook it. *Ungrateful thing.* She'd done it exactly right. What would everyone think of her at being unable to roll a simple bandage?

"You're supposed to behave. Save lives," she whispered at it, hoping the low conversation around her would cover the sound. Everyone in her section of the tent wore black—or as much black clothing as they could scrounge—all having lost a loved one in the recent fighting. Ramiro's mother, First Wife Beatriz, had discovered Claire's own loss and bundled her up in a black dress donated from someone. Claire hated the color, but it was cooler than the old dress and trousers she'd worn to hike across the swamp a week ago—and cleaner. Yet, for its benefits, the black material would have done better made into bandages as it couldn't magically wipe away grief.

Fronilde took the failed bandage out of her hand. She wore a black band around her upper arm over a gray dress. "Watch." The older girl rolled the material and fastened it in half the time it had taken Claire, while the matrons around them nodded in approval. Fronilde did everything well. Claire could see her as the perfect wife for Ramiro's perfect brother. Now Fronilde made the perfect almost-widow. Almost, because the second set of banns had never been read by a priest, or so Beatriz explained it.

Claire sighed as a loud laugh and a chorus of giggles sounded from another section of the crowded tent. Everyone inside was female, except for the one guard set to watch First Wife Beatriz by her husband, *Alcalde* Julian, for fear she'd martyr herself again. Before the invading army panicked, Beatriz had gone in her husband's place to the Northerners with the rejection of their terms. But something about the bodyguard made Claire uneasy—his eyes watched her more than Beatriz.

In their corner, where the widows and orphans flocked, no one laughed. They talked only quietly, of somber things. Sadly, as an orphan herself, she fit right in. But she couldn't understand this muted mood. She remembered her mother with pride, and laughing at memories helped her heal. Like the black garments, these women embraced sorrow. It was almost as strange as their belief that bodies needed to be committed to the ground instead of burned properly to set the spirit free.

"You'll learn the trick of it," the miller's widow said, her fingers busy over her own work. Most of the females sitting around them were related to him, daughters and granddaughters. Pedro, the miller, had been an important man on the city council, and had an equally important family. Beatriz said getting their approval could establish Claire as someone to "know."

"Thank you," Claire said meekly. "I'm sure I will." She liked these ladies, especially Beatriz and Fronilde, but it was hard to be herself around them. They weren't the friends she used to dream of giggling and telling secrets with, though with time Fronilde might get there. They wouldn't argue or banter with her. They didn't tease and embarrass her. Gossip about fresh losses flowed somberly from their tongues, but as Claire didn't recognize any of the names, it made no sense to her. She could be more herself with Ramiro than these women.

She glanced outside to the darkening sky. "Shouldn't Ramiro be back by now?"

It was the wrong thing to say. Beatriz started and put a handkerchief to eyes filled with sudden worry. Fronilde and the others stared, their eyes shimmering with unshed tears.

"I mean," she stammered, "I'm sure he's well . . . I just . . . um . . . I miss him."

She'd put her foot in it now. Beatriz's eyes narrowed. The woman didn't like any mention of an association between her remaining son and a witch.

"We all miss him," Fronilde said too quickly. "And all the menfolk. The voting will have started."

Claire blessed Fronilde for changing the subject and leaped on her distraction. "Aren't you going to vote?" It was all they talked about yesterday: which candidate to support for councilman. Beatriz had been the most vocal of all, spreading her assertions far and wide.

Again the stares took aim at her, this time puzzled. "We don't vote," Fronilde said. "The men do that."

"But I thought you could," Claire pressed. To her understanding, several of the members of the city council, including Pedro, had been killed, and the people gathered to elect new ones. Any man who'd earned his beard or woman who wore her hair up could vote. With her blond braid coiled atop her head by Fronilde this morning, Claire wondered if that applied to her also.

"Certainly we *can*," Beatriz said. "It is our law. But

we don't *need* to. We tell our men folk what we think and they take care of it."

"But the decisions affect you, too. *None* of you are going to vote?"

"If our menfolk feel they need our vote, they'll cast it themselves."

Claire's mouth hung open. "They cast your vote for you?"

The ladies around her smiled. "If we cast our own votes, then they'd start telling us how to run the households or raise the children," said one girl who couldn't possibly be old enough to marry.

"Men have their areas and we have ours," Pedro's widow added.

"And if you know what you're doing, you run both," Beatriz said as others nodded their agreement.

"Oh," Claire said blankly. The idea of men doing anything for her was foreign. Her mother impressed upon her that men tried to control women and here was proof. These women could vote and had been tricked or scared out of it. It was just like her mother always said: Men couldn't be trusted. No Woman of the Song had anything to do with men. With the possible exception of Ramiro, Claire added to herself. Though if he tried to vote for her, she'd show him what she thought of that. "But isn't this sort of an emergency?" She gestured at the tent. "Is rolling bandages the most important thing to be doing? I mean things are different. I thought you'd be out in front . . . you know, helping . . . taking a larger part."

"Exactly," Beatriz said. "We are helping, by remembering how things work. When normalcy is stripped away, we carry on like it is not. So many are hanging on by their fingertips, especially the children. We remain calm and show them things have not changed so much."

Claire opened her mouth, but she couldn't argue. The children did need reassurance—likely the men folk did, too—and keeping things stable made sense. The calm these woman provided had comforted her, after all.

Yet still, the growing inactivity was starting to drive her crazy.

A little girl with curly brown hair appeared between Claire and Fronilde. She touched Claire's blond braid with a dirty finger. "Does it look like straw because of the magic?"

One of the matrons yanked the girl back before Claire could answer. Another girl, who had twined bandages around her wrists instead of rolling them, looked up. "Can you kill men with it?"

"No," Claire said, shocked into a hysterical giggle. She flushed as the women around her shushed the child. Why would anyone think that? She had killed no one.

"Silly," the curly-haired one said. "She makes men go mad with her voice. My pap said so. Can you show us? Try it on him." She pointed at the guard standing behind them, and the man flinched.

A chill passed over Claire. She'd not used her

magic since *that* day. "Frogs don't hop for fun," she said with a frown. "The magic isn't a game." By the Song, now she used the very argument her mother always employed to counter Claire's demand to practice her powers. But the words felt right.

"Where are your manners?" Pedro's widow said with a frown. "You've upset our guest." Women rose and quickly dragged off the inquisitive girls, taking them right out of the tent with scolds and whispered warnings about politeness. Claire's face grew hotter. Were they really worried about etiquette . . . or about letting their children close to a witch?

A fresh wave of laughter came from the other side of the tent, and this time Claire picked out the actual word "witch." More laughter and unsympathetic looks followed. The women sitting around Claire suddenly found other places for their eyes, avoiding her gaze, and hastily returning to their work.

Claire's shoulders dropped. Words shouldn't bother her, but moisture rushed to her eyes and now she blinked to hold back tears. Did they think her brainless? She knew they only tolerated her because her magic saved them or because Ramiro insisted. Still, it seemed that if there was a time to get over such pettiness, the tragedies they'd all faced would be it.

These may be Ramiro's people, but they seem nothing like him.

Strangely, that thought led to another: that she missed Teresa, though she barely knew the woman. The woman who dressed like a man and taught at the university would have stood up for her. But Teresa had been left behind in the swamp. Who knew if she even lived?

Not for the first time, Claire reconsidered her decision to stay when Ramiro had asked her. She'd lingered out of curiosity—and truthfully because it felt good to be needed—but they didn't need her now with the Northern army defeated. She could return to the swamp and away from so many people. Despite her hopes of friends and community, she felt awkward here. Reason said she'd get used to their ways, but being around so many folk made her want to hide. Everything pressed down. The walls of the tent shrunk, pinning her in, and smothering her. It became hard to breathe.

She reached for a fresh strip of cloth, only to have her hand shake. She snatched the material and began to roll it, trying to shut out everything else, including her own doubts.

Before she could find a semblance of peace, though, someone shouted. Ladies screamed. Claire looked over her shoulder at the noise. A brown-bearded man in a poncho and a floppy hat ran in her direction. "My family is dead, because of the evacuations. Because of you."

Claire gasped. He seemed to be talking to Beatriz, then his gaze found Claire.

"Witch!" His outstretched hand suddenly held a long butcher knife. "Witch! Stay away from us! Murderer! Abomination! Die!"

Fronilde dropped to the ground, but Claire couldn't move. Surprise robbed her brain of a Song to stop him. Even the words of the Hornet Tune, which she knew as well as her name, deserted her. The man closed as everyone scrambled out of his way. Then Beatriz sprang from her chair to stand over Claire, holding up her hand. The tall black-lace mantilla atop her head waved like a flag. "Stop."

Something about the authority in the First Wife's voice—or maybe her simple resistance instead of cringing or scrambling away—brought the man up short, making him pause for a moment. Just the moment the bodyguard needed to crush the lunatic to the floor and overpower him, wrestling free the knife. More guards came running from outside.

Breath rushed back in Claire's lungs. Beatriz sniffed and touched a spot on her chest over her heart and then her forehead and stomach areas. "Imbecile. He didn't know who he was dealing with."

Laughter exploded from Claire. It simply took over, pushing past her common sense at the ridiculous sight of the motherly figure as her savior. She threw her arms around Beatriz and, despite the woman's flinch, sobbed into her shoulder, all the frustration and fear working loose. The loss of her mother hit home again.

"There. There." Beatriz patted her back awkwardly. "He was just some poor soul who can't handle his loss. I told my son I'd see you safe. I'll not have him come back to find you dead. That would never do. He'd never forgive me."

Claire pulled back to see if the woman was joking, but Beatriz was wiping a tear. Claire scrubbed the tears from her own cheeks before the women getting to their feet around them could notice. The guards hustled the man and his knife outside.

"He tried to kill me," Claire said. The world reeled around her. How could this happen? They didn't like her and called her witch, but to try to kill her? "Why? I saved them."

Beatriz sniffed. "My husband would say grief makes people do crazy things. They need someone to blame. You are an easy target. Julian may be partly right, but I think there's more. I say they forgot their God and their good sense. It could just as easily have been Julian they went after, though he came here for me. I've seen it often enough—thankfully usually with words. Call it the price of standing out from everyone else."

"But I don't want—"

Beatriz gave a nod. "Did you think to escape notice? Sorry—the world doesn't work like that. Now then, it's over. It doesn't help to dwell on it. Let's talk about other things. I told Ramiro to keep an eye out for my dogs, you know, when he is out patrolling. They should be with my maid. If he finds them, you shall have one. Wonderful how dogs can make a body feel less grief. When you can't have your husband with you . . . they can make a death . . . like . . . a son's . . . easier."

A sob burst from Beatriz. "Salvador. My baby . . ."

She closed her eyes for a moment and her throat worked before she recovered. "But enough of that. Tea. Tea is what we need now. Tea and a visit to Father Telo. Fronilde, you, too." The First Wife strode for the nearest opening. "Come along, girls. Don't dawdle."

Tea? How would tea help? As if it wasn't hot enough? But it did sound good to depart this tent. Claire lifted her skirt to step over a basket of spilled bandages, trying to push aside the uneasiness that made her want to flee home to the swamp. Her knees wobbled, almost betraying her, the shock still fresh.

Despite Beatriz's instruction, she couldn't stop thinking about the man's attempt on her life. Maybe he was extreme and had never met her, but did the others feel much different? Were they being polite when they shushed the children or did they fear her magic? She felt small and lonely, caught in a world she didn't understand.

As she followed Beatriz from the tent, she couldn't help but review her hasty decision to stay here. Besides her curiosity about the city people, she'd also stayed to have someone she could rely on as she practiced the Song. But she barely saw Ramiro, and he was really the only person left she trusted. But no—he was always off with the other soldiers, honoring *his* duty. And so she'd not let the Song touch her lips since she'd sung to scare the Northerners. A shadow descended over her at the notion of using the magic again.

She shivered, feeling sick to her stomach. The longing to run built.

Her mind skittered away from that line of thought, unwilling to define it, grasping at weak excuses. Her magic could not put out fires or rebuild walls. She was of no use here. All she did was miss her home and cause awkwardness when these people had enough to deal with.

She nodded; the decision made. She'd talk to Ramiro. They owed each other that much. When he came back from patrol, she'd tell him her doubts—her wish to return home. Feeling better at having made a decision, she took Fronilde's offered hand and hurried after the First Wife.

CHAPTER 3

At long last camp neared and Ramiro wasn't sure whether he and Arias were more relieved or the civilians they escorted. Ramiro found it hard to keep his eyes from drifting to the grave of Colina Hermosa, as though somehow, if one watched long enough, the image would change, become whole again. Even with the setting sun outlining the city in brilliance and blinding the eye, the changes leapt out. What structures remained standing above the protective walls—such as *they* were—were blackened and dull, the usual mass of pristine white buildings gone. Smoke rose in spots, unquenched after two days, and a cough persisted throughout the camp. A perpetual haze hung over the once grand city, barely parting when the wind lifted, making it impossible to see the gaping hole where once the citadel stood at the crest of the center hill. The great bronze gates hung yet, the heat unable to melt them, but they were now buckled and warped, never to close again. Forcing himself to look at it brought no closure.

Only more anger.

And he knew who deserved that anger—and it wasn't just the Northerners. If only the other *ciudades-estado* had just banded together, his city would still exist. His people would have homes.

Instead, Colina Hermosa had become a scar on the desert soil. Soon enough it would return to the sand and leave nothing but a legend to mark its last resting spot.

His father, *Alcalde* Julian, had made camp on the vast plain before the city, in the same spot abandoned by the Northern army. There, they remained, with hearts too fragile to move far from their destroyed home. To leave would be admitting it truly lost.

But it was lost. And the futility of that thought fueled the slow-burning rage in his soul.

As if feeling something similar, Lupaa touched heart, mind, liver, and spleen. "And no one has been inside?" Behind her on the second horse, her grandsons wept.

Ramiro had no tears left. "No. Well, yes," he corrected. "Some tried, but found it too hot. They didn't have much success. The *Alcalde* posted guards at every opening to keep the citizens away. It just isn't safe with so many fires burning to have people roaming all over. They have sent in a few teams to uncover the nearest wells, though. Water will soon be our biggest concern." They were already rationing it, even having confiscated the supply left by the enemy army.

"Perhaps something can be saved when it cools. Rebuilt."

Lupaa said what was repeated whenever two of his countrymen met, the phrase recurring so often it seemed on everyone's tongue. Ramiro had said it himself more often than he could count. Now he grunted and let Arias answer her. Some things went too deep for words. The loss of a city. The loss of a brother.

Sancha whickered unhappily, showing the whites of her eyes. Ramiro patted his mare's neck. Either she caught his unease, or somehow she sensed the burnt hulk marked the destruction of her kind also. Sancha had saved his life so many times and now that opportunity to bond was lost to others for the foreseeable future. Before the Northern army began the siege around Colina Hermosa, they'd brought all of the precious *caballos de guerra* bloodline inside the walls to safeguard them. All the dapple-gray horseflesh that made pairing with a *pelotón* soldier so special, including the breeding stock: all the mares that were pregnant or in estrus, the foals—and worse—the stallions . . .

When the fire started, no one had come to their rescue. Most guessed they died still inside their stable. Alone and in terror of a horse's mortal foe: fire. The image twisted Ramiro's guts to knots. The majority of *caballos de guerra* that survived were mares like Sancha or geldings like Arias rode. It would be years before new *pelotón* members would be able to form the important, unbreakable bond with their horse again—if the bloodline ever fully recovered.

Just one more depravity to lay at the Northerners' feet. One more failure of the other *ciudades-estado* for not aiding. The people of Colina Hermosa had done their part and almost succeeded. The anger threatened to overwhelm Ramiro, and he fought to remember that many still lived. To dwell on such dark thoughts would be to sit down and never get up again.

And there was still so much to do.

The camp sprawled out ahead of them, guardsmen nodding and calling greeting as they approached the perimeter, recognizing their own. The people of Colina Hermosa spread over three camps, with this settlement being the largest, and like Lupaa, stragglers filled the open countryside in between. A second camp was organized halfway between Crueses and here; and a third lay nearly to the swamp of the witches. He hoped Teresa had taken charge of that one, but no one had yet returned from making contact with it. Patrols like his brought in more people every day as they waited on the *Alcalde* and the *concejales* to decide where to go and what the people should do.

Though Ramiro had only been gone a day, improvements in the camp abounded. More makeshift tents had risen, made from blankets. People filled the pathways, going about their usual tasks as best they could. With no water for washing, women strung clothing from lines and beat them with sticks or the ends of spears to knock off sand and ash. Children ran and played as if a battle hadn't just happened here. With unspoken agreement, the site had been laid out along the same lines as the city. The tent of the *Alcalde* resided at the center, exactly like the citadel. It was there Ramiro aimed his steps.

The pathways through camp mimicked the roads of Colina Hermosa, making it easy to find his way. Even without anything to sell, merchants set up their bedding on the same avenues where their shops and homes had once stood, leaving space for missing neighbors. Residential areas sprang up to correspond to their old locations. Priests marked out cathedrals and more modest mud-dab churches, laying comforting hands on the dying and speaking wisdom to the worried. Soldiers bedded down at the perimeters. It all felt very much the same, while looking vastly different. Only the large healer tents for the injured were new.

The largest of the Northern tents had been given over to the wounded or sick—a situation Ramiro hoped would go unneeded soon. The people of Colina Hermosa had bought their peace with much sacrifice. It had to last. The thought of the Northerners returning sent a flood of cold across his skin. The unease, which had started on patrol, lingered. The sight of the slaughter continued to flash before his eyes. He walked faster, eager to finish his duty and be free to find Claire and his family.

In silence, they reached the center of the camp and the area set aside to replicate the citadel. Ramiro bypassed the carpets stretched over spear points assembled for his parents' sleeping quarters. It was clearly empty. The council tent next door had its flaps down, and bodyguards with crossed spears out front said *Alcalde* Julian held a conference inside and interlopers would not be welcome. Claire's small tent sat halfway between, but as a person had to crawl their way inside, Ramiro doubted she spent her free time there. No, the girl would be off with Beatriz.

Ramiro tamped down his disappointment and led the group behind his parents' tent to where the citadel servants had used Northern wagons and planks torn from others as a makeshift kitchen area. They'd turned industriousness to inventiveness: a cutting board stood atop a flour barrel, spurs pounded in a plank became hooks for cookware.

He helped Lupaa slide off Sancha. The head chef hurried forward with a grandson under each arm to be engulfed by her fellow cooks, grooms, butlers, and the other servants who had always kept the thousand-year-old citadel a shining masterpiece. They welcomed her in like the family they were, giving her time for only a small wave and a thank you thrown to him over her shoulder. Later, she'd have a snack for him, and while it wouldn't include her famous honey, she would find something special.

He smiled, happy to see her settled and safe. Relieved for even a bit of happiness.

"I'm headed back to barracks for a drink and shut-eye," Arias said. The older man had removed his helmet and gauntlets since they'd entered camp, and tugged at the top of his breastplate to let in a breath of air. "I can report for the both of us, if you want to stay here."

"Hi-ya," Ramiro acknowledge gratefully. "I owe you."

Arias waved it off as he turned his horse. "Nothing owed between brothers."

Brothers. The word cut like a sharp slap, though Arias meant it kindly. And he was right. Ramiro had not just one brother, but hundreds of them, all watching his back, all invested in his life. His military brothers didn't replace Salvador, but they would try. Ramiro dashed at his eyes before someone could see the wetness.

"Come on, Sancha. Where do we find Claire?"

The mare rolled an ear and stamped, raising a puff of dust. When he pulled on the reins, she stayed stubbornly in place.

"Here?" Ramiro asked her. "Claire's not here. Come on. We need to find her. She could be in danger."

Sancha started forward, going straight to the rocky ground where the servants had staked out sleeping spots and left their few possessions. She stopped before the oiled tarp covering Ramiro's own things and shook as if brushing off flies.

Ramiro rolled his eyes. "It's not time to bed down. Claire." He remembered the people torn to bits and shuddered. That couldn't happen to Claire. Yet rushing out to find her without a plan wasn't likely to succeed. He stared out at the camp. It wasn't as big as the Northern army, but large enough.

His mother had resumed all her usual activities, and knowing her, she was probably dragging Claire with her. Beatriz could be anywhere: visiting the injured, at one of the many makeshift, outdoor churches, paying calls on the other ladies, sitting with Fronilde, or having tea in a tent somewhere. While he searched one spot, she could have moved on to another or even doubled back to someplace he'd already been—if he didn't walk right past her. He groaned. It might be faster to wait here. Besides, there would have been some outcry if something had happened to Claire, and she did have a guard.

Sancha pawed the ground again. "You win," he told the mare. "We'll wait here." His instinct didn't shout out a warning as it had before when they'd been close to the Northerners. What he felt was more like the electric smell of the air a day before a storm arrived. Trouble hadn't happened, but it headed in their direction. Waiting might let him reach Claire sooner than rushing around like a chicken butchered for the soup pot, but if she didn't come soon, he might tear apart the camp to find her.

He couldn't say why, but he knew time was definitely a factor.

Ramiro took off all his armor and padding and left it on the tarp to be cleaned later. He kept his sword belted on and his knives securely in place, then removed Sancha's tack and got out his curry comb and hoof pick. He could placate his horse if nothing else.

By the time he finished and got the mare settled, the first stars graced the sky. He stared at the lights inside the council tent, outlining the dark human shapes around an equally dark table. The meeting went long. What would become of the people of Colina Hermosa? Would they return to the nomadic life of small groups they'd lived before the arrival of Santiago and the other saints thousands of years ago to civilize them? The men inside that tent, including his father, would decide. He prayed the saints sent them wisdom.

Claire took a seat on a flat-topped rock low to the ground. After being with people all day, she was glad to find Ramiro alone except for his horse. Or as alone as possible in this camp. Servants bustled about a few yards away, but the darkness seemed to wall them apart. The stars made a river above them, as lonely and distant as her heart.

Not only would speaking to him alone make telling him about her decision to depart easier, she was grateful for the quiet. How did Beatriz stand doing nothing but talking all day? Of course as the First Wife, she had others to make her food, wash her clothes, and even smooth her bed. But to do no chore other than flit from place to place all day? To never have the satisfaction of producing a successful batch of soap or storing enough food for the winter?

How did a person live without accomplishing anything?

Ramiro hadn't noticed her approach, facing the other direction with hands on hips. Claire remained as quiet as a pack rat. Even before they become friends, she'd enjoyed tricking him, creeping up on him, or doing the unexpected. It never got old. Unfortunately, she had a task to do and couldn't spend time amusing herself.

She tossed a pebble, creating the clink of stone striking stone. She bit back a snicker when Ramiro jumped and turned to discover her on a rock not a yard from him. He'd been so deep in thought he hadn't noticed her approach, despite the light now blazing across the sands from the lamps in Beatriz's tent not twenty yards away. Sancha whickered a greeting and went back to her grain. Claire tossed another pebble, then smiled at Ramiro.

"When did you get here?" he asked. "I was just going to look for you."

"A few minutes ago." She placed her arms around her drawn-up knees, a pleasant glow flickering inside at sneaking up on him. Shadows melded his skin into his equally brown clothing, still the width of his shoulders stood out well enough. "You didn't even hear me."

He squinted one eye. "You used magic, is what you did."

She wiggled on the rock, uncomfortable at the

reminder, not wanting to admit that she hadn't. Her failure this morning still stung. She hadn't protected herself, but had let Beatriz stand between her and the knife. The words and the will just hadn't appeared, not even to save her life. Perhaps Beatriz had accomplished more than Claire gave her credit for after all. "Maybe. Your patrol went well?"

"Well enough. We found three lost souls and brought them back. Didn't see any living Northerners." He paused as if he had more to say, but then said, "And you? You're well?"

"Well enough," she echoed. She ducked her head down, finding it hard to tell him of the knife man. It would only make him fight her decision more.

"Mother kept you busy?" When she didn't answer, Ramiro frowned. "What happened?"

She struggled for a lie, but her mother raised her too well. She couldn't even think of a way to tone the words down to sound better, but if she didn't tell him, someone else would. "Someone tried to kill me."

Ramiro had his knife out and moved to stand over her, before she drew a breath. His jumpy reaction surprising her. They were safe enough at the moment. "A Northerner? How did they sneak in?"

"No." Her head stayed down. She hated to disappoint him. She'd hoped he wouldn't ask. Why did he always dig so deep? "One of your people."

"My people." The knife in his hand trembled. "No. They couldn't . . ." She watched him stop as realization that they could and had grew across his face.

Anger tightened his features. "Of all the ungrateful—" he sputtered.

"It's over, and I'm not harmed. But . . . I was thinking"—this was even harder to say—"maybe I'll go home—just for a bit."

"No. You told me you'd stay." He rammed the knife back into its place.

The decisiveness of his answer made it her turn to be surprised. "You have your soldiering and your family. You'll be busy enough . . . and I'm not really needed anymore. The Northerners are gone." All true, if she could just convince him.

"Rubbish." He took a step back, eyes narrowing. "Don't put on that mulish face. That's nothing but excuses. What's really going on? Was it mother? Did she say something?"

"No. She was . . . she supported me."

He swung around to stare off into the night. "They hurt your feelings. Called you witch. Well, to hell with them. You'll stay with me from now on. I'll make time for you."

She climbed to her feet. "Now who's being mulish? When you're on patrol? Guard duty? That won't work. It's best this way. I don't fit in here, and I never will. They're nice enough, but I make them nervous." If she left, Ramiro could go on being the hero, and no one would look at him funny because he protected the witch anymore. They would stop whispering behind his back. If saving their people didn't earn their gratitude, nothing would. Staying would only drive him to step away from the people he loved most in order to defend her.

Clearly he disagreed. He turned back and caught her hand, as if he could physically keep her from going. "Give it time. They will."

She shook her head sadly. "It's not just about them, you know. This isn't my home. Maybe it's about what I want. I wanted to learn about this place and I have. Maybe I miss the swamp. I'm ready to leave."

Deep down a tiny voice called her out, shouting *liar* at her. Wasn't the real reason because if she went back to the swamp she could keep hiding from her magic? Stay here and Ramiro or someone else would pressure her to use it, thinking it what she wanted.

He dropped her hand. Now she'd hurt his feelings. He'd never believe his home wasn't the place for everyone. That their ways, possibly, weren't best for all.

"And if the Northerners come back?" he asked.

"Well, you'll know where to find me." They'd discussed that possibility. He'd agreed never to force her to sing that Song again. The Song had removed the Northerners, but had been foul, evil. She couldn't stand to touch on the memory of that magic—

Or any magic.

Her legs wobbled and she sat back on the rock before Ramiro could see. But his sharp eyes missed nothing.

"What else is wrong?"

She tried to say "nothing," to laugh him off, but the words tumbled out. "When the man came at me with a knife today, I froze. I couldn't use the Song. I forgot all about it until too late. Your mother stepped in front of me. I put her in danger." Cold swept over her, the fear from that moment returning. What if it happened again and someone died? What if instead of her, it were an innocent or a friend's life in danger? Would she freeze again? "It was a stroke of luck that I stopped the Northerners. I don't know anything about the magic. I'm not really any good, any use—"

"Rubbish," he said again. "If anyone is strong, it's you. I see it in you every day. You wouldn't have let my mother be hurt. Turning back the Northerners was no fluke. The only fluke was today. It won't happen again. And you can learn about the magic. I thought that was your plan."

A blush spread over her features at his compliments, and she was glad he couldn't see it. He'd always believed in her more than she did. "That's as may be, but I'm still going."

"I can't let you do that. It isn't safe for you to leave camp or be alone." Then he told her of what he'd seen on patrol that day—the people torn apart by some new Northern cruelty—and his anxiety that they would come after her next.

The cold wasn't in her imagination now. Frosty tendrils of fear spread out from her heart, snaking down each limb, and turning her fingers to ice. The Northerners killed and killed; they delighted in nothing else. Mules, children, women. What would they do to the one who had disrupted their army? The one who made assured, confident men run off a cliff? She knotted stiff fingers together as bile rose in her throat.

"Perhaps it was some new torture of their priests' magic," Ramiro said.

Claire followed his gaze into the darkness where Ramiro bedded down to sleep. Both knew what lay rolled up in his extra shirt and hidden at the bottom of his pack: a slim white rod as long as a forearm that they'd taken from a Northern priest. The rod that could kill with a touch. It had to be magic of a kind they couldn't understand. Neither of them had the desire to bring it to the light of day, but now they might not have a choice.

Though it didn't tear bodies into tiny pieces or rip off arms as Ramiro described seeing today. As far as they could tell, the rod simply caused hearts to stop—although there was nothing quite so "simple" about it. The only other thing they knew was that it had failed when it touched Ramiro wearing his entire suit of armor. Something about the metal had repelled the magic so it injured and caused pain, but failed to kill.

Ramiro pointed at the council tent. "My father might be able to tell us more about it. He gets reports on everything."

"And if he can't, I think I know someone else to

ask," Claire said. One of their visits today had been to Father Telo. The dark-skinned priest had been unusually hushed, listening more than speaking during their brief time in the healer tent. He'd suffered the loss of his hand, cut off in some Northern sacrifice. But the man had spent time as a prisoner with the enemy. He'd be the most likely to know what their magic could do—if he would speak about it.

"My father will also know if the Northerners are regrouping," Ramiro said. "He sent scouts after them within hours of their stampede. He'll have ideas, so we can figure out what we're facing."

Claire wanted to laugh. Wanted to say they faced nothing at all, except too much imagination. That she could walk back to her swamp alone and face nothing scarier than the animals who lived there. Yet, the feel of unseen claws sinking into her shoulders kept her silent and hunched her spine against eyes that weren't there. They both felt it. Men were the worst sort of beasts.

"You'll stay until we know more, even if I have to sit on you," Ramiro said.

A picture rose in her mind's eye of being alone in the swamp, milking the goats, and having dozens of Northerners creep up on her. Of her magic sticking in her throat and refusing to save her as a horde tore her apart.

"I'll stay, but only until we know more," she said finally. "And don't think it's because you said so. I make up my own mind." She expected him to smirk at that, but his face remained grave.

"I'll speak to my father as soon as he's free."

They both turned to look at the council tent, filled with light and old men arguing the future of a people.

CHAPTER 4

Inside the tent, Julian let the arguing and raised voices of the *concejales* float past him. Since the battle he found it harder and harder to put an effort into anything he did. Where before he would have intervened and steered the *concejales* in the direction he preferred, now he couldn't decide on a heading, let alone chart a course. His certainty gone, he sat lifeless, hands folded around his chin, lost in contemplation as he pretended to study the reports in front of him.

Years and years ago, he'd begun work on what he termed his landscape of self. In his younger days, the terrain had been hard to negotiate, filled with cliffs and valleys, rough and ever-changing and driven by whim. As he aged, he'd filed down the hills of self-doubt. He'd filled in deep fissures of uncertainty with set principles and goals. He'd groomed confidence in his choices until his inner landscape became a flat plain of stone. A broad and easy road ran down the center, allowing him to make his way wherever he needed to go. Every day took him a step farther down the road, certainty making it a little smoother.

Then the Northerners arrived.

His inner landscape grew bumpy—boulders appeared—but he'd navigated them. They were a slowdown, not impassible obstacles to his convictions. The years of work he'd done on knowing himself allowed him to conquer difficulties.

Then came his eldest son's death.

Suddenly, a chasm opened down the center of the road and grew deep and wide. When Beatriz had surpassed his expectations of her character and gone to the Northerners in his place, it had terrified his heart and resulted in his left arm having a weak grip. Hours later, the city he'd sworn to guide and protect burned, and the chasm began to grow with each minute that passed. It became a bottomless canyon, stretching to the horizon, and no longer stable—the landscape shook as if suffering a constant earthquake. His decisions that had led to the failure of his family, of his city—were the cause. On the outside, he tried to appear as before, yet inside, he teetered on the edge of the canyon. He hadn't the ability of a younger man, such as his son Ramiro, to rebound. In this, age was not his ally.

For two days, he'd let the people remain without direction. Oh, he'd done the smaller things: providing organization of food and water, sending out scouts, setting up protection, but at the larger issues he'd failed. It wasn't like agreeing on the amount of an olive oil subsidy or deciding where to put the tax to pay for a new city park. The choices made here would affect his people for generations to come. How could he decide where his people should go—how they should act—when he couldn't find his own way? After the damage he'd wrought, how could he ever trust he had the correct answers?

What good came of learning to live in the present, if the present were unbearable?

Words of resignation hovered on the tip of his tongue. He would tell the *concejales* of his determination to step aside and let one better equipped become the leader. Let him put the yoke aside in order to focus on healing himself and his family. That was enough burden.

Julian opened his mouth to tell them, and *Concejal* Lugo's hand came crashing down on the table, jarring the water in the cups by their elbows. Everything in the tent, from the water to the chairs, came from the Northerners—all except the icon of Santiago that *Concejal* Diego had carried next to his heart during the evacuation. In the small painting, the founding saint of Colina Hermosa held a book and his staff, and his eyes beamed at them serenely with perfect conviction. A conviction Julian could no longer find.

"We remain here," Lugo said. "The city will cool and then we can go back inside. Something must be salvageable. We will rebuild."

Julian had expected this from Lugo: all his worldly wealth was tied up in his stores, to leave them would be impossible for the grasping merchant. Julian also expected to see two other heads nodding along. The two craftsmen on the council, Osmundo the potter and Sarracino the weaver, sold their wares in Lugo's stores, derived all their income from it, and their votes corresponded accordingly. But he hadn't predicted agreement from landowner Diego, though it made sense. Diego would no more want to leave his acreage than Lugo his stores—burnt or not. The other landowner, Adulfo, had died in the evacuation, advanced age and his heart unable to handle the excitement. That made four votes in favor of staying and two seats at the table empty with the additional death of Pedro.

Lugo continued, "There is no sign the Northerners intend to return—"

"Yet," Antonio interrupted. "The scouts have not reported." Most of the scouts forsook horses for better stealth on their own feet. This would slow them down.

"Yet," Lugo allowed. "We are better off here—inside broken walls is better than no walls."

"Whole walls would be the wisest of all," Antonio repeated for the third time, being as stubborn as the bulls he sometimes slaughtered in his occupation as butcher. "I say we break our people into groups and send them into the other *ciudades-estado*."

"There is no guarantee the other cities would accept our people inside their walls," Lugo said.

"If each group included a *pelotón* of soldiers I believe they would," Antonio argued. "Every city would give much for more trained soldiers. Our people would be safe."

"But we would no longer *be* a people." Lugo sneered. "You would have us split up. Our identity would be lost. Colina Hermosa would truly cease to exist."

"But our people would *live*. Isn't that the point of everything we've done and everything we've lost?"

Lugo looked away, his face set in disgust. "And if it had been done differently, would we have lost so much? If the attack on the Northerners had been held back to the agreed-upon time—at dawn—the city might not have burned. We would have had men inside the walls to fight the fires."

Julian stared at the papers before him. And so the blame started.

"The witch girl rid us of the Northerners," Osmundo added. "We could have stayed within the walls. It was a mistake to evacuate in the first place."

"That's unfair." Diego stroked his long beard as he did when agitated. "No one could have predicted—"

"No, we could not," Lugo agreed. "As we didn't even know such an expedition had been sent to the witches in the first place. How could such a thing have been attempted without the consent of the council? It is against law—against precedence." The potter and weaver nodded along. "It is a crime worthy of expulsion from the office of *alcalde*."

"You would not have agreed," Julian said tiredly. "I did what had to be done." It made no matter to defend himself—words could not undo the loss or make his guilt any less heavy. He didn't need the *concejales* to bring it home. It was already burned into his bones.

"And with the result that we've lost the city—after losing many of our children to your mistakes." Lugo stabbed a finger at the table. "I say we bring it to a vote. *Alcalde* Alvarado moved up the attack for personal reasons—to save his wife. He cost us the city with that faulty decision."

Antonio shot to his feet, knocking over his stool. "That decision was made by myself and Pedro."

"And we know how independent *your* thinking is. You follow our leader like a dog." Lugo rose from his seat, the normally mild merchant going nose to nose with the hulking butcher.

"*Caballeros*," Diego interposed, wringing his hands. "You forget yourselves." Sarracino jumped between them, pushing them apart.

Tempers ran high today, not a usual occurrence. The elderly men of the council seldom acted the part of young hotheads, more apt to think first than react. The last days had shortened many levels of patience, and not just among the *concejales*. Julian witnessed it everywhere.

Julian sank lower in his seat, squeezing his fists, the left refusing to close fully or tighten, the strength gone from it. A reminder of all he'd done wrong. Still, there were procedures to follow and he'd stick to that.

The end would come soon enough. "A vote will be held on my removal—once the two empty seats are filled. So says the law."

Antonio and Diego regarded him with deeper furrows on their already-lined brows, obviously concerned by his lack of defense and leadership at this meeting. *And they should be—that's why I do this.*

"So says the law," Lugo said more bitterly. A vote now would guarantee Lugo's wishes prevailed. Yet, his chances remained just as good once the seats were filled on the morrow, Julian knew. The candidates rumored to be the favorites were cronies of Lugo's or likely to be swayed by him. With that knowledge, the store owner sat, drawing his chair closer to the table.

"We may handle smaller matters while we have empty seats, day-to-day matters," Lugo said, as a satisfied smile crossed his sour face. "I bring to this body that we should have a stiffer guard on the witch. Why is she allowed to go where she will, with the highest citizens of our people? She is dangerous and should be locked up, just like the Northern demon and other soldiers we captured. She puts us at risk."

Julian couldn't repress a frown. For the first time, anger tightened in his chest. Attacking him was one thing. Now, they attempted to lower him by going after his associations, his family. Did Lugo harbor that much bitterness from competition years ago between their stores? Regardless of Lugo's reasons, Julian wouldn't let this stand. "We owe *Claire* much." He put all the emphasis on her name he could muster. They all knew it, choosing not to use it was another insult.

Lugo tried to wave that away with his hand, like shooing a buzzing fly. "Yet, she is a witch and unpredictable. For the people's safety, she should be watched. And for her own safety. Some peasant did try to kill her today."

"There *is* a guard on her, and when he is not there, my son is with her."

"That guard is assigned to your wife, is he not?" Sarracino asked. "And your son has other duties . . . though he is the one who brought the witch here in the first place." The weaver rarely spoke in council, had always been of a dreamy, inward-turned temperament. He'd made a success of putting those dreams into the designs of his tapestries and rugs. But he'd been sweet on Beatriz as a child and never accepted Julian winning her over. *So another old rivalry uses our tragedy as opportunity.* "Beyond the risk of being unattended, we also can't have the witch leave us. What if we have need of her again and our lack of vigilance allows her to escape?"

"I don't believe she has any intention—"

"You know the witch's mind so well?" Lugo said quickly. "You are privy to her thoughts?"

Antonio rushed to defend Julian again, and the arguing grew heated enough that the entrance of a messenger boy went unnoticed by all but Julian. He took the scroll of paper the boy held out, then watched the boy leave the tent before unrolling it.

Even the curly paper they were forced to use was left behind by the Northerners, and it had their unreadable writing upon it. Julian wondered vaguely if they could persuade the captured priestess, Santabe, to read it for them. So far, she had refused to speak in their language, though they knew she spoke it. There, he agreed with the council to keep her in chains and under heavy guard both to protect her and others as she awaited trial. The woman was unpredictable in her violence, and given her angry rants in her coarse language, likely insane. She deserved execution, and would get it once a trial could be arranged, but others argued with the right persuasion they could get useful information from her.

He wasn't so sure, however, and what he should do with Santabe was yet another choice on his shoulders. Speed forward her trial or delay it in hopes of breaking her?

How am I supposed to choose wisely anymore?

Julian set the paper upon the table, placed rocks on the corners to hold it down and studied the words scrawled in the margins. The news, though not unexpected, hit like a stab in the dark, making him wish for his brandy bottle for the first time in ages. He rubbed his eyes, suddenly exhausted, with no strength to say the words aloud. He'd hoped for better things. Yet, the council must know.

"*Caballeros*, our first scout report."

Instant silence greeted him. Those on their feet

settled back to their chairs, although most sat at the edge of their seats.

"Aveston is still besieged. The army around it has not retreated or been reduced. Those Northerners stand strong." Julian did not need to say any more—they all knew the implications. That second army around their nearest neighboring city might be a little smaller and lack siege engines, but if it turned on them as they sat in the desert, they would be flattened. The same fear rocking his belly shone from their eyes.

"Time runs out," Osmundo said. "We must make decisions now."

"We lack a quorum," Julian said with trepidation. He dreaded what would follow. The decision could only take one direction—a heartbreaking course. How could they not regret choices made in fear and haste? "The votes are not counted for the replacement councilors."

Lugo nodded. "Based on this news, we must not wait for the voting to be tabulated. Do we so agree?" Every hand rose. "Then I say we start with the witch girl," Lugo continued. "We must be the ones to guide her. She's a woman. She'll do what her menfolk tell her."

All eyes swiveled to the merchant. "What do you know of it?" Antonio asked with a smirk. "You don't have a wife. I guarantee no one here gets their wives to do *anything*." Nervous chuckles rose, but they all knew Antonio had spoken true.

"Lugo is right, though," Diego said, setting aside the humorous moment to return to business, touching mind and heart. "Saints forgive me, we are spread too thin. There is no choice. It is to protect the people. *We* must decide her future."

Heads nodded and this time the eyes found him. As the closest to the girl, they would make him present their judgment to Claire.

Julian closed his eyes as his inner landscape shivered and fell to pieces around him. Once again the words of resignation rose to his tongue. After the way Claire had saved them, they owed her better than this—deciding her life for her as if she didn't have a voice of her own. He knew their methods. They'd try a clumsy-handed persuasion and then use threats against her first, and with the girl's lack of confidence that might be all it took—he recognized a person struggling with their own concept of self when he saw one. And despite the power of the girl's magic, it was clear she didn't really trust the strength of her own abilities enough to strike back at them. Tampering with her fragile self-image might crush her at this point and render her useless while making her hate them as much as the Northerners. Besides the fact that forcing an ally to act contrary to her convictions went against everything Julian believed in. And then there was his son. Ramiro had befriended the girl; he would take it hard as well.

Julian grasped at the principles of honor and pride he'd tried to instill in his sons and they all seemed to slide through his fingers. Then one stuck, and he straightened in his chair, opening his eyes. One didn't avoid responsibility simple because it had become unpleasant. To do so was to be a coward. A quitter. That was not the way of his family. Not what he wanted to show to his remaining son. In that moment, he decided not to resign and take the easy way out. Let that decision be on someone else's head. Not that it mattered all that much—the situation would not last long. In days they would have the votes to remove him and he would be free from this torture. But until then, he would do his job, the task he swore to Santiago to perform. Yet, even as his resolve stiffened, he knew that his role must diminish. They all believed his decisions had caused their recent suffering—and there he couldn't blame them, his own lingering thoughts tended the same way—and so his standing shrank to the lowest it had ever been. These men had been chosen by the people, too, and he would respect that if nothing else.

Just as my people hurt, so will I suffer through whatever decisions the council reaches, no matter how I disagree with them. He hadn't the energy to do otherwise.

He slumped further in his chair and let the debate swirl around him.

CHAPTER 5

Fog encased Ramiro, shutting him in a gray world. It surrounded but didn't touch him, leaving no cling of moisture on his skin. He turned slowly, feeling sand move under his boots, though the fog concealed even the ground. He was still in the desert, then. But how had fog gotten here, and where had the camp gone?

As he stared, fighting the unreality, the fog changed. It didn't thin, nor did it part, but he could see through a section, enough to glimpse Colina Hermosa and its broken walls with gaps of darkness where stone had fallen. He was no longer near the gates, but at the rear of the city. A wisp of it moved to his right, and Ramiro saw a figure standing ahead of him, closer to the dead city. He'd recognize this shape anywhere.

Salvador.

His brother focused on the city, unaware of Ramiro.

Salvador wore his uniform surcoat over full armor, the cloak depicting San Martin on his back. From one hand hung his official helm with the eagle feathers Salvador only wore when he wanted to stand out as an officer. The other hand stretched out toward the city in longing. Uncertainty turned to joy in Ramiro's chest.

He tried to dash ahead, but his legs refused to cooperate. It took every ounce of energy to push them a single step. They dragged, as if his commands from his brain didn't connect, moving so slowly as to be standing still. Hard as he fought for each stumbling step, Salvador remained as distant as ever.

He couldn't get close to his brother.

Frustration turned to panic. His heart thudded, icy cold sliding up each limb. His knees lost all strength, buckling and declining to hold his weight. He couldn't reach him.

"Salvador!"

His brother turned his head. Their eyes met. Ramiro was surprised that he didn't see the eyes of a ghost, cold and dead, but of the Salvador he remembered in their brown depths. They held warmth, love—and worry. Ramiro read a weight of concern, as Salvador had shown the time Gomez had accidentally laid open Ramiro's scalp with a wooden sword during a practice bout.

Without breaking contact, Ramiro tugged at his legs, desperate for their cooperation. He must reach Salvador. Ask his brother what was wrong. Touch him one last time. Tears of frustration pooled in his eyes, blinding more than the fog. He could get no closer.

"Wait! Speak to me!"

Salvador's eyes narrowed, commanding Ramiro's attention as they did before a fresh military order. Then his brother deliberately turned his back on the city. His hand holding the helmet hung raised for a heartbeat, then the helmet dropped, falling from his brother's hand with a ringing crash of metal on rock. Salvador vanished into the fog.

Ramiro screamed his frustration—

—and woke with a gasp. His heart pounded and his breath came much too fast. Fear ran in rivers through all parts of his body. For a second, he still couldn't move, but then sense returned and he sprang to his feet. A dream—nothing more—because he missed his brother. He wiped cold sweat from his face, feeling its chill everywhere.

He'd fallen asleep waiting for his father's meeting to break up. Claire had gone to her tent hours ago, but he'd sat on a blanket waiting. He looked that way now and saw that only one lantern remained lit in the council tent. The guards had gone from the entrance. Behind him were lumps in the darkness where the servants had bedded down. The camp around them had gone silent, except for the occasional cough and the flickering of fires. Across the sand, the flaps of his parents' tent were closed. Ramiro frowned—he'd missed his chance.

Or had he.

Perhaps like at home in the citadel, his father stayed awake in his study long hours after his mother had retired. They hadn't a study now, but . . . Ramiro shook off the last effects of the dream and headed for the meeting tent. Maybe he could at least hear about the latest scout reports.

Hidden bodyguards came into view as he got closer. They recognized Ramiro and drew aside in permission for him to enter, but inside the tent, he stopped short. Julian was here all right, but so were the entire collection of *pelotón* captains at the camp, all in formal uniform. Ramiro snapped to attention, silencing the babble of apologies for interrupting that bubbled to his lips. A few of the captains, including his own, acknowledged him with a nod of the head. The others bowed to his father, clearly taking their leave.

The captains normally reported straight to their *concejales* or the current bishop, except in times of special circumstance. Clearly the present situation counted as such, and now they all came to the *Alcalde*.

Capitán Muño touched Ramiro's arm on the way out. "Don't forget to rest, kiddo. Report first thing in the morning to the meeting of *capitáns* to discuss Northern fighting styles. You being the closest we have to an expert, you know more than most."

Me? They want to speak to me as an expert? Before Ramiro could shake off his astonishment, they were gone.

"Congratulations, my son." Julian looked up from writing on the reports. His face looked worn and his hair and beard now contained more silver than brown. "I know how much that must mean to you."

Instead of answering, Ramiro approached his father. The table had been created from a single plank—no tree that size grew in the desert—and ingeniously fashioned with hinges to collapse for traveling. Teresa would say to take note of the Northerners' creativity; it meant they came up with solutions. Ramiro wished she were here now.

Julian waved him to a seat without lifting his eyes from the many reports. "You wished to speak with me?"

Ramiro fidgeted with the edge of the table—it wasn't like his father not to put things aside for family, even if only for a few moments. In his worry, he found himself babbling, instead of getting to the point. "I don't know what to tell the captains. The Northerners seem to take orders from the priests—the ones in white—sometimes. At least, that's what I saw in the swamp village. Though I heard from Mother they had another leader."

A scroll crinkled as Julian let it roll back up. "Ordoño. A Lord Ordoño. He was one of our people. I got some information about him from Father Telo and have hopes he can tell us more—if I can find the time. We do know Ordoño escaped us." His father gave him a brief glance, not quite making eye contact. "The priests lead the soldiers—a good bit of information to tell the *capitáns*. I'm sure it will be useful. Did you have something you needed?"

"I came to ask about the scout reports." Ramiro sat up taller in his chair at the reminder. "Any word on the Northern army? You heard what we found on patrol this afternoon?"

"Aye, the massacre. It was not the first."

Ramiro touched liver and spleen surreptitiously as his father had never favored superstitious reactions. He couldn't help it, though—*there had been other incidents of people torn apart?* Why had he not heard of such horror? And why wasn't his father more concerned? "More massacres? Like what we found today? Some new evil of the Northerners?"

"What? No, nothing like that. Just more refugees found dead. What you saw must have been animals." His father continued, "We have no news on the larger army from any scouts who've returned."

"That's well, then." No signs of regrouping was hopeful, as was no other twisted killings. Maybe Ramiro overreacted and it *was* animals. Claire would be relieved. When Julian kept his head bent, Ramiro frowned. "But what is the matter?" Ramiro waved a hand to get his father's attention. "You are not yourself."

"I'm simply busy, my son." Julian gave a weak smile. "Nothing to worry about."

Ramiro stared, feeling like the world had shifted for the third time within a week. He'd never seen his father like this—he fumbled to put his thumb on it—so almost normal, yet something off. "If you won't tell me, then you should tell Mother." His parents kept nothing from each other, so it had always been in good times or bad.

Julian sighed and scrubbed his face with his hands. Ramiro rose from his chair. His father's left hand shook with a tremor. He pointed at it. "What's going on? Tell me. Should I fetch a healer?"

"No. And you won't tell your mother. It's nothing. A momentary ailment. Do you understand?"

"I won't understand until you tell me."

Julian sighed again. "We have only supplies for a few more days. The Northerners remain around Aveston. I do not believe the others have gone—it's not in their character. And here we sit, undefended, with no one able to agree on our next move."

"But you'll find the answer."

"And if there is no answer?" Julian shouted, banging his hand on the table, then seemed to collapse back into himself. Quieter he asked, "Or if any answer makes things worse? I'm not infallible, nor is the council. I don't . . . But leave that for now, my son. It is not your problem. This, however, is: The *concejales* insist Claire be taken to use her magic on the army around Aveston. I'm to carry that message to her."

His father's word rushed by Ramiro in a flood, impossibly defeated, like a man given up, inspiring dread, until the last struck a raw nerve. "But that can't happen. I promised her."

Julian met his eyes. "I doubt the *concejales* care for your promise, my son."

"You weren't there," Ramiro said. "You don't know how the magic felt . . . it's wrong." Like everyone else who'd heard the Song, he found it hard to speak about the feelings it raised afterward. None of Claire's other magic had ever left an impression like this, not even when used against him.

"I was close enough," Julian said. "I felt it—as did some of the *concejales*. That has not dissuaded them." If it were possible even more weariness entered his father's voice. "They see it as the solution, but not only that, they see it as the *only* solution. Do you understand me? They will not let it go. I haven't the energy, and maybe not the right, to override them anymore."

Ramiro's jaw tightened. "She doesn't know what she did—how to replicate it. Or even if she can. She barely knows more about her magic than we do. Plus, she needs time to recover. She's worried; I can tell. And besides, won't the Northerners be expecting it this time? We won't fool them again." He launched into the best argument he could pursue. "Salvador said so. He said the Northerners were smart. That repeating tricks would not work."

"Trick or not, it might be our only option. The *concejales* have a point there." Julian stretched out his hand and took Ramiro's arm, guiding him back to the chair. "I'm not saying I agree with them or that I like this directive. I just don't see other choices."

"The other *ciudades-estado*," Ramiro said bitterly. "They should step up and do some of the work. Why is it only us fighting?"

"Because it is human nature, my son. We are in the line of fire and they are not. It is an avenue I have tried and failed—repeatedly. Their turn will come soon enough.

"I'll delay speaking to the girl until evening—it's the longest I can stall," his father continued, refusing to make eye contact. "If she says no, there will be consequences. She will be compelled."

Ramiro couldn't wrap his head around it. How could his father approve of this? "What are you saying?"

Julian looked at the icon of Santiago on the tent wall. "God help me, I'm saying if she plans to refuse, don't let her be here in the morning. They'll make good their threat, putting guards on her or worse."

"You mean torture." Ramiro felt stunned in more ways than one. "But you wouldn't let them."

"It's not their first choice, but it *could* come to that." Julian shook his head. "Son, they outvoted me in this. Send her back to the swamp if you want her free. But know this: taking that option could be the death of Colina Hermosa. If she can't defeat the Northern army, we have no choice but to go begging to the other *ciudades-estado* to take in our people in bits and scraps. To break us up into groups and live off others' charity until the Northerners come for the other cities. It's her or all of us. Do. You. Understand?"

Ramiro forced himself to breathe, as his lungs seemed to have forgotten how to do the task. No wonder his father wasn't acting in his old way. How could one function with such a weight bearing down? And when he spoke to her that weight would be on Claire.

"I tell you this for the sake of decency. She means the most to you," Julian said. "It's right you know the facts. It could be she'd go to Aveston and succeed, save us all again. Or it could be the death of her and all of us. Maybe you can talk her into working with us—I'm sure the council would terrify her. I'm sorry to pass the burden to you, but better the message comes from you."

Ramiro felt horrified on more than one level. *Always see first to Colina Hermosa*. As *alcalde*, Julian had to follow the same precepts. "Father, you're breaking your oath of office to tell me this." Yet, if Ramiro warned Claire—wouldn't he be doing the same?

His father simply grunted. "As your mother says, 'there is a time for everything.' I don't make this decision lightly, but some choices are too much for the soul—compelling the girl would be one of them. Tell her and let the decision be hers."

Ramiro nodded as his father smoothed his path. As an order from the *Alcalde*, he would be acting for the city and not breaking the precepts. Yet, he felt little better. Still, he said, "Hi-ya. If Claire doesn't want to help, then I'll escort her home and return. She'll need someone who can handle a weapon."

"I forbid it. Your duty is here, my son. Warning her is enough, leave the rest to the witch girl."

Ramiro drew back. His father never spoke that

way, had never forbidden him or his brother anything—no matter how foolish the childhood demand. Always he believed in letting them take their lumps and find out the hard way. "But a few days. I'll not be missed—"

"Absolutely not. There is no wiggle room on this. The *concejales* already accuse me of favoring family. And they're right." His gaze turned inward. "With your brother gone, I know for sure that family matters the most. But I won't be able to protect you if they find out you warned her—or that I warned you. If you choose to send Claire off, make sure no one witnesses. Be at that meeting of the *capitáns* when she sneaks away. Don't wait until evening." Julian took the rocks, one by one, from the scrolls and let the paper roll up. "Likely we'll be blamed no matter what. Saints help us all."

"Saints help us all," Ramiro echoed. He turned and stumbled from the tent, accepting the dismissal and having no other response to give. Once again their salvation rested on one girl's shoulders—only this time, Ramiro didn't think she had any more to give. The leader who had always had all the answers suddenly had none. Where before the picture had simply been bleak, now, as if firm ground had become quicksand, his world turned on its head, burying him to his eyes and leaving him fighting for his last breath.

CHAPTER 6

Teresa lugged another bucket of mud as she supervised the building of a fresh hut. The camp of villagers and evacuated children from Colina Hermosa spread out around her in a large clearing right against the swamp lake. Women prepared food or tended babies, and children of all sizes trotted back and forth on errands or hunted dry wood for fires. Everyone had an activity to keep them busy—even her. No one wanted to go back to the village in case the Northerners returned, so they were creating their own refuge deep in the swamp.

Teresa tuned out the pain of the blisters on her palm, rubbed by the bucket handle. What would she be doing if she were back at the university? Browsing at the library? Buying a traveler a meal in a tavern to learn more about their city? Working on her latest thesis? Without the constant din of church bells to mark the time, she couldn't tell the hour, but no matter what time it was now, her life was *very* different.

Somehow this manual work felt more rewarding. The injury to her collarbone barely throbbed anymore, and she'd lost some of the weight she'd earned sitting at a desk all day, though her shape remained conspicuously round.

Nothing to do about that, though.

"We need a bigger branch at the back," she called to Sebastian, the oldest of today's helpers at ten winters. "There's a gap."

She eyed the hazy sky. It had a brownish tinge to the gray like she'd never seen before. Another rain might be coming and they needed to finish.

Once Bromisto had shown the other youngsters how to construct shelters, the children found it a wonderful game to make a rough form out of branches and slather a clay-like mud over it. When finished, this one would cover five more little ones from the frequent rain. Teresa discovered she had a knack for organizing the tiny army of small volunteers to do whatever she asked.

She set her bucket by a team of four small girls and watched them dive in and begin slapping the clay over the branches. Teresa smiled. Adult workers from Colina Hermosa wouldn't have half their enthusiasm.

"Very good progress," Alvito said.

Teresa rolled her eyes before glancing over. A huddle of young women sat and waved at the flies trying to settle on Alvito's prone form as he reclined in the shade of a hut. For the three-hundredth time that day, Elo squatted down beside them.

"I'll just check those bandages again," Bromisto's sister, Elo, said. Instead, the girl mooned at Alvito's face, a faint pink staining her cheeks, and played with the thick coil of brown hair atop her head, indicating her marriageable age. Teresa knew her own cropped-off hair had mud in it—it might be unfashionable, but it kept her cool—and would draw no one's eye. The other young women around them giggled, undeterred that Alvito could hear their brazen flirting. Teresa had been hearing them for a sevenday, ever since they'd found Alvito more dead than alive and brought him back to camp. If only she could shoo the girls like the annoying flies. Luckily, an older woman called them all, except Elo, back to tend the cook fires.

Teresa tilted her head, trying to discover what was so fascinating about Alvito. A man's face had never made her heart quicken. This one was no different. Sure, his was more regular in feature than some others—the beard more square, the nose straighter. But pain tightened the corners of his eyes and made his skin pale. And while his lack of shirt showed off well-defined muscles, it also displayed the bandages wrapping his chest that hid wounds to his lungs. And, despite his injuries, he primped his mustache—the first thing he'd done upon waking was wash himself and trim his beard. The man had more vanity than any woman. Not that it mattered—the perfect man was never going to be right for her, let alone this cocky soldier. Though Teresa admitted he also had plenty of bravery—or the saint's own luck.

When they'd found Gomez's body partially eaten by panthers, they'd assumed the same fate had met Alvito—his body dragged off by the big cats. That was until Elo noticed the reeds cut in small pieces by the lakeside. The man had somehow used the reeds as hollow tubes to clear the air out of his chest wounds. His horse had defended him as he had crawled to the nearest tree and climbed into a defensible position. To escape the predators, he'd waited there three days until help arrived. A deed worthy of songs.

Since Elo's instructor, the healer Fagilda, declared Alvito would live, Teresa had given up on advancing her friendship with Elo. Teresa admired the young woman's questioning mind—so much like Bromisto's. She had offered to take the girl to Colina Hermosa and acquire her a place at the university to study healing. Now it seemed Elo was more likely to become a soldier's wife.

Teresa sighed and walked over to stand by them. The girl needed lessons in hiding her feelings. Lessons Teresa had mastered long ago and put into play to conceal her disappointment. She wasn't unhappy that Alvito would live—that was wonderful—just that Elo would never notice her. Teresa shook herself out of her own heartsick mooning. Love may be out of the question for her, but she still had her career and her friends. The girl was too young for her anyway, and by that measure, too young for Alvito also, who was nearer to her age.

"Any news today?" Teresa asked.

"Oh," Elo said with a grimace. "I forgot. My father is back."

Teresa exchanged a look with Alvito, and the man used his elbows to lever up to a half sit. They'd heard nothing since Suero reluctantly told them Ramiro had left the village with the witch girl—apparently she'd joined him of her free will as Suero said nothing about her being tied. That had been over a sevenday ago, and she and Alvito craved to know more, to no avail. None of the villagers would consent to go to Colina Hermosa, and Suero had forbidden his young son, Bromisto, when Teresa had attempted to bribe him.

Elo brightened. "You go ask him about your other friend and I'll sit here."

Of course she would, Teresa thought unfairly. She tried to push the mud from her arms and hands but only smeared it more. "Where—"

"With the hunters," Elo answered before she could finish. She pointed vaguely toward the western end of the camp.

"Bring him here, and I'll handle him," Alvito said, a fierce frown darkening his face. Teresa doubted Suero would be intimidated by a man who couldn't stand on his own feet, and rolled her eyes. When it came to handling the obstinate village leader, she was on her own.

Before Teresa took two steps from her post, a small

girl caught Teresa around her thick waist in a brief hug and then ran off into the crowd, dragging a tree branch behind her. The children of Colina Hermosa had adopted her as their mother figure. She didn't quite understand it—she had never exactly thought of herself as maternal—but she realized her city clothes and accent must reassure them in the strange world they found themselves.

And she wasn't complaining—their attention had become the best thing about her time in the makeshift camp. Unused to cooking or chores or children, Teresa had been thrust into overseeing a hundred of them with more arriving every day. She had promised Ramiro to see to them, and see to them she would, even if it killed her to stay here with no news. It was the least she could do after losing his horse within the first day. Sancha had run off when they'd been rescuing Alvito. Teresa wasn't sure whether that was reassuring or worrying. The *caballos de guerra* stayed loyal for life, which meant the mare should have stayed put as Ramiro commanded. Did Sancha sense Ramiro was in danger and so hurry to him? Teresa feared somehow the horse knew more than she did about Ramiro's situation.

Nothing she could do about it now.

As she searched the moving crowd for signs of Suero, a boy about the height of her shoulder—a little bigger than Bromisto but less familiar with the swamp—showed her a pouch full of blueberries.

"Did you watch for quicksand?" she asked. He

nodded, but his beaming face fell in disappointment. Teresa adjusted her words, trying to remember how fragile children were. "A fine job. Just what we need for our dinner. What would we do without you? Take it to the women at the cook fires, please."

A smile reappeared across his face as Teresa clapped him on the back. "Have you seen the hunters?" she asked before he turned.

He pointed in the direction she'd been going, and she saw a group of figures at the edge of the clearing by the trees. Teresa broke into a trot. If Suero was back, maybe this time he had fresh news. She wished Bromisto was there to back her up, but their guide through the swamp was likely hiding to avoid more chores.

Halfway there, two small girls appeared in front of her, forcing Teresa to a halt. "My sister is sick," the taller said, her voice shaking. "Her eyes." Tears made clean runnels down the older girl's dirty cheeks.

As Teresa looked closer, she added baths to her list of things to arrange. The smaller girl had little blogs of yellowish pus at the corners of her eyes, but the whites of her eyes were clear and not bloodshot. She stood tall as if to show her bravery, however a little whimper came out.

"I want my *mamá*," the small one said.

Something tightened in Teresa's throat. She wasn't prepared for this responsibility. "Your *mamá* will be here soon," she lied. "It's just a cold from the damp swamp air," Teresa added to reassure them. "Nothing to worry about. Go to Alvito's blanket and have Elo look at it. She's a healer. She'll know what to do," she added more confidently than she felt. Hopefully, her words were true.

The sisters darted off, but not before grubby hands caught Teresa in a hug. Teresa hugged back, some of her worry lifting with their childish gesture. The university was full of adults—she had had no idea of the satisfaction that could come from such innocent expressions of gratitude.

The crowd parted to give her a clear view of the dozen or so hunters and Suero at their center. He stood with his back to her. Bits and pieces of armor covered his arms and legs. A long sword hung from his belt. A frown pulled down Teresa's mouth when she saw him—those were Ramiro's. Worry and anger warred inside her for dominance.

Anger won.

The village leader claimed he'd found Ramiro's gear, but every word out of his mouth could be a lie, including his assurances that Ramiro lived. She couldn't believe Ramiro would leave a sword behind.

That said, the rest of his men could have stolen weapons and armor off the dead Northerners and *pelotónes* members, but superstition stopped them. They feared the ghosts of the dead haunting them more than they desired weapons. It was that which gave Teresa hope Ramiro really did live and Suero spoke the truth for once. Unless . . . her friend had been robbed before they killed him.

She hurried the rest of the distance, grabbing Suero and pulling him around. The bent man was her height, but weighed less, though heavy shoulders made him seem bigger. Like most village men, the only thing he respected was confidence, and the ability to back it up. He was used to women with none of either. His affected attitude when around her reflected that, and speaking with the wiry man always made her want to wash.

"What news? You've been out hunting?"

His squinty dark eyes regarded her without blinking. "It's a man's job, *woman*." Suero spat and stared at her dirty trousers then made his way to her man-length hair. "But you seem confused about that. Can't tell which is which."

Teresa kept her feet steady, refusing to let this vile man make her back down. Her studies had taught her some about the outlying villages and their culture. Elo and Bromisto offering her blankets assured her of guest rights, guaranteeing her the tolerance of their father. He could beat his own wife and daughters, but for any non-relative females, violence was taboo. That didn't prevent him from lying to her and edging as close to disrespect as possible. Their distrust of anything from the cities made lying their natural reaction.

"Any news?" she repeated doggedly.

"Aye," the village leader said reluctantly. "Found more of your city brats." He gestured where a handful of children entered the clearing led by two of Suero's unfriendly men. "More mouths to feed. I said I'd take them to a safe spot, but the rest is up to them."

Teresa hesitated then nodded. She'd manage more children somehow, thankfully most of the women were willing to help feed them. "We pull our own, in case you haven't noticed. We earn our keep."

Suero grunted, and she turned. There was only so much of this man she could stand at a time.

"And smoke," he said.

She spun back around. "What?"

"I said 'smoke.' You asked for news." Something distasteful lit up his eyes. "We saw a vast plume of smoke . . . to the east. That's the direction of your city, isn't it, woman?" He gestured to the hazy air. "A *vast* cloud of it. Didn't you notice?"

Teresa stood transfixed.

The haze.

Not clouds.

Smoke.

"Oh saints!" Now that he mentioned it, she thought she could smell it in the air. But could this be another of his lies? "You're certain? It was east. How can you tell?" The trees—many of them towering sycamore—made it hard to see much of anything in the swamp, including the sky.

"Because we went back to the village, woman. That's how I could *tell*. There's an open view there. It's east—a great thick plume of it. Blots out the sky."

Denial rushed to her tongue. "You swear."

"I swear by the strength of my good right arm. May it weaken and wither if I lie. Does that satisfy you, woman?" A sly smiled crept over his face. "Seems there's something amiss with your city."

"If there is, you should be concerned, too," she snapped.

"Why? We know how to survive here. Which is more than I can say for you city folk," he said with a sneer.

Worry made a drumbeat in her chest. Instead of rounding up the new children, she stood fixed like the rawest student on his first day to class.

Something tugged on Teresa's poncho, and she turned to find a toddler with big brown eyes. "I's hungry," the girl lisped.

"I know, Ines," Teresa managed to say. The toddler said as much at least fifteen times an hour. "We're all hungry." The little girl's eyes only got bigger. "Go over to the cook fires and tell them I said you could have some blueberries until it's time for supper."

Ines hurried away, and Teresa found that Suero had used the distraction to escape back into the group of his men. No doubt he expected her to keep to a female's place and respect the hunters. His ways were not hers. She cut right through to confront the village leader again.

"Send someone," Teresa pressed. "Send someone to see what happened."

Face tight, Suero held up his hand. "You think I've got men to spare to see what happened to your fool city?"

Teresa let her anger show. The man would respect nothing else. Any other response would be considered weakness by their culture, as their own women were *encouraged* to be submissive. To keep her place she must act as confident as any man. "Then go yourself. It concerns you as much as anyone. The Northerners are your threat, too. Find out how things stand."

"I've got all these people to feed. Go yourself, why don't you. A woman can be spared. Unless you've got something to bargain."

She glared. He meant Alvito's horse and gear. Well, that wasn't hers to give and she wouldn't trade it if it were. *Stupid, stubborn man.* He'd rather perish than admit a woman might have a good idea.

Suero turned his back on her, and she let him go. There would be no cooperation here. If she took his advice and went herself, what would happen to the children? Who would care for them in her absence? Suero would see they got nothing. She felt torn apart and her feet stumbled taking her back to her shelter.

"I *should* go," Teresa said aloud. "Ramiro might need my help."

The boy who had shown her the blueberries stood at her side. He twisted his shoe into the wet ground. "I just wondered about blankets. There's not enough for everyone."

"I'll see about it," Teresa told him distractedly. "Would you greet the new children for me? Start on settling them until I can get there. I'll just be a minute."

She sent the boy on his way. With another group of children, there would be even less to go around.

A cloud of what she now knew was smoke passed over the sun—its shadow a reminder of how chilly it would become when night fell. Teresa glanced around at the weeds and grasses of the clearing. The newly arrived children stood grouped at the edge, near the trees, at a loss for what to do now with no adults helping them. The children would have no idea how to take care of themselves. They couldn't even start fires.

Ramiro's motto came to her: Always see first to Colina Hermosa and its civilians. But which civilians: the ones here or the ones at Colina Hermosa?

Teresa knew.

She dragged her pants higher by its rope belt and strode toward Alvito. He could take over for the short time she was gone—just to find out what happened at home—to prepare for what might be coming for them. She'd take one of the mules and be back in . . . five or six days. The thought made her heart wilt, but they couldn't go on with this worry and doubt. Best to know the worst, she'd always believed.

"It's smoke," she said, pointing to the sky. "Suero says it's coming from Colina Hermosa. I've got to go. I've got to know what's happening. If it's the worst . . . we'll need to go deeper into the swamp."

Alvito and Elo stared at her as if she'd lost her wits. Alvito snapped out of it first. "I'll go with you."

"You can't even stand," she huffed, bending to

grab her saddlebags. "Plus, I need you to stay here and take care of the children. Someone has to, Cat." The nickname he'd given himself seemed even more appropriate now that he'd avoided being eaten by panthers.

Alvito levered himself to a sitting position. "Take Suero with you. The man is a born brawler. He'd be handy in a fight."

"No offense, Elo"—she gave the girl an apologetic glance while answering Alvito—"but I don't think your father would exactly stand by me. And besides, he lives in a squalid village at the edge of a swamp—ambition is not his strong suit." *Not without a hefty price*, she thought but didn't voice. She thrust clothing and a blanket into the bags.

"You'll get lost," Alvito insisted.

"I'll follow the road. I can tell whether a church is located in Aveston, Zapata, or another *ciudades-estado* just by looking at the altar cloth. I'm not a fool."

"The road is suicide. Your book learning won't serve you now. I'm coming with you." Before she could tell him no again, he'd climbed to his feet, wavering unsteadily with a white face. She glimpsed a flash, and was surprised to see a knife quivering in the bald spot of the nearest sycamore trunk. "I'm weak, not helpless."

"That would be impressive *if* you could go and fetch it," Teresa said. But once again to her surprise, he made his slow way over to the tree and wrenched out the knife.

"I might have been feeling better than I let on." He shrugged and winked. "So I like being waited on."

She scowled, but noticed he still leaned against the sycamore. He wasn't that much better.

"I'll be riding," he said interpreting her look. "Not walking. I can handle it."

"No. Then who'd look after the children?"

"I will," Elo said, getting to her feet. "I can do it. I'll make Estefanio help me."

Teresa couldn't help but smile. "Not if you call him by his real name." He'd dubbed himself Bromisto, meaning trickster, and didn't care much for his older sister's bossing to start with. "Let me ask him."

"Then it's settled?" Alvito asked.

She thought on it. It did make sense—injured as he was, he could still handle himself better then she could alone. She nodded. "It's settled, Cat. But if you fall off your horse, I'm not picking you up."

"You know you'd do anything to touch this body."

Elo blushed at that, but Teresa just rolled her eyes and went to find Bromisto, Alvito's laughter following her.

CHAPTER 7

Ramiro sank onto his bedroll, struggling to come to grips with his father's words. He must make a choice: the fate of his people over the feelings of one slim girl, who wasn't even part of his race.

A girl he'd known only a handful of days.

It shouldn't be a choice. There should be none of this confusion, no questioning of his honor. He'd promised not to force her to use her magic, but how did that compare to the lives of thousands? Yet...

He pictured her face with its pale scattering of freckles lifted up to look at him. The little upturn to her nose. Her blue eyes so trusting lately...

Saints. Why was it always one more thing piled on another? Why couldn't it end?

With no chance of sleep, he glanced over at Sancha. The mare slept, her head down in the way of horses. He thought he detected the flicker of an eye in his direction. Unlike other animals, *caballos de guerra* didn't mind being alone. Other horses clumped together when put into a pasture. The dapple-gray animals were as likely to stand off by themselves as in a group. Unbonded youngsters stayed together, but once a *caballo de guerra* matched with a human, they seemed to need nothing more. Sancha was content alone here as long as Ramiro was near. Plus, the servants spoiled her rotten with small treats from the kitchen.

It would be selfish of him to disturb her now, just because he couldn't settle down. He stood, intending to walk. Surely tiring himself out on top of a night of no sleep would make his decision all the better, he mocked. Perhaps he would go by Claire's tent, though he didn't know what to say to her.

"Come with me," a voice said, and he nearly jumped out of his skin.

"Mother? What are you doing here?"

In her black clothes, Beatriz blended into the darkness, even standing a few feet away. She'd removed her tall lace mantilla from her hair, but otherwise looked as if she hadn't considered going to bed. Like his father, she'd aged in the last days. Unlike Julian, care had not taken the color from her hair, but instead added lines that pinched around her mouth and eyes. "I've been watching over my children for twenty-five years. You think I don't know when something is troubling them? Come with me."

"What? How did you—"

She took his arm and led him through the quiet camp toward the quarry. "I saw you go into your father's tent, and I saw you weave like a drunkard when you came out. As if a child of mine would drink at a time like this." She sniffed. "Then you sit here at this time of night. You who sleep like the dead waiting for the saints to raise them. I knew."

They walked awhile in silence. All around them were tents and blackened fires, the people long abed, though somewhere sentries patrolled. She took him out of the shadows to where the moon gleamed silver on the sand. It slid and gave under his boots. The wind and clouds were nonexistent, holding their breath for the coming summer rains.

"What is it, my son?"

In everyday matters, he found his mother often silly or capricious, more likely to say something ridiculous, or put all her faith in the saints. But when push came to shove, as when he'd decided to enter the military, she showed a more thoughtful side. So he told her everything: How he knew where his duty lay, yet burned under the dishonorable treatment of an ally . . . a friend; the way his father forbid him to leave the camp with Claire.

She listened until he ran out of words as he babbled his uncertainty, then said, "Your father believes Lord Ordoño will rally the Northerners. That that army will return for us. I can see it in his face."

"Is he a prophet now? He can see the future?" Ramiro joked as the tension pressed down and he needed some release. And because he didn't want it to be true. Either of the groups of Northerners would only have to realize his people sat outside the walls, like chickens without a henhouse, and they'd be finished.

His mother took his words at their face value. "Father Telo told me and I'm sure he told your father. It is what the priest believes, and he's the only one who spent time with the Northerners. They are driven by bloodthirstiness to appease their god. Why sacrifice your own people..."

"When you can use ours," he finished for her. He had suspected as much, had witnessed at the swamp village how they killed by cutting off first a person's hands, then head. They'd started the process with Father Telo but been unable to finish because Ramiro stopped them.

"Father Telo doesn't believe they are the type to go home," Beatriz whispered as if saying it aloud would make it so. She stopped them close to the edge of the quarry, yet not so near that he could look over the edge. Here, they were truly alone, except for the stars. "I felt what the witch's magic did."

"Claire," he corrected automatically.

"I felt what the magic did." She ignored his correction. "It was wicked. I don't sense that in her, but what she did to frighten the Northerners, it was wrong—evil. God will punish us for that."

He stared at her. Never had she preached to him of a vengeful God, but always of one loving and kind. A

God who had sent the saints to protect and guide his children. The saints that had led them to establishing cities, giving up their nomad ways.

Her eyes didn't look at him, but out over the quarry. "It was wrong to use it the first time. It would be worse to do it again knowingly. Sometimes . . . sometimes it is better to accept your fate than fight it with evil." She shook herself and tugged at his arm, turning them around. "But none of that helps us. Done is done.

"Here you are worried about what you must do and what's right, just like a man. But it isn't up to you, is it? The one who really must decide is the witch. You must tell her what you told me and let her make up her mind. That is the right thing to do."

"Claire," he corrected again halfheartedly.

And again she ignored him, instead pointing at the sky and then waving her finger under his nose. "But not before light. It isn't right to consort with an unmarried woman—especially when she's a witch—before morning. One should wait until after noon, but I suppose I can pardon it this time."

"Mother."

"I know. I know. You don't want to listen to your mother. Let me just say this to you. My mother was not thrilled with my choice of husband. She wanted me to marry a landowner, not a merchant. But Julian wasn't a foreigner or . . . from a swamp." She gave a nod. "You don't know how this disappoints me."

Ramiro rolled his eyes. "I think I do. But we are just

friends—Claire and I—nothing more." There, he'd said it aloud and made it true. They were friends—not that that would convince his mother. So he went for a better argument, one she would heed. "*Sangre* kin because of our relations killing one another. In that regard, she's your kin, too."

Beatriz pursed her lips in a pout. "Don't be ridiculous. *Sangre* kin does not include—her kind."

He squeezed her arm, pleased she hadn't thrown *witch* at him again. From his mother that was progress. "Her kind? I believe you're warming to Claire. And what would Santiago say about excluding people from his laws? It isn't fitting of a godly people."

"You leave the saints out of it." She *humphed* and then chuckled. "You are too smart for your own good. Just like your father." She released his arm and raised her chin. "Speak to the girl—after first light—and come see me afterward. No, better yet, leave it to me. I know your father can't show you any favoritism, but I can."

Father Telo said the prayer for the dying. One hand gripped the unconscious soldier's arm, the other reached for his triple-rope belt, the symbol of his office. His nub dragged against the rough cloth of his robe, and Telo's prayer faltered as pain rode up his entire arm to his shoulder.

The Lord giveth and the Lord taketh away.

Telo gritted his teeth and managed to cross heart,

mind, liver, and spleen as he finished the prayer and collapsed back on the camp stool the healers had set out for him. This was the first day he'd dressed and put on his sandals, and his feet were none too steady yet. He'd no taste for meat or drink, leaving him weak—though life continued. All around him, people moved in the large healer tent, but he sat in an island of quiet with only the ragged gasps for air of the soldier before him.

The Lord taketh away.

He glanced at the bandaged nub of his left arm, then back to the dying man. The Lord had left him much more than this poor soul—passing alone, without even his family for comfort. A patrol had apparently run into a small party of Northerners. The enemy had been dispatched, but this soldier went to meet the saints. No amount of healing skill or prayer could hold back the inevitable.

One-handed, Telo tucked the man's blanket closer to his chin and smoothed the gray wool on the man's chest. Would that he could do more.

Father Vellito always complimented Telo on his generous heart. Yet, he found compassion a small thing in these troubled times. Scripture taught to have faith and look to hope. Faith, hope, and charity.

Well, he could provide the last, but the other two were in short supply.

Telo shook his head at his poor wit. Not even the loss of a hand seemed to dampen his mind's ability to be irreverent. Would he never learn? And at a death-bed no less. "Lord have pity on this poor soul and send some for myself. We both need it sorely."

Compassion he had, but silent vigil had never been Telo's strong suit. All too soon his mind wandered, so he stretched out his arms, examining what remained. His right hand sported callouses on the dark skin and prominent knuckles, proof that as a wandering friar, he'd done his fair share of labor and even brawled with bandits of the desert. The other ended two inches above where his wrist should be. Cut off at the direction of the Northern priestess, Santabe. She had never liked him from the unfortunate moment they'd met, having small allowance for priests of other faiths—or anyone, for that matter. He prayed she found tolerance in her captivity, but not even Santiago himself could work that miracle.

Telo should have lost both hands and then his head, but the First Wife's son had interrupted before they could finish the job. Divine intervention the bishop and Father Vellito would homily. Telo wished that it had come just a few minutes earlier and saved him much agony.

Or a few minutes later.

Perhaps it should have.

If he had not harbored impure thoughts—if he'd been more worthy of rescue. If he had not considered using these very hands to strangle the leader of the Northern army.

He tucked the nub of his stump across his chest and under his armpit, where the pressure he exerted on it somehow brought comfort. The unhealed wound throbbed in time with his heartbeat as he reflected on sin in all its guises. There could be no worse transgression than the sin of murder. Though he hadn't followed through on his thought, he'd given it consideration. Didn't that make him just as guilty as actually committing the sin?

Wasn't that why rescue had come late for him?

Ridiculous, his mind rebuffed, but deep in his heart, his conscience said that was the case. For the last few days, it had struck him repeatedly as truth. It made no matter that the priest who confessed him waved it off as the remorse of an injured man and bade him do penitence for pride. Perhaps it was pride to believe the Lord would take notice of a lowly friar. Telo gladly did the penance and went beyond with extra, but that did not erase the belief deep inside that the loss of his hand had been a lesson.

Oddly enough, he'd never been one to look for signs. Needing signs from the saints—whether that be in the form of a tomato with San Pedro's face or a burning bush—had never interested Telo. It was asking for proof, requiring that one see to believe. Faith had always been enough for him. *Have faith in Me and the Lord will have faith in you.*

But . . . things changed.

Telo frowned. If the loss of his hand were a sign, what did it urge him to do?

Its loss came from sinful thoughts, then ought he to act in the opposite manner? To give more compassion and tolerance? To forgive? He had struggled with this for days to no avail, waking from feverish dreams of being a captive of the Northerners.

A captive.

He was no longer the captive. Instead, he'd changed places with Santabe in that regard.

Now, the answer came to him in a blinding light: He must forgive the heathen priestess.

He must go to Santabe and say the words—speaking them in prayer was not enough. He would make this right with their Lord by doing right by their captive.

With a start, he realized the area around him had gone quiet. Healers still bustled around the large tent and men still moaned and cried out in suffering. But the dying man in front of him had ceased to breathe, had passed in peace.

Telo said the prayer of passing and tugged up the blanket over the poor man's slack face. The Lord worked in his own time. One never knew when it would run out. He would go at morning's first light. It was time to leave this tent and return to the world. He had much to do.

CHAPTER 8

As Claire crawled backward out of her tent, a voice at her elbow said, "Good, you're up." Claire jumped, tangling her head in the top of the tiny tent. When no hands grabbed her or knife came at her, she ignored her thudding heart to turn and see First Wife Beatriz waiting on her.

"Put on those trousers I gave you. We're going riding."

Claire gaped. "Riding?" As far as she knew, Beatriz never left the camp. And had certainly never appeared this early before.

"Yes, riding." Hands went to hips and a no-nonsense gleam appeared in the First Wife's eye. "Stop dawdling. I swear you're as slow as my sons . . . son." A quiver hit her lip, there and gone in an instant. "Well, hurry up. Breakfast is waiting."

Claire obediently crawled back in the tent and

struggled to pull on the trousers—black like all the clothes given to her—in the tight space. Something odd was going on, but there was only one way to find out what. Refusing would achieve nothing with this woman. Besides, one listened to one's elders. Her hands faltered. Beatriz reminded her in one crucial way of her own mother—just as determined and controlling.

"And pack up all your things while you're in there," First Wife Beatriz called loud enough to be heard over half the camp. "We're getting you a bigger tent!"

Claire froze. Now she knew something odd was going on. She quickly stuffed her few belongings into her bags, rolled up her blanket, and had hardly escaped the tent with her boots and bags before a group of servants descended on it, pulling up the stakes and laying the canvas out flat.

She hopped up to Beatriz, pulling on her boots and settling her golden braid over her shoulder. She pulled pins from her pocket to fasten her hair up with. "What's going on?"

"We're having breakfast first, that's what. Come along. And leave your hair down today. It makes you look younger."

Claire stuffed the pins back in her pocket. All the women had always urged her to wear her hair up like an adult, and she was happy to comply. Why in the world would they want her to look younger? She needed someone who would give her straight answers. "Where's Ramiro?"

"Meeting with the *capitáns*. They summoned him for his expertise." Beatriz's spine stiffened with obvious pride, but once again, the words came out much too loud.

Claire frowned, but before she could say anything a thin little man with wispy brown hair that allowed his scalp to show through joined them.

"*Concejal* Lugo." Beatriz's eyes had gone flat as had her voice.

"First Wife," the man said with false pleasure. "Where is your husband? I expect he would have something important to say to our gracious guest." He gave Claire a stiff bow, but she couldn't help but notice how he kept his distance, as if he would be contaminated if too close to the "witch."

"As it happens, *Concejal*, he asked me to see to it," Beatriz said. "A woman's delicate touch as you know."

The man stepped closer. "I don't believe that is part of the duties of a First Wife, but I bow to *Alcalde* Julian's expertise. Allow me to sit with you."

Beatriz gritted her teeth. "Not necessary, good sir."

"I insist."

He took Beatriz's elbow and reached for Claire's arm. Claire stepped back, tense. Whatever was happening here was all about her, and her instincts said to run.

The First Wife threw her forearm across her face, covering her eyes. "This man is bothering me," she pronounced loudly. "I shall faint."

Instantly, a wall of green and gray uniforms formed

between her and the man called Lugo. As Claire watched, the soldiers stepped forward, making the little man retreat before them. He tried to dodge around them and was smoothly intercepted and forced back.

"Return to your tent, sir. The First Wife doesn't want to be bothered," one said. "We will escort you."

"I am a *concejal*!" The man Lugo blustered and complained, but it did him no good. The soldiers pushed him farther and farther back without ever laying a hand on him until they vanished into the camp.

Claire turned to catch a smile being wiped off Beatriz's face. "Some friends of Salvador's," Beatriz said. "They watch over me. Ramiro might have suggested they be here this morning." The woman gave a nod. "Come into the tent. His spies are still out here."

Claire followed, trying to look everywhere at once. There were a lot of people about near the *Alcalde*'s tent: servants, messengers, and more soldiers. Several people without an obvious reason to be there loitered about. It could be any of them. A half dozen in rather dirty clothing, wearing the ponchos Claire had learned were favored by the poor, waited on their knees. They stared openly at her.

"Is it them?" she asked, trying not to point too directly.

"Oh no," Beatriz said, leading the way into the large tent. "Those are here to look at you. They think you caused a miracle and want to see if you'll perform another."

Claire blinked, her astonishment growing by the second. "Me?" The sun beat down on her head, making it ache—or perhaps it was the activity already this morning.

"That's the third group today." Beatriz came back to fetch her as Claire stood at the entrance. "The belief in your saintliness seems to be catching on." A servant slipped Claire's bags out of her hand and set them in the shade. Beatriz gestured, and a soldier began getting the kneelers on their feet and sending them on their way. "You're quite popular in some circles," Beatriz said.

"A miracle? It was magic."

"Aye. But where does the magic come from?" Beatriz regarded her quizzically, then her eyes softened. "I never thought of that before, but we are all the Lord's creatures after all . . . Claire. Scripture says the Lord plays no favorites. Why not a witch as a saint?" Beatriz looked like she wanted to bite off her tongue.

Claire choked, whether because of the idea or because Beatriz had used her name, she couldn't tell. The next thing she knew, she was sitting at the table with the First Wife. "My mother never told me where the magic comes from. It always was. I didn't think to ask." How could she be so foolish and have never dug deeper when she had the time? She regretted every lost opportunity now.

Beatriz nodded. "That would be like asking why you have thumbs. Why should you?"

The First Wife's words made her feel a little better, but she still blamed herself for her lack of curiosity. A servant set a plate of eggs in front of each of them and another poured water into tin mugs.

Their conversation made suspicion creep up Claire's spine. "What's happened?"

"Nothing good," Beatriz whispered. "Now eat your eggs and we'll go riding. We are off to fetch some honey."

As if on a cue, a large, solidly built woman in a brightly colored apron emerged from the back of the tent with a bowl of strawberry jam. "This is my head chef, Lupaa," Beatriz introduced. "She's a wonder in the kitchen, can manage anything, but she's especially amazing with honey."

Like the rest of this strange morning, Claire fumbled for words. "Nice to meet you?"

Lupaa deposited some jam on her plate. "I so thank you, First Wife, for going to see if my bees and their honeycombs survived the Northerners."

Claire covered her ears as the woman shouted her reply loud enough to scare the birds off the trees—or would if there were trees here. Unless she were very deaf, this Lupaa was in on the mystery, too. Worry fought its way into Claire's stomach. The feel of a thousand eyes watching made her skin crawl. Claire had to force herself not to hunch her shoulders.

They stared at her, waiting for her to take up her part in this farce. Claire put a smile on her face and said brightly and loudly, "That sounds pleasant."

The rest of the breakfast passed swiftly with Beatriz scowling whenever Claire tried to ask a question. The First Wife's skirts rustled stiffly as they left the tent, and Claire wondered how she would ride a horse in them until two boys brought a set of small steps and Beatriz climbed to sit nimbly sideways on her saddle. Claire used the steps to mount the brown horse with white-striped knees they brought her. Ramiro had taught her how to ride alone, but she felt far from comfortable doing so. Or maybe it was the feeling of eyes at her back that had her so nervous she dropped the reins—twice. Either way she was glad to escape camp with their two bodyguards and leave it all behind. Unlike the soldiers of earlier, these men wore neither armor nor uniform, but hard leather vests, and rode regular horses instead of the dappled-gray ones of the military.

Somehow in the bustle of departure, a servant strapped her bags of possessions behind her on the saddle, making her more curious.

She expected Beatriz to explain once they were alone, only to be disappointed. The woman would talk about nothing but yesterday's election and the weather. Neither of which were favorable, apparently. According to Beatriz the summer rains should have started and helped with their water shortage, and none of the elected were allies of her husband. Bad news all around. Claire suspected the reason for this trip to be more of the same.

As the ride lengthened, Claire wilted under the

increasing heat. Though she seemed to sweat less here, no shade existed to escape the burning sun. The taller cacti produced only thin skeletons of shadow, and the few times they ended on the cool side of a hill never lasted long. Her skin reddened on arms and hands where the sun hit it. All the black clothing protected her from the burn, but also absorbed the sun and made the heat worse. Beatriz, in black from head to toe, should have felt it more, but the woman looked positively fresh.

Finally, they entered a grove of olive trees, though the twisted trunks weren't tall enough to make a decent shade, it did seem cooler here. One of the bodyguards stood in his stirrups and pointed ahead to a small cluster of dwellings.

Claire sighed with relief. Surely they'd have water there. "Is that where we're going?"

"Aye," Beatriz allowed. "The bee farm."

"Then you'll tell me what this is all about there?" Claire hoped Ramiro's mother wasn't taking her out to the middle of nowhere to dispose of her. The idea had occurred to her that perhaps her blind obedience hadn't been wise, but she wasn't exactly defenseless and she'd rather give Beatriz the benefit of the doubt.

"It's about getting honey," was all the answer she received.

The cluster of buildings turned out to be one white stucco house, a stable, and dozens of tiny, little mud-colored domes on rickety platforms. Bees buzzed literally everywhere, making Claire hold very still to avoid angering any of them. Some of their little domes had been pulled apart and bits of honeycomb lay scattered on the ground. Claire eyed the mess with concern, hoping it was animals.

Their two guards—whose heads turned so often they might have been on swivels and whose hands were never far from their weapons—seemed to grow even tenser here. They got stiffly down from their horses. "Wait here, First Wife, while we scout," one said.

Claire dismounted and warily took her horse into the shade as their guards split up to enter the barn and house. Fewer bees bothered her here, and she looked for Beatriz to follow her, but the older woman wandered among the beehives. Claire twiddled the reins between her fingers. At least she was doing something for the camp out here. Certainly, she enjoyed the exercise better than sitting in a stuffy tent and rolling bandages—but she found it difficult to believe they really came for honey. A bee investigated her braid and she tried not to flinch. As long as she didn't move or accidently touch one of them, the bees would ignore her.

Beatriz finally came to her side, and Claire leaned close to whisper, "Is this about a threat to my life?" She couldn't imagine why else they'd want her out of the camp. It must be about that massacre Ramiro encountered on patrol. Claire frowned. But then wouldn't she be safer *in* camp? It didn't add up.

"Ramiro will tell you all about it. There's no time. Do you remember the collapsed tunnel entrance?" Beatriz pointed. "It should be that way. Can you find it?"

"Tunnel entrance?" Claire echoed, mystified. Ramiro had taken her there in an attempt to sneak into Colina Hermosa only to find it caved in. "I remember it. But why?"

"You'll run from us and go there. Ramiro will meet you." Beatriz pulled her closer and hissed low, "You'll have to use your magic on us to escape. Make it look real. The bodyguards aren't in on it."

"I figured that." Claire shook her head as her stomach started to roil. "But I don't understand. Why all this—"

"Later. They'll be back any second."

Claire sniffed, feeling slightly sick—and it wasn't from the strawberry jam. It seemed to her Beatriz simply didn't want to be the one to tell her. There had been plenty of opportunity. It must be very bad news indeed. Almost more than the reason for all this, however, she feared resorting to her magic again. What could she do that wouldn't hurt anyone too much? Her brain was all a tumble, making it impossible to think. Her hands got cold and sweaty at the same time.

Silly, you're a Woman of the Song. You can manage anything.

But it was easier to think such words than to believe her own reassurances. She leaned against the side of the house to hold her up. The stucco was cool to the touch. It was such a little house, not more than three or four rooms. Why were their guards taking so long to search?

She was about to ask when a man, wearing yellow and black like a bee, rushed out of the house. He moved fast, reaching them between one breath and the next, and slashed at Beatriz with something silvery. The First Wife cried out in pain, and he shoved her down.

The silvery gleam—a long knife—swiped at Claire. She screeched and twisted, and it caught the edge of her shoulder instead of her chest. Material ripped as she jerked and scrambled from the Northern soldier.

Before she could catch a breath, the Northerner followed, slashing again. She darted to the side and managed to put one of the haystack-shaped bee houses between them. Undeterred, he seized the short table it sat upon and batted it away with such force it crashed against the house. Hive and table broke into pieces. Bees flew everywhere, their careless meandering turning into an angry buzz.

The soldier shouted in a harsh language she couldn't understand. His narrowed eyes promised her death.

By the Song, she'd gotten Beatriz killed. Was about to get herself killed. She couldn't let the man win. Anger struggled with fear and conquered. Her mouth opened, but a lump in her throat threatened to gag her; the Song emerged as more of a wheeze,

> *Sting*
> *Hornets*
> *Wasps*
> *Bees*
> *Pain*
> *Swarming*
> *Sting*

He swatted at the air, but the magic didn't distract him from stepping toward her. She couldn't seem to put any force into her Song. Instead, bees stung her arm, her neck. Too many bees already for the deception of the magic to work. The Hornet Tune wouldn't sidetrack him. The magic was useless. Claire stopped singing, sought desperately for another Song, but her mind locked up, words wouldn't come to her.

The knife struck at her again.

She jumped back, toppling another hive. Bees went for her face, blinding her. Their stings made tiny pricks of pain on the bare skin of her arms.

She tried to run, but a hand seized her clothing, pulling her back.

Claire closed her eyes, as if that could make this vanish. Where were their bodyguards?

Something collided into her, staggering her back. Her eyes popped open. The Northern soldier clutched at her to keep himself upright, his knife pressed against her arm. He was so close she could see the individual hairs in the stubble on his face.

Beatriz swung a plank from the broken beehive into his back, pounding the soldier with an audible whack. Beatriz had her face averted and disgust covered her expression as if she'd been shown a mouse or a particular hairy spider.

Claire wiggled free, and he fell. The knife tumbled in the dust.

"Run," Beatriz shouted. Fistfuls of her hair had fallen in a scraggly mess. The comb holding her mantilla was tipped askew, lace wrapped around her face to keep off the bees. Something wet stained her dress down her side.

"Wait. The weapon." Claire snatched up the knife, and the man's head came up. His hand darted out, wrestling her for possession. Knowing she was the weaker, she dropped the blade. When Beatriz just stood there, she grabbed the plank. It weighed more than expected, dragging down her arms. He kicked out, catching Beatriz in the stomach and sending her sprawling. His other leg connected with Claire's shin, creating a fresh wave of pain. Instead of giving in to it, though, she brought the heavy plank down on his head with a sickening crunch. He went limp.

Back protesting like an ancient grandmother, Claire managed to straighten.

What if there were more of him? What if he got back up?

By the Song, Beatriz was hurt. What would Ramiro think of her for letting his mother be injured? More than that, they had to flee. Where were the horses? The frantic buzz of the bees matched the frantic pace of her thoughts.

She kept the plank raised. Her breath came in short pants. Before she could control her thoughts, Beatriz clung to her as bees stung them both. It was the bee stings that drove them into the house, forcing them to close the door.

"Well, we handled that well enough," Beatriz said,

her voice shaky. She turned. Her eyes went roundish and she clutched at her throat. "Dear Lord."

Claire followed her gaze. Their guard lay by the back door with his throat slit. The surprise on his face suggested the Northerner had been hiding in the tiny pantry or had sneaked in the back door.

Bile rose in Claire's throat, but she fought it off. The horses. They must have bolted when she struggled with the soldier. They should go for the horses before they were too long gone to catch, but Claire couldn't force herself to leave this sanctuary. A few bees buzzed her, but most stayed close to the oiled covers on the windows. "Do you think the other bodyguard is dead?"

Beatriz leaned against the well pump in the corner, eyes darting. "He must be or he would have come at all the noise. So would any more of *them*, saints save us." She touched forehead, heart, and stomach, then the First Wife closed her eyes. When she reopened them, she straightened her headpiece. "That man won't be getting back up anytime soon. We'd best see to ourselves. Water, cold water for the pain and to clean the wounds. Pull out the stingers. Just as I used to do when the boys got stung."

The problem was, the woman just stood there, as if expecting a servant to appear and do the task for them. So Claire stumbled over and worked the pump one handed—unable to bring herself to set down the plank. Pain stung her shoulder where the knife had made a shallow cut. However, it was no worse than the numerous bee stings, which were already swelling. She felt proud her hands barely shook; maybe she was getting used to people trying to kill her. At least this one hadn't been after her specifically.

Water gushed over her hands into the small washbasin and she patted her face, bringing some relief. Moving aside, she let Beatriz join her. "A deserter," Claire said. "He must have been brought here by the well and the shelter." Rumor among the womenfolk said there were many Northerners out there, separated from their army or possibly scouting.

"Julian is going to be so upset. He'll lock me up and toss the key after this little stunt. And the bodyguards, the poor souls. It's my fault." Beatriz hissed in pain as she looked up from examining the knife cut along her ribs.

Claire bent to look, setting the plank at her feet, but Beatriz waved her off. "Barely a nick—though it's ruined my best steel-ribbed corset—just a lot of blood. But I've seen plenty of that." She laughed ruefully and splashed water from the washbasin over herself. "It does take me back, though. I haven't scuffled like that since I was a girl. Wrestling. Fighting over the biggest piece of pie. I used to run with all the boys, even beat Julian in races."

"I believe it," Claire said with a smile. "We wouldn't be alive if you hadn't found that plank."

"It was a grand time. Then my grandmother insisted I put on skirts and act the lady." Beatriz put her hands over her face. "Listen to me. Reminiscing like we were at tea."

"It's the shock," Claire said. She located a stinger in her neck by touch and pulled it out. "I never had anyone like that to play with, unless you count the goats." Now with her mother dead, she had even less. Only a grandmother she hadn't seen since infancy and couldn't remember.

"Goats. Certainly not." Beatriz dropped her hands. "That's a shame. There are always so many kin and close kin here—"

"*Sangre* kin."

"Aye, that, too. So much kin, you can't turn around without stumbling over them. And all your kin's friends. Always someone to get you in trouble. I'm sorry you missed that. Still, you did pretty well out there yourself . . . and there's always room for more kin."

Claire looked up from examining her arms for stingers.

"Ramiro made me promise to let him tell you why we're out here. Stiff-necked child. I don't know where he gets it—must be his father. But that's why I didn't say anything." Beatriz busily straightened her clothing, keeping her eyes on that task. "Don't tell him I said so, but I think you'll make the right choice."

She held out her hand, and Claire grasped it with a tinge of delight.

"We paid a dear price today," Beatriz said, shaking her head. "But possibly it was worth it."

CHAPTER 9

Father Telo made his way from the healer tent rather later than he planned—he intended an early jump on an unpleasant task—but when a sufferer wished to speak to a priest, such demands came first—even if the man just complained about the taste of his food and the need for clean bedding.

Misery didn't make *everyone* more spiritual.

Children called to him as they ran through the camp. Women put down their work to bend head and knee for a blessing, and soldiers gave him quick salutes. Even if he hadn't been wearing his brown robes and triple-rope belt, a priest was immediately spotted by his lack of beard, conspicuous like the Lord intended.

He headed for the most logical spot for the heathen priestess to be confined—the very wagon where he'd been a prisoner. The chains that bound him still lay there after all. He set his steps toward the quarry. As he made his way through the camp, however, he could sense a shift in mood. All around were whispers and drawn faces. Something had occurred—and recently. He finally stopped a sharp-faced boy to find out what it was about. Certain children knew everything, and he had learned to spot the type. A copper from his pocket loosened the boy's tongue.

"Why, the witch has left, Father. Some say she escaped. Some say *el jefe* got rid of her. Nobody really knows."

Telo grunted and handed over a second copper. Tempting though it was to find out more, he was out of that now, no longer at the center of things, back to being a simple friar instead of a confidant and sometime spy of the *Alcalde*.

As it should be.

The Lord cared not for those who made themselves important. Simplicity had always been his guiding light. More reluctantly than was good for him, he turned from the center of the camp and resumed his walk toward the quarry.

The little house on wheels sat where it had always been, though someone had removed the carpet and altar of the Northerners that had been across from it. The spot where they'd taken his hand. The place where they'd killed children. The memory made his blood boil. He tucked his nub under his other arm and straightened his spine.

Asking forgiveness of the murderess who'd ordered that deed would take all his strength. But the Lord commanded it of him, and he would obey.

To his surprise, Farmer-face and Taps proved to be the guards outside the house wagon, the very scouts who had gone into the Northern camp with him. If one were looking for omens—which he wasn't—you couldn't find a better one.

"Peace be upon you this fine morning, my friends," Telo called out heartily. He really should have learned their true names—Farmer-face for his lined, weathered appearance and a face that looked tough enough to pound nails, and Taps for a resemblance to a cheerful Father at his first monastery who brewed such good beer.

"And to you, Father." Taps's plump face beamed. "So glad to see you recovered from . . . the unfortunate incident. We owe you thanks, I believe." For all of looking like a friendly tavern keeper, both these men were at the top of their profession, lethal, and able to survive many missions into enemy territory by their wits.

Telo waved that off with his good hand. "Doing as the Lord moves me, as should we all."

Farmer-face rolled his eyes, but Taps clapped him on the shoulder. "Indeed, Father. What can we do for you?"

"A visit to the prisoner. Some spiritual consolation."

"No one allowed inside," Farmer-face snapped, crossing his arms.

"She's been violent, Father," Taps said more mildly.

"Refuses to speak our language, though we all know she can."

"You coddle her too much," Farmer-face accused his companion. "She doesn't need blankets or chamber pots. She should be chained to the bare ground, like she did with our children. I don't see why we even have to have a trial."

"And wouldn't that make us as bad as her kind," Taps said. "She is a woman, after all."

"A devil is more like."

Telo had to agree with Farmer-face. He'd seen Santabe's work up close. It didn't surprise him that they received no cooperation from the priestess. But he didn't need her to talk. He'd come to say his piece and leave. "No one allowed inside, is it? What about opening the door to give her some fresh air?" With the wagon so small, they could converse just fine with him outside.

Farmer-face shrugged, and Taps pulled out a key. "We had to install a lock in addition to the bolt to keep her inside. She frightens the passersby." Knife in one hand and key in the other, he climbed the three steps, unlocked the door, then quickly stepped back before turning the knob. He leapt from the small platform to the ground. Farmer-face had his sword out and held ready.

"I've seen less caution from men approaching deadly snakes," Telo said, elbowing Farmer-face.

Farmer-face grunted. "Deadly snakes only bite."

"The weak-willed priest. Come to let me finish the job of killing you?" Santabe poked her head around the doorframe. Red glinted in the strange light coloring of her hair. It hung uneven as if hacked off jaggedly by the handful. The usual pristine white of her robe was stained with blood and dirt. The Northern priestess stood as tall as Telo, but thinner, her bare arms corded with wiry muscle. An earring in the shape of the sun dangled from one earlobe.

"You still don't find kindness is a virtue, though it's the only thing keeping you alive." Telo shook his head. Always first with the clever tongue and forgetting to think before he spoke. He shouldn't be engaging the woman—she thrived on it.

"You've caught her in a good mood," Taps said. "That's the first time she's spoken so we can understand. Her first day here she chewed off her own hair and ripped up the clean clothing the *Alcalde* sent."

Santabe left the doorway, and a chain clinked on her ankle fastening her to the inside of the wagon. Telo knew from experience it only reached to the small porch and the steps. He'd worn it over a sevenday.

Her eyes burned with a light that made Telo want to step back. She glanced toward Colina Hermosa's walls. "We've razed your filthy den and soon we'll cleanse the rest of the animals. Weak. You're all weak. Only fitting as sacrifice for Dal. Lord Ordoño will be back and then you all die."

Before anyone could react, she twisted, kicking out with her unchained leg and catching Farmer-face in the chest, punching him back. One arm caught Taps and pulled him into the wagon. They crashed to the floor, and she wrapped the chain around his neck, then yanked.

As Telo sprang up the steps, Santabe took the knife from beside Taps and slashed the guard's throat. Blood sprayed in Telo's eyes, but he seized her hand before she finished the stroke. Farmer-face appeared, seizing her other side. Too late, sadly. Much too late as life fled from Taps.

Santabe grinned with red teeth. "Such is what happens to the weak, fools. Dal takes his blood."

"Hello!" Claire called and echoes bounced back to greet her. She smiled and then ducked her head. Probably not the wisest thing, to be shouting all alone like this, but the temptation had proven too strong. She'd always wanted to hear an echo and this seemed the place to create one.

"Think we'll be there soon?" she asked her horse in a brave whisper. They'd found three of the four horses wandering in the olive grove, including this one carrying her baggage. Beatriz had led her to this trail and then they'd split up, the First Wife going back to camp to seek help in retrieving their guard's bodies. Help was also too late for the Northern deserter—the man had died from the injuries they'd inflicted. Claire's guilt had grown as the shadows lengthened and so did another worry.

Claire had walked the narrow trail Beatriz pointed out to her, guiding her horse behind. With her limited skill at riding, being on the ground seemed wisest. The First Wife said the trail would take her straight to the tunnel where she was to wait for Ramiro. Beatriz hadn't mentioned it being so rugged or rocky. Nor did Claire know how long the journey might take, or even the length. Twin hills rose fifteen feet or maybe twenty feet on either side of the trail, their sides sheer, leaving her in a deep gully. The air was quite a bit cooler than when she'd been on the flat desert. Not much grew at the bottom but the tiny cacti about the height of her foot and lichen. How Beatriz even knew about this trail was startling in itself.

Despite the First Wife's mule-headedness and obvious enjoyment for giving orders, Claire found herself missing the woman and hoped she'd make it back to camp without further misfortune.

Claire clicked her tongue at the horse for some noise—the return to silence after the echoes died made her skin crawl more than the echoes had. And to think, she used to look forward to being alone. Well, she had the horse, so she wasn't completely on her own, but near enough.

The horse flicked an ear and looked at her with uncaring eyes. Claire sighed. Ramiro's horse had always seemed to understand what he was saying. Apparently, her horse was just a normal one.

"Maybe Ramiro will beat us there and be waiting."

If horses could yawn, this one would. Even with a horse she felt inadequate.

"I hope it doesn't rain." She had no doubt where all the water would go if it did.

Up ahead, the narrow split between the steep walls changed, climbing upward. Claire increased her pace and saw that it widened. She stumbled over loose rock and stopped. The gully ended, leaving her on level ground, but the trail split in two directions, heading toward different hills.

"Oh."

She looked at the horse for inspiration, but it hadn't the decency to look back. "Maybe they both go to the same place?" Perhaps one was the easy way and the other the hard way. Wishful thinking and not at all likely. Why hadn't Beatriz mentioned this?

"Let's see." The tunnel entrance had been west of the city, directly on the path from her home in the swamp. They'd gone south and west in the morning—possibly? She hadn't paid much attention. If she picked the one most to the west, would that be a good notion? The sun would give her direction. She cringed, feeling sure it was a bad idea, but pulled the horse toward the trail that angled toward the sun. As good a reason as any, she supposed.

"If we don't arrive by dark, we'll turn around and come back." The horse didn't disagree and she took that for a good sign.

The trail wound for hours through cacti of all

kinds: fat ones, tall ones, flat ones, and the extra spiny variety, before dumping her out in front of the tunnel entrance.

"There it is. Impressed now?" she asked the horse to no reaction. "You know, goats have more personality than you. I guess it would serve you right if I name you Horse." The insult flew right over Horse's head, and the idea made her giggle until she remembered she was stuck in the middle of nowhere with only Horse. Ramiro had not beaten her here, and she soon found the light didn't penetrate farther than a few feet inside the tunnel. Anything could be hiding in the darkness.

"So we wait out here."

She looked helplessly at Horse. From watching Ramiro, she knew she should do certain things to make Horse comfortable, but she didn't have food or water for it, and taking off the saddle meant trying to put it back on later. It looked heavy. She settled for tying the reins tightly around one of the tall cacti—while avoiding thorns—and sitting on a rock in the shade. She munched on the trails rations from her bag, hoping the wait wouldn't be long.

What could be the reason for sending her here, and why hadn't Ramiro brought her himself?

Several answers occurred to her, but as they all involved danger, she tried not to dwell on them. Instead one thought kept intruding: When they'd defeated the Northern army the peril was supposed to be over. She'd be accepted by Ramiro's people and make a new home. Everything would be roses.

Naïve, that's what she was.

Loneliness swept over her, making her think of the people back at the camp.

Fronilde would make a wonderful friend—when the young woman wasn't quite so sad. Claire would have liked to be her shoulder to lean on, but she didn't know if that would happen now. It saddened her that things hadn't worked out as she hoped. So many things. Because it wasn't just losing the chance to become friends with Fronilde. She also had to leave just when Ramiro's mother had started to like her.

Nothing she could do about that now. With no one around, this was the perfect time to practice the Song. Immediately that lump in her throat that seemed to appear every time she thought of magic formed along with a cold shiver.

Later would be a good time, too.

Claire squinted up at the first brightening of stars. High overhead hung the Half Note. And there, just peeking over the hill above the tunnel, the Staff glowed. The familiar sight reassured her that some things stayed the same. And inside, she was the same Claire no matter what around her changed. That's what her mother would say anyway.

What would her mother think of her situation now?

She'd tell her not to trust men or the magic, that's what.

Claire considered. The sky might seem flat to some, like the plank she'd used on the Northerner, but it wasn't. She'd seen stars move in it. Her mother's advice took humans—especially men—for flat, that everyone behaved the same, had no variation. Like the sky, people were more complex. Some couldn't be trusted and others always proved their worth.

Metal scraped on stone, and Claire sat up. A dark shape moved on the trail. The fading light showed the figure waving to her, and she smiled in relief. Ramiro. She'd seen many shapes and sizes of people now, but his always seemed the best to her. Slim hips, but wide shoulders, as if he could carry a heavy load.

"You made it. You are well?" he asked before he even got close enough to see his features.

She fingered the lumps of bee stings on her neck, some felt less swollen. "Well enough. And Beatriz? She is well?" She stood to better hear the answer.

"Home already and facing Father's wrath. She told us of the skirmish and your part in it. Also that you escaped afterward. There are search parties everywhere hunting."

"Hunting me?" she squeaked.

"Aye," he said as he dismounted from Sancha. "Hunting you. I'm part of the patrol, looking for you, too."

"And here I am."

"And here you are."

Claire stepped closer and touched his arm. He wore his breastplate, but his helmet and the other armor hung strapped to Sancha. The smile lingered on his face, though his eyes held uncertainty. He didn't appear eager to bring up why they were here, and suddenly neither was she.

"The bees got you worse than Mother." His warm fingers touched her face, turning it up to the remaining light, and somehow making her shiver. "It must hurt. I've got a salve." He dropped his touch to turn to Sancha.

She took the plunge. "Why did you send me here?"

"The scouts reported the other army around Aveston is intact. They didn't break." He handed her a small glass jar. "Mother sent this."

"Thanks." She held tight to the jar. "What does that mean for me?"

"The *concejales* want to send you as our answer—let you scare the Northerners again. They've bullied my father into insisting as much to you." His face expressed concern, sympathy. "Father warned me they plan on holding you until you agree."

The jar of salve fell from her fingers. This morning, she hadn't time for fear, the attack had come too swiftly, and all she could do was react. Now, terror settled over her like a second skin, sinking deep and turning her insides to jelly.

"I can't," she whispered.

He helped her back to the rock where she'd been sitting earlier, kneeling beside her. "I explained to Father you didn't know about the magic. That the first time was more accidental than planned. Of course, no one will believe that. Look, I wish this wasn't so, but—"

"This is a smaller army, right? Can't you fight them instead?"

"If we send all our forces, we'd be a match for them in size. Perhaps with the element of surprise . . . but that means leaving the people undefended, you understand." Bitterness entered his voice. "None of the other *ciudades-estado* will help us. Worse, Father expects the first army is regrouping. We're on the plain . . . exposed—with nowhere to go."

She looked at him with wide eyes, disappointment filling her heart. "You want me to do it."

"No." He stood and walked toward the tunnel, showing her his back. "Maybe. I don't know. It doesn't matter——it's *your* choice. I want you to decide. It's just that there doesn't seem to be any other option."

The betrayal sank deep into her heart, tears forming. "It was wrong. Using the magic like that went to a place no one should touch. And you said it wouldn't work again, wouldn't catch them unaware."

"I know," he all but shouted, then calmed as he paced. "I know what I said. And I meant it—at the time. Now I'm not so sure."

"I can't," she said, and it cost her more than she'd expected. They needed her help, would probably die without it. She let Ramiro down. Let herself down. Not only did she fear to do as asked, the thought of using the magic again stung more than the bees. It hadn't worked today. Moreover, she hadn't the will to use it. There were so many variables. The subject had to be receptive to the thought she put in their head—and the conditions had to be favorable. What if she got there and the magic failed like it had at the bee house? And that was with only *one* Northerner. What if showing them their god had only worked that time because the sun was rising? What if it stuck in her throat again?

"I just can't."

She couldn't see Ramiro's back stiffen in the dark, but she felt it.

"That's no way to treat a horse." He strode over to Horse and began working on the strap under its belly.

She gave in to his avoidance, feeling limp and washed out. "I wasn't sure what to do and didn't have supplies for it. It's not like I knew I was going for a journey."

"I brought some." He swung the saddle to the ground, then he leaned against Horse, still not facing her. "Look, I understand. That's why I sent you out here—to give you a choice. Just . . . just think on it overnight. I'll come back in the morning. Don't leave until then. Promise me."

She smiled through the tears. Without him to saddle Horse she really couldn't go anyway, except on foot. She remembered Ramiro's stubbornness in finding her before when she'd run off in the swamp. She wanted some of that stubbornness now, only used to stand up for her. "I promise." She believed he'd be true and wouldn't force her to use the magic. "Think on something for me: other options. Maybe . . ." She grasp at reeds in quicksand. "Maybe my people would help, Women of the Song. We could try."

"You said you didn't know any."

"Well . . . I don't. But my grandmother is there. I think. I'd hope that she would listen to me at least. She is kin. It's a possibility." She'd considered it yesterday when she decided to leave, going to her grandmother for a home. As she said it aloud now, it felt even more like the right option. "She knows more about the magic. Maybe she'd teach me. Then I'd know what I did wrong last time." The lump rose in her throat again.

"That would take weeks. My duty is with my people."

"Yes," she said sadly, feeling hopeless. Though she said "we," she hadn't supposed he'd go with her. Duty and his responsibility as a soldier meant too much to him. More than she ever would.

He finished with Horse and came back to take her hands. "We'll both think about it and meet in the morning." All too soon he released her. "There are torches inside the tunnel. And there should be a cot for the guards who used to be stationed there. We can make you comfortable, too, before I head back."

"Sure," she whispered, thinking that neither one of them would sleep much tonight.

CHAPTER 10

Alone at the council table, Julian listened to Lugo's voice coming through the tent, as he announced to the crowd the results of the no-confidence vote and the special election coming in eight days. That was quickly followed by his intention to assume the post of *alcalde*, if the people would have him. The "if" rang with false humility to Julian. Scattered shouts came from the crowd, but most received the news with indecipherable mutterings.

The loss of Claire made the no-confidence unanimous among the *concejales*. Not even Antonio, stubborn friend as he was, had stood against it. The fact that the girl was with Beatriz when the escape happened had proven the last gust of wind to begin the sandstorm. There was no stopping it now. Though the hour was late, guards had to hold mobs of people back from showing their displeasure to Julian first-hand. They may have hated and feared the witch, but she was their salvation at the same time. Even without opinion being against him, Julian had already made up his mind to seek no votes—to let the office go without a struggle.

The voices moved off, gone to announce his shame—his failure—to the rest of the camp. Julian felt no blame toward the *concejales*: The people called for his blood and it would be political suicide to stand against it. And weren't they right?

All true, he acknowledged.

His left hand shook, the whole arm feeble. He sank deep into the self-pity and doubt of his broken inner landscape, unable to move from his chair.

The cold touch of metal pushed against his neck right below his beard. A presence pressed beside his back. Julian froze, not daring to breathe. He hadn't thought they literally wanted his blood, at least not enough to come at him through the back of the tent.

"You do not look so well, old fox. What is all this silver in your hair? Why your beard is entirely gray." Amusement tinged the words, but the knife didn't waiver and kept its keen edge against his throat. "I call that first round a draw—you lose your city, I my army—but it seems your people see it elsewise."

"Ordoño." Julian did not give the man the dignity of a title.

"The old fox and the young fox. But no, no longer an old fox. What is this? Now an old, whipped dog." The knife lifted. "There is no fun in killing a dog with its tail between its legs. You disappoint me—letting them strip you of your rule. Who does that?"

"A people who follow the law."

Ordoño came around the table and took Diego's empty chair. The first time they had met, the leader of the Northern army had acted the part of servant. Now he wore a worn poncho over torn trousers several inches too short. Dusty sandals covered his feet instead of boots. A scruff of a dark beard graced his jaw. With his ordinary face, no one would have picked him out of a crowd of peasants. Julian couldn't help but be impressed with the man's recklessness. The Northerners, with their pale skin, eyes, and hair, could never hope to blend into the camp, but Ordoño was one of them.

He sat, flipping the knife first by point and then by hilt. "Where's the thrill in following the law? A fox makes his own rules. I already have my army back. While you, you have nothing."

Julian considered calling for help and dismissed it. He wouldn't learn any information that way. "Did you come here to gloat?"

"No. I came to kill you. But this punishment seems much better. Why ruin it? I will even order my men not to touch you." He grinned. "Does that add salt in the wounds, old fox? Because to me you will always be that: a fox. Only a fox could manage to bring an enemy like the witch and rout my army. Your citizens are fools to lose you." Ordoño caught the knife by its point and gestured with the hilt. "You delight me with your unexpectedness. So creative. It's almost a pity. I should kill your competition to let you keep your seat, but I'm not insane."

"You could have fooled me," Julian said drily. "Is there anything you haven't learned while spying?"

Ordoño shrugged. "I know more than you. People talk amongst their own, after all. Would you like to question me?"

"Where is your army?"

"Near Zapata. Do you plan to attack it? We both know that would be suicide on your part and no one would follow you anyway." The man leaned forward in his chair. "I'll admit, you didn't make it easy for me. I'm still dragging in odds and ends—had to make many examples. How I hate superstitious fools. Such a waste."

"My sympathies."

Ordoño slapped his knee. "You and I, my friend, so much alike."

"Hardly."

"Careful, old fox. Keep up this spirit, and you might earn your throne back. You're showing your teeth." He stood and slid the knife into his poncho. "One thing to think on before I go. I also know your witch is gone, and I can take your people anytime I like. The question is shall they be appetizer or dessert, before or after Aveston, my army's main course?"

"You might find us pricklier than you expect."

"Don't bluff when I can see all your cards. You are defenseless without your walls. I know why your witch was here, and I know why she left. I know there is only the one. A witch alone is easier sport. Shall I hunt her? Or perhaps, I'll save my knife for your son. Women are so fickle. Killing him will ensure she never comes back. A girl will do many foolish things for a handsome face, but if that face is gone—so is the incentive."

"Guards!" Julian shouted as he jumped to his feet, but the man was out of the tent in a flash. By the time Julian reached the flap, he caught sight of the end of the poncho vanishing into the crowd, gone.

"Sir?"

Julian hesitated. There were hundreds, maybe thousands, in the camp to match the generic description he could provide. To bring up this encounter would be a waste of valuable time and resources. Julian modified his words. "Would you tell my son to come see me—immediately?"

"Right away, *Alcalde*," one said with a sympathetic nod. "He rode back into camp a few minutes ago."

"There he is!" someone from the mob shouted.

Julian looked at them, almost expecting to see Ramiro, but no one could have heard him from this distance. It was him they had caught sight of, and with the crowd ready to overreact, it made sense to stay inside the tent and let someone else fetch Ramiro. Though he saw almost as many hands held out beseechingly as fisted in anger.

"Make another miracle for us, *Alcalde*," a woman shouted.

She was immediately shoved to the side by a taller man. "We need no more of those kind of miracles! My family is dead!"

"You let the witch get away. Your wife did it!"

Julian shrank back, as arguing broke out for and against. His inner landscape rocked with doubt. Maybe some still supported him, but the majority felt like the *concejales*. The scorn in Ordoño's eyes flashed in his brain and the world steadied, solidifying with anger.

At that moment, a thought struck. "And have someone check on the captive woman Santabe, and try and find Father Telo and escort him here." After the fiasco that morning with Santabe killing one of her jailers, Julian had tripled the guard on her wagon—he needed to hurry her trial, but there had been difficulties. He did not believe Ordoño had come to free the priestess, but the man may have a twisted sense of loyalty, and if he wanted her, then her rescue would have taken place already.

Julian ducked back inside as the guards issued orders and sent men running. The *concejales* would say Ordoño had a death wish in coming here, but Julian knew the wisdom of sending the right tool for the right job. Ordoño was the right tool. The hazard had been acceptable for the potential gain. In his place, Julian would have put most priority on finding out how his army had been disrupted. Ordoño must feel the same. Maybe they were somewhat alike in that they both accepted risk.

For the first time in days Julian's inner landscape stayed firm. His mind worked, tumbling through possibilities, rejecting some and holding fast to others. He stared at his left thumb, willing it to bend. With much pain, he forced it to touch his palm, the merest brush before he relaxed the effort.

Julian stuck his head out of the tent again. "Fetch back the *concejales* and find me all the priests."

"*All* the priests?" a guard said. "In the middle of the night, sir?"

"Aye, now. They'll need to begin work at first light. There will be changes."

Ordoño might live to regret this visit. Julian had eight days before his time ran out as *alcalde*. If he could hold on to his resolve, he could still bend the situation and this round would be his. Then they would see who was the whipped dog.

After leaving Claire and returning to camp, Ramiro felt as if tied to two horses running in opposite directions. They took his heart one way and his brain the other, dividing him. He couldn't sit still. Couldn't concentrate. He started to groom Sancha only to walk off distractedly and find himself yards away, holding the curry brush. A quick return to work, and the next thing he knew, Sancha nudged him with her nose as he stood doing nothing again.

The camp reflected his mood—it seemed alive tonight. He swore he could hear it breathe, though the servant section was empty with not a soul in sight. The desert beat with a suppressed excitement. It seemed no one could sit tonight, despite the late hour, let alone sleep.

Saints.

One minute he resolved to let Claire go and stay for his people. An instant later, he wanted to throw it all away. He owed duty to both. It was his fault Claire was here. If she should die on her own . . .

If the people should perish for lack of fighting men . . .

His father forbade choosing Claire . . .

He leaned over and heaved until bile filled his mouth. San Martin had never faced this. Santiago never doubted his path. The Lord knew Ramiro was no saint, but he'd always thought his path clear.

A week ago following orders was enough—he let others tell him what to do. Then his mother was in the hands of the Northerners and he'd made his own commands. Now, he found no clear sense of direction.

He spat the bitter taste from his mouth and ran a hand through his hair. What was he to do?

What Claire said about other witches made sense, but he doubted there would be time—if any of the strange women listened. Using her magic was a surer answer to the Northerners. There would be no right choice to bring to Claire in the morning.

A messenger boy collided with him in the darkness. "The *Alcalde* wants you immediately," the boy got out in a breathless rush. "Immediately," he repeated.

Ramiro touched his sword hilt, some of the boy's urgency transferring to him. "I'm on my way."

The guards at the council tent fell back to give him room. Ramiro lifted the flap and entered. "What's happened? I heard shouting. You sent for me?"

His father paced the room with more energy than Ramiro had seen in days. When Julian turned, the spark of life lit his eyes again.

"I don't like the look of that crowd outside," Ramiro said. "They didn't want to let me through."

"What? That? It is nothing, my son." Julian waved it off and took Ramiro's arm, drawing him close. "I need you to leave your unit and take a message to Crueses."

Ramiro drew back, brows coming down. "Crueses? That's a two-day trip. I have patrol tomorrow afternoon. They might send me out again tonight to look for Claire. What's happened?" Did his father know of his dilemma and resolve to make the choice for him?

"Things have changed. It's a new day, my son. I am in charge of all the *pelotónes*, am I not? Surely I can order one of its number. I'm still the *Alcalde* with control of the troops, and the council has to listen to me—whether they like it or not. I have a message for the leader of Crueses. I will explain to your *capitán*."

"Why bother to go to Crueses? They won't help us. And they don't deserve to share our information. Let *them* suffer as we have. It should be their turn for the way they let us down. If they'd been there . . ." He trailed off, the anger too deep to speak.

His father had bustled over to the table to turn over papers, now he looked up, shock on his face. "What's this, my son? Hate, from you? This isn't like you."

"I've changed more than you know."

"So had I—or so I thought." Compassion spread across Julian's face. "Hate is not the way to success, Ramiro. It clouds the thinking process. What I do I do for Colina Hermosa and our people. If it benefits Crueses, then that's as may be." He turned back to his papers.

"And what about Claire?" Ramiro asked.

"Where is the ink? What about her? She has returned to her home, has she not? Unfortunately, the Northerners know all about her, but I trust in her skills to defend herself. She has a head start on them and will be fine."

"Fine?" Ramiro said, disgusted. The Northerners knew of Claire? His worst fears were realized. "But how do you know this? How did the Northerners find out?"

"I just know, my son. Leave some worries to me. I need your obedience on this. Take the message to Crueses for me, and when you come back we can talk." Julian looked up. "I think your mother was right—never tell her I said so—we should not use the magic again. As you said, they'll be expecting it. There are other ways to save our people." He looked down again. "Saints, *where* is that ink?"

A guard stuck his head inside. "We are still locating the *concejales*, sir."

As the bodyguard disappeared, Julian crossed to Ramiro and took his arm, leading him to the exit. "I need someone I can count on. I'll send a runner to you with the message and I need you to go with haste. Right away. Do this for me?"

Ramiro reeled from the tent, his father having accepted his silence for assent. What had been hours to make up his mind just became minutes. He didn't want to see the smug, satisfied people of Crueses in their homes when he had none. And going to Crueses would make it impossible to speak to Claire again . . . to say goodbye.

Things had been so much easier when he'd been nothing but a *bisoño*, yearning to earn his beard. He longed to lay this before someone for advice, but his military brothers would all say the same thing, would not even see the dilemma. Speaking to his commanding officer would likely get him arrested for desertion. His closest friends to whom he could confide were dead at the hands of Claire's mother. And the one—his breath caught—the one of his blood, yet closer than a mere sibling, who always listened to his troubles, could never help him again.

His vision blurred. Ramiro jabbed at his eyes with his knuckles before someone saw his weakness. He wanted to pound something until it was beyond dead, wanted to yell until his throat was raw. Yet, such acts were childish. Salvador would scold that sort of self-indulgence. Ramiro stumbled forward, eager to leave behind the desperate people around the council tent.

A shape broke out of the darkness. Sancha nudged his chest with her nose. "Felt that did you, girl. Sorry to wake you up." It didn't happen often, but he must have been upset enough to alert Sancha through their bond. "It's a mess, and I don't know what to do." He touched her warm flank. Should he disappoint his father or the girl?

The moon rode high in the sky, large and bright and uncaring. Its beam lit up the dark walls of Colina Hermosa like something out of a dream.

A dream...

Ramiro's heart skittered. He'd seen this before.

The dream where Salvador had dropped his helm and turned his back on him. More appropriately, he'd been facing the city, had turned his back on it. Had it been a message for him from his brother? Had Salvador been trying to say something to him besides farewell?

"That's senseless," he told Sancha, but indecision fled and his stomach settled. He thought back to the dream, to what Salvador had showed him.

He knew what he had to do.

CHAPTER 11

When Ramiro entered the clearing, the moonlight showed Claire precariously balanced on a rock, her saddle on her shoulder and both arms up to keep it there. The saddle blanket hung askew across her horse's back, and every time she shimmied closer with the saddle, the animal ambled its backside away. A laugh burst from him before he could hold it back, followed by a surge of annoyance.

Claire tipped off the rock, arms waving, as her saddle hit the ground just missing her toes.

"Trying to leave without saying goodbye?" It was hours before they were supposed to meet. If he'd waited until the assigned time, she'd have been long gone. He'd never expected her to be the one trying to avoid the other. He slid from Sancha to face her with hands on his hips.

She frowned right back at him. "I didn't think you would show, and if you did, I didn't want to say no again."

He strode over and took the blanket off her horse, giving it a hard shake to free any clinging hair or dirt, and refolding it to the cleaner side. "You need to learn how to treat a horse. It was never going to stand still for you."

"I'd have managed," she said crossly.

"Really?"

She stuck out her tongue, and he resisted the urge to do the same. How could one tiny girl make him so angry? His mind inserted another question he didn't want to think about: How did she manage to look so appealing with her tongue out, a smudge of dirt on her cheek, and her braid done crookedly? He shook that off as unproductive for this moment. "I'm not here to ask you to reconsider."

"Oh?"

"I'm here about the other option. Your idea of finding more witches to help. I think it has merit."

"It does?" She blinked and her hands dropped off her hips. "Of course it does."

A few scratches and reassuring pats to her horse and the mare knew exactly who was in charge. He bent to retrieve the saddle. With his face hidden, he said, "And I'm going with you. Father has a new plan for protecting our people—he likes your idea and doesn't need me hanging around for his. That frees me up to go with you."

Also technically true, as he'd arranged for Arias to take the message to Crueses. Claire didn't need to know his father had forbidden him to go with her, or that he was deserting from his *pelotón*. His mother's support would likely be gone, too, if she found out what he was doing. He pushed aside the wave of guilt—and loss. He knew this was the right choice.

Claire clapped her hands at his lie, a beaming smile crossing her face. "I don't have to go alone. You're coming with me. That's a relief—erm . . . I mean"— her eagerness dropped—"I can make space for you."

He rolled his eyes at her lack of guile, but inwardly smiled. At least someone was happy about his decision. "Then it's settled." He set the saddle and started adjusting the straps. "Find yourself something to eat from my bags."

"I had breakfast, thank you very much. I have my own bags this time."

Ramiro refrained from reminding her that Beatriz had managed that. He finished up the breast collar on the mare and double-checked the cinch strap. Her saddle bags sat beside the rock, and he lashed them down tight.

He'd decided on the ride over that he wouldn't bring up the Northerners or that they knew about Claire. Why scare her more with her already reluctant to use her magic?

Just as he wouldn't mention his desertion.

"Then we're ready to go."

She came and took the saddle horn in her hand, then stood there. Even in the moonlight, he could see her face flooding with color. She mumbled something.

"What?"

Again came the mumble and finally, "I can't reach the saddle on my own."

"So you need my help?"

"Stop torturing me," she snapped. "You know I do."

Instead of giving her a leg up, he grabbed the back of her breeches and tossed her up. "That's for trying to sneak off." She clung to the horse on her stomach and managed to inch a leg over. It struck him then that sneaking off was just what *he* had done, and once more a wave of misery and doubt spread over him.

Am I doing the right thing?

The thing was, there was no time to turn around. Right or wrong, the decision was made. So he ignored the little voice inside as best he could, keeping his face from showing his conflict just as Claire faced him.

"Thanks for that." She scowled in his direction.

"Any time." Sancha lifted her upper lip as if to join in his amusement. He sprang into the saddle with just a touch on the horn and Claire's glower deepened.

"Show off."

"Teresa is better with horses." He flashed her a grin. "And yeah, I know, you only had goats."

"I hope you brought plenty of socks. It's going to get wet." She dished out their old joke from their previous time in the swamp with a lifted chin and a glow of pure mischief. He hadn't the heart to take the last word from her. He feared on this trip her successes might be too few and far between. Soggy boots would soon be the least of his worries.

Teresa had worried the mule would slow them down—that the shorter legs of her animal compared to Alvito's tall mare would hold them back from reaching Colina Hermosa. An hour was enough to disabuse her of that notion, when Alvito asked to be tied to his saddle in case he fainted. She'd refused, insisting they stop more frequently to rest instead. While he sat white-faced and stoic, she'd become the guide, making sure they headed the right way . . . and she became the squire, too, taking care of the animals and establishing camp, doing work she'd never dreamed of in her routine life at the university. Always she'd been a small gear in a larger mill with others to give the direction; now she knew how Ramiro had felt when he'd been left with the responsibility of the hostile witch girl—terrified.

The second day had gone smoother with Alvito regaining some of his strength and riding for longer periods. They even made it to the abandoned village late into the night and slept with a roof over their heads.

With the sun cresting the horizon on a cloudless morning, Alvito rode without a word. The flirtatious smirk or light comment she'd come to expect from him were gone. His eyes focused on the brilliance before them, and Teresa read a sadness festering there.

"It's always pretty, no?" she asked him, gesturing at the sunrise. She was no healer, but it didn't take one to know some things were healthier not held inside, and military cultures were notorious for bottling their emotions. She should know, she'd spent a whole year studying the subject. When he didn't answer, she teased, "Or have you never noticed the sight before because you've never been without a woman to hold your eye instead? Or perhaps it was too many aching heads in the morning."

He flipped his reins toward the sunrise. "Is my shallowness that apparent?" His sudden grin faded. "It's . . . I . . . didn't expect to see many more of them."

"Ah. The fear of death can bring soberness to many a man, Cat."

"Yes . . . No, not that. Just, there were better men . . . Why did the saints spare me? Gomez practically raised me . . ."

She waited, sensing silence was needed.

"Salvador. He was thoughtful—a leader. Better. We were kin through our mothers, you know. And Ramiro's out there alone. I owe it to Salvador to watch over him . . ." His mouth quirked with bitterness. "I didn't expect to still be seeing sunrises after this." He touched his chest where his wounds lay hidden.

"I expect many of us have felt the same on this trip," she said. "We cannot understand how the Lord works. Or why the saints underwent so many trials.

But it helps to know they faced difficulties such as these, too."

He nodded at her trite words, keeping his eyes before him. "I don't know how the witch made us do it. The best of friends . . ."

"Why you attacked one another? But you know it was the magic, right?"

"Yes, but *how*? How could it make us . . . I killed them—my best friends."

His pain brought tears to her eyes. She couldn't speak, not to give him more empty words. But he expected something from her, needed wisdom. Finally she said, "And *they* nearly killed you. I think—no proof, mind you—but I think the witches delve into our deepest fears. You all feared the Northerners would find us before we could save the city. How could you not see enemies everywhere? Even mistaking them for those closest. The witches' magic deceives—it's what it does."

"But how," he pressed. "How did that witch know?"

Teresa frowned, shrugging in turn. She had considered this puzzle through the long days of waiting for news and for Alvito to heal. She had turned it over in her mind; after all, she made study her habit. How had the older witch known? How had she disabled them so easily? "Perhaps it's instinct, an inborn talent of the magic in the witches. At least, so I hope. Because that would mean the young one Ramiro has could be powerful, though she denied it. Claimed she hadn't come into her full command yet. But—"

Alvito turned to look at her. "But?"

Something that had been niggling at her burst to the fore of her mind, and she shuddered at the thought. Finally she answered Alvito.

"But if it's not instinct, how would the witches know we feared a foe appearing? That would imply the witches know more of our situation than we ever expected."

A few hours later, Teresa sat up tall on her mule to see forward. A long, low bridge waited ahead, spanning a wide creek and a morass of wetland. A large camp had been set up across the bridge and down either side. She saw figures out front who must be guards, but couldn't make out details. A shiver rode down her spine, and she gripped her medallion of Santa Catalina, patron of scholars, through her pocket. It could be Northerners.

Before she could voice her fear, Alvito spoke, "They're ours. I see the uniform—and horses. But they have a mass of civilians with them."

She envied his superior eyesight, even as the specifics cleared and she made out the greens and grays of the soldiers. Twenty or more of them guarded this end of the camp, with many farther inside among what must number a few thousand civilians. A group of unsaddled, dapple-gray horses grazed nearby. The Northerners had no such animals. The sight of the unconcerned *caballos de guerra* reassured more than words, reminding her of Ramiro. She held on to her curiosity and urged her mule faster.

The guards came forward to greet them with easy smiles and words of welcome, due no doubt to Alvito's tattered and patched-together uniform and the dapple-gray color of his mount. More than ever she was glad he offered to accompany her, and not just for his companionship. Soon one was leading them deeper inside the camp, through the staring eyes of the civilians, to their commanding officer. There, she hoped to find out what all these people did in the middle of nowhere and another day and a half hard ride from Colina Hermosa.

Alvito dismounted to walk by her side. "Soldiers of the third *pelotón*," he whispered for her hearing alone.

She'd recognized the stripe on their shoulder from her studies and knew them to be of *Concejal* Pedro Martinez's *pelotón*.

The civilians consisted of men and women, the old and the young as well as those in the prime of life. Many sat listlessly on bunched blankets, but others slept. A group of men farther back laughed easily, dog-eared cards held in their hands. There, a cluster of women with young children talked together. Some stood as they spotted her to ask, "What word? Has the *Alcalde* forgotten us?"

Their guide waved them off. "You'll know as soon as the *capitán* hears something."

Teresa glanced to the sky where the haze of smoke had once existed, but it had dissipated, leaving empty blue—almost as if she'd imagined the whole thing. She prayed that she had and their city had not burned.

A tall man, wearing a pristine uniform, met them by one of the few tents. He wore the double brass star on each side of his collar of a captain. His armor had been set aside, but a sword hung belted to his waist, and a knife fit on the opposite side. With skin dark enough to rival the rocks called coal burned in Suseph, his beard had been sheared so short as to practically be nonexistent. A style Teresa had always found seemed to match with men who preferred a minimalistic lifestyle, the type who didn't care for small talk, yet didn't accept shortcuts.

She often found the beard matched the man inside, just as Alvito's excessive grooming bespoke him a dandy before she'd ever exchanged a word with him.

"What news of Colina Hermosa?" she asked.

"I would ask you the same, but see you come from the other direction," the man said, then turned his attention to Alvito. "What does a man of your *pelotón* do out here? I believe your unit was recalled to the city? Let's see your orders, *alférez*."

Alvito drew to his full height with barely a wince for his wounds. "Lost, sir. Along with both my superior officers and the rest of my mission."

Teresa reached into her poncho and retrieved the paper concealed in her shirt. Dirty and waterlogged, it had seen better days, but most of it remained legible. "My orders, *capitán*. I'm afraid they were submerged in quicksand for a short time."

One slim dark brow rose as he took the smudged paper and noted the intact seal of the *Alcalde*. He broke it open, read, and took a long look at her, eyes lingering on every detail but giving nothing away. "An official ambassador, designated two sevendays ago, to the 'Women of Mortífero Swamp. To be afforded every resource.'" He gave a short bow. "Madam *Embajador*, won't you come inside and sit, while we talk. I am Captain Gonzalo."

As he spoke two oldsters, several obviously pregnant women, and a man with an infant emerged from the tent. "I share my space with those less able to bear exposure to the elements," Captain Gonzalo said with another bow.

"I would not put them out," Teresa protested.

"Official reports must be heard in privacy during a time of war, Madam *Embajador*, so says the law. We will hurry so as to inconvenience them less. *Alférez*, wait here," he told Alvito.

Teresa followed him into the tent that held empty blankets and nothing more than a map pinned to one canvas wall. "What news of the city, Captain?" she asked again. "We saw the smoke."

"I have no confirmation, but the scout who came to us reported Colina Hermosa was burning when he left. How badly it fared, I do not know. We were to take our group of evacuees to the swamp for protection, while others fought a diversionary battle to break them free, but the scout brought orders to remain where we were and await further instructions."

"Then the city was evacuated? The people got out?"

"Such was *Alcalde* Alvarado's plan, but again, I lack confirmation. The scout said the Northern army was in full retreat, though that was news a day old, which came to me two days ago. We have waited in place as ordered ever since."

Retreat? "Why would the Northerners retreat? They have the numbers." She couldn't keep astonishment from her voice.

Captain Gonzalo gave a short bow. "I could only speculate, ma'am."

Teresa wondered if the captain speculated in the privacy of his own head, but it was apparent he wasn't going to do so with her. Obviously, he had nothing more to tell. Answers would have to wait. Which meant she needed to continue her journey to Colina Hermosa. But perhaps she could do something here for the children she had left behind first.

"The people seemed restless." She could well imagine the word to halt coming as they were crossing the bridge, and the Captain settling them down right upon it, exactly as they were, and remaining that way—in the full glare of the sun. Dismissing the elderly and sick so they could talk alone, he was a man to follow orders to the letter. She chose her words with care. "As you mentioned it is exposed. Less than comfortable."

"Comfort is not in the vocabulary of a soldier, ma'am. We lack for food is all, though not for water.

And there have been several skirmishes with bands of the enemy, but we have beaten them off. The *Alcalde* will send instructions soon."

"No doubt," she said hurriedly. "An official ambassador speaks with the voice of the *Alcalde*, so it says in the uniform code."

"Yes, ma'am. That is correct—on any matter pertaining to their official mission. Yours is with the witches."

She heard the hint of a question at the end. The man was not above curiosity, despite the stick up his butt. How had the miller, Pedro, dealt with this martinet? She walked to the map on the wall and found the swamp village upon it, then traced with her finger to her best guess of the hidden camp where she'd left the children.

"My mission was partly successful. We recovered one witch." When he gave no sign he knew anything about Ramiro or the witch girl, Teresa continued, "However, I left nearly a hundred evacuated children in this spot—alone and unprotected. It's next to a lake with shelter and abundant resources. Food could be found there for your collection of evacuees. Protecting evacuees is your mission, is it not? I believe that would include these children, who have no one but a few reluctant village men to guard them." Elo would try her best to be an advocate for the children, but she was no match for her father. Teresa wanted someone better equipped to be in charge of them.

"Our orders are to stay in place."

"And if I ordered you to stay in place *there* instead of here?"

"I would have to regretfully decline, ma'am. You would not be speaking as an ambassador, but as a woman with a soft heart. Highly commendable, but it does not countermand my current orders."

Teresa cursed and dropped her finger off the map. "Does sending scouts countermand your current orders, sir?"

"No, ma'am." He nodded, his face relaxing. "A team of scouts or even a whole unit could go that way, looking for resources to bring here. Of course any refugees we found would have to be brought back as well. My orders do say to provide for the refugees. A hunt for food in that direct would not be out of order. It will be done within the hour."

The breath went out of her in a rush, and she smiled. "Thank you, Captain."

A whisper of an answering smile met her. "Perhaps I also have a soft heart, ma'am. Can I ask your intentions now?"

"I return home for news. Let it be good."

"The saints make it so. I can spare two men for escort—bands of Northerners continue to roam and your own escort seems weak." She admired the way he avoided directly saying Alvito wasn't fit to protect her. All true of course. He continued, "With the consideration that my men be returned when you reach your destination."

"Gratefully accepted, Captain. I shall send them back with news to report and all the information of my own mission." Now his favor had been returned, and she could rest easy about the children.

If only she could feel the same about Ramiro and Colina Hermosa.

CHAPTER 12

Julian looked up as a guard poked his head inside the tent. He'd been studying maps, reassuring his memory as to distance and timing, considering whether it would be possible for him to go to Suseph and Crueses before venturing to Aveston. Less than a mile apart, the twin cities, with their more temperate climate, were the breadbasket of the *ciudades-estado* and the closest with the exception of Aveston. Losing them would be devastating to the rest. That's why this foreign incursion had to stop now. With luck, he could reach them *and* Aveston before his time as *alcalde* expired.

If it expired, he reminded himself. The vote had yet to take place, and he was no longer determined to just let Lugo wrest control of the city. It felt good to have a purpose and goal again. Ordoño's presence had reminded him what they fought.

"Father Telo as you requested, sir," a guard said.

Julian rolled up the maps and set them aside. He'd hoped for the *concejales* first, but they would prove more difficult to track down in their numbers and more varied habits. He admitted, too, that they were probably less inclined to heed his call, even if the office was still his. *One thing at a time.* "I need you to do a task for me, Father." He noted how the priest cradled his wounded arm under the opposite armpit. And while he needed the priest, he also knew the man had paid enough. He let his face soften. "A less dangerous task this time."

The dark-skinned priest shrugged. "'Look not to weariness or toil if the work be for the glory of the Lord. The Lord is thy support.'" He walked forward and plucked a shining bit of metal off the table—the hostile priestess Santabe's earring. "May I have this?"

Surprised, Julian waved permission. "Take it, Father. I have no use for it."

"Thank you, my son. What can I do to help?"

Julian frowned. Father Telo sounded as hearty as before, yet a note of hollowness entered the words that had never been there—not as if the priest didn't mean them, but as if they had been reduced to less. It was clear the loss of a hand would take the heart out of any man—even a priest.

"I wish I could give this task to another and let you rest further, Father, but you and I have been around Ordoño the most. Other than a few guards, no one else has been close to him—not and been aware of it anyway."

Father Telo looked up sharply from pondering the sand. *"Aware* of it?"

"Yes. Obviously I require your complete discretion, Father."

"Of course." And for the first time since he had entered the tent, Telo's eyes held a certain brightness.

"Ordoño has been here, in this camp. He may still be here. Besides spying, he came to kill me and then changed his mind. Giving a description of him to a search party would do no good. He's so damn ordinary. I suspect he has already changed his clothing. I need you, and a sizable party of soldiers, to look for him. Make sure he's not lingering."

Telo swayed on his feet, and Julian jumped up and rushed a stool to the man, easing him down onto it before he fell. "I had no idea you were still so unwell. I'll find—"

The priest waved that off. "He came here to kill you, you say. Then didn't. Why, my son? What changed his mind?"

Julian glanced to the side, embarrassed. "I think he came to gloat . . . for my . . . failure to act. Indecision has been clutching me for some time. In fact, Ordoño's threats helped wake me up."

"Threats?" Telo seized his arm, his grip strong despite his injury. The white of the bandages on his other arm stood out starkly against his dark skin. The burst of energy from the man was like someone awakened violently from a doze. "Who else did he mention?"

"Why, my son and the witch girl, but they are both out of the camp. Ordoño could not gain access to them. He was just trying to upset me. To rattle me."

Instead of relaxing, the priest's grip tightened. "Remember everything he said. Nothing he does is without purpose. It's important. Don't you see? Everything he does, everything he says has an aim. Ordoño didn't fall into leadership of the Northerners. He *took* it. Clawed and schemed and, no doubt, murdered his way into it. Fought tooth and nail, and now he controls these Unbelievers enough to send them out of their land and into ours—sent them into war. He accomplished all that, and he isn't of their race, my son. How much easier it would be to take over our people? He didn't get where he is by letting any opportunity pass by."

Julian pulled free, his heart starting to beat fast as Telo's words penetrated the fog he hadn't fully gotten beyond. "He wasn't just here to spy. It's an assault. He plots out our weak points and exploits them." He passed a hand over his beard. "Saints. I'll send a rider after my son. There's nothing I can do about the girl." He started to turn and Telo grabbed him.

"Did he threaten anyone else? The slightest mention?"

Their eyes met, the priest's filled with a cold rage. "My competition," Julian said. "But he passed it off as a joke."

"Who would that be?" Telo demanded. "Which *concejal*? Or is it someone else?"

Julian felt limp, unable to think. "It changes depending on the subject under consideration and the moment. Diego and I sometimes clashed over subsidies. Loyalties and allegiances shift. With Pedro and Adulfo dead..."

"But who is your opposition since we've been here? Since Ordoño was in the camp."

"Lugo."

"Where is he now?"

"I don't know. I asked for them all to be brought here, but none have come. They were announcing the election for *alcalde*. They might have finished and disbanded. They could be anywhere in the camp." Julian rushed to the entrance of the tent, the guards snapping to attention at his appearance. "Where has *Concejal* Lugo been living?" he asked them.

"Why on the recreated Market Avenue, sir," the guard answered.

Julian may not have ventured through the camp much, but he knew the location of everything in Colina Hermosa and had been amused that the camp replicated the structure of the city. Like every other merchant, Lugo had chosen to camp in the spot corresponding to where his stores would have been found. Before becoming *alcalde*, they had been neighbors.

Julian bolted from the tent, guards falling in around him. Market Avenue had been right down High Street, one of the largest avenues in Colina Hermosa, built of stone and surrounded by white stucco storefronts, kept swept and immaculate. Now, a track through sand with rolled blankets and hanging laundry alongside, the new version was not fit to be a goat path, let alone an avenue. It was also hard to distinguish one camp spot from the next, let alone pick out the one he wanted. Julian reached what would be the middle of the street and took the north side, scurrying through campsites, checking faces. Disturbed sleepers sat up in dismay. Voices called out asking his purpose, failing to recognize him in his hurry. He didn't stop.

"Here," a guard called.

Julian jumped over a kettle hanging over a small fire. His knee twinged, almost throwing him off his feet and sideways, but he righted and ran. Beatriz would laugh at him for forgetting his age. She might be right as there didn't seem a need for worry. All was quiet. The guard stood over a peaceful form rolled in bedding.

Lugo had no wife or children, only an elderly mother somewhere. He claimed his stores were all the family a man needed. With that kind of thinking, no wonder he refused to leave the burned shell of Colina Hermosa.

Julian reached out and shook the *Concejal*. Instead of upbraiding everyone for being disturbed, Lugo flopped over, his eyes staring at the sky. Something sticky coated Julian's fingers. Telo pulled up beside them touching heart, mind, liver, and spleen with his remaining hand.

Lugo had been stabbed repeatedly in head, chest, and stomach, as if to mock the priest's gesture.

"Blessed saints," Julian said respectfully. No fan

of religion at the best of times, yet he felt sick at this mockery of their values. No one deserved this—not even Lugo. They may have worked from different opinions on most matters, but the man had cared about the city and the people. Ordoño was twisted.

He looked around, knowing he needed to warn Ramiro, perhaps even assign a guard to his son—and send someone after the witch girl, for all the good it would do. He should—

"Look," one of the guards said, pointing at the body and leaning toward it with his torch. The civilians who had followed moved in to see.

A small paper had been pinned near the feet, undeniably to avoid being soaked with blood. The words scrawled across it read, *"For the Alcalde."*

Julian could picture Ordoño throwing out his arms and laughing at this last piece of impudence. Horrified whispers sprang up. Rumors would run like wildfire that Julian had arranged this murder of his rival. Trying to keep it secret or asking people to keep quiet would cause them to spread faster. A great sinking feeling lodged in Julian's stomach. He very much feared that Ordoño had won this round.

He was even more afraid the madman was likely to win all the rest.

Julian wait until Lugo's body was respectfully taken away for burial, then headed back to his tent, followed by a handful of extra-attentive guards, flanking him like toddlers attached to their mother's side. But long practice had taught Julian how to tune out such distractions. Being surrounded by guards was the nearest equivalent to being alone. He'd remained vigilant while Father Telo said prayers over the body, and then sunk deep in his own thoughts—they were very dark indeed.

A painful tingle ran down his left arm, and he gripped the limb close with his right. He foresaw no simple maneuver out of this mess. Ordoño could have struck at no surer way to discredit him and keep him from using his influence to win reelection, and acting to save his people. Nothing he said would be believed. Every order he gave would be analyzed for hidden motive, even by those who supported him in the past.

He scanned over anything he might have said to Lugo that could be taken the least bit threatening, finding way too many words that could be taken the wrong way. After all, rumor was like a snake with a thousand heads: Strike down one and a dozen more would spring into life. Any innocent expression he had ever uttered could be taken the wrong way with just a little twisting. The people were already torn over supporting him and an election had already been called—this death added upon that would look more than suspicious and would drive the numbers against him.

It wouldn't matter that he was never alone and the guards could testify that he'd never left his tent. Any defense he brought to bear would be matched with something equally discrediting. The personal animosity between himself and Lugo was too well known. The people who wanted him guilty would always assumed he'd bribed the guards or paid someone to act for him—either a family member or a devoted supporter. His innocence would count for little against those determined to believe or even those who just loved a scandal.

It didn't take actual wrongdoing to ruin a politician.

His inner landscape rocked and shook, threatening to bury him with the guilt, as he recalled the conversation with Ordoño to the best of his ability. Had he said anything or implied anything that would drive his enemy to kill Lugo? Had anyone else been killed? Was this his fault?

Lugo was bitter and stingy with his money, and his respect. He might object and be obstreperous, but only because he honestly disagreed on the correct course, never for personal reasons. And never for outright personal gain. Stubborn as a mule, like the rest of them, he would change his mind if he could be brought to see a wiser path. Harsh, but fair, others said of him. Fairer in politics than in his business dealings, certainly. They did not like each other, often worked against one another, but Julian did not wish *this* upon him.

Try as he might, the words he'd spoken to Ordoño slipped through Julian's fingers, made vague by shock.

He stumbled into the tent, sinking onto the bed,

barely cognizant of the guards remaining outside and spreading out around the structure. As he stared without seeing, the light dimmed as someone closed the tent flaps, then the rope-strung bed gave as another sat next to him. Chilly hands touched his face, and sense returned.

Mere inches distant, her eyes filled with concern, Beatriz said with a fierceness he'd come to expect of her, "It isn't true. No matter what they say, it isn't true." His wife wore a dress robe over her nightclothes. Her hair twisted up in bits of rag to make it curl, but she looked no less ferocious for that.

Before the conflict, in the early years of their marriage when first elected *alcalde*, their days were often spent apart, engaged in their own different pursuits, but evenings were always reserved for family time. Gradually, the boys had gotten older and drifted into their own hobbies and concerns, leaving just the two of them to meet each night for dinner or to spend their evenings in quiet reading or sometimes entertainment with friends and colleagues. They enjoyed the time when their sons were present, but were content, as well, to be the two of them. That, too, became a habit. Since the Northerners invaded, more and more Beatriz was forced to wake if they were to have any time together. Neither would have it so, but circumstances dictated and they adapted.

Julian worked to extend a weak smile. He always knew lines of rumor and gossip ran deep through his people in a master web of communication, and every segment of it reported straight to his wife at some point. It was no surprise the news had beaten his return and been urgent enough to keep her from bed.

"No," he agreed. Deep inside, he knew the fault was Ordoño's, not his own, but that didn't make accepting it easier. Nor did the worry that someone else might be dead and yet to be discovered. "But I should step aside, and let the council rule until the election."

Beatriz bristled, her hands dropping. "That would be to admit responsibility—at least indirectly."

"No one would believe the truth if I spoke it now. Who would accept that I saw and spoke to Lord Ordoño, yet told no one, warned no one, until after Lugo was dead? It would seem the words of a man backtracking to cover himself."

Beatriz gasped when he admitted speaking to the Northern enemy, but stayed silent to let him continue. "To say nothing is to make it worse. To speak out is pointless. It's like the man knew just what to do to make my position untenable, *mi amor*." It was so and there was no getting around it. Ordoño had acted with deliberation to cut out his legs and leave him nothing to stand upon. The man seemed to find Julian responsible for the loss of his army and attempted the most intimate revenge possible. To a man of such bitterness, death would indeed seem too easy a solution—no wonder the madman had not cut Julian's throat when he had a chance.

"If there is no way out, then you will do what is right."

Julian came out of his abstraction to see Beatriz sitting tall on the bed, a light of determination shining in her eyes as she took his hands. "Now and forever," she said. "I am not just the wife of the *Alcalde*. I am the wife of a *good* man. What is the right thing to do?"

"Save our people."

Her eyes glittered with unshed tears. "Then forget political concerns. Do you know how to do that? Do you believe your wisdom the best to accomplish that?"

Julian hesitated, staring at their joined hands. Did he? Could not someone else lead them perhaps just as well, if not better? He thought of the *concejales'* timid response at their most recent meeting. With their position so exposed and hopeless, they would be almost as likely to roll over for Ordoño, like dogs showing their bellies, as fight him. Julian had a sense of the man now, and it was clear appeasing him would not dissuade him from his vicious course.

Beatriz squeezed his hand as if to force an answer from him. "I do have an idea," he said reluctantly. "But it is as likely to destroy us as save us. Try as I might, I find no other sound alternative."

"Then act to make it happen. The power is still yours."

He considered her words. *Was* the power still his? Would anyone follow him if he gave commands? Without doubt the military would. The *pelotónes* captains would stick with him no matter what due to his years of support of them. He had increased their funding, gotten them the supplies they craved. They loved that both his sons had found homes with them—*ah saints, Salvador!* Grief rushed in, and he struggled to push aside the pain of his loss to focus.

Yes, he could count on the loyalty of the troops. And the *concejales*?

If the councilors opposed him, his actions to save their people would flounder. But . . . without Lugo, the councilors would be cut adrift. His was the leadership that brought the rest together in opposition. Osmundo and Sarracino were used to being followers. The new council members would be struggling to find their feet. And Julian still had support on the council. Without Lugo's presence, they might not be able to get the votes to veto his commands. He doubted they had the backbone to supersede law and speed the election. And some might even approve his plan, at least the parts he told them about.

The people would follow where the military and the councilors led, and he should have the muscle to control them for the time needed.

He nodded. "I should have the power for eight days."

She leaned in and kissed him softly on the side of his mouth. "Take it from a woman: Much can be done in eight days."

He let her surety wash over him; always he felt stronger when they were in accord. His resolve hardened. Julian refused to go down without a fight. "Pack your things. I'm putting forth orders right now that the camp is to move in the morning—sooner is better to catch the *concejales* off-balance, before they can react." *God, let the remaining concejales be alive.* He wanted no more deaths on his conscience. Their situation was never worse than today. And he had never been a politician to bully his decisions onto the people—much as he'd offered an out to the witch from the council's bullying—but that situation was different. His people had voted him their approval to make decisions for them and Claire had not. He tried to put aside the small voice that said that had been true about his people at one time and was no longer. Indecision got them nowhere. He either exercised the power or he did not, and the choice had been made.

"You opposed my leaving you before," he said, patting her hands. Of all he had asked of her as a political wife, this might be the most difficult. The death of their firstborn could have driven them apart, made her blame him. Instead, they had drawn closer than ever, devoted in all things. "Now, I require your support on our separation, though I don't go to the enemy. I go to Crueses and Suseph, then Aveston to prepare the way. I need you here to be my good right hand, showing strength to others as our home is left behind and making sure my orders continue to be followed. The military will be your support in this. Just keep the *concejales* squabbling enough to not fight me directly. Normally, I wouldn't have to ask . . ." They both knew he spoke of Salvador's death and the fragileness they felt now. In happier days, there would be no one better equipped to manage the task he needed done, but Beatriz dealt with their son's death and he worried at adding to her load and separating from her when she needed him. "Can you endure this for me?"

She blazed up like tinder when a spark hits it. Beatriz stood with hands flying to hips. "Blessed saints, Julian Alvarado, do not say a word more! Do you honestly think a woman cannot put love of self and family below the needs of her country, cannot feel patriotism, just as a man? Can you, of all people, believe so low of me! I've trained you better than that!" As quickly as it came, the anger leeched from her. She settled back on the bed, close enough for their hips to touch. "Tell me this plan of yours, and I will do what has to be done—for us, for our family—for our kind—the Lord bear witness, if I can find value in a witch and consent to her being around our son, I can handle this."

"What is this?" He frowned. Why would she bring Ramiro's relationship with the witch up? That was over and Beatriz wasn't one to dwell on what was handled. "Ramiro is on his way to Crueses. I sent him there myself. He is not with the girl any longer." A dawning realization hit. "Or is he?"

Beatriz shook her head and *hmmphed*, making light of his words. She mumbled something under her breath, of which he picked out "blind," then shook herself. "We both remember what it is to be young and led by the heart. I suspect Ramiro is with that girl, though I have no proof. And you would have known as much if you weren't so preoccupied. I arranged for him to meet with her, but he returned afterward. Now, however . . . But that is too late to be remedied. First things first. Tell me this plan and then we will speak more of our son."

Despite his shock, he did as she asked and shed the worry, putting an arm around her to draw her closer. "When a difficult problem exists in mathematics or life, a wise man cuts it into bite-size pieces. So with my idea . . ."

CHAPTER 13

Teresa swayed with the fast walk of her mule, feeling not a little proud that she finally had achieved the knack of riding and barely even wobbled anymore—not that she enjoyed it. People of her girth weren't meant for swaying atop animals. Ahead, Alvito rode with the other two guards, chatting and trading quips. The brotherhood of soldiers apparently overcame differences of unit, rank, or temperament. Teresa quirked her head and made a mental note, but she had no interest in joining them. She preferred to consider Captain Gonzalo's words to her about Colina Hermosa: the city on fire and the Northern army in retreat.

Two things that didn't fit well together, unless, improbably, the army retreated because they had destroyed everything and everyone. But it seemed fairly certain the *Alcalde* was not dead and was still giving orders. Surely, Gonzalo would have acted more evasively with her if he had knowledge to the contrary and wished to hide it from her. She did not believe that to be the case, so why would the Northerners retreat? Had they even done so?

In times of uncertainty, Teresa fell back upon her university training—considering first the source of the data given her. Gonzalo had not seen these things himself; he was not an actual witness. Teresa was skeptical of anything secondhand.

Teresa sighed. Having little actual evidence reminded her of scripture writing. But unlike thousand-year-old scriptures, and their aged recounting of miracles, at least this data was fresh. The accounts of the earliest miracles from such saints as Santiago were millennium old, and the latest miracles still three hundred years in the past.

Sure, there was enough outside documentation to show that such a person as Santiago or San Martin had actually existed. Yet, not enough to ease the skepticism Teresa felt about religion—the doubt that marred her reaching for true belief.

Most of the miracles performed by the later saints and quite a percentage of the earlier miracles were what most at the university termed private events. They had been performed with few witnesses, such as the healing of a family member of a follower. There were thousands of reports of the lame walking, the blind seeing, and the severely injured recovering—such as Alvito—and little proof for any of it because of the small number of people who had been involved.

The news from Gonzalo, however, was more like a large scale event, the kind commonly found in the early miracles from the more important, major saints: Santiago calling the rains to change course and make the building of Colina Hermosa possible, the lack of decomposition of San Martin's body, San Pedro cleaving the great rock that became Aveston's citadel. If the Northern army *had* fled, then it had been seen by thousands.

Which meant she must do exactly as she already planned and go to Colina Hermosa to see for herself. Talk to those who had actually been there. Otherwise, there just wasn't enough information for any of this to make sense to her. It wasn't as if she'd been sent dreams or visions where she talked with God as some of the past saints. How much easier it would be if she had, but she must rely on other means. And if there's one thing she was good at, it was rooting out information.

Teresa rolled her eyes, staring at the reins in her hands without seeing the leather straps. She had run far afield of her true concerns about Colina Hermosa. As if the time of miracles had anything to do with—

A heavy force struck her and drove her off the mule. She collided with the ground with a man atop her. The air rushed out of her lungs, as much from astonishment as pain. The man was dirty and unshaven, and when breath returned it brought the unmistakable odor of someone who hadn't washed in a long time.

Bandits.

Criminal outcasts from the *ciudades-estado*. Her heart gave a great jump, and she opened her mouth to shout. A grimy hand covered her mouth as a dagger pressed against the soft skin next to her left eye. "Not a sound, *campesino*," the man hissed.

She heard shouts and realized her companions had been set upon. They would rescue her; she had no doubt of that. Her position allowed her to see nothing, and she did not dare move in the slightest. Seconds became an eternity as she waited, focusing on the bloodshot eyes of the man atop her, but her ears grasping at any sound.

Rescue was taking too long.

Would she survive the quicksand in the swamp to die by the hand of thieves? Ramiro wasn't here to pull her out this time.

Her teeth began to chatter as fear took hold, chasing away reason.

The man moved as if uncomfortable. His blackened teeth coming closer as he leaned nearer, bringing fetid breath. Teresa winced and rolled her head to the side.

"Not a *campesino*," he said in a fresh gust of stench. The look in his eyes shifted, becoming more calculating. "No, a *campesina*."

The hand across her mouth loosened fractionally. She tried to give a sharp twist and pull free. He rolled with her as though expecting it. His hand without the knife grabbed her shoulder, pressing her against the sand, then he slapped her across the face, hard enough to spin her head around.

An angry whinny split the air. Teresa glanced up to see dappled-gray horseflesh rise above her. Forefeet pawed the air. The dark, expressive eye high above was set in fury. Dagger-sharp hooves came down. Teresa rolled with all her power, the bandit still clinging to her. The horse struck the legs of the bandit, stamping.

"Valentía!" she screamed. As the bandit shrieked under the stallion's hooves, she scrambled free on hands and knees, fighting to her feet.

How had Salvador's horse come here? The last she'd seen of him, Ramiro had sent it off with his master's dead body strapped across his back.

She caught a quick impression of bandits everywhere—twenty, thirty—too many.

A bandit in a gray poncho came upon Valentía from his flank. A long knife swung and red droplets filled the air, carrying the horse's blood. The stallion screamed.

A man ran at Teresa, and she ducked under his reach, spinning past. Teresa's hands formed into fists. She had ridden Valentía for only a few days, but they had almost died in the quicksand together. The horse had come for *her* out of nowhere. Felt companionship for *her*.

The stallion whirled, snapping with his teeth. The knife struck at Valentía again.

Teresa bellowed. "Nooooooooooo!" She rushed forward, pummeling the bandit attacking the stallion with pathetic buffets about his head and ears, screaming with rage all the while. She scratched and clawed. Hands grabbed her, pinioning her arms. She wriggled like one berserk. A weight struck her head and she knew no more.

Teresa woke to pain trying to separate her skull from her body. She took a few breaths and the agony localized to the back of her head, becoming nearly bearable. When she tried to open her eyes, the bright midday sun blinded like stabbing knives. Around her, she heard the wheezes and sobs of people crying. A few more attempts and she managed to hold her eyes open, though the world rotated around, spinning like a top. She retched, bringing up bile, and the people alongside her shifted from her.

People—as in more than the three men *she was with*?

What had happened? How did she get here?

She wiped at her mouth with hands bound together with leather straps and forced her eyes to stay open. She sat—or half lay rather—on a dirty blanket, surrounded by a crowd of men and women. Outside their group was empty desert. She attempted to count and retched again, having to stop, but guessed they must number fifteen to twenty souls. The bandits must have brought them all here—but why? Some looked as injured and as weak as she felt, others sobbed or huddled against their neighbors. One and all, they could have been from Colina Hermosa, though she recognized none of them. They all wore nooses of thick rope around their necks and trailing off into long leads.

Her hands came up, touching her own neck and found a noose there, too. *A hangman's noose.* Her pulse ratcheted skywards. She closed her eyes to ward off a fresh bout of dizziness but that made it worse. The woman closest to her avoided her eyes when Teresa tried to gain her attention to ask what had happened. Then she noticed one of those unconscious: Alvito.

He slumped, huddled in a ball on the outside of their group. She struggled to see if he was breathing, but she couldn't tell. Then she saw the bandits.

The entire band stood between the prisoners and . . . an equal number of men dressed in black-and-yellow uniforms. The Northerners had hair the color of sand, and eyes in every shade of blue, green, and gray. There was not a black head or brown eye among them. Everyone had a sword out, and there was a noticeable separation of soldiers on one side and bandits on the other, the eyes of both were sharp and glittering with watchfulness. One bandit and one soldier met in the halfway point between, doing more gesturing than talking.

The desert still spun dizzyingly around her, but at

a slower pace now. Although a handful of the other prisoners also focused on the exchange going on, the rest looked anywhere but at their captors. The bandit leader was the one who had attacked Valentía, the one she'd attempted to beat off.

The lead bandit held up ten fingers twice and pointed at the prisoners. The Northern soldier singled out several of the slumped prisoners, including Alvito, shook his head and held up ten fingers and then five. Their bartering went on some time, until they reached an agreement in the middle. The soldier counted out something from a little bag and handed it to the bandit. At last there were cautious smiles and nods on both sides. The bandits began backing off, never turning their backs or lowering their weapons.

Teresa thought she'd never be as frightened as those few minutes spent sinking to her death in quicksand. How wrong she'd been. What did the Northerners want with the prisoners? Why pay money for them? The only ones able to speak her language and give her answers slowly slunk away.

Panic struck as a bold wish hit. *Oh saints! Oh saints!* Her breath came too fast. Would she sit here like a coward or do it? *You're not a coward. The situation can't get much worse. Do it, fool.*

Several of the Northerners began taking the long ropes attached to their nooses and fastening them to iron rings on the back of a wagon shaped like a little house with a canvas roof.

Teresa got up on her knees. "Bandit! Bandit! You

sold us to the Northerners. Your own countrymen—and women." She felt like she was babbling now, but he looked her direction. "What do they want with us? Where are they taking us?" she hollered.

"Shut up, *puta*," one snapped.

"Have compassion," she persisted. "What do they want with us? Where are they taking us?"

A soldier shouted at her and made a slashing motion with his hand, warning her in no uncertain terms. She kept to her knees but held her tongue.

The bandit leader looked at her, his eyes cold as a winter morning. "Zapata. They take you to Zapata, *puta*." Then the bandits faded into the desert and were gone.

"Zapata," the woman next to her in a silk shawl whispered, hands clenched under her chin. "The city is burned. Why take us there?"

Teresa had no answers, but Zapata was north—toward the enemy's homeland.

The world made choppy circles around her, still revolving. The movement made it hard to think, and her skull continued to throb with a sickening pain. From the look of things, they were expected to walk. Maybe the wagon was for the ones too injured. Should she try her feet or go with those who couldn't move, like Alvito? Surely, when she could think clearly again, she could find a way to escape. Or a *pelotón* would find and rescue them.

Before she could make up her mind, two soldiers waded into the prisoners. There were scattered cries from those avoiding their boots and shoves as they pulled out one of the unconscious: a middle-aged man in well-tailored clothes. They dragged him out onto the sand, where they stood him up. His head lolled back, eyes closed, blood painting gristly patterns over his face and down his shirt. They released him and stepped back, and he promptly fell. This brought the limp prisoner sharp slaps and shouts in their harsh language. A second time they held him up and let him fall.

The lead soldier, a man with eyes green like an avocado, said something with a shrug. A sword came out, and Teresa couldn't see what happened next. There were three thunks and plenty of shrieks from the prisoners closest to the scene. Prisoners tried to shuffle farther back only to be caught up against their neighbors.

Teresa caught her lip between her teeth, horrified, as they pulled out another man, this one elderly with a belly wound. Despite the world spinning, Teresa jostled through the crowd, fighting her way to Alvito. The rope attached to her noose trailed behind, tangling and snagging on other people. It would be easy enough to remove, even with her hands bound, but such an action would surely bring her captors down on her. They eyed her progress with hostility, leaving her alone for now, but she wasn't going to push her luck.

She inched forward. Alvito wasn't going to die—not if she had anything to say about it. The other two guards from her escort didn't seem to be here. She didn't know what had become of them or Valentía, but by the Lord, she wasn't going to be left alone with barbarians who bought people and killed the injured.

She reached Alvito's side and shook him. There didn't appear to be any new damage, perhaps he'd just been knocked out like herself. His eyes flared open briefly. "Wake up, Cat," she commanded in a quiet hiss. "Wake up." She shook him again. "They've sold us to the Northerners and they're killing anyone who can't stand." The prisoners around them edged away, unwilling to be guilty by association.

This time his eyes stayed open.

"You have to walk," she urged. "Do you hear? You have to stay on your feet."

She didn't know if this would work. Alvito was the only prisoner in uniform. Perhaps they'd kill him no matter what. She glanced over her shoulder. Was there time? The elderly man stood on his feet, face scrunched in determination, though hunched over his wound. The leader gave a nod, and they pulled out a woman holding her arm to her chest. Her injury didn't look too bad, but she sobbed so hard it was difficult to tell. More ropes were attached to the wagon.

Teresa turned back to Alvito. "They'll be here next. Can you stand?"

He stirred beside her and nodded, coughed, and a tiny amount of blood ran into his beard from a split lip. "Constanza. What happened to Constanza?"

Her heart lurched as he begged for information on his horse. "I don't know. Sorry. I didn't see. But we'll never find her if you don't get up."

"And our companions?"

A sob stuck in her throat at giving him the truth. "The other soldiers? Most likely dead. Not here anyway, saints preserve them."

Alvito's eyes that had been slack burned with a white heat. "I'll stand. These bastards won't win again today."

She slumped in relief. No matter what happened next, at least she'd survived this far.

If only she knew if she'd come to regret it.

CHAPTER 14

Claire frowned at the sky. Her earlier words, "It's going to get wet," proved an understatement. A steady rain had settled over them for the last few hours, ever since they'd reached the border of the swamp and left the empty village behind. They looked like drowned rabbits. Her mare shook, sending water into Claire's eyes. It only added to her lingering humiliation. Ramiro had asked what direction to take to find her grandmother, and she had to admit that south was all she had to go on. Ramiro didn't say anything—his incredulous stare said it for him. They both thought her a dunce.

But she didn't mind that so much. The moisture in the air, the scents in her nose, even having trees and greenery around her made her feel like she had come home. Oh, she might not be *at* home, but close enough.

Whether they were out under the open sky without a tree in sight, or tucked among tight hills, she hadn't realize how odd that made her feel—like an itch inside her ear she couldn't scratch—until they returned to a proper land. She had spent plenty of time in the rain before, after all; chores didn't stop because of a shower. Claire just wished for her oiled cloak and hood. Her frown turned into a goofy grin as an idea struck.

"We should stop at my home," she called ahead. The trail only allowed for single riders and Ramiro insisted on taking the lead. As if trouble couldn't sneak up on them from behind just as well. "I have supplies we could use. And I could check on the goats."

Ramiro turned his head to regard her with a raised brow. "I think the goats can take their chances, but Teresa would be on the way. We could check on her also—take her with us. The problem is: Your home isn't south."

"Rain makes you grumpy."

"I just mean that we don't have time for larks. 'Time is a thief'—have you heard of that one?"

"I know that," she grumped back at him. She hadn't heard that expression, but she wasn't about to tell him that. "As you keep pointing out, *I* don't exactly know where we're going, so you have to trust I know best. My mother always said, 'Don't look for a Woman of the Song; she'll find you.'"

Doubt turned to outright skepticism on his face. "So we blunder around until she finds us? That doesn't sound like a good plan."

"What's wrong with that plan? Have you got a better one?"

His face went suspiciously flat, and he turned back to the front, almost sheepishly. "Point taken."

Claire pulled a seed ball from a dangling branch of a sycamore as she passed, yanking off a few of the large leaves with it. *Home.* Her own bed. Her mother's things. The little ache in her heart grew, but it would be so good to be home, even if they couldn't stay. She pulled the leaves off the seed ball and tossed the hard green knob of seeds into the air, catching it again, letting herself dwell on memories.

After a few minutes, she said, "I'm naming this horse Jorga after my mother's favorite goat, since you don't like me calling it Horse."

"After a goat? That's an insult to a decent horse."

She caught the seed ball and held it. "Goats are intelligent and stubborn. They remind me a lot of you."

"Then don't forget wickedly handsome."

The seed ball left her hand and hit him squarely in the middle of the back, making a ding sound on his breastplate. He turned enough so she could see he was laughing at her. She laughed right back. "I'll allow wicked."

"Speaking of names, what about your grandmother? If we run into some witches, what name do we ask after?"

Her laughter wilted. "I don't know. My mother just called her 'my grandmother' or 'Mother,' when she mentioned her at all. Mother's name is Rosemund, if that helps." Even as she said the words, she knew they weren't much to go upon. She dredged her brain for another memory that would help them find her grandmother and came up with little. "What else can I tell you about her? She and my mother didn't agree. Grandmother is a real believer in using the magic and training with it. Mother . . . well, she felt different. That's why they parted." At this point, Claire wasn't sure who was more accurate in their views. Knowing about the magic could have helped her in so many ways. Yet, that time when she'd scared the Northern army had felt wrong—evil. What if her mother was right?

Something inside her seized up, curling tight. She found it hard to think of the magic without feeling sick.

"They didn't get along?" Ramiro asked tensely. "You didn't think that was kind of important?"

"What—what do you mean?"

"I *mean* she could include you in this grudge thing they've had going. That she could strike out at you."

She wilted even more under his unexpected ridicule, her voice dropping with her spirits. "She came to see me when I was born and she wanted my mother to use the magic. They weren't trying to hurt each other . . . they just didn't get along. Surely, if I come looking for a teacher . . . You think she'll reject me?" She barely refrained from adding a "too" onto the end that would be entirely too whiny, remembering how poorly she'd been received among his people.

Ahead, Sancha halted and Claire's horse obediently followed suit. "I'm sorry—I didn't mean to further upset you. I just think that it would be something to keep in mind. We shouldn't assume she's going to welcome you with open arms." He smiled gently. "Let's just worry about finding her and figure out the rest when we do," Ramiro said, and Sancha began moving again.

Claire bit her tongue. She never knew what might upset him or shift his emotions. Ever since he'd come back to her wearing plain browns and grays and not his uniform, he'd been so moody. Sometimes distracted and staring at nothing. Sometimes snapping at her instead of their playful sparring. She didn't think Ramiro realized how he hurt her feelings and she didn't think he meant to do so. Something had him preoccupied. She had a pretty good idea of the reason but wanted to hear it from him. He wasn't telling her the truth about what had happened before he met up with her, and trying to press him on it hurt her almost as much as him. She couldn't seem to make herself ask him outright. What if he overreacted and got truly mad at her? What if he left?

She didn't want that to happen, and it had nothing to do with his protection. She had gotten used to his face, the way his short beard ran along his jaw. The way he cocked his head and rolled his eyes when she said something silly. The shape of his body . . .

Friends. It's because we are friends.

Friends meant that you preferred to be with that

person and that you forgave them when they stepped on your toes, especially if it was unintentional as she believed his most recent snappiness was. Friends made you feel good—most of the time—or so her mother had explained it. She hadn't mentioned the little tingle Claire got whenever she saw Ramiro, but her mother had said that friends shared things and feelings.

Maybe if she shared, he would, too.

"I'm really looking forward to meeting my grandmother. It's exciting."

"Let's hope it's not exciting because she's trying to kill us," he grumbled. "Lately, everything has been trying to kill us."

"That won't happen."

"Either she accepts you or she doesn't, but how do you plan to explain me?"

She coughed and choked like she'd swallowed a bug. A flush of embarrassment shot through her at the idea of discussing the plan she'd come up with. "I've got that covered. You're my protection because I can't use the magic well enough yet." She hoped he'd leave it at that. Women of the Song had one requirement: producing a daughter. She planned to call him her consort—the word even in the privacy of her head made her face hotter—if the question came up. Women of the Song usually lived in the villages for a year or two to meet their requirement. Perhaps, sometimes, they brought a man home with them.

"It will all work out," she said more confidently than she felt. "I'll vouch for you."

"That makes me feel better," he quipped, but smiled before turning back around.

She lifted her face to let the rain patter against her skin, glad that she didn't feel like everything would work out. She'd rather be worried. The last time the world seemed to be going her way, her mother had died.

"I can protect myself, you know," he said, "when we find the wit—er . . . song women. Have you thought about how you're going to convince them to help us? That will be the tricky part."

Claire clutched at her saddle, a sick little knot working itself deeper in her stomach. That's where she drew a blank about the future. "It'll come to me," she said, this time feeling just as cynical as he looked.

Ramiro sat watching the ashes of their fire, the girl next to him, just within reach. He had set them up in the center of a large clearing that was as dry as anything got in the rainy season. They used their saddles as cushions against the wet ground, and he tried not to think about what it would do to the leather. Claire had laughed at his surprise when they couldn't find much wood that wasn't damp. He hadn't expected everything to be wetter and the ponds deeper than last time. "Wait until we reach the lake," she'd warned, smiling at the dismay on his face.

Already they let the fire die so it wouldn't draw attention, having boiled their drinking water. The fire pit gave out small cracks and pops as the last pockets of wetness hit the heat. The horses were just out of sight in the darkness, close enough he could hear their occasional stamp. Vapor swirled upward from the pot set over the dying flames, making phantom patterns in the air in which he could lose himself.

He picked over and over at the festering wounds in his heart, unable to let it go, knowing he made for poor company.

Claire broke the preoccupied silence that had descended on their duo, showing thoughts equally as murky as his own. "Funny how when it's dark every task seems impossible. What if Northerners find us? We avoided the main roads and all, but they could be anywhere now. Or what if the Women of the Song attack instead of talk when we find them? Worse, what if they judge me based on my magic and find me wanting? How will I ever convince them with the little I can do?"

Before he could answer, she charged off again, words tumbling out. "My Hornet Tune isn't good enough. It's failed already. I need more, something foolproof. What would stop you in your tracks during a fight? I mean, people who are determined enough can suffer through the hornets—or there might be bees there already. What else would work?"

So that's what her moping was about. Ramiro shrugged, caught off guard by her flow of words. She'd been so quiet, apparently locked in her thoughts, and now so vehement. He said the first thing that popped into his head. "Panic worked pretty well on me before."

She tapped at the ground with a half-burnt stick. "Yes, but you weren't trying to kill me at the time, only catch me. And I had a specific source to use on you, too."

"The campsite? Teresa and I talked about it. You used our fear that the Northerners would locate us through the remains of our campsite. That and my own doubt in my leadership."

Claire nodded along as he reasoned that out. "I had time to study you. Your ways. Your worries." He agreed that they both had plenty of anxieties and that hadn't changed. "But most situations wouldn't give me time for study," she continued. "What could I use then?"

"Fear," he said instantly. He remembered his first battle, the one atop the wall of Colina Hermosa. How fear had turned his insides to pudding. How only anxiety of acting shamefully had kept him moving. In the fight that had earned his beard, there hadn't been time for fear. It happened so fast that he'd acted and the fear hit afterward. Good thing. If it had come earlier, he might not have survived. Fear was the most powerful motivator before, during, and after a combat.

Claire laughed. "That won't work. Look at me." She scrambled up and set her feet apart, hands out, and fingers curled like claws. Her braid hung around one shoulder. She was a slender vision of innocence even with the serious expression on her face. She looked like a child playing pretend, and he had to cough to cover a laugh at her idea of ferocity. That, of course, was her point.

"I've got no weapons," she said. "I don't intimidate in the slightest. Mother warned me fear would never work for us. We don't make men fear for their life or prepare for death. They aren't going to be ready to run at the sight of me."

He hesitated, had never wanted to tell her this, but this might be the best opening. "That was before. There was a spy inside the camp. The Northerners know about you—about me, too. They know you broke them; they'll suspect you can do it again. If they recognize who you are, you'll intimidate the shit out of them. Use it." Any Northerners hunting a witch would have been told about their unusual coloring—Claire's hair would give her away at a glance.

She gaped at him, her face going white. "They . . . know about me? How long? You're just telling me now? But that would mean . . ." Two steps and she was close enough to bend down and poke him in the shoulder with a stiff finger. "You're just telling me now! They're *hunting* me?"

"Maybe. There's no way to be sure, but it seems likely."

"Hunting me. Looking to kill us specifically. And you didn't warn me?" She made a funny little growling sound and poked him again. "And to think I was worried about hurting your feelings when you've been keeping all sorts of secrets from me. What about this?" She took his sleeve and pulled. "Armor, but no uniform. Is that part of a disguise for the Northerners or is there something else? Time to come clean. No more hidden stuff between us!"

He recoiled and dropped his eyes back to the fire. "It's nothing."

"Nothing?" she persisted. She crouched down to his level, scooting closer so he had to lean back on his hands to avoid bumping heads with her. "I know it's not a disguise—like that could hide us. Out with it. I shared what was worrying me. Your turn."

"It's nothing that affects you. I don't want to talk about it," he practically shouted.

Ramiro braced for a tongue-lashing, but she dropped to the grass beside him. A pressure squeezed his hand, and he realized their fingers were laced together. Her head rested on his shoulder, her weight leaning on him.

"A friend listens," she said. "I'm listening."

He'd expected more anger, was prepared for that. He hadn't fortified against this. "I"—something unclenched in the cords of tension along his neck and down his body at her touch. The pressure gripping him for two days uncurled—"I don't have permission to be here. My father forbid me. My commanding officer doesn't know." Her hand tightened on his, and he pushed out the rest. "I deserted. At best they'll bust me back down to squire. At worst . . . at worst, they'll flog me and lock me up for life . . . if they don't hang me."

Saying it aloud tore at him. He wanted to crawl under a rock with the other slime. How could she ever look at him again? He was the lowest of villains: someone who deserted his brothers. Ran off without even trying to explain himself. Shame stabbed, like being beaten with cactus needles, only no squirming could hide him from his own mind. He'd abandoned responsibility, forsworn his oaths. He could never be trusted. She'd hate him now. *Oh saints*. He squeezed his eyes shut to conceal the moisture gathering.

She touched his face, hand curling along his jaw, fingers in his beard, and she pressed closer. "You did that for me?"

"Maybe." His voice sounded broken like a *niño*. He forced it to come out more normally. "It seemed like the right thing to do at the time. Worse to let you leave alone."

"And now? If . . . if you can't live with it—you should go back."

This time he squeezed her hand. "I'm living with it. It's still the right choice."

Her hand dropped from his face to rest on his knee. He got back enough control to open his eyes. Nothing had changed, yet everything had. "I'm disappointed in myself. That's not a strong enough word. Disgusted. Sickened."

She pulled away, sitting up so their eyes could meet. "For doing what you thought was right?"

"For not doing it the *right* way. I could have stood

up to my father. I could have resigned. Instead, I slunk out, like a thief in the night. I shame my family. I shame myself. I'm no leader, like Salvador was."

"No, you're just someone who avoids responsibility. A drone who follows orders without thought. You didn't save a village full of people when everyone else did nothing. Didn't make a girl believe in you enough to leave her home and face an army. Didn't save his entire people, single-handed." She shook her head. "Are we done feeling sorry for ourselves yet or do I have to keep going? Maybe you didn't do it right—"

"Those were . . . accidents."

"Then you're the luckiest man I've ever met."

"And you've met so many."

She sniffed and folded her arms. "I was going to say I believe in you, but not after that."

"You compared me to a goat."

Her chin went up, but her eyes sparkled. "I was right about that."

"Because you like goats."

She got to her feet and returned to her own saddle. "I do like goats, and it's a good thing for you. For one thing—you both have such wonderful beards. Besides, who else would put up with your misery for the last two days, except your mother?"

"That makes two extraordinary women in my life—extraordinarily odd." Ramiro set aside the teasing. "I thank you for not . . . for putting up with me."

"We muddled through it last time, and this will be no different," Claire said stoutly and turned back to the dying fire as though the matter were settled. "We both need to remember that."

He wished he had her conviction. It was good they had cleared the air and he'd told her everything, but it was only words. Nothing he *said* could make it right. It would only be right when he returned and surrendered, accepting his punishment. The momentary relief he felt vanished as the weight of guilt returned. Only in movement and keeping busy did it remain tolerable. Too much time to think killed him.

He stood, suffering her look of surprise. "I'm going to check on the horses."

And with that, he walked away from the camp, the darkness swallowing him inside and out.

CHAPTER 15

Claire sighed as she watched Ramiro stand and leave her, witnessed whatever comfort she'd provided during their conversation eaten up. Maybe being with his horse would help. Sancha often seemed to make things better for him. She wished she had such a bond to improve her own mood. Though she'd mentioned some of her doubts about the magic, she hadn't told him of her fear of using the power at all.

Everything just seemed to become worse and worse. Now, she was no longer an unknown weapon against the Northerners—not that she was much of one to start with. Did they have her description? Could they recognize her on sight? Just how much did they know? If she could even Sing, would they be ready for her magic next time?

Useless questions. She would assume they knew all and move forward. There was nothing else she could do. What was important now was creating a new Song. A Song of fear. Maybe if she had something more dependable, stronger and surer, she wouldn't avoid the power so much. Perhaps something of that sort the soldiers couldn't ignore.

She dug her toe into the soft ground as she worked this through. Of course this couldn't be simple like the Hornet Tune. After all, unlike bee stings, everyone experienced fear differently and for different reasons. How did she pack that all into one Song to cover every contingency?

Common sense prodded that nothing would happen unless she tried and practiced. She gave her toe one last twist in the dirt, then put her hands in her lap, sitting up tall, feet together as her mother had taught her for Singing, and began a hum under her breath, keeping it quiet so it wouldn't reach anyone or anything else.

In her head, she laced the magic, feeding in thoughts and feelings. *Death. Loss. Failure. The end of all things.* The magic ran through it all, would make it come alive in any listener's head. To her it was only ideas and music, to any other ears it was reality. Or would be real, if she found the courage to Sing it aloud. The words came more slowly as she tried and discarded options.

> *Fear, panic,*
> *Cold hands,*
> *Icy shakes.*
> *Knees buckle,*
> *Strength flees.*
> *The grave waits, darkness.*
> *Loss, Emptiness, Defeat.*
> *Foe's too strong.*
> *Strength fails.*
> *Heart stills.*
> *Pain, Agony, Suffering,*
> *Luck fails and failure comes.*
> *Death reaches.*
> *Unmade.*
> *Nothingness.*
> *Inevitability.*

Claire repeated it several times, tweaking and refining, making sure it locked into her memory to be pulled up at need. Once it was settled firmly in her mind, she relaxed a bit. Granted, it was only sounds and syllables tied together. Logically it could harm no one. From anyone else's throat it wouldn't. Yet, from her mouth, it might be deadly.

Or simply the last random words before a knife plunged into her heart.

It wouldn't stop a rampaging bear for example. Bears might feel fear, but they wouldn't experience it in the same way as a human. Who knew if animals worried about death? If they dreaded failure? An animal would most likely hit her Song and keep coming, unaffected. The Song had to suit the listener, that's why her mother always said Women of the Song had to be quick on their feet—always thinking.

Claire's eyes widened.

Why hadn't she thought of it before? The Hornet Tune. All along she'd assumed magic didn't work on the Northern priests. The Hornet Tune had done nothing to slow them—the magic apparently a failure. She'd considered the silly notion that the Northern priests had grown up living in a swarm of bees, and almost smiled before her thoughts turned somber once more. She didn't even know if her Song that sent the enemy army stampeding had affected them either, or only the regular soldiers. What if instead the priests' minds worked differently than most humans? Maybe magic did work on them, but she'd used the wrong Song. Maybe it wasn't the Song that failed; it was her choice that had or the level of her determination and will.

A rush of energy jumped through her, excitement and joy. Her magic's failure had deadened her spirits more than she realized, making her feel hopeless, as well as helpless, as if a familiar tool had let her down. She'd felt much the same when she'd thought Ramiro wanted her to use *that* Song again. But he hadn't, and what if she was mistaken about the magic's potency as well!

Claire thought back to tea with Father Telo and

Beatriz. Beatriz had quizzed the city priest all about the Northerners, and she'd taken in every word, fascinated. The enemy priests in their white robes didn't believe in kindness, something about this world being a test from their god to make sure they were good enough. Would that mean they shrugged off personal injury and pain? Could go right through her Hornet Tune and not care?

She tugged her braid, trying to think deeper. "If they don't care for themselves, what sort of Song will work on them?" she asked the dying fire. Ideas darted in and out of her head, but none impressed her as likely to work. She slumped. Here's where her mother's experience would have helped immensely. She just didn't have the knowledge or skill to figure out the answer on her own.

In theory, her grandmother would know even more than her mother—if they could only find her . . . and if her grandmother would speak to her or want to help. She'd made assumptions about the Northern priests, she didn't want to do the same about her nearest relation. Her only choice was to find out.

Claire glanced around for Ramiro, to tell him her ideas about the priests and ask his opinion. Nothing moved around her but the little beetles that came out since the rain had stopped to flash the lights in their tails. While she waited, she slipped into a daydream of showing her grandmother her latest Song, of working together to make it stronger. Grandmother would hug her and give her a piece of cake because that's what grandmothers did—or so her mother had reported when she'd begged to hear about village life.

The daydream shattered.

Maybe that's what other grandmothers did in the villages, but Claire couldn't believe that would be true even in a fantasy. Somehow, the idea of her grandmother baking just didn't seem realistic. The woman from her very vague childhood memory was all sharp edges.

Beatriz, however, would pat her on the head and give her cake—cake someone else had baked, naturally. That she could imagine. A new daydream formed of Beatriz liking her and feeding her all sorts of sweets. Claire sat contentedly in a rosy daze as the last of the firelight went out and the sliver of moon rose higher.

Finally growing cold and giving up on Ramiro, she slid into her bedroll. Ramiro could hear about her Song in the morning. With luck, she'd reach home tomorrow, could maybe spend the next night in her own bed before they moved on. She heard Ramiro's low voice talking to his horse and felt warm and cozy. He wouldn't let anything happen to her. In her head, she ran through the words from the Goodnight Song she'd been Singing to herself as long as she could remember to help fall asleep.

Rest
Close your eyes
All is well
All is safe
Loved
Wake to a new day
Wake to . . .

For the better part of the night Father Telo had wandered the camp, giving support where he could, watching the people pack their few belongings. Despite much grumbling and vocal resistance, this morning, the majority had departed for Crueses with the First Wife as their unofficial figurehead. No one wanted to be left behind as the military pulled out on Julian's orders and a majority of the council had voted with the idea to leave. *Alcalde* Julian had left hours earlier to ensure their safe passage into the *ciudad-estado* and to enact whatever other plan he had in his head. The man was incapable of setting aside responsibility, even when the responsibility would soon no longer be his.

Again, Telo missed not being in the thick of things—he'd enjoyed his time being counselor to kings perhaps too much—but he had his own destiny to follow. Pray God they both had an equally successful conclusion.

If you cannot do great things, do small things in a great way.

What was left of the camp had the empty ring to it that spoke of loneliness, the sort of feeling one got the first day inside the walls of the seminary when you missed the fullness of life. He walked past the blackened rings of campfires littered with the occasional trash or ripped and cast-aside blankets. With the women, children, and warriors gone, all that remained were various soldiers doing clean up and making sure nothing of importance was left behind.

The sort of nothing such as a single, lowly friar and a dangerous prisoner.

Telo walked toward the wagon holding Santabe. He'd chosen the time carefully, well aware that most of her guards took a break for their meal at noon. Santabe was to move out last, staying well separated from the civilians, and bring up the very rear of the long train of refugees.

Telo fingered the weapon inside his robe and hoped he followed the Lord's will in this. The council, forced to wait for a trial and having trouble finding anyone to defend their prisoner, had failed to act. His people seemed content to keep Santabe chained up and put aside the decision of executing her for another day, more concerned with their own survival. Telo thought their priorities skewed, but honored their reluctance to kill in haste and outside of true justice.

He'd debated again and again over this choice, afraid of the lengths it would take him—the sin he would commit. Thoughts of it kept him awake at night, made food taste like dust in his mouth. Yet, the murder of Taps and *Concejal* Lugo, the audacity of Ordoño in infiltrating the camp in broad daylight, urged him to this point, made his duty, if not clear, then apparent.

He'd been thinking the wrong way after the loss of his hand—the loss of his city. His loss wasn't a message from the Lord about forgiveness, but the opposite. Instead of passive, he needed to be aggressive. He'd failed to act when Ordoño was right in front of him.

Fear the sword: For wrath brings punishment to evil, that they may know there is a judgment.

By the Lord, there was no one else. Dealing with Ordoño rested on him alone, even if it took his life—or worse, pushed him into grave sin.

The situation at this moment called for his affable face to be shown to the lone man leaning against the wagon and looking bored. Telo had spoken with him before in his tour of the camp. He had taken pains to become familiar to all the guards. Compared to the hard-as-nails Farmer-face and Taps, this one with his unlined features could have been a child. No doubt he was the one all the others bullied around, as he had been picked to miss his dinner.

"Greetings," Telo called, "a hot day, is it not?" He wiped his forehead and pulled out his flask, almost putting it to his lips, before seeming to recollect himself. "You first, my son."

"Thanks, Father," the guard said eagerly. "From you, this is truly holy water." The guard winked, and Telo had the grace to feel ashamed. Telo reminded himself the lad wouldn't be hurt. He'd only take a nice nap and be embarrassed at his gullibility when he woke.

"Santiago blessed the wine and Santa Teresa used it for her sacred healing, but I like to think they preferred beer for their own libations."

"Amen to that, Father." The guard tilted up the flask for a second pull, then handed it back, and Telo tucked it away.

"How goes it with your prisoner?" Telo asked.

The lad's face soured and he spit. "The same, Father, still rioting and too violent to approach. It is kind of you to take an interest in her, as everyone else wishes her dead. I wish the trial would start and get it over."

"'All belong to me,' sayeth the Lord, 'from the small to the great.' My interest is the least I can do after the unfortunate incident I caused earlier." Telo hung his head. The death of Taps had indeed been his fault. He would see that corrected, come what may. Justice may belong to the Lord, but the saints didn't hesitate to make it their cause. A nudge to balance the scales from a lowly friar wouldn't be the end of the world—probably—though it might damn him.

The guard gave his shoulder a squeeze. "Had nothing to do with you, Father. She was waiting her chance, and that's for tr—" He brows drew down in surprise and then his face went slack. Telo caught the lad as he slid to the ground. The little herb he'd added to the flask worked fast once it took effect.

Telo arranged the guard in a more dignified position, then, one-handed, he rifled through the lad's clothes and found a set of keys. Telo let out a breath. He'd hoped the other guards followed procedure and left the keys with this poor fellow, but he wasn't sure they would. Without the keys, he'd planned to turn back from this course. "Thanks for showing me the way," he said to the clear sky, unsure whether to be relieved or downcast. He mounted the stairs to the wagon.

One key on the ring opened the door, the smaller intended for another lock. Santabe must have heard the rattles for she stood waiting when he entered.

"Come to offer yourself for the next sacrifice?" she said without preamble. The tall priestess looked much the same as before, dirty and disheveled, her hair hacked raggedly short, but now her earlobe hung torn and bloodied, the sun-shaped earring gone and actually in his pocket. Dark bruises covered her face, and Telo saw more peeking out above her shirt at her collarbone—someone had taken a toll for Taps's death—and they'd managed to get fresh clothing on her, a bright yellow shirt of the type peasant women preferred and an equally bright-colored skirt of pink. It hung several inches too short, revealing her ankles. The chain attached to her waist and the far wall of the wagon had been shortened considerably, giving her less range. On the wooden wall where the chain was bolted were splinters and gashes as though torn at by fingernails in a mad frenzy. This one would fight every step to her hanging.

She rushed him. Telo had expected it and set his feet. He hiked his robe and kicked her squarely in the midsection. She tumbled back, all the air gone from her lungs, and collapsed atop her pallet.

"The Lord has many faces," he said cheerfully. No remorse hit him for striking a woman. Her orders to kill children, her viciousness with Taps, proved she was more devil than human. Some souls couldn't be redeemed, no matter what scripture said. "Just as I wasn't always a priest. Before I found the Lord and left the slums to take orders, I used to earn coin in the brawl pits, wrestling or boxing for others to wager on. Even spent a few seasons with bandits." Telo flexed his brawny arm. The woman may have been tall and fit, but he was the taller and outweighed her easily. He had little concern for who would come out on top in an honest fight—if it wasn't for the loss of his hand.

And then, it was up to the Lord.

She sat up, holding her chest, unable to do more than send him a glare that turned his blood cold. He went to the chain in the wall, making sure not to turn his back upon her, and found the key to unlock it.

"Come for your revenge?" she hissed. "That doesn't follow your pathetic beliefs of charity and kindness."

"As I said, our Lord has many faces. Some of the saints came to show us of the Lord's love and tolerance, others to prove his thirst for justice and righteousness. San Martin led an army against those who opposed him. Santiago smote the unbelievers. I'm not yet sure which He wants to see from me." Telo held her chain securely and showed her his nub. "I'm no saint, but I take this as a hint that I wasn't going about things correctly. Our Lord believes in second chances. Whether I am to save or execute you will be revealed in His good time. For now, you come with me."

"Why?"

"Because in polite company when one goes calling, one takes a gift. You are that gift." He locked her chain to a corresponding one he now wore beneath his triple-rope belt and put away the keys, then pulled on the links until she had been dragged to her feet. She snarled and growled under her breath, and he wondered if she would bite. He didn't intend to let her close enough to try.

Out of his robe, and the hidden pocket one of his healers had obligingly sewed for him, he produced a slim white rod. He thought this better than putting a sharp object within her reach. Telo had discovered the weapons were harmless when held by a single person, only when they touched a second did the magic kill. Her eyes widened upon seeing the magic weapon. "Several of these Diviners were found scattered on the battlefield. Dropped by your priests, I think. Our *Alcalde* ordered them secured until he could decide what to do with them, but they just might come in handy. I know how this works. You will cooperate or I'll test it on you. 'Justice is mine,' sayeth the Lord, and you are long overdue. I won't hesitate. As Lord Ordoño didn't take you when he was here, he shouldn't mind too much."

"You take me to Ordoño?" He read the repeat of surprise on her face and felt the relaxing in her posture. As expected, she would go back to her kind willingly enough. "Then you are a bigger fool than I took you for, priest. Dal will finish you."

That threat sent a chill down his back, but he showed none of it. Weakness was invitation with this one. "Or the Lord will be my shepherd. Either way, I'll find out. Whether you do depends on your behavior." He gestured with the rod. "You first. Walk."

As before, no one was around but the sleeping guard. Telo set a fast pace and kept a tight grip on the Diviner, hoping not to use it and to escape the camp before her absence was discovered. They quickly left the wagon behind, heading out into the desert. Telo had studied the maps and knew where to reach the road going north. An overheard scout report informed him the Northern army camped near the ruins of Zapata. Ordoño would be there now, Telo hoped. He certainly wasn't here—two days searching the camp assured Telo the Northern leader had left. It's true he could have gone to his second army at Aveston, but Telo didn't think so. The man would return to take charge of the larger army. He only hoped Santabe could get him close again.

It was a risk bringing her. He might be able to approach Ordoño without her. But she spoke the language; she would open doors he might not be able to manage. Plus, her presence would be either a boon to Ordoño or an alternate target against which to expend a first reaction of rage. Telo found Ordoño a thoughtful man, considering before striking out, but if he judged wrong perhaps Santabe would be the enemy leader's object and not his humble self.

Either way, he needed to get close.

In the brawler pits, they said life is a gamble. Telo had missed an opportunity to fulfill his destiny and stop the army. He had every chance to clasp his fingers around Ordoño's throat and keep the wildcat of his army from running again. The idea made him sick, but he intended to rectify that mistake, even if it led him to the gravest sin a man could commit. For a second the world wavered. *To do this thing...*

Everything inside him screamed at him it was evil.

He looked at the priestess, and resolved himself. *That* was the face of evil.

Telo kept his steps firm, his hand on the Diviner unshaken, no matter his inner turmoil. The Lord gave him a second chance and he'd make it count—even at the cost of his immortal soul.

CHAPTER 16

Julian stared at the feast spread before him: bread, fowl, beef, and other meats, a variety of cheeses, two types of wine plus ale, vegetables marinated in rich sauces giving off a heady aroma, bowls of olives. He had not seen this much food in one place since before the Northerners split their army and set their siege around Colina Hermosa. The rationing he'd ordered had been citywide. But his ride through Crueses and glimpses of the markets said the excess wasn't confined to the palace. Everywhere plenty of food was on display, nor did prices seem elevated. It was as if they weren't worried at all. Yet, their military seemed alert enough.

An escort had reached him and his attendants while still two miles out—the message of his approach apparently having reached them. Upon arriving at the city, the soldiers had refused admittance to the majority of his guards, leaving him with two, both of which had been restricted from this room and kept in the vestibule of the palace. Surprisingly, they hadn't insisted on searching his person, not that they would have found any weapon—he carried none.

So why wasn't their *alcalde* here to meet him? The whole situation gave him an uneasy feeling.

Appetite fled, and it had nothing to do with the wastefulness before him. Julian pushed his untouched plate forward so he could rest his elbows on the table. Two days of riding nonstop to speak with the *alcaldes* here, only to be kept waiting for hours. Why would they do that? He was sore and tired and a knot of emptiness rested in his chest, the same lump he got every time he was separated from his wife and children. Even without a clock in the room, time pressed down upon him in a silent ticking of the seconds. Rather than pacing, he adjusted his tunic and coat, rehearsing his speech once more in his head, but he couldn't settle.

The leaders here would know such delaying tactics to be useless on a man of his experience, thus the slight was either because they found him, the leader of the largest *ciudad-estado* with one of the biggest militaries that could break them twice over, unimportant—unlikely—or they were well and truly flustered at his arrival. He could grant that his presence was unwanted. They must guess at his reason for being here and would oppose it. Nor did his plan satisfy himself—for a moment his inner landscape rocked, and he tried and failed to tighten his left hand into a fist, then he regained control, pushing aside the doubt.

The plan was flimsy enough against what faced them, but the alternative was to roll over and let Ordoño win.

That Julian would never allow, not until the last breath left his body. He would try whatever it took to convince the leaders here to listen, including anything that might keep them off-balance and likely to concede. He arranged the throw pillows—Beatriz might have had a hand in decorating this room from the amount of plush and lace—against his back in the throne-like chair and laced his hands over his chest for a nap. Although a sham, let the *alcaldes* see him perfectly at home and relaxed, not a frantic man, flinging out desperate ideas.

In the end, the long day's ride did send him into a light doze, a pleasant-seeming dream where he walked hand in hand with Beatriz through their favorite garden while the boys ran around them. It harkened of days that would never come again, bittersweet bliss. When the door creaked open, he woke with a smile on his face and an ache in his heart. Three men entered. He recognized *Alcalde* Juan of Crueses and *Alcalde* Ramón of Suseph.

Juan and Ramón were similar enough in feature and figure to be brothers though decades separated them in age. This was not surprising—their families had been intermarrying for generations. The term *alcalde* was only a formality here, their elections a mockery, considered more of a quaint tradition, as the eldest son always succeeded the father as ruler. Both had long fingers and high foreheads with sloping chins. *Alcalde* Ramón ran to jowls under his beard and a comfortable paunch around his middle. He kept his beard full to touch his chest. As the younger—and Julian's contemporary in age—Juan still wore his hair in curly ringlets to his shoulders, a fashion in their cities for younger men that Julian found made them look more like women. He wore his beard short over the chin and lips, but with great bushy sideburns. Their clothing could have been selected by the same tailor: bright colors that didn't necessarily match and puffy sleeves on the short doublet the wealthy seemed to favor worn long over green hose. Despite being prepared as they had met many times before in better times, their colorful attire hurt Julian's half-asleep eyes.

The third member of their group was a priest. Julian gave him a cursory glance as he climbed to his feet and offered a bow. The elderly man was so old as to be hunched over under the weight of his own shoulders. He wore the black robe of a bishop under the traditional triple-rope belt. Another aspect of their cities that did not surprise Julian. Instead of an advising elected council, Crueses and Suseph relied on the clergy. This bishop must be their leading counselor. Oddly enough he wore a curling mustache dyed a startling black. Julian did a double take. In his fifty-four years, he'd never seen a priest with facial hair before.

"Turn right back around," Juan said before they'd cleared the threshold. "We know what you're about and we're not having it."

"We are not the shelter for the entirety of your *ciudad-estado*," Ramón added. He waved a ringed hand. "Turn your people around and take them somewhere else."

Julian felt glad to have the worst out—it did save time—though it *was* odd that they didn't seem to be *guessing* about his purpose. Their posture spoke of certainty. There were rumors that the twin cities employed birds as messengers, and he knew it must be true—no runner could have brought word of the number of civilians headed this way this quickly. "There is nowhere else."

"There are plenty of other places," Juan interrupted. He remained standing while Ramón dropped into a chair and dipped his fingers into the olive bowl. "Go deeper into the desert. Head for Vista Sur. It is too many for us. You are not welcome."

"Not welcome," Ramón repeated, holding out a hand in a warding gesture. The man had a vain fetish over displaying his plump, smooth hands when he talked. It had always been so—Julian used to laugh about it with Beatriz—but today it irritated.

Julian pushed the pillows on the floor. "There isn't time for this, and you know it. You are talking nonsense, not the wisdom of an *alcalde*. The people of Colina Hermosa are coming here and that is that. Will you open your gates or will you force our hand?"

Lips curled at Julian's threat, but there was also a touch of fear in both men's eyes, for it was not an idle one. Julian was perfectly prepared to batter down the gates to the twin cities if needed to provide safety for his people. The smaller *ciudades-estado* would be unable to stop them. It was a gigantic waste of time and resources, though. People would die on both sides. No one wanted that, but they knew it was not a bluff.

They would do the same in his place.

"Be reasonable. We cannot absorb so many, Julian," Ramón said, placing a hand on his heart. "On our honor. We'll all starve."

Julian looked at the overloaded table with an eyebrow raised and his patience drained another notch. "I have a solution for that. You will only be taking our civilians. The fighting men will go with me to Aveston." He held his breath for a heartbeat. Getting the people inside was not his fear. Here came the tricky part. "And we will take your *pelotónes* as well. That will save your provisions for a time."

Ramón pushed himself back from the table, the chair legs screeching on the tiles. Fury overtook Juan's face. "You bastard."

The bishop touched mind, heart, liver, and spleen. "Hold. Hold," the priest said. "This is a conference. We will talk it out. Be cal—"

"The Northern army around Aveston is the smaller

army," Julian shouted over the priest. "Together, we can take it down. That will be one less part for Lord Ordoño to bring against us. One less group of fighting men to resist." The remaining army would continue to be huge; Julian feared them unbeatable. But he had seen one miracle in the last sevenday. Given time, could not another be worked and brought to save them? "We would free Aveston, so their men could join us. Together we can pressure the other *ciudades-estado* to join us, too. If all our cities send their armies, we have a better chance."

Juan raised his chin. "We care not for your chances. Engaging the Northerners at all is delusional."

"Delusional," Ramón echoed the younger man, punctuating it with a raised fist. "We are small, vulnerable. Fighting is not our choice."

Julian frowned. *Not their choice.*

As if the Northerners are giving us a choice.

"Do you think to buy the Northerners off?" he scoffed, standing. Crueses and Suseph were wealthy cities, but no one with half of a mind would think that a possibility. Or not anyone who'd met Ordoño. "I can tell you have not talked with Ordoño. I've seen him myself, and we had an insider close to him who knows his mind. Father Telo assures me the Northern leader will not be dissuaded. Look how he burns his victim cities. He's not interested in riches."

Ramón had pulled his chair back to the table as Julian spoke, piling a plate with thin-sliced pieces of beefsteak and pouring turnip gravy over it. Juan took a seat, leaving the bishop as the only one of the three still standing. "You mistake us," Juan said.

"Wha—" Julian snapped his mouth shut. "You . . ." The word wouldn't come. "You aren't buying off the Northerners. Or rather . . ." He looked at the men, his vision almost wavering. "*Saints.* You . . . you are taking their terms." His legs trembled and he sat abruptly, unsure whether he was more shocked or horrified. "Do you not know what that means?" His voice rose. "They demand a portion of your population—for sacrifice. How can you accept them?"

"We'd planned on a lottery of all nonessential persons." Ramón's knife paused. "It is the only logical way. Fair to all."

"Fair to all," Juan repeated. "We have no power to fight, and they recognize it. This way we save our city. We will not burn as your Colina Hermosa."

"So you sacrifice your people"—Julian waved his hand around the room—"for this? You give up your people in favor of buildings? You haven't told them, have you? Your people don't know you intend to do this."

"We act to save our way of life," Juan corrected. "It was not an easy decision. Our people will be told when the time is right. Do not mock us because you were too selfish and lacked strength to make the hard choice."

"Strength? What you do is a mockery. You will not keep your way of life. The Northerners will not leave you that. You will become the fodder for their knives until there is nothing left of you. Can't you see that? You might think to protect yourselves"—Julian pointed at the three of them—"but it will not succeed."

"*Caballeros,*" the priest hobbled forward. "Our Lord gave everyone leave to follow their own path. Our differences make us as various as clouds in the sky."

"This isn't about differences," Julian shouted, incensed. "It's about insanity!" Were they so isolated in their rosy palaces as to have no feel for the common people? What deal had they struck with the priests to gain the support of the church? Could they be so foolish as to overlook that if you opened the door for one rat, it was impossible to keep the rest out?

It all smelled of rot to Julian.

The elderly bishop stepped forward to scold again as Juan and Ramón shared a look. Ramón raised a plump hand and sent the bishop back to his corner. "You will not change our mind, Julian. It will be announced to the people when the moment is right and accepted. They will see there is no other way. The failure of your city is a fine example for them. We will do you the concession of taking your people into our shelter if you choose to go fight." Both *alcaldes* focused on the table as if unable to look him in the eye. "But you may not have our fighting men."

Julian blinked, suddenly understanding and feeling like a fool. They'd maneuvered him perfectly. All along, they'd been ready to accept his people, counting on it. Who better to throw to the Northerners as the first victims? They spoke of lotteries they no longer had to hold—not right away on any count. Why sacrifice their own people when Julian provided replacements? They'd give the people of Colina Hermosa to the Northerners.

And what choice did he have?

No wonder they waited so long to see him. They *should* be ashamed to show their faces to the world, let alone to him. How could they act so? The cities had always squabbled—sometimes to trading blows—but to betray each other like this before outsiders . . .

He couldn't go fight the Northerners at Aveston and leave the people of Colina Hermosa undefended and without walls around them. He'd already debated that point. That was the reason for sending them here.

"It doesn't have to be this way. If we all joined together—"

Their eyes snapped to him. "Drop it. We are decided. Continue to force the issue and you will not leave this room."

The bishop swung open the door, revealing a dozen guards with swords drawn. Chills ran down Julian's back. *Alcaldes* had been murdered by rival *ciudades-estado* in the past. Precedent existed. "Would you kill me to prevent me from stopping my people from coming?"

"You're a smart man," Juan said. "You know they must come here with or without your support."

"We don't want to kill anyone," Ramón added. "Especially you. You are our brother *alcalde*."

"It would be a poor return," Juan agreed. "Think

of leaving your people with us as insurance and payment to us as you go to incense the Northerners more. We allow you to have your fight, with your soldiers. We keep your people safe, feed them, clothe them, and tend their ills. If worse comes to worse, they save our people."

Julian worked double time assessing the possibilities and hit a blind alley. By the saints, they'd have his wife as hostage. They might as well have beaten him senseless with sticks, the result was the same. "Supposing I accept this quietly, have you a way to contact those inside Aveston?"

Again, the *alcaldes* exchanged glances and Julian took that for yes. Ideas clicked in his head. To be able to slip a message inside Aveston would be invaluable. Could he let his people go for this concession? Could he betray them with a smile and a wave of the hand, in an instant becoming the biggest traitor in his people's history? All for the chance to strike a feeble blow against his enemies. Without the extra military units it was even odds they could win.

The thing was: Did he have a choice?

The fingers of his left hand closed enough to manipulate his thumb over them, though it brought enough pain to draw tears from his eyes. He'd let himself be outmaneuvered. Saints forgive him his failures, for Julian would never forgive himself.

"For our people . . ." he whispered.

"For our people," Juan and Ramon echoed, their grins turning his stomach.

CHAPTER 17

The horses' hooves sloshed through puddles from the recent rain. The marshland where Ramiro had camped during his last trip to the swamp had changed beyond recognition. There, where he'd tied Claire to a slender birch tree, a latrine had been dug. The grass was trampled and matted from the passage of many feet. The trees where Claire had tried to escape him had been hacked down. Dozens of little mud huts, more like lean-tos in height, dotted the area. A large camp had been here, but now only a few eyes stared out at them from inside the small shelters, most of the structures empty. Claire echoed him in glancing around uneasily.

It wasn't right. Why hadn't Teresa greeted him? Ramiro had expected there to be more . . . life about the place. Why were there so few children in evidence? There should have been dozens.

"The *ciudad* man returns."

Claire let out a yelp of surprise. Anger tightened Ramiro's muscles at the sound of that swaggering voice. Signaling Claire to remain in place, he held himself together, descending from Sancha before turning to look, giving his temper a chance to settle. He wanted nothing so much as to pound Suero into a greasy stain on the ground. The man had stood aside to let the Northerners kill him. Only Claire's unexpected interference had saved his life. They'd had a deal and Suero had kept it by the slimmest of margins, abandoning Ramiro as soon as allowable. Now it appeared Suero had failed to protect the children of Colina Hermosa as well.

And just like a cheat and a liar, the leader of the village had deliberately let them go past to move in at their backs. It was a wonder he spoke and didn't just fill them full of arrows, though Ramiro guessed it was more about their lack of skill with such weapons than any idea of honorable courtesy.

Back bent like he was hiding something, Suero stood with feet spread apart, Salvador's sword held at his hip by a length of rope. He sported bits of Ramiro's stolen armor on upper arms and thighs. Spots of rust dotted the metal, in places as big as a thumbprint. Armor needed constant scouring in such a wet place to avoid corrosion. Suero had done none of that. The anger swelled again and it had nothing to do with the armor.

"Where are the children? Where's Teresa?" Ramiro

squeezed his fingers into fists, ready to grab for sword or knife. If Suero had altered that part of their bargain, nothing kept Ramiro from taking back his brother's sword—and enjoying doing it.

"Gone and gone."

"Hardly an explanation."

"Why are you back, city man?" Suero's hand reached up to scratch his dark beard, the only full and generous thing on his otherwise pinched and suspicious face. He stared with obvious greed at their horses and equipment. "Five *ciudad* people enter my swamp, and only three leave. This time I think none will."

Ramiro faltered. *Three?* Teresa and he were the only ones to survive. What did the man mean? Certainty returned as he guessed the traitorous little man had added Claire to the mix. That would explain the higher number.

"Stop with the threats," Ramiro said, making note of the other hunched men hiding behind shelters. No doubt they waited with heavy cudgels in hand. As sure as the sun rose in the morning, Suero would fight dirty, but Ramiro had allies now.

Or did he?

Claire was conflicted about her magic. Could she hold the others off as he took Suero down?

It didn't matter. He'd fought dirty himself in street contests as a boy. He'd just as soon do it again today. Take out Suero and the rest would slink away. He took a step forward, hand going to his sword. "Let's get this started."

"Wait." Claire shook her head at him in warning or maybe exasperation, and he stopped. "What good does fighting do? Aren't there more important things than ego right now?"

She was right: It was more important to find answers to his questions than take out his frustrations. "Taunting seems to be all you can do," Ramiro called out. "It's pathetic. Tell me where Teresa and the children have gone and you never have to see us again."

"Why should I care? Do you have something to trade?"

"I'm sure you prefer to steal," Ramiro snapped. "It's a wonder you can show your face after you dishonored our bargain. What kind of man are you? Did you hand them to the Northerners?" Claire's disapproval or no, his conscience wouldn't bother him to end this treacherous sneak.

Suero spat. "Speak for yourself. City men have no honor."

Ramiro started forward again, his anger on a hot simmer, then he noticed the boy. Still shirtless and brown, Bromisto stood near the edge of the huts, watching. He couldn't very well beat the father with his ten-year-old son looking on. Ramiro kept his voice low, spreading his fingers wide as a sign of peace. "There are still greater enemies to deal with. Just tell us so we can go."

Suero sneered but visibly relaxed, as if he, too, didn't want to be less in front of the child or, more likely, he'd noticed the tightening of Claire's face and wanted no part of a witch. "Your people left of their own choice. Your bossy woman went to see what fared with your city—saints scourge it to the ground—and soldiers took your brats."

"What soldiers?"

"Your city ones. They took back their own, and I had no call to keep them. Glad to see them gone. Now take your *sirena* and get, and don't look to me for a guide this time. We are quits. Me and mine have no more to do with you."

Turning his back and returning to his horse sent a shiver of unseen eyes down Ramiro's spine. Much like a snake, Suero was dangerous exactly because of his unexpectedness. You could never tell when he would strike, and it wouldn't be from the direction you predicted.

Sancha and Claire gave him the same blank stare, like they had practiced it. "What?" he said to both.

"You could have been less aggressive. They aren't our enemy."

"I had to know."

"You know. Can we leave?" Claire said. "I don't like this place." Sancha snapped her tail in agreement.

"Gladly." He slid into the saddle with a nod of farewell to Bromisto. He would have liked to speak to the boy again—he seemed nothing like his father—but not at the expense of remaining another minute. His conscience stung briefly that he hadn't warned Suero that the Northerners may push deeper into the swamp, but the man had dug his own tomb with his hostility.

The women in the tiny shelters watched him with frightened eyes as he directed Sancha to the lake. They didn't deserve to be here either, with such husbands and fathers, but they had made their choice.

He took Claire a ways down the shore, where he was sure Suero couldn't watch them cross. Reeds cracked under the horses' hooves and frogs jumped ahead by the score. The tension slowly left Ramiro as he put Suero out of his mind. They had a mission to find the witches—Women of the Song—there's where his attention must lie. Not with Suero—or worse his desertion.

"Those people wouldn't accept me," Claire said, breaking into his thoughts, "and I wouldn't be happy if they did."

"What?"

"Mother always said men dominate the women, and that's true here. You can see it in the way they hide, unwilling to look in my eyes." Her head tilted as if listening to a voice on the wind. "But the women from your city haven't been crushed. They have their own spirit."

He frowned at her. "Who said they didn't?"

"Never mind," she said, suddenly interested in arranging her clothing. "It's not about the voting. Beatriz was right about that. I can tell the difference now."

He considered asking if her brain had too much sun today—perhaps he should see she got a hat—but other considerations intruded. The slime-green lake stretched out before them, waiting to be crossed. Ramiro sighed. He should be used to it by now. This would be—what?—his third trip across?

"Stay on the horse—"

"Jorga."

"Stay on Jorga. I'll lead you across."

"I'm not a butterfly. I can manage on my feet."

"You're a fragile and delicate flower, remember," he added, referring to their argument of what seemed years ago. "I'm the one who takes on the fragile and delicate stink. It's what I do."

"You do it very well, too," she agreed too quickly and threw in a sly smile that warmed her whole face, putting a devastating dimple in her cheek. "Your mother would agree I should stay on Jorga."

"I'm glad that's settled, though I wish you'd leave my mother out of it." He didn't need the reminder that she wouldn't approve of his desertion.

"I'm sorry Teresa wasn't there," Claire said. "I was hoping she'd go with us."

"Aye. Me, too. We must have missed her on the road." Ramiro prayed she was safe and had made it back to Colina Hermosa—or what was left of it.

"You can take me," a thin voice said from a clump of reeds. Ramiro whirled, his sword in his hand, only to see Bromisto step out. "I'm ready to go with you." The boy's brown eyes snapped with anticipation, a smile on his thin face. He hadn't donned shirt or shoes, but a small bag hung over one shoulder.

"No," Ramiro said automatically.

"Who is this?" Claire asked. Before he could stop her, she half climbed and half fell from her horse. "A child. He's so cute." She reached out to touch Bromisto on the head.

The boy slapped at her hands and stepped back. "I don't need another sister or a mother. What's wrong with her? Your *sirena* is *loca*."

"That's not very friendly." Claire stepped back, a hurt look on her face. "I won't harm you."

"Who said you'd be able to? I can take care of myself."

Ramiro put a hand over his eyes and counted to ten. When he removed it, he found a wary standoff with Claire smiling hesitantly at the boy, and Bromisto frowning and keeping an arm's distance between them.

"You travel with her. Maybe I change my mind."

"You *can't* come with us this time, Bromisto," Ramiro said. "It's too dangerous and we don't need a guide. Claire can lead me."

Claire's face brightened. "That's true. Maybe another time, little boy."

"I can lead you better than her. She's just a girl. What does she know of the swamp?"

Ramiro secured Claire's horse before it decided to wander. "Claire can barely explain *me* to the Women of the Song. How would you explain you? It's too dangerous."

"I'm sorry, little boy. He's right. It just wouldn't be safe for you." Claire reached out to touch him again as if to express sympathy, and Bromisto dodged.

Ramiro sighed. "Bromisto, you have to stay here and help your family. This is where you're needed."

"That's nothing but chores and more chores. The excitement is where you are."

Bromisto's eyes shone in a way that reminded Ramiro painfully of too many occasions of being turned back from following his older brother, being left behind again. His resolve began to slip. Maybe it wouldn't be the end of the world if the kid tagged along. Claire shrugged, and Sancha twitched an ear in indifference.

"Everyone else says yes," Bromisto wheedled.

Something burned in Ramiro's chest. It felt like the sunshine vanished behind thick cloud cover. "I just spoke to Suero, and your father forbade it. He said there is to be no more contact between his and mine. A son should obey his father. You stay here."

The boy's shoulders slumped. "You'll be sorry not to take me." But without another word, he turned and vanished back into the scrub and out of sight.

A weight like a rock settled in Ramiro's stomach. "It's the honorable course," he called after the boy. "It would be too dangerous," he repeated to himself.

Claire had her hands on her hips. "He isn't you."

"What's that supposed to mean?" he asked tiredly as he held Jorga's reins out to the girl.

He froze in the middle of pulling off a boot and

rolling up his pant leg, when Claire said, "Just because you didn't *obey* your own father, doesn't mean you should decide for the boy. You can't make up for your own guilt by keeping the child from it. You did what you decided to be right. Your father will forgive you."

"Will he?" Ramiro pulled off the other boot, holding it in his hands. Likely his father would understand—more easily than his mother, anyway. The catch in his throat came not from fear of his father's anger, but from letting him down. His father would forgive, but Ramiro couldn't forgive himself. The military was all he ever wanted. He'd thrown that away, too. "Does it matter the reason I sent Bromisto back? It needed to be done."

For that Claire had no answer, but the light touch of a hand on his back. There then gone, yet it eased the guilt inside him. He removed his armor and tied everything atop Sancha with a lighter heart, ready to face the lake again.

They crossed the rain-swollen lake without incident, avoiding quicksand, poisonous spiders, and most of the leeches—disgusted, Ramiro pried a few loose from private places within the safety of a blueberry bush while Claire had a good laugh at his expense, then he put on his armor again over his civilian clothing. Conversation stopped as they went through the area where their kin had died, each locked in their own thoughts. Claire took the lead, seeming to become more certain of her direction as the hours passed.

As the day grew later, Ramiro had them walk, more to stretch his legs than to give the horses a break. They followed a slender path, wide enough for goats but not horses. Branches brushed against them as they passed, like welcoming hands. The ground was drier here than any other spot in the swamp, smelling less like mildew. His feet didn't squish or sink in. No doubt why they'd chosen it for their home.

The silence drew out, not clumsy and awkward, but with mutual acceptance, like a comfortable blanket. Claire spoke only to repeat they were close, excitement in her voice. He glanced over to where she walked ahead, leading her horse, to see her wiping at tears with the heel of her hand.

He almost said nothing, but the ache of sympathy pulled. "For me the memories were the worst on patrol." When she didn't respond, he stumbled on, "All the uniforms. It . . . was painful. Always reminded he isn't coming back."

She nodded, pointing to a tree. "She used to watch me climb that one. Apple trees are easiest. She let me start out on apple trees." Fresh tears welled, her throat working as she swallowed. "I used to hide there to avoid cleaning the stable. She always found me. Memories . . . everywhere."

"Aye," he said against the tightening in his own throat. He'd been ashamed at the tiny part of him glad his home was burned just so he wouldn't have to be there without Salvador. It was selfish when so many others lost their homes, too. Sancha nosed his shoulder. "I . . ."

She stopped to let him draw even with her as the trail widened out. "What?"

"It's silly."

"I want to know."

"I dream of him sometimes." Moisture burned his eyes, and he jabbed at them angrily, trying to hide the motion with a scratch at his temple. "I pretend Salvador is speaking to me about things, still cares about me."

"Of course they still care about us." Claire stared out into the distance and another tear rolled. "They do. It isn't silly."

"Reading into dreams. Likely just too much stress." He touched mind and heart. "It was only twice."

"I think it's nice. I wish I dreamt about Mother."

"Perhaps you will tonight."

She took his hand and it felt right not letting go—after all she needed the comfort more than he. Hand in hand, they started walking again. She pointed ahead with the hand holding her reins. "Just there, through those bushes and down in a hollow. I wonder if the goats will still be there. After all this time, likely they strayed without anyone to tend them."

Her pace increased, drawing him along with her. They broke from the bushes to find a low wooden house cleverly built into the side of the hollow. Flowers bloomed in boxes under the windows. A churn stood on the porch. Beside it was a stable roofed with sod, grass growing atop it and blowing in the slight breeze, and several smaller outbuildings. A garden had a rail fence around it. It was a place that bespoke tidy, snug owners who tended their home with care.

A warning went off in his head. It was altogether too neat for a home abandoned for over a sevenday.

Claire dropped his hand to clap and bounce on her toes, her eyes glowing. "Home! It looks the same!" She turned on tiptoe to grasp his shoulder and her lips brushed his with an electric tingle. The hurried kiss lasting just a second.

He stood in shock as she gave him a giddy smile, not even realizing what she'd done, and ran down the path. He tried to call for her to wait, but her kiss stunned him.

The door to the cabin opened, and Claire stopped with a jerk as a woman in a brown dress stepped out. Tall and slim with a lined face tanned by sun, her white-blond hair hung in a single, thick braid.

The woman's eyes traveled over Claire. "Granddaughter. Where's your moth—" But then the eyes caught on him and filled with fury. Her chin lifted, hands going to her side just as Claire did before singing.

Then everything around Ramiro went dark.

CHAPTER 18

Ramiro existed in a whirl of blackness. It buffeted him, swallowing him whole. Howling like a hurricane without a breath of breeze. Unlike a sandstorm, there was no variation of light and color or any break from the suffocating darkness. Instead of the danger filling his eyes and mouth with sand and triggering his determination to live, it deadened the senses, reduced thought, turning him into a shell. He couldn't think, couldn't react—could only feel.

Every dark emotion he'd ever harbored bore in on him. Grief. Shame. Fear.

He wasn't worthy. Shouldn't tarnish the air by drawing breath. Everything he did produced failure.

Deserter.

All he loved found him repulsive. The core essence inside his body that made up *him* shrank into a ball of agony, rebelling against a force that sought to blot him from existence. Yet the force wasn't foreign or an intruder. It could only be self—speaking truth. It showed his self-importance, his reasons for living were nothing but a lie, an illusion he built up of himself. The light that was *him* dimmed, unable to fight.

He couldn't fight off himself.

Dimly, he heard screaming. As self-loathing swallowed him whole, he latched on to the sound where there was nothing—and held on. Gradually it resolved into words. Someone screamed his name over and over, along with "stop." The darkness weakened.

"Ramiro! Grandmother, stop!" The desperation in Claire's voice tugged at him. "Stop!" The need of others meant more than self. The darkness faded.

A force had ahold of his arm, pulling.

He blinked and daylight returned. He smelled the moisture in the air. Claire had seized onto his upraised arm with both her hands, dragging it down with all her weight. His hand gripped his dagger, pointed only inches from his eye.

He jumped and shouted, dropping the knife. With his resistance against her gone, Claire hit the ground, overbalanced by the lack of force. She lay gasping.

Saints.

He'd been trying to drive his knife through his eye socket and into his brain. Tremors ran up his body. Amazement struck him dumb. His brain lurched into action again, lifting his eyes from Claire to the woman on the porch.

She had done this.

The woman could have been Claire in looks, if Claire had aged forty years and had spent that time chewing rocks. She was Claire shaped to a hardness, with every bit of fun or kindness removed. His hand shot to his sword belt. Again Claire seized him. "Stop. Both of you stop. This is what killed my mother!"

The woman on the porch bowed her shoulders. "Rosemund is dead?"

Ramiro let Claire draw his hand from his sword. She clutched it as if doing so could keep him from violence. "Grandmother, I need Ramiro's help. And so do you, though you may not know it. We came here for you."

The reminder of their mission drew the last of the anger from him, but he didn't release his distrust. The power this witch had used against him made Claire's seem like a gnat in comparison. Even her mother's magic had been lighter the one time used against him. He'd been able to see through it eventually. Without Claire's desperation to awaken him, he would have never recovered from this woman.

"I thought the magic could only work *with* what is in a man's head," he said gruffly.

The older woman's sharp eyes pinned him down, lingering on their joined hands. "Do you think we all don't wish for death in some way? Then you are a child. Tell me of my daughter."

Ramiro freed himself from Claire, fumbling in the grass for his knife. "The apple doesn't fall far from the tree," he shot out. "She greeted us with the same tricks, and paid for them."

Claire's grandmother drew herself up again, and Claire rushed between them arms upraised. "Please stop," she pleaded. "There's no need for that attitude. We are all friends here."

Ramiro gave her a disbelieving glare. He'd expected this reception, but not that Claire would lump him in with *her*. "She tried to kill me, not the other way around." He cleaned his knife on his pant leg, did it again just to be sure, before ramming it home in his belt.

"I'm not blaming anyone," Claire said. "Maybe you should take care of Jorga and Sancha while we go inside and talk."

"I don't need taking care of from any man," the woman from the porch said.

Ramiro frowned and then it came to him. "You're Jorga." Dark laughter welled up. It suited his mood. He turned to Claire. "I stand by what I said earlier: You're insulting a good horse."

Claire scowled at him. "Not helping." She swept toward the house, leaving him to fetch the horses. Suddenly, the air outside felt much preferable. He had no desire to go inside that house.

He hadn't given Sancha a good grooming in a while. He needed that peaceful time as his thoughts spun and his nerves felt shaken. He kept flashing to the knife inches from his eye. Perhaps a touch of Jorga's magic lingered, because he couldn't seem to shake the dark thoughts. Did he really want the witches among his people? With the swiftness of their reactions? What sort of damage could she do there? Inviting in the Northern army might be a better choice. He'd done nothing but breathe and she'd tried to end him. What would she do with a city full of people calling her witch? His second thoughts spun faster.

He stroked Sancha's forelock, letting Jorga nuzzle his pocket for a treat, and cursed ever heeding a vision of his brother to steer him on the right path.

Claire followed her grandmother into the house. The temperature cooled when she crossed the threshold, helped by the wide overhang of the porch keeping the sun from the small windows. A fine mesh covered them to add further shade and keep out insects. The back of the two-room building had been built right into the hillside, rendering it further insulated.

Inside contained mostly crude, homemade furniture: stools, a makeshift box-like structure as an extra cutting surface in the kitchen area. The only better-made article of fixtures was the table and one square-backed, spindle chair that her mother had brought from the house of Claire's father. The sole thing in the structure that he must have touched. The wide wooden arms and bottom had gentle slopes worn inward from the depressions of much use. Her grandmother went straight to it, but Claire lingered to take in the sight of home.

An unfamiliar shawl hung on the peg her mother used for that purpose, the cornmeal crock sat slightly out of place, and the cold room door where their food was stored hung open—an occurrence never allowed—but all else looked the same. There was the pillow her mother gave her on her tenth naming day. The wicker baskets where they stored their spare clothing. Under the porch window, her mother's bed where they had lain safe and cozy when storms raged, was neatly made. Her own bed and small private space was above in the tiny loft. She wanted to crawl into it now.

Her lip quivered, and she bit down on it hard. She might shed a tear in front of Ramiro, but to do so in front of this stern stranger was unthinkable. She used closing the cold room door to give her time, before taking a stool, and settling her hands in her lap.

"Tell me what happened to your mother." The command was sharp and clear; no hint of emotion softened the woman's cold face. Claire's first instinct was to run and hug this woman for her similarity to her mother and their shared loss. But what happened outside and a darker instinct held her back. While her mother usually looked nearly as forbidding, her eyes were softer than this woman's. Even when angry, the love showed in her mother. In Jorga, there was nothing but ice.

Somehow Claire got out the story without her voice cracking, focusing on the way her jagged thumbnail—which she hadn't had time to smooth—

snagged on the fabric of her trousers. She told how the city men had encountered them. How her mother had struck first, much as her grandmother had done moments ago. The tragic consequences of her mother killing the men, but being given her death blow in return. The tale grew easier as Claire related being taken prisoner, her escape, and encountering Ramiro saving the village. Her change of heart toward him. Before she could describe the foreign army or the Song she had used against them, she was interrupted.

"Tricks and lies," her grandmother snapped, her face unchanged. "They took you in with tricks and lies, and you knew no better than to go along with it. A Woman of the Song needs no other people. Are you that soft, child? What did your mother teach you?"

"She taught me to recognize truth when I saw it! You weren't there!"

Jorga waved a bony arm. "Tsk. You speak as if truth were the same for all. When you reach my age, you'll recognize truth is a sphere of mirrors with many sides. It shows you what you want to see."

Claire stared at her jagged nail in silence, biting back a harsh answer. Her mother had babied her for her entire life, made every decision for her until she died. She could see that. But there was no way she wanted to fall into that again. Right or wrong, she made her own decisions now.

"We came back here with the intention of finding you, Grandmother. We need your help."

"*Jorga*. Your mother swore you'd never call me grandmother. I'll honor her wish on this. Foolish though it might be."

Claire frowned, looking up. Mentioning that her mother had put that name on a goat wouldn't help the situation, she needed to stick to arguments that would. "Aren't you curious? Don't you want to know why I need your help? Why I think you will need our help in return?" The woman hadn't batted an eye to hear of her daughter's death; what did it take to disturb her? And for that matter, why was she here in the first place, after visiting once in seventeen years?

"It doesn't need much intuition to figure it involves that man. So the answer is no."

The stool toppled over as Claire sprang up. She felt sickened, knowing this same sort of shut off life, uncaring of the world around, is what she had placidly accepted for her entire life. "It involves an enemy that kills the weak and helpless. Is that good enough for you? They chop off hands, heads. Kill children. They won't stop with killing the desert people. But you are worse. You make your victims do it themselves." Her hands fisted at her sides. "I wish . . . I wish I could make you see. See what I've seen."

"Then why don't you, girl. Show me." The woman sat straight as a pine. Her back never touching the chair.

"What?"

"Show me. Are you the one deaf? Use the magic and share memory."

Claire could only stare at her dumbfounded. "The magic can do this?"

"You can't be that ignorant. What did your mother teach you? Spill it, girl."

"The Hornet Tune."

A hand twitched in impatience. "And?"

"And that was all."

"All? You're telling me you know the first spell taught to an infant and nothing more?" Lips pursed. "This must be remedied. None of my flesh and blood can remain this ignorant. You will train with me. There is to be no argument."

"That is what I want. But my friend. Will he be safe from you? More, will you actually help us?"

Again the lips pursed. "I give no help to men. But . . . I will make no hindrance either. If he is to die, then it will be upon him, not me. Don't accuse me when he has an accident. That is the only promise I will give. Take it or leave it."

Slowly, Claire righted the stool and sat. "I don't want it."

For the first time, the frozen façade broke, swiftly there and just as swiftly gone. A twitch of surprise, hidden in the blink of an eye.

"I don't want any part of someone who won't listen to me," Claire said. Her grandmother was stubborn, but she was cut from the same cloth. "I'm not sure I want to learn and I know I don't want to learn from someone so closed-minded. Nor someone who would hurt those I call friend. I'll find another Woman of the Song to help us—on my terms."

"You'll not go begging to the others. Not while I'm alive." Jorga stood and moved to her shawl, snapping it off the peg and around her shoulders. "I'll . . . I'll not interfere with him. You have my word. Your training starts this moment. Obviously, there's nothing to build upon. We'll need every instant. Tomorrow, we head for my house."

Claire sensed the control she'd won slipping. Her grandmother was a force that once it got rolling, bowled over anything in her path. "There isn't time for that. The need for help is urgent. Will you listen?"

"There is always time. What I must have for your training is there. I'll not have you staying ignorant."

"You're evading my question," Claire said. "Will you listen to me?"

"When I feel you have the basics—enough to survive—you can speak. Convince me then. Prove this army is a threat to us."

Claire frowned. "I never said anything about an army." More thoughts bothered her. "And how did you know to come here? Why were you waiting? How did you—"

"Are you one of us or of them? No secrets will you learn from me until I know. Now, show me how you stand properly to Sing."

At the command in her grandmother's voice,

Claire found herself climbing to her feet, even as she wondered what the woman meant by "them or us." She very much feared she'd fallen into quicksand and gotten in over her head.

But which do I fear more—the magic or my grandmother?

CHAPTER 19

Teresa checked the burning sun as it stood a palm-length above the horizon. The noose around her neck tugged, and she stumbled forward another few steps behind the wagon house across the loose sand, trying to do her best to avoid being tripped or tripping another prisoner. She panted at keeping up this pace, but she feared stopping for the evening even more.

Two nights ago, a few of the Northerners had picked out the younger and prettier of the female prisoners and taken them into the darkness beyond the wagon. Teresa had been ignored, but that hadn't blocked her ears against the screaming. It left her sickened, guilty, and enraged. Yet those emotions paled in comparison to feeling fearful and helpless. Only some of those girls came back, more dead than alive, and most had been murdered the next morning when they'd been unable to walk. Teresa had helped carry one of the two survivors.

The next night, the Northerners had picked out an elderly man and held him down as they shaved his beard off with a dull knife, taking large swaths of flesh with the hair, laughing and joking and leaving him bleeding and scarred. They had repeated the ridicule on several other men, all the while eyeing Alvito as one eyed a scrumptious dessert. The memory sent fresh waves of fear through her. Before they could select another victim, however, the officer had intervened in their indecipherable language, and shortly after their captors had settled into blankets, leaving the prisoners shaken and afraid.

Who knew what deviltry they had in store tonight?

The only time they had a reprieve from the violence was when they walked, and that, only if they didn't falter. Anyone unable to keep pace was swiftly dispatched. They didn't dare speak, and barely dared to share glances. The prisoners were given water, but little food, and that as much as exhaustion made it hard for Teresa to lift her knees for another step.

She moved a foot forward and promptly bumped into the wagon, looking up in surprise to find that it had stopped. She turned to the woman—little more than a girl who just put up her hair—next to her to see her on the ground, curled into a ball with arms around her knees and head tucked in. Eva's eye was swelled shut from the abuse two nights ago. She emitted a continuous keening whimper. Teresa hunched next to her and rubbed circles on the girl's back, helpless to provide more than meaningless comfort, although ready to thrust the girl on her feet if anyone so much as looked their way. Shouts from up front caused Teresa to stand.

By Santiago, it's too early to camp.

Hope flared and Teresa quickly tamped down on it. The shouts didn't sound like a rescue, more like astonishment. A glance at Alvito showed him bent over with hands on knees, catching his breath. He gave her a small wave then looked away. They'd agreed to interact as little as possible to ensure they gave no leverage to their captors. Logically, she should use the time to rest as well. She cursed as curiosity drove its hooks into her.

It was curiosity that had induced her to say yes to the *Alcalde* in the first place and leave the security of the university. Should she have resisted? Even now, her heart couldn't decide if she'd made the right choice. A part of her wouldn't have missed this adventure for the world. The other part believed the mission would be the death of her.

"Stupid, woman. Keep your head down," she hissed to herself. Captivity was not like drowning in quicksand in one respect: It went on so long that the panic had receded out of necessity. One could only exist on the edge of mindless terror for so long. There were moments of clarity between the gibbering fear.

Teresa felt for her Santa Catalina medallion before she remembered the Northerners had taken it, along with everything else in her pockets. "You're too stubborn for your own good." But perhaps what happened up front could be used to her advantage. *Knowledge was never bad*, the braver part of her whispered.

She edged around fellow prisoners to move past the wagon. An older woman with her hands clamped onto a black silk shawl followed. This prisoner had enough gray in her hair to be a grandmother twice over. None of the five guards paid them any mind. They both peered forward, seeing nothing but Northerners studying the ground.

"What is it?" Teresa whispered to her companion. Talking was a quick way to draw a lash with the whips the guards kept close, but she couldn't help it.

The grandmother shrugged, when nothing happened, turning to make her way back, but Teresa held her spot as the officer spoke at length, pointing to something. He, too, seemed to shrug, then gestured and the men took their spots again on the wagon shafts. The Northerners employed manpower to draw their wagon instead of draft animals. As much as she was glad it wasn't the case, Teresa had tried and failed to find an explanation for why they didn't use the prisoners to pull the box on wheels. No one rode in it, nor did the officer sleep in it. It apparently contained their supplies and nothing else.

The wagon began to move, and Teresa hurried back to her spot, careful to retrace her steps so the rope around her neck wouldn't tangle with anyone else's. She got a shoulder under Eva and lifted the girl onto her feet as the nightmare resumed. Teresa tried to fasten onto Eustance's Principles of a Useful Life as she had the first two days, but exhaustion drove the litany out of her head. Eva leaned on her heavily, Teresa's feet throbbed, and her stomach twisted with hunger. Instead, she latched onto a child's rhyme as distraction.

Saints above,
Saints below.
God's hand spiritual,
God's rule made flesh.
Covet not the miracle,
It brings death.

With the tune playing over and over in her head, the rope around her neck pulled, dragging her onward. To what, she didn't know. Imagination took her to frightening places, giving anticipation almost worse horrors than reality. It was only her exhaustion that kept her from truly succumbing to the horrors in her mind, and that was the only blessing of her horrid existence.

Her ankle gave, twisting, and she stumbled. She'd stepped in a place of wet sand, likely where a Northern had done his business. That's what she got for not paying attention. Then she noticed another and another, some large and some small. All brownish discolorations in the sand. The prisoners around her stirred, noticing them, too. More and more of them appeared. One splashed across a rock, revealed by the sunshine, and Teresa gasped. Not urine.

Blood.

Puddles of blood lay all around them. She caught sight of a patch of rabbit fur, and scanned the sky searching for the hawk. It was empty, but it wasn't long before they passed a hawk's distinctive feather. The wagon wheel turned and in its track lay something roundish. Instead of a pincushion cactus, she retreated from a skull. The wagon wheel had run over the feathered head of a bird of prey.

Over there lay a haunch of some black-furred animal, and her sinuses were assaulted with the putrid smell of skunk. The prisoners around her touched mind, heart, liver, and spleen as Teresa felt cold eyes at the back of her head. She turned to find nothing there, yet shivers of dread rippled up and down her spine.

More animal carcasses crossed their track. The puddles of blood became tiny rivers—the width of a teardrop—that worked their way through the hillocks of sand. The jabbering terror returned, and her hands knotted on Eva's clothing. What had done this?

As quickly as the scene of death came, it ended, providing no answers. The eyes at her back vanished, taking the sense of doom. Her heart slowed to a more regular beat.

Maybe there are worse things than stopping for the night.

Teresa sat huddled among the other prisoners as the Northerners ate. It wasn't much protection since they now numbered fewer than thirteen. The twenty or so Northerners didn't bother with a detailed camp, just blanket rolls laid out in a circle around the wagon and two fires. The leaping light cast sinister shadows more than cheer.

The prisoners had each received a dipperful of water and naught else. The smell of stew cooking in metal pots over the fires caused Teresa's mouth to water and her stomach to complain, making her head swim with hunger. If she didn't eat soon, she'd be one of those who couldn't carry on in the morning. Her legs trembled with weakness more than fear.

Once again, she thrust such thoughts aside and tried to focus on why the Northerners wanted them. They weren't given any tasks as a slave might be forced to do. The fact that they weren't put to pulling the wagon or carrying anything still confused her. If they were wanted for more deviant desires, why keep the older or more unattractive prisoners? She had thought perhaps they intended some sort of ransom, but the few in silks, like the grandmotherly woman, were treated no differently than those in plain woolens. It made no sense.

Another oddity—she had noticed, they almost never killed a prisoner after dark, only during the daytime. She glanced at the night sky but felt no relief. Death wasn't the only terror.

A heel of bread pelted the prisoner to her right, tossed with a laugh. A mad scramble ensued, and Teresa found herself diving for the food like everyone around her, driven by desperation. Another heel tossed on the other side sent the fight in that direction. The Northerners took obvious enjoyment from the scramble. A man with cuts across his face from having his beard removed kicked her in his haste to keep the morsel he'd secured for himself.

"No," the black-shawled grandmother whispered. "We are people of Colina Hermosa, not animals. We will share."

"Aye," Alvito agreed.

For a moment, Teresa thought reason would prevail, then the next crust of bread landed in the center of them and a fierce free-for-all with pushing and shoving broke out. The small bit of food was torn into shreds. She set her jaw and refused to participate.

She had underestimated the Northerners' lack of humanity. They kept the prisoners not for profit, but for fun. The creatures enjoyed seeing other humans suffer and debase themselves. They were nothing more than entertainment. Of all she had witnessed, this divisiveness sickened her the most.

"Look at yourselves," Teresa hissed. "You should be ashamed. Are we not one people? Control yourselves." Some had the grace to look ashamed.

Alvito flexed his arms. "We share or I throttle the next."

"So you can eat it all," Eva whimpered.

Teresa didn't even mention she'd carried the young woman the last day. "The lady with the shawl will hold the food and you divide it equally," Teresa said instead, choosing those two at random simply because they seemed more reasonable. "We'll all watch to make sure it's fair."

The next crusts were seized and reluctantly passed over. With no more mad scramble, the Northerners soon lost interest and ceased tossing tidbits. Eva sorted out thirteen pieces and they all got one mouthful. Teresa chewed as slowly as she could, but it was gone all too soon.

An hour later, the officer instructed the emptied stewpots be set in front of them. They arranged the pots in the center of their huddle and took turns at the blackened remains in the bottom of the pots. With no utensils, they scooped out the cooling stew with bare fingers. Not enough for a meal, it still left a warm comfort in her complaining stomach and a gleam of pride that they'd refused to act as animals.

She managed to scoot next to Alvito. "I don't believe they want any information from us. They've asked no questions." Not that they could with no one speaking the same language. But there had been no attempt at intimidation. "They don't seem to care about us at all, other than to take us along with them. I don't think it matters if we hide our connection or not."

Alvito raised a brow. Despite the lack of food, his body continued to heal. He had not the same pale cast as before but had taken back his normal honeyed tan. "It wouldn't matter anyway. They'll come for me tonight. I see the anticipation in their looks."

Teresa had seen it, too, but refused to say as much. "A beard is just a symbol. It is not worth dying over. It's what's inside that counts."

"I know it's not nearly the same comparison, but would you tell the girls taken beyond the wagon not to fight? To lie there and take it? It may not be the same violation, but maybe my resistance can help them—because I can barely live with myself now."

Teresa fought back tears at his words. She had known her entreaty was wasted breath.

"I couldn't help when they took the women. I did nothing when they shaved the men."

"There are too many of them," Teresa protested.

"Salvador wouldn't have cared. He'd have tried and died. So would Ramiro," he whispered, eyes turned toward the firelight. "I did nothing to protect the citizens of Colina Hermosa.

"I went into the military with barely a thought," he continued. "My cousin Salvador did it, and it seemed easier than other types of work. The uniform set off my looks, helped me entice women. Alcohol flowed freely for soldiers. It was only supposed to be the occasional border dispute." She had never seen his face so grave. "But honor is more than just a beard. It is what treatment we will accept and what we will fight. I never took much seriously before. Eat, drink, and be merry was my motto. I must set the example for every soldier they ever capture. I keep my head down no more."

"Hi-ya, Cat." Her voice wobbled. "Take a few of them with you."

They came for Alvito minutes later—six of them. She watched him go quietly as they dragged him away and forced him down by the fire, refused to watch as they held him while a seventh displayed a straight razor. Eva huddled against her, sobbing softly, while the silk-shawled grandmother clenched Teresa's arm in a viselike grip. The taunts and laughter, though in another language, were indisputably clear. No amount of clamping her hands over her ears could shut them out.

Then the tenor of the voices changed, becoming alarmed. Teresa scrunched her eyes tightly closed, unwilling to witness the end, but the grandmother took this for invitation to comment. "Your friend knocked one off. His arm is loose. He has the razor. A stab to the neck. One is down. By the saints, they're on him again. Oh! They have him down."

"Stop!" an unfamiliar voice rang out. "Tell them to stop and drop their weapons."

Teresa started up. A burly man with black skin and wearing the brown robes of a wandering friar had appeared from nowhere and stood at the edge of the firelight. One arm was awkwardly placed around the neck of a tall woman. Teresa scooted apart of the huddle to see his arm ended in a swath of bandages and no hand. The woman's hair had been hacked off raggedly, and though she wore clothing from the city, her coloring proclaimed her Northern. The way she stood, so straight and undaunted while completely controlled, said she was used to her position being otherwise. In the friar's single hand, he held a slim white rod pointed at her throat.

Where did they come from? Teresa thought, knowing instantly she'd never seen them before.

"Tell them to stop and drop their weapons," the friar said again. This time he followed the words with a shake and a tightening of his arm around the woman's neck.

She spoke in their language, her words a sharp command. The Northern soldiers looked uncertain. She spoke again, a quick roll of syllables that blurred together to Teresa's ears. Their officer spoke and a short interchange between him and the woman led to weapons being dropped. The men on Alvito got up. Feet shifted and the Northerners withdrew slowly toward their wagon, never turning their backs.

"Tell them to keep going or I kill their priestess," the friar said. Then his attention fell upon the prisoners. "Remove the ropes! Run! Get away before they change their minds. I can only hold them off so long."

Some of the people around her began to comply. Teresa pushed the noose from her neck, then did the same for Eva. "Go. Go," she urged.

Then everything fell apart.

The tall Northern woman the friar had called a priestess turned as swift as a snake. She shouted out in her language. The Northerners' indecision turned to anger. They rushed forward, diving for the dropped weapons. The friar released the woman and struck her a blow across her temple that felled her.

As a Northern soldier rushed past her, Teresa reached out and seized him around the ankles, bringing him down. She felt other prisoners doing the same. Eva bashed the head of the man she'd tackled with a rock. Teresa saw Alvito stab one soldier with the straight razor, then launch a knife he'd scrounged from the ground into the officer's chest.

The friar retreated from the first soldier to approach him, holding the white rod back as if to shield it. The soldier reached for the friar's arm; at the same time, the friar twisted. Instead of grabbing the friar, the soldier's hand encircled the top of the strange weapon. To Teresa's astonishment, the man went rigid in a spasm, then dropped boneless.

Alvito brought down another with a fresh knife toss. Her fellow prisoners struck out with anything they could find. Teresa threw sand in the eyes of the nearest Northerner, bringing him to a painful halt. The man who had stolen the first bread crust kicked that soldier in the knee, then in the head and belly when he fell.

The few Northerners still able ran from the camp. Teresa lay upon her back, staring up at the night sky and panting as the stars twinkled distantly. She'd helped to kill. Rather than remorse, a fierce gladness pounded in her heart.

When she sat up, she saw the friar pulling the tall Northern woman to her feet again. The other prisoners exchanged glances as if they couldn't believe their good fortune. "Hurry," the friar said. "You'll need to be gone before they regroup."

Knowing good advice when she heard it, Teresa hastened to Alvito. The Northerners hadn't managed to cut his beard. The perfection of his features was untouched. A half dozen dead Northerners surrounded him. Then she noticed it: He sat with his hands around his thigh. Bright blood spurted in a stream, staining his pants and the ground. An artery had been hit. All her joy evaporated as their eyes met. "Bring them home for me," he said through gritted teeth.

"Aye, Cat. That I will, thanks to you."

He nodded to her once more, then said, "Go."

She turned, not so much at his command, but because she didn't want him to see her tears.

CHAPTER 20

They buried the *pelotón* soldier at noon the next day. Telo spoke the words over the man called Alvito and the other unknown prisoner who'd perished in the short uprising. As a wandering friar, he officiated many funerals for people he'd never met. Usually improvisation and inventiveness got him through the difficulties of such ceremonies. After the events of the night before, he didn't feel confident enough to carry that off and stuck with the memorized words from San Lucius's book of sermons—though the dead men deserved better.

As their hero, the man Alvito had slain seven of the enemy single-handed, apparently securing their knives when Telo had ordered them dropped. The other prisoners had helped, but it was Alvito's removal of the officer to which they owed their lives. They could only assume his loss kept the Northerners from regrouping and returning to find them as they floundered around in the darkness.

What haunted Telo and stripped his confidence was the death he had caused—accidental though it was. The Northerner had grabbed the Diviner even as Telo had attempted to avoid using it.

If we confess our sins, He is faithful and just to forgive.

Telo didn't think that applied to the sin of killing.

As the words of the sermon flowed from his tongue, he glanced down at the rocky burial mounds at his feet. A soldier's job was to protect and that could mean taking lives. The Church instructed that the Lord understood and overlooked that sin from soldiers. Without question, they would say the buried soldier went to his just reward and wouldn't face judgment in the afterlife. Part of Telo's mind mocked that—otherwise how else would they find men to be soldiers?—but his trust in the Church held.

He refocused on the job at hand. "May almighty God bless you, He and all the saints." Telo touched heart, mind, liver, and spleen as he concluded the ceremony—ever mindful of the chain linking him to Santabe and that she remained enough distance away, so she couldn't kill him as easily.

His thoughts returned to his own soul. The Church would say the Lord forgave him this one death for the lives of many. Once he'd made the decision to intervene to save the prisoners last night, to the Church's eyes that made him a soldier of the Lord and gave him the same exemption. His soul felt tarnished just the same.

"Would you like to say a few words?" he asked the roundish peasant woman in the poncho. She seemed to know the fallen best. With her shorn hair and trousers, it had taken two looks to make sure she was a woman.

She nodded, then to his surprise launched into a child's rhyme:

> *Saints above,*
> *Saints below.*
> *God's hand spiritual,*
> *God's rule made flesh.*
> *Covet not the miracle,*
> *It brings death.*

"Be at peace, Cat. I won't forget what you did for us."

Telo remained at the grave as the other prisoners shuffled off to gather up the few possessions they'd poached hastily from the Northern wagon before their flight. They couldn't take too much, burdened as they were with the bodies. After hearing all his news, they intended to head east, toward what remained of Colina Hermosa and then on to Suseph and Crueses. Despite their liberation, they were a silent group; after the suffering of captivity, the news of the burning of their home had struck particularly hard. Even the food they'd taken from the wagon of the Northerners had not loosened their tongues. Telo could respect that sort of grief.

A tug came from the chain securing Santabe as the woman fidgeted, reminding him that he should get moving also. What he had seen only steeled his resolve to find and deal with Ordoño. Instead, he moved closer to the roundish woman in the poncho—*Teresa*, his mind supplied the name randomly from the confusion of last night as it often did with names—pulling Santabe with him. Calling Teresa plain was to be generous. With her mannish clothing and hair, Telo was not surprised the other prisoners left a space around her.

"That was an interesting choice of words, my child. Why that poem, if I may ask?"

Teresa looked up, then rubbed at her glistening eyes. "It seemed fitting. He survived a wound that should have killed him a sevenday ago—miraculously one might say—only to die today. Like the Hypothesis of Morales."

Telo's interest grew. Few people had heard of that theory. It wasn't something the Church wanted bandied about. It was only because Father Vellito in his first monastery took interest in a bandit-turned-wandering-friar's questioning mind that Telo had been taught about it. Most considered miracles as something to covet, a sign of divine favor. Morales postulated that as most who suffered miracles perished as martyrs; it was a punishment sent by the Lord, not a kindness. It was from Morales's hypothesis that the childish rhyme had grown nearly two thousand years ago, though few enough knew of the correlation. Telo had always wondered if the Church played a part in covering it up.

"I subscribe to the Suseph Decree, my child," Telo said to see if she'd heard of it. The Church in Suseph had created an alternative theory that was now widely held.

"Because it is the stance taken by the Church," Teresa said. "To forsake it is heresy. I've met few priests who don't toe the line."

"Not for that reason, no." Telo shook his head. "I subscribe to it because it speaks of hope. I prefer to believe our Lord has put off a chosen saint's death, given them more time to prove their true worth. To see what they will do with it. We are all sinners in our Lord's eyes, yet still he gives us hope in return for faith. It's an opportunity, a second chance, you might say, to work His will, not a death sentence." Even as he said those words, though, to cling to them like the lifeline he hoped they were, they slipped through his fingers, like the summer rains that would not come.

"I had not considered the Suseph Decree in that light," Teresa was saying. "Interesting. I thought of it as just more dogma to give the Church a positive spin."

"Only partially. It depends on your point of view. The Church is neither black nor white, as you'll find of most people. You are university trained, my child, to know these things?"

"An expert on anthropology and cultures. In Colina Hermosa."

Telo smiled. "It is one of the best."

Teresa smiled in return. "Then you hail from Aveston, because only an Aveston man would say there are others as good."

"Raised in the streets of the slums there," Telo acknowledged. "Though I never attended that great facility."

"Church trained, then?" she asked.

"And self-trained. I was a little too independent. My vows are to Our Lord, not to the Church—though it has my full support."

"Interesting, Father. A man who only looks for the gray in people, instead of seeing good or bad. Then tell me why such a man of God has a woman chained to him?"

Telo admired how she looked him in the eye as she asked, since most would have had second thoughts of speaking. In fact, none of the other prisoners had asked. Most avoided looking at Santabe or himself, for that matter. He didn't blame them, seeing how he wasn't sure exactly what the answer was. He considered what to say to this strange woman, knowing the need for confession ran in every man, even those priests who offered solace. He wished some of the burden off his own chest by sharing it, and he believed her more than intelligent enough to have an open mind and not to judge. This Teresa was unique.

And yet, for all that, he knew that to tell her everything wasn't an option.

He sighed. "It is a long story, involving this"—he raised his nub—"but I believe God gave me a second chance after I failed Him. I let something go when I was with the Northerners that I could have finished." Telo winced for the covering euphemism, but it was the closest he felt able to approach the truth. He'd let the wildcat run and the destruction continued. "This woman is more devil than flesh and blood. I've witnessed her handiwork. To chain her is only fitting, but she can help me back into their camp.

"I've told you the Northerners wanted you and the others for a sacrifice to their god, Dal; she is one of those who gives those orders and sees them carried out. She is my method back to finish my quest—if you will allow such egotism from a humble man. I don't consider the Lord has laid his hand on me so much as he put opportunities in my path."

She shifted her balance to her back foot as if deciding. "I, too, had a mission. From what you say, it succeeded. I was one of those sent with Ramiro by the *Alcalde to find a witch*, and you say he and a witch drove off the army for a time. My job would seem to be over, but I feel discontented with that. The witch succeeded more despite me than because of me. The university—my home—is gone."

"You feel you have not done your part," Telo supplied. He could see where the rescue and the death of her friend would lead her to feel this way. She suffered survivor's guilt. A grimace tightened his face as he considered whether that applied equally well to him. Again, the doubt rose whether what he believed was nothing more than a justification of his guilt.

Now she did look away. "It must seem foolish. Here I am, a woman highly trained in understanding people and other cultures. Yet, you've learned more about them than I."

He hesitated to encourage her. He could hear the question in her words, and his stomach churned at the thought of what she was asking. Finally, though, he voiced it. "You would come with me into the lion's den, my child. I do not think there will be a return trip."

"By your own words, I was saved from death. Perhaps my path is not finished."

"Or perhaps it was no more than good fortune," Telo said. "The Lord works beyond our understanding." He regarded Santabe, sitting meekly—or as meekly as she ever did, a constant sneer never leaving her face. Regardless, she was obviously listening with all her might. The stump of his arm still throbbed from his recent scuffle with her. Had the Lord sent him the test of the captives to see if he deserved help? He could use the help, especially from one who seemed so capable and intelligent. It was true that a job halved was a job sooner done, and better for the company. And with his disability, he might need the assistance.

Alcalde Julian would fault him for thinking in platitudes again—for looking for signs. What he should be looking for were answers to his questions.

Did he have a right to draw a woman into this?

Just as important, did he have a right to keep her out?

"The Lord gave free will to all. If you come, stay

far from her reach, my child. She kills as quickly as drawing breath. And have you skill with *Acorraloar*?"

"*Acorraloar*? The game? Strange that you would ask, but I was university champion once—that was most definitely fortune, as it never happened again." She shrugged. "Let me tell my companions to go on without me. I promised Alvito to see them home, but he couldn't know of this more crucial opportunity." She walked off to join a gray-haired woman in a black silk shawl, waiting at the head of the group of fellow prisoners.

"Fortune or God's will?" Telo asked. "You would call her a test," he told Santabe, though speaking more to himself. He knew from the few conversations he'd had with her that Santabe believed this world nothing but a test of will and audacity. From what he'd seen of her and the Northerners, he'd learned that those who survived were the only ones worthy of their sun god, Dal. Or perhaps one didn't need to survive in their culture, only show the most cruelty while they lived. Who knew whether they believed in an afterlife or what use Dal had for them there or here?

Santabe shifted in her chains, watching for any weakness on his part as she always did. What she didn't understand was that weakness was not a flaw. Those who knew when to accept help were the strongest of all.

Julian hunched over the desk, putting down the last words and checking for errors. He picked up a piece of blotting paper and dabbed carefully. Ten other copies already crowded the desk as he set down the pen, satisfied.

Juan and Ramón had installed him in a luxurious suite and not a dungeon. They might have removed anything resembling a weapon, including his razor, and assigned guards outside his door to keep him inside, nor would they let anyone speak with him, but they feared to antagonize him too far. After all, they needed him to take down the army around Aveston and thin the Northerners for them.

That said, their "courtesy" only went so far—they had confiscated all the documents he had with him to peruse themselves. Included in that number was the copy of the Northerners' terms of surrender. Luckily, he knew whole passages of it by heart and the rest well enough, and the desk contained plenty of writing supplies. He'd made fair enough replicas of the important points of the Northern terms.

Let the people of Crueses learn the Northerners demanded all weapons be confiscated, churches be closed, and the military disbanded in each conquered city, along with Northern soldiers to be billeted inside. Or that trade could be inspected at any time. When they found out the Northerners expected the blood of one in ten men and women, and one in thirty children, there would be riots. No, Juan and Ramón thought to leave those little nuggets out until the terms were accepted and the Northerners in the gates. There was no way for Julian to judge how far communication between Crueses and the Northerners had progressed, but he could take a hand in making sure the common people knew the facts.

Maybe Juan and Ramón were ignorant of parts of the terms. Well, his fellow *alcaldes* knew *all* the details now with the papers they'd taken from Julian. He pictured them shaking in their colorful tights and having to have their valets wipe their bottoms. Then he sighed and put aside such petty thoughts. He was not some youth to wallow in dreams of revenge. They got him nowhere. If he didn't want to be named traitor, then he had a coup to arrange, and none of it would begin if he couldn't ferret these papers out.

He blew on the ink of the last copy, touching it to make sure it didn't smudge. "Arias."

After Beatriz's concern about Ramiro's conflicted feelings but lack of information on his actual choice, it was no great surprise to find a soldier other than Ramiro here. In some ways, it was a relief. His son might be safer elsewhere. He teetered between worry that Ramiro was with Claire and the hope it was a good thing—if the witch would protect his last child. He put that aside as something he could do nothing about in his present situation. A man must know his own limitations.

Arias stepped up beside him. Julian had asked to have all his entourage with him; they'd allowed him one. The others still waited outside the palace. Julian hoped they housed the men well. It might be a long wait.

A plan of switching clothing with Arias and leaving the palace as a soldier had occurred to Julian—occurred and been discarded. Though he and Arias were of an age and size, both gray bearded, still their features looked nothing alike. And Julian was just too well known in this *ciudad-estado*. Besides the fact that leaving would accomplish nothing but saving his own skin. He would find another way.

Julian began folding the sheets up small. "Put these under your clothing and guard them well. Once outside, you are to take some to the largest squares and pin them up for the civilians. Take the rest to the popular taverns and make sure they are seen." He quickly rattled off a few names from previous visits to Crueses. That should do well enough to start. "Do it quietly, you understand—don't be flashy—and use the guise of procuring my supplies. You have coin for that?" In his few interactions with Arias, he judged the man had little imagination but plenty of capability for following through with orders—just what he needed.

"Hi-ya," Arias said with a short bow, rattling his pocket. "I have coppers. I understand. But how—"

"Leave that to me."

As Arias tucked the last broadsides from sight, Julian cleaned off the desk and moved the table with the *Acorraloar* board to the seating area. His left side still couldn't pull as strongly, but a few days ago it wouldn't have gripped at all.

He went to the door and found it unlocked. Three soldiers of Crueses in orange and white paid him full attention as he stepped into the hall. "Very sorry, *Alcalde*, you are not allowed exit from your rooms."

Julian put on a smile. "So I understand. I don't need exit, but I do need help. *Acorraloar* is much more interesting with three people and some betting. Any volunteers—if it wouldn't be against your duty?" Their duty being to watch him, he supposed, it hardly mattered whether that be inside the room or outside. Throw in a chance of profit, and at least one would be tempted.

"I would be honored to join you, *Alcalde*." The lieutenant bowed and followed him into the room. Julian didn't miss the disappointment on the enlisted men's faces. They were not paid as well as they would like obviously. Julian stored that fact.

Once inside, he gestured and said briskly, "In today's climate, the professional soldiers should pick sides first. After you, gentlemen." The lieutenant chose white and the opportunity to move first, while Arias took black. Julian settled happily behind brown, taking third.

He then did what he did best: put constituents at ease. As the moves began, he launched into small talk about the surprising lack of rain, the fish and light vegetable diet Beatriz had installed him on, demonstrating the lack of mobility of his hand, and anything that came into his head, using the soldier's language he'd heard from his sons so often. Soon the lieutenant was laughing at his poor table fare, sympathizing with a henpecking wife, agreeing on the lack of rain and relating his memory of the drought ten years ago when the rains failed altogether. Julian was careful to keep his *Acorraloar* game masterful, but not domineering.

In just a few more moves, the first question came and Julian hid a smile of triumph behind a sad face. "Hi-ya, it's true. Colina Hermosa did burn to the ground. But we routed them in return, though gravely outnumbered."

To his approval, Arias chimed in with exact troop numbers and deployments for both sides, giving details, and ending with, "And the *pelotónes* escorted the civilians, leaving the nonmilitary men to fight. Men such as our *Alcalde*."

The lieutenant leaned forward on his seat, hardly noticing as he placed his flat chip of white stone. "And is it true you only survived because of the help of a witch?"

"Aye," Julian said. "She saved us and our civilians. We'd have been massacred without her. She should be coming this way with my people." True enough. Claire *should* be with his people . . . if the *concejales* hadn't forced the issue and frightened her off.

"I wish I could have been there," the lieutenant said. "We've had no fighting here."

"We've had all too much. Our men have been well-tempered. And they might be tested again—the Northerners have completely regrouped and are strong again.

"Once the *pelotónes* arrive we leave the civilians here and go to fight with Aveston," Julian continued. He didn't miss the tightening of the lieutenant's face.

"We could use you there. But I dare say, you're happier here in reserve, playing guard to civilians and old men. The menfolk of Colina Hermosa will manage—somehow."

Julian couldn't resist a last dig before changing the subject, keenly aware of the look of a young man anxious to prove himself. "I'm sure *Alcalde* Juan knows what's best for his city and his soldiers. I am altogether too reckless, always bringing our troops to battle instead of thinking about their lives."

The lieutenant sat back in his chair, suddenly quiet, and Julian began talking about a Zapata wine Beatriz forced him to drink nightly and the herbs she insisted were for his health, satisfied with the barbs he'd left. He might not be able to reach the garrison, but he could bring the garrison to him.

Julian waited until the lieutenant won more than he lost, and then ended the game, getting up stiffly from his chair. "It's hard to admit when your wife is right, gentlemen. But Beatriz might be onto something with her Zapata wine and herbs. My joints are sorely aching. Alas—I didn't think to bring any with me. Stubbornness, I suppose." He assumed a forced smile. "We make do with what we have. It was a pleasure. Thank you for entertainment this noon."

Arias muttered sympathetically.

The lieutenant paused by the door. "I don't believe it would be against orders for your man to go out to market to buy what you need. We are to see to your every comfort, just not to let you out or allow you to converse with any others. We can search him well when he returns, if that suits you, sir."

Julian beamed. "Very generous. My wife thanks you and my joints thank you." He handed over a pouch of money and watched Arias amble out the door. He settled himself, feeling no guilt for the damage to Juan or Ramón's reign. His inner landscape held firm. Undermining the rule of another's *ciudad-estado* was never his preferred path. Saints forgive him, nothing was normal anymore. Paths had to change. He'd do what had to be done to win this war, and if that involved taking down collaborating *alcaldes*, then so be it.

If they side with the Northerners—if they would let harm come to the people of Colina Hermosa—than they are not my allies.

When Arias returned hours later with the hard-to-find vintage and packets of herbs, he gave not so much as a nod or a wag of his gray-tinged beard to indicate success, but Julian read it in his calm demeanor as he was searched. What was more exciting were the three lieutenants and a captain who stood in the corridor, all eager to hear details of the planned fight at Aveston. Soon his whispers would bring their highest ranks. The doubts about the leadership would grow among the military and the populace. Revolutions could start with a whisper and Julian had just uttered the first words. *Alcaldes* who crossed him could be double-crossed. For one thing was certain: He'd lure the men he needed for Aveston and the safety for his people, or die trying.

CHAPTER 21

"Who refuses to ride horses?" Ramiro asked. Sancha turned an ear his direction and the hop in the horse's normally smooth gait grew more pronounced. "Of all the bloody commandeering, stubborn . . . goats." Goat described the old woman very well. Ramiro saw now why a goat—and a horse—had been named for Jorga. He felt more sympathy for Claire's mother than he ever had before. No wonder she turned out so badly, being raised by such a shrew.

Jorga demanded they leave immediately for her home without giving the slimmest of reasons. Then she refused to ride despite her all-fire hurry. Further, she refused to teach Claire anything if Ramiro remained in earshot. He'd tried following behind, but his irritation and Jorga's constant watching—as if he were some dirty slug who'd crawled out of her cabbages—drove him to move ahead where he could be out of eye-line as well.

"Stubborn goat!" he repeated, not caring if she overheard, though logic said the women had fallen far behind and some of the thickest underbrush he'd yet encountered in the swamp surrounded him. Oaks and sycamores mixed with shorter bushes like raspberry and honeysuckle vine—vegetation so unknown to him that Claire had to teach him the names. No, they wouldn't overhear. The women walked so slowly. No doubt done purposely by Jorga just to irritate him more. He knew his emotion to be petty—it felt like the time his brother and Alvito had gone to spy over the school wall into the girl's section without inviting him—but he didn't care.

"And Claire's just as bad." He knew that for a lie before the words left his mouth. She'd tried to speak to him alone, but every time, her grandmother popped up like an unwelcome louse. She'd only managed a hurried whisper that Jorga had agreed to teach her and she was working on getting the old woman's support against the Northerners. "Good luck with that," he said now.

Sancha gave a huff as if to agree with him, and he felt a little better.

"It's not your fault," he told the mare. The hop dropped out of her walk, and she picked her way down the narrow animal trail more smoothly. The only direction he had to go upon was Jorga's vaguely pointed "that way." Getting any speech from her was like carrying rocks uphill.

He pulled out a strip of dried mutton and took a snappish bite, chewing noisily because his mother wouldn't like it, irked by the whole female race at the moment. He started to feel this trip was a gigantic waste of time.

"You're getting another name," Ramiro told Claire's horse who followed on a lead. "We have enough Jorgas. How about Fronilde?" Now there was a woman who didn't put herself forward. Salvador's fiancée was all kindness and consideration—Sancha shot him a look—and to be truthful, dull and timid. He much preferred Claire and her spunk.

Salvador would council patience and he'd be right. Ramiro had no reason to feel . . . *jealous*.

By the saints. That's what he felt. *Jealous*. Like a total dunce. Jealous because someone else had more of Claire's time. Always before it was he with other obligations, and Claire waiting for his time—

"Hell and damnation!" In a fit of temper, he threw the leftover bit of jerky into the brush and scowled.

From out of nowhere, a shiver went up his spine and not for his thoughts. For a moment, his name hung on the nonexistent wind. *Ramiro*. A call in Claire's voice, demanding his attention. There and gone in an instant, leaving him doubting his own ears, but full of urgency. A call. It felt like the Sight that ran in his family, but not—somehow different.

With a start, he realized he hadn't heard it with his ears, but somehow in his heart. The Sight he felt over his whole body . . . or so it had always worked before.

He touched mind, heart, liver, and spleen, glancing around uneasily.

Sancha had stopped without a signal from him. She never did that. So much moisture gathered in the air today that it formed on the leaves, sliding down to drip on his head as they sat still.

"Blessed saints. Did you hear it, too?"

Sancha's mane danced as she shook herself, sending water splashing up into his face. The cold drops awakened him.

Witchcraft.

Claire.

What if she were in danger? Hurt?

Sancha backed easily as he turned her on the narrow trail. It proved more difficult to turn Claire's animal. The beast shied every time a branch touched its hide.

He didn't dare put Sancha in a gallop in the confined space, but he urged her to a cantor. Five minutes down the trail, he spotted a broken branch dangling. Just beyond and north of the trail hung another. There was no other sign of a struggle. Nothing to indicate foul play—just two sets of feet going off-trail in the soft ground.

His scowl returned. There could be only one explanation: The women had tried to lose him. They'd purposely let him explore ahead and gone another direction.

Without an animal trail to follow, he had to dismount and lead the horses, pushing aside bushes and saplings to make room for them. His irritation rose with each difficult step, vines and brush grasping at him. Why? It made no sense. Surely, Claire wouldn't change sides so quickly. They had to know they'd leave a trail behind. Doubt strangled his irritation, resulting in a vague hurt.

The wet ground showed their footsteps. The only sounds came from his efforts and the water dripping around him. He took his time, trying to come up with an explanation and finding none. Branches tried to scratch his face, rebuffed in other places by his body armor, sending water flying. Sancha stamped, letting him know she didn't like this one bit. He couldn't agree more.

The thick woods opened up into a small clearing full of dead leaves. A thick tree canopy above had kept it relatively dry. And there they sat on a downed tree. "See," Jorga said. "Incentive makes it easier to work the magic."

"What in the hell just happened?" Ramiro demanded. "Saints! Did you try to lose me?"

Claire left the log and hurried to him, her feet rustling the leaves. "That's not it at all," she said, reaching for his hand.

He pulled back. "It sure feels like it to me."

"Grandmo—Jorga is trying to teach me my first

lesson, to Speak on the Wind. She said I'd progress faster if I was anxious, so we left the trail. It's not really a true Song, but supposed to allow me to communicate over distances. Did you hear my voice calling you back? I'd been trying for hours, and Jorga said it would work if we gave me extra incentive. It could be a very useful skill. Did you hear it?"

"I thought I felt something," he said reluctantly, hating to disappoint her. Common sense begrudged it would be a useful skill. But common sense and pride rarely coexist, and his insides remained bound in angry knots.

Her face brightened. "Then it did work. I swear I only let her convince me because it sounded reasonable. I wasn't trying to lose you. I left the branches for you to find. You do believe me, right?" She peered into his face.

He let her catch his hand. "I suppose I do. But I don't like being the fool." He glared over her shoulder at Jorga. "How does it work? Could you send messages to troops on a battlefield? All the way to Colina Hermosa to speak to my parents?"

Claire bit her lip. "It's not quite that effective. More like it lets you send emotions, and if you're really good, a word or two. It only reaches as far as my magic—so not far. Like I told you before, the wet air does give me a longer reach." Her voice rose hopefully on the last, as if waiting his reaction. "It's not really good for fighting, but it's the first magic I've worked successfully with . . . Jorga. And it was because of you."

A little more of his irritation drained, leaving him not sure what to feel, but she appeared somewhere between proud and nervous. It reminded him of how hard he'd sought Salvador's approval. "That was good work. It was your effort, to your credit, not mine," he said gruffly, all too aware of their third wheel. He lifted his eyes to find Jorga at his side, looking like she'd bitten a rotten olive. She'd done this purposely to put a wedge between them. He wasn't about to let her win. "And you—"

Leaves rustled outside the clearing, and Ramiro jerked that way. The level of their voices should have frozen any small animals within hearing as it had the silenced the birds. Even larger predators would probably be intimidated by a group of humans. And water droplets off the trees couldn't make that amount of noise. So his mind went to the one threat he could think of.

Northerners.

He drew his sword even as his body took action, dropping the reins and running for the trees. A flood of rustling erupted ahead at his approach. Ramiro dived behind a tree and instinctively seized a figure much too small to be a Northern soldier. "Bromisto?"

The boy gave him a wave and a weak grin. "Surprise?"

Ramiro released the boy and stepped back, still holding his unneeded sword. "You followed us," he accused.

Bromisto took it as praise, beaming wider. "Pretty good, eh? You didn't notice me at all."

"Great," Ramiro muttered even as Claire pushed him aside.

"Look. He's back," she said. "Isn't he cute?"

Jorga appeared in the creepy way she had of seeming to spring somewhere without motion or noise, back straight, face expressionless. "No more males. One is too much. He's spying on us. I'll get rid of it." Exactly how she'd *get rid* of the boy was clear in her tone.

"He's a child!" Ramiro roared, moving between them. "You'll do no such thing." Even for ten winters, Bromisto was scrawny and underfed. All his ribs showed in the way of active boys without a shirt to cover them. He didn't reach Claire's shoulder. A wave of protectiveness shot through Ramiro. No witch was worth this—even for Claire he couldn't let a child be harmed. But he was sure she wouldn't want this either.

"I allowed one city man," Jorga said. "No more."

Ramiro swung the tip of his sword under her chin, touching skin. "By the saints you will. Make one move and I'll remove your head."

"Would everyone just stop," Claire said, wringing her hands. She stood in front of Bromisto. "You're both driving me crazy. No one is getting rid of anyone or chopping off any heads. Can we all just stop! Why does it have to be this way? Just don't!" She burst into tears, but when Ramiro reached for her, she swung on him, shoving him away. "Just don't! We've been together one day, and all there's been is hate." She ran off to bury her face in her horse's mane.

Jorga regarded him without a flicker of emotion, never even glancing at Claire. "You've made my granddaughter cry. Can we dispense with this?" She touched the end of his sword.

"Can you dispense with . . . being you?" Ramiro shook his head and removed the blade with a sigh. "Let me handle the boy. You just . . . go."

Inscrutable eyes watched him. "I don't think you want that. I'll train no more with spying eyes around."

"I said I'd handle it," Ramiro said as Jorga glided away without a backward glance. "I hate that woman," he whispered.

Bromisto stood in a crouch as if prepared to run. Ramiro couldn't blame him. And honestly, that's exactly what he wanted the boy to do, anyway. But he needed to make sure Bromisto understood so he wouldn't follow once he recovered his nerve. "It's all right. There won't be any magic." He clasped the boy's shoulder, man to man. "But it isn't safe for you here. I need you to go home, Bromisto."

"But I want to help. That *sirena* is *loca*. You need another man."

"You've got that right," Ramiro muttered.

"Are you building an army of *sirenas* to match the army of pale soldiers?"

"Something like that," Ramiro said doubtfully. He pulled the boy toward the trees. "I have to ask a favor: Could you go home? I know it's not the way a brave man like you should be treated, but you saw how touchy they are. Even with your skill and cunning, she's likely to lose her temper. The way you can help is keeping an eye out at home for what the pale soldiers are up to. Letting me know when I come back. You understand. This is sort of a one-man mission at the moment."

Bromisto nodded and tapped at his chin thoughtfully. "Aye. I can see that. That *sirena* has more touchy feelings than an older sister."

"Exactly. They have so much touchy feelings there's not room for four." Ramiro wondered if there would be room for three much longer. His whole plan looked more and more insane. His head ached. He'd left everything for this . . . Plus, he could feel time ticking away. The Northerners wouldn't wait while Claire trained. Their army could be up to anything. It could already be too late. He put on a confident face, though. He'd rolled the dice, now he had to live with it. "Can you do this for me?"

"Hi-ya." The boy drew himself up an extra inch. "I can watch for more signs of the pale soldiers. I saw one of their trails not fifteen minutes ago."

Ramiro blinked at him, feeling suddenly dizzy. "What are you talking about? Why didn't you tell me that first?"

"You didn't let me." Bromisto pointed. "The trail is off that way. I saw three or four of them since I followed you. Maybe the same men. Maybe different. I just saw the trails they made, crisscrossing, like hunters."

Ramiro put a hand on his sword and looked back

to check on the women. Jorga had Claire sitting on the dead tree as they sipped from water skins taken from his saddle. Claire gave him a limp smile and a nod when she saw him looking. Moisture sparkled in her fair hair, the drops like gems.

"*Mierda.*" News like this, he'd have to tell them. "Show me."

CHAPTER 22

Ramiro knelt over the trail Bromisto had found. Vegetation had been hacked and cut for the width of two feet, leaving a clear path through this woodsy section of ground. Every bush, every sapling, every overhanging branch to a height of seven feet—or a man's arm's length when holding a sword or machete. Everything thinner than three inches had been cut down. The handiwork ran straight and true for yards and yards, with only the occasional large tree for obstruction, before being lost to view.

Ramiro touched a clear boot print in the soft ground. It was larger than his own. How had he missed this? This sort of total destruction must have made plenty of noise. And why go to this trouble of clearing everything? Even more worrisome, they'd practically walked right past it. This trail was only minutes from the one they'd been following. They could have blundered into Northerners unprepared.

"How long ago?" he asked Bromisto, who knelt on his right to keep as much distance from the two women as possible. None of his skills had taught Ramiro how to read signs in this sort of terrain. In the desert he knew everything about tracking. Here, he could only guess.

Bromisto nudged a leaf on a sliced branch. "It's not wilted. Less than five days."

Ramiro grunted. That left a wide margin for when the Northerners had been here and where they might be now—or how many units of them there might be. "I'd say five men. Do you figure the same?"

Bromisto nodded.

"You don't know it was your enemy soldiers," Jorga said stiffly.

Ramiro just stared at the women—no one could be that stubborn to what was right in front of them. Only this . . . witch. He'd wanted to leave her behind when they went hunting Bromisto's trails, but having her out of his sight was a worse idea.

Bromisto laughed. "No hunter would do this. It frightens the animals."

"No man from a *ciudades-estado* would waste the energy," Ramiro agreed. "Or want to leave such a clear sign they've been here. We tiptoe around *witches*." He gave the word deliberate emphasis. "The Northerners don't fear you enough yet. Respect, maybe. And I've seen their work before. They did this same sort of stripping around Colina Hermosa for their camp. Cut down every cacti. Hopefully, whoever is here now is just some soldiers and not one of their priests."

"Why are they here?" she asked. "I assume you have something to do with this."

Ramiro tossed a fragment of bark in Claire's direction where she stood on the other side of Jorga. Instead of looking worried or fidgeting, she met his gaze, eyes troubled. They should have foreseen this coming. "They're here for your granddaughter." Guilt did a number on his conscience. Claire would never have met the Northerners if not for him. She'd have stayed safe in her swamp if he hadn't been on the mission. Of course, then he'd never have gotten to know her or admire how she faced the world on her feet.

Focusing on the now, Ramiro ticked the reasons off on his fingers as he spoke. "They had spies in our camp. They know she scattered their army. They know her name and where she went. Their leader is from one of the *ciudades-estado*. He knows of witches and what the legends say you can do. He wants to make sure she doesn't come back. And if one witch is a danger, imagine how they'll feel about a whole group of them."

Stubborn disbelief shone in Jorga's eyes and her chin thrust forward. She'd hate him even more for bringing, not just Claire, but now *all* the witches into this. But if one Woman of the Song could disrupt the army, a collection of them was a bigger threat and even Jorga was smart enough to see that.

"If I was him," Ramiro said, "and had two armies to finish off—Colina Hermosa and Aveston—I'd see to them first. But I'd send my crack units to look for the burr in my side. Once the cities are finished, with their numbers, I'd bring my whole army here and root out *every* witch, burn down every acre to make it so. That's what I'd do, and I'm no general. That's what my father would do. That's what any good leader would do. They'll come for you. And they won't care that you want to be left alone."

"I know they're here for me." Claire said. "If I left now—"

"It wouldn't matter," he said. "You've proven yourself a threat. That makes all Women of the Song threats, whether they cooperate with us or not."

"How many will they send?" Jorga asked.

Ramiro shrugged. "We've no way of knowing. He could have sent half his best units or all of them. No telling how many he has . . . Or how big of a threat he assigns to Claire. Time shortens. Don't you see how important it is we have your help? They're coming for you next, if they aren't already."

"And if we defend ourselves, we make ourselves bigger targets." Jorga glared and snapped her shawl across her shoulders. "By the Song, you made sure we don't have any choice in this."

"Not on purpose." Ramiro said, feeling his face heat at the admission. There was no way he could have anticipated it. "I didn't think ahead."

"Men never do!"

"Smoke," Bromisto said, pointing.

Ramiro stood to see over the trees better. A lazy stream of gray broke the blue, rising from deeper in the woods—in the exact direction they'd come from that morning. It was too large to be a campfire. With the moisture still dripping it was no forest fire. No, something large and dry was being burned. "Looks like they found your house."

He moved to Claire, taking her arm, and she leaned on him as if the strength had gone out of her legs. Her lip trembled. Ramiro's fingers tightened on her arm. Again their lives mirrored each other. First losing pieces of their family, and now both their homes. Her loss was his own.

By the saints, he very much feared he would cost her life next.

"I will ride your horses," Jorga said, startling him out of staring with worry at Claire. Urgency lifted her voice into something almost human, though her spine remained as straight as ever, and her eyes as cold. "No more training for now. We go to my home fast."

"Have you got a fortress?" Ramiro asked. "Twenty-foot walls? That's the only thing that will protect us. Hurrying to your house isn't going to help. In fact, we have to travel with more caution now."

"How well did your walls protect you?" Her chin held that stubborn cant again. "We're not in the desert, city boy. No—we hurry. My son is there. Alone."

Ramiro noticed Claire gaped just as much as he did. "I have an uncle?" she gasped.

"It happened after your mother left. You wouldn't know as I told no one."

"Well, that sounds like you." Ramiro gave Claire a last squeeze and moved to the horses. "I agree, though—we hurry. But I'll need a scout. I've already missed too much. Bromisto comes with us." He hated to involve the boy, but the kid was here and his people were at risk, too. Bromisto's skills might make all the difference in keeping everyone safe. Besides, he wasn't sure the boy wouldn't just follow them anyway. Ramiro scrubbed a hand over his face, rubbing his beard. Life had certainly been easier before he'd grown it.

Bromisto practically danced with excitement. Jorga didn't lose the sour look, but she nodded, showing even the perpetually dim could exhibit a little sense. "Done. You have your scout. Get me home."

It was two very different things to expect to be hunted and to actually know that you were. From her place riding double with Ramiro, Claire tried hard to let go of the worry and tension, but she still jumped every time the undergrowth rustled or metal on the horses clinked. Much as she wanted to be relaxed like Ramiro—riding with hands resting easily on his thighs, reins dangling from his fingers as if he didn't need them—she couldn't seem to focus on anything else. A Woman of the Song shouldn't be such a coward. Look how well her grandmother bore it, riding ahead on the second horse, eyes on the trail, without a word in hours. That's how Claire should be.

Instead her hands shook, clammy with sweat, and her eyes darted. She wanted to babble with panic and hide in a hole—not be riding across an open stretch of swampland. The cover of the trees had vanished, replaced with marshy ground and stagnant pools. Usually she could find the beauty in any type of view—not today. The thick mass of cloud cover didn't help, rendering everything gray and dismal.

She leaned against Ramiro's broad back in front of her, shut her eyes, and let herself scream silently in her head until she had to breathe. Somehow, letting the fear out, if only in her head, helped.

After a few seconds, she sat up and poked Ramiro in the shoulder. "Socks still dry?"

"The ones in my saddlebag." He gave the leather satchel a nudge with his knee. "You?"

She held out a foot to show water leaking in slow drips. "Squishy." The boots Beatriz had given her worked wonders, but even they had their limits. She felt grateful she'd been able to change into some of her own clothing and take a few things from her home before . . . She made herself finish the thought—before it was all burned. The only memories of her mother now existed in her head and, more tangibly, her baggage.

"So," Ramiro said, "you have an uncle."

She made a grunting sound of agreement. "I

wonder if he's older or younger. My mother was gone a few years before she had me. He could be older."

"Or the same age."

Claire considered, but that didn't make it seem real either. She supposed she should be pleased to have another relative.

"I thought Women of the Song didn't have boys," Ramiro said.

"Mother said it was rare."

"After seeing your grandmother, I'd think they'd drown them at birth. I wonder if the Women of the Song are all like her. She doesn't care for me."

"You're an acquired taste." Claire gave him a push to show she was teasing and smiled. A ray of sun escaped the thick mask of clouds to dapple the ground on the trail ahead of her grandmother. Claire's eyes drank in the color and life of it. Somewhere out there, the little Bromisto scouted, under strict orders to run if he saw any Northerners. She and Ramiro made up the "rear guard"—as he called it—of their tiny party. He'd told her being relaxed was part of being ready for anything—an idea that only confused her.

He made a click of encouragement to Sancha, then said, "I almost feel sorry for any Northerners who run into your grandmother."

"I think she feels the swamp is her own personal property and any trespassers will answer to her. Being around her makes me feel two years old."

"Did she tell you much when you were alone, give you much insight?"

"Just the Speak on the Wind Song." And the few well-placed questions Claire managed—which she didn't feel like talking about with Ramiro—had been instructive. It seemed recently invented Songs could work just as well as ones passed down through generations, like the Hornet Tune. The magic lay not in the words, but in the user, allowing any Song to be effective, whether improvised on the spur of the moment or practiced for years. The key lay in being ready to act and being flexible in guessing the mind of the audience, finding the Song that best fit the situation. And in practicing—the lump returned to her throat at the thought—practice kept you prepared and always ready to strike first according to her grandmother. Having the Songs drilled into your brain so they sprang forth without thought helped, too. Practice could make her a killing machine like Jorga—an idea that made Claire slightly queasy as she remembered the Song she'd created days ago.

She started to tell Ramiro about it, and the words stuck. She latched onto something she did feel like sharing. "But Jorga told me a story. Do you want to hear it?"

He turned enough to see her out of the corner of his eye as if she were having him on. "A story? She doesn't seem the story type."

"Do you want to hear it?"

"I'm listening." Then more quietly, "I like the sound of your voice. It sings even when you aren't."

A warm blush ran up her neck and face, and she

remembered how she'd kissed him on the spur of the moment in front of her home. Did he think of it, too? Or, what if he considered it brash and forward? Fronilde never would have done such a thing. Her blush turned hot with shame. Maybe that's why he never spoke of it—to keep from embarrassing her.

She plunged into the story to have something else to think about. "The Great Goddess is the world. Her breath the wind, her breasts the mountains—"

"That's some image," he scoffed.

"Shhh. I'm repeating it as she told it to me. Do you want to hear or not?"

"I'm listening. I'm listening."

"All right then. Her breast the mountains. Her tears the seas. She is our home and our shelter. The Great Goddess is life and womb, giving life . . . And some more things I forget, but sometimes she walks among us in human form. On one such day, she took the form of a simple farmwife in woolens with a basket on her arm and walked the world."

"So she walked on . . . herself? Because she's the world."

"Shush. It's a story. If I talked like this, Jorga never would have told it all to me." Unexpectedly, his ridicule stung. She shared something that resonated with her and he mocked? When he kept quiet, she tried again, "She walked the world to see the state of her creations. Everywhere she looked, she found harmony. The fish swam and ate and minded their lives. The fox took no more food than he could eat.

The rabbit gave up its life for others to live, but not before the next generation was born. Life had balance, devoid of gluttony or greed. There was death, but it held purpose. Nothing was wasted. Then the Great Goddess came to the lands of humans.

"The first thing she saw was a man beating his wife and children because grain had spilt in the roadway. Man, woman, child, the Great Goddess had given all a role to play to ensure all lived complete lives. None were meant to be master over the other, but to man—who had the greater strength to bear physical loads, while woman had the inner strength—an imbalance had sprung. Against the will of the Great Goddess, men used their strength to dominate and as proof they were the greater sex. The Great Goddess became angry. The skies darkened and thunder rolled. But the Great Goddess did not interfere with her creations. She gave them the will and the wisdom to order their own lives."

"So she didn't do anything?"

"Not yet." Claire took a breath and started the next part. "Then there was some more about what the Great Goddess saw until she came to two sisters. The two sisters worked the land, producing abundance from what the Goddess gave them—in harmony. What they did was well done and the Great Goddess felt that there existed a kinship between her and the sisters. Here were ones who lived in her image.

"As she lingered, bandits came from the woods as the sisters worked alone, and well . . . forced their will upon them. The Goddess was incensed at the misuse of her greatest gift to man and woman, but did nothing as was her wont.

"This time, however, the Great Goddess did not walk away. When the men had gone, she revealed herself and touched each sister, transporting them to the Great Goddess's favorite spot among her creations where variety thrived: She brought them to the swamp to heal. Here, where quicksand could shield, poisonous snake could protect, even double-bite spider could keep the world of men out, she put the sisters in a safe area and the Great Goddess shared her Song with them to mute their pain before she went her way.

"But her touch and music lived on. For though the sisters separated to each nurse their injury and grieve alone, both bore daughters, and remained connected as only sisters can be. And each daughter brought forth the Great Goddess's Song and shaped it in their own way. Thus did the Women of the Song have the gift to protect themselves evermore. And that's the story she told me."

"Hmmm," Ramiro said tactfully. "That's some story. And this is what your people believe?"

"Jorga said it was as good an explanation as any for where the magic came from."

"And this Great Goddess did nothing to change her creations out in the world? Didn't smite the profane or send anyone to show them a better approach?"

"It's not her way." Claire shifted her seat. "It's not the way of Women of the Song. Mother always insisted we mind our own lives."

"That's what I'm afraid of," Ramiro said. "That they can't be brought to help, and they won't even train you quickly enough to be of use—it feels like Jorga is dragging her feet on that. This whole thing could be a wild goose chase. Jorga would still rather walk away from helping my people. A waste of time when I could have been doing something else. Supporting my father among them." As if sensing he'd said words that might wound, he added, "It was worth a try and you needed to return, if only briefly." He rushed onward, "I feel like we're a *pelotón* of two. We work well together. A team. Don't you think? It would be wrong to break it up."

Startled, astonishment kept Claire silent. He worried about losing her, about her staying here. Somehow, he could sit here calm and composed when Northerners hunted them and babble at the thought of splitting up from *her*. Warmth and hope grew in her heart, then dimmed. Was it as simple as losing the companionship of his military company and his brother had made him latch onto the nearest person? Or did it go deeper?

"I . . . I agree," she said, suddenly too shy to say more. "We feel like a team. But don't give up on the Women of the Song—or—me yet. I have a feeling this isn't over."

"Aye. I trust your judgment. We'll give it a little more time."

In response, she leaned forward and rested against his back again, putting her arms around his waist. A smile bloomed across her face when his hand encircled hers.

CHAPTER 23

Ramiro stood in the gray world. All around him fog clung, thick and impenetrable, but not touching him. This time, in this dream, there was no city rising from the murk. No sign of Colina Hermosa. The ground didn't slide in the way of sand. It splashed when he stepped, water cold against his feet. The swamp, then.

He circled in place, searching for Salvador, and the fog let him see through it to reveal his brother at the crest of a small hill, looking upward, with his back turned. Ghostly shadows of trees lurked deeper within the white, rising like distant, dead things.

Salvador wore no armor this time. A priest-like robe covered his brother, but white instead of brown or black, and no triple-rope belt cinched his middle. The robe fell unhindered to the ground. For a second, Ramiro, too, wore the same outfit, then it flickered and he stood in his undertunic and trousers, barefoot and unarmed. The clothing he'd worn when he'd fallen asleep.

Ramiro stepped toward the hill and once again time slowed, pulling against him like quicksand, leaving him unable to make progress. In the way of dreams, he knew time and strength held no meaning here. No matter the effort expended, he'd never get close—to touch, to take his brother's hand, to feel his life whole again.

"Salvador!" he shouted, his voice raw with longing.

As before, his brother turned slowly. Almost Ramiro expected to find him beardless as a priest, but the same face met his gaze, the brown eyes seeing him for an instant of recognition and turning in dismissal.

Salvador pointed to the sky. The fog obediently became translucent again.

The sun was a black disc.

Ramiro jumped, his whole body going cold. Unlike with an eclipse, there was no foreign body between the orb and him. The sun itself had gone dark as ink, though still giving light. A light that felt foul and tainted.

Before he could react further, the fog reformed, covering everything and leaving him alone. As if from a far distance, one word drifted in Salvador's voice.

"Hide."

Ramiro woke with a gasp, his heart racing. *"Hide."* Panic turned his insides to water.

A dream. A dream and nothing more.

Sancha slept. She would have alerted him if anything threatened. She made a better guard than any human. He was safe among his bedding, weapons lying close. Bromisto lay curled in a ball in his blankets, snoring lightly near the ashes of their small fire, muttering in his sleep now and then. Next to Ramiro, Claire sprawled, one hand holding his blanket as if with a need to reassure he was there—or maybe in some delusion of protecting him. Moonlight glinted pale off the skin of her face, arm, and hand lying inches from his own, the white of her contrasting more sharply so close to his honeyed-brown coloring.

Warmth at having her so near pushed aside the terror. Slowly, he brought heart and breathing under control. It was just a dream, no matter how real. This was reality.

Reality left a bitter taste in his mouth.

In his dreams, he was not the Ramiro who had turned his back on his father. Not the Ramiro who had left his *pelotón* and his duty. He used to have joy, despite the fear, as when he'd gone on his first ride, or the day he'd earned his beard. He'd forgotten how to laugh—how to smile. In his dreams, he had a brother.

Now, he tasted only bitter ashes.

Deserter.

Claire had become the shining beacon who got him through Salvador's death. For that, his heart of hearts knew he'd followed her. Yet, in the darkest hours, it couldn't make up for what he left behind. He let the guilt swallow him whole, giving it time to fester, then asserted an effort to block the feelings and not think about them. With just such denial, he got through each day.

He sniffed the air. From years of sentry duty and early morning practice, he judged it to be some hours until dawn. A smile touched his face as he studied Claire's sleeping form, still so innocent and naïve despite the death she'd seen. He wrestled with the desire to lean just a few inches and taste her with a kiss. No gentleman would act so. If this war were over and he were home, he would seek out her family for permission to court her, then he might indulge such wishes. But he wasn't home and she had no family.

Jorga.

The bitter taste grew stronger, but he levered himself up by an elbow. Jorga sat on the other side of the fire from them. Her shoulders actually slumped instead of being held straight as a spear. Ramiro sucked in a breath, his eyes rolled from just a glimpse of her.

Claire's family. Duty dictated his behavior. Her answer would be no, but that didn't excuse him from asking.

He got to his feet, gathered his weapons, and in an echo from his dream, his legs refused to respond, but this time because of actual reluctance. He cursed and walked over to her, sitting down none too gently, putting dagger in his lap and sword against his knee. The old woman's eyes flew open with a start, and he realized she'd been asleep sitting up. The moonlight reflected off the paleness of her skin also but without kindness, revealing the knobby and twisted joints of one with severe rheumatism. A fact she kept hidden during the day. She shook her sleeves down over her hands almost before he could blink.

"It pains you to sleep lying down," he said in a moment of insight.

She stared at him coldly with eyes made black instead of blue in the darkness. "What do you want?"

"Permission to court your granddaughter."

She laughed without mirth, a dry rasp, lips pulling back to show large, square teeth. "Why bother to ask? I see how she looks at you."

"That's why I ask. You are wrong about me. Wrong about most men."

"Am I? You would take her to your cities. And what would she be there? Hated. Feared. Made a second-class citizen, not her own person. A reflection of you, having no life of her own."

"Not in my—our household. My mother raised me differently."

Again came the dry laugh. "Think you see her as equal? Then why ask my permission? Do I own her? Is she incapable of directing her own life and making her own decisions? Would any man ask permission in how they run their life? Did you run to your parents before coming here?"

Ramiro sat stumped and speechless.

"I see you. You would protect her, wrap her up like a piece of priceless glass. Give her no choice of her own. She sees the danger around her and chooses it with her eyes open, but you would take the choice from her to ease your own fears of breaking her. She is as capable as the rest of us of fighting her own battles, city man. All women are. It should be up to them to choose."

"My request was meant as a courtesy," he said, stung. "To show her respect." He drew his knees up to his chest, his weapons moving with him as he sat back on the damp ground, thoughts flashed in his head, there and gone lightning fast. "I thank you. I spoke in haste. You are right. I spoke and acted dishonorably toward her." It smarted to admit as much, but justice required it. Jorga had responded to him with the most civility she'd shown so far.

Her gnarled hand grasped his knee, squeezed, and vanished. "I trust my granddaughter. If she looks at you with such eyes, there's a reason. That's why I let you live. But she is my last kin."

"You have a son."

"A son cannot carry on the line—he has no magic. My line goes back three thousand years and more. Can you say as much? My kin walked this swamp with chin held high when your kind were still nomads of the desert. We watched you settle in your cities, thinking you owned everything. She can no more turn her back on her heritage than you can learn respect. It is in her blood. I won't let her dismiss us."

It would certainly be easier for them if Claire did just that, once this whole thing were over—if they survived. If she set aside her magic they would be accepted more quickly; their lives could be normal . . .

once more he realized he was falling into the role Jorga expected of him. His jaw firmed.

"I would never ask that of her. As you said, it is her decision. Not mine. Not *yours*. But we'll see which life she prefers."

"All the better," Jorga said before countering with shattering words. "Are you worthy of her, city man? Has your life been as blameless and clean as hers? Or will your love muddy her and cast a shadow on her?"

Deserter.

How could he ask to court Claire when he could end in prison or hanged? Cast out by his own people? Could he visit that shame on her?

Against his will, his head dropped, a cloud over his heart. *Never.* He could speak nothing to Claire until he had settled his own life.

Ramiro made his muscles relax, settling his legs back to the ground and shaking out his hands. "Ready yourself and wake Claire. We move now. Before it's light." He eyed the sky, remembering the black sun and Salvador's advice to hide. "We need to move at night."

To his surprise, she didn't argue, glancing at the sky as if she, too, felt something. She gave a nod and held out a bony hand. "Help me up, city man. We'll be there by morning."

CHAPTER 24

The day dawned hot, windless, and dry with few clouds and the promise of great heat to come. The only shade came from the taller cacti and was as skimpy as their rations. As the priest requested, Teresa stayed well back of the prisoner as they walked down the main road to Zapata. Santabe had the height of a man. The wiry muscles on her arms were more than enough to convince Teresa she could be dangerous without needing the description of her crimes from Father Telo. Santabe had the sort of athletic figure Teresa often admired, though the harshness of her personality would keep it from going beyond appreciation. Teresa preferred gentleness in a woman in order to inspire love—or lust.

Yet, Santabe showed nothing but a docile nature at the moment, acting in no way like one compelled, looking awkwardly out of place in a bright yellow peasant blouse with bell sleeves and pink skirt next to the somber browns Teresa wore and the priest's robe. A smug, self-satisfied smile proved her habitual expression. Teresa suspected the woman could have overpowered the one-handed priest at any time and chose not to.

Teresa shook off that worrisome thought as well as her doubts for accompanying the strange pair. She'd come along to find out more about the Northern culture, not find a lover.

Yet, she couldn't ignore the woman either. Once again in her life curiosity outweighed self-preservation. Finding one of the Northerners who could speak their language had to be fate. Teresa couldn't let this opportunity slip away—she just hoped she had the chance to report what she learned so it could be recorded. If . . . if she could learn anything. This Santabe didn't seem like the chatty type.

Well, she'd interviewed plenty of difficult subjects. She straightened her poncho and hurried her pace to draw closer, road dust puffing around her scuffed boots at every step. Most people wanted to talk about themselves, no matter how much they resisted at first. She'd start with something smaller and try to build to her larger questions.

"Horses? Is it true Northerners don't use horses because you prefer your own feet?" The question again sent her worrying whether Valentía had survived after trying to protect her. She prayed the stallion lived. A lump in her throat reminded her that she'd lost enough friends already. There had been loss before in her life—her parents' deaths—but then the world had gone on as before. Somehow that had helped support her. Now it felt like every beautiful thing in the world was being stolen, leaving only the ugly and cruel.

As if in confirmation, the prisoner's only answer was a sneer.

"They call themselves the Children of Dal," Telo supplied.

Teresa tried again. "The Children of Dal avoid horses perhaps because your god shunned them? It's amazing how many different customs have their start in a religious cause," she said for the priest's benefit. "Altar cloths and candles for instance. Santiago started the practice by spreading a napkin on a rock before one of his famous homilies. He used to light a candle before he prayed and others imitated him."

"But where did he learn it from?" Father Telo asked. "Was it his invention or was the origin still older? We can only guess."

"Oh, to have been alive then," she said with a smile. "Back when great things were happening." When the struggle to give up their nomad ways had begun. Even as she romanticized it, though, she knew it was hardly the wondrous moment she wished it to be. It had been a nasty time of civil war, with many martyrs created and ordinary people killed. Hardly safe.

Much like now.

"I guess we have our own great things happening right now," she said. "No matter the outcome of the war, there will be change to the culture of the *ciudades-estado*."

Telo shook his dark head. "I very much fear so. It has begun already."

Santabe laughed, startling Teresa into a small jump. "You are weak. Doomed to fail. There is no mercy from Dal, only his sufferance. Stupid priest, taking me right where I want to go. You think losing your hand was painful. Wait until I am back among my people. I will make you suffer slowly, oh so slowly. What you had from me before will be as—what is that you say—a needle stick." Even with the accent her words were clear enough. The expression on her face held something close to bliss, and Teresa shivered with revulsion.

"Pin prick," Telo corrected in a mild voice. "So you've told me many times in the past days."

"If you are so certain of winning, then why refuse to talk?" Teresa demanded. "What can it hurt to tell me of your culture? If it is so great and we are so wrong, then prove it." She had little hope such a jibe would work, but the priestess raised her chin, seeming to preen under her words.

"True enough. Your kind shall lose and perish. Dal commands we speak of Him when asked, even to infidels and blasphemers such as you. I will answer your questions, ugly woman, stupid as they are. We walk because the Children of Dal do not keep *pets*." She put a world of scorn into the word. "Animals are meant for two things: meat and blood sacrifice."

Teresa ignored the rude comment toward herself. The attitude toward animals stung more, striking on the kinship she felt toward the missing Valentía. "Blood sacrifice appears to be an important component to your culture. You do so to appease Dal?"

Santabe looked toward the sky, directly at the sun. "Do not speak his name unless you wish to draw his attention. His attention would be the end of you."

"You spoke his name plenty and never minded when I did so," Telo objected.

"That was before," came the smug answer. "As you mentioned, times change."

"Their god is a sun god," Telo said. "And very touchy. With, apparently, very good hearing. But I shouldn't ridicule. Did not our Lord appear as a burning bush?"

"I believe most take that for parable—myth, not fact," Teresa said.

"Once I would have agreed. Now, I'm not so sure."

Teresa clicked her tongue, angry at herself for letting the discussion veer off track. She hadn't gotten an answer to the question she most wished to know. "But why the blood sacrifice?"

Telo winced, and she knew the subject to be hurtful. To him the why probably didn't matter. His hand was gone and not coming back. But it wasn't just curiosity. It was such a key component of their lives, their mission, and to have insight into it—as repulsive as it was—might be useful. She pressed on. "The usual reason would be to direct their god's anger elsewhere," she continued. "To spare themselves from his wrath or appease it."

"You know nothing, ugly woman," Santabe said. Her step never slowed, but Teresa got the feeling the priestess was pleased that Teresa had missed the mark. So she stayed silent, knowing someone who believes in the truth of themselves will want to talk about it. Soon Teresa was rewarded when Santabe said, "Blood feeds the Great Dal. Gives him power so that his influence grows and we see his actions among us again."

"Then he has time periods where he doesn't show interest in your world. When he isn't active? Would you term it sleep? What happens when he wakes?"

"You should pray to your weak god that you never find out," came the gloating reply.

"Interesting," Teresa couldn't avoid saying. "Most gods are omnipresent and omnipotent, but yours chooses to detach himself." She pushed aside the useless wish for pen and paper. An inquiry of Father Telo had yielded nothing. He apparently packed more necessary supplies than writing implements. She'd just have to hold everything she learned in her memory and hope it didn't fail. "How often is your god awake compared to asleep?"

"That is your wording, not mine," Santabe said harshly. "To speak of such is blasphemy."

A cloud passed over the sun, sliding a shadow over Teresa and making her jump as if she'd dropped a book in a library. She was too jittery, skittish, and to tell the truth, downright frightened. Following this priest and his hostile prisoner was more than foolish. What did she hope to accomplish? Damn her curiosity. She should ask a few more questions and flee to the remains of Colina Hermosa as fast as her legs would carry her.

Telo glanced back. "Perhaps inquire on something beyond the spiritual, my child. Most everything is blasphemy to the Children of Dal."

"Your leader is a foreigner, not of your people," Teresa said, finding his advice wise. "I did not know you were welcoming to foreigners. Is this Lord Ordoño an exception?"

"Lord Ordoño is always an exception."

"How did you meet him? Or more precisely, how did he climb your ranks?"

"By proving he was not weak."

Teresa frowned for the short answers. "And how does one prove that?"

"There is no word for it in your language, but 'ruthlessness' comes close."

"Your ability to speak our language is very impressive. How many years did you study?"

"Six of your years."

"Your superiors must have been impressed." Teresa slipped in a compliment. If done carefully enough, those often helped hostile subjects to open up.

"My superiors were all chopped into tiny pieces. Their blood fueled many Diviners."

Bile rose in Teresa's throat as an image of that

formed. The woman said it so coolly, as if speaking of the weather. She couldn't help a glance toward Father Telo's robe where he wore one of the weapons close to his skin. "Why? Is that routine?"

"They resisted the rule of Lord Ordoño, refused to see his wisdom, where he was taking the Children of Dal. They fought against changing their doctrine."

"Fascinating." And she meant it—Teresa found it hard to believe Santabe had been open to change of any kind, let alone to doctrine. "Tell me more of this change. What did Ordoño suggest differently?"

Teresa exchanged a look with Telo, trying to caution him not to interrupt. He looked as enthralled as herself. She held her breath, but there was no need. Santabe spoke without further prompting.

"They continued to believe that we remain in our cities." Her accent rendered the last word close to unrecognizable. "They believed as we'd always believed that we discovered Dal and he was our destiny. But his touch made us strong. Ordoño saw our strength. He taught that we didn't need to keep the Great Dal to ourselves. That our fortitude and numbers would overcome all other people. That we would bring the Dal to the rest of the world. Now the Great Dal is your destiny also." A wicked smile curved her lips. "The Children of Dal no longer must bear the brunt." The woman fell silent, striding up the road as if she'd said nothing extraordinary.

"Why continue to sacrifice your own people, when

you can use ours," Telo said, almost to himself. To Teresa, he said, "They see it as a gift to us. We now know their god. They count us as the lucky ones."

Teresa shook her head. "Perhaps not. They might have felt responsible. She said that they 'discovered' him. What if before the Northerners kept to themselves to contain their practices? Perhaps they thought they were acting as a buffer, keeping Dal in, protecting other cultures."

Santabe hissed. "Do not say His name, ugly woman."

Teresa waved her hand in acceptance. Better to go along with the priestess's wishes, if she were to keep her talking. "I will remember."

"And Ordoño came, somehow his influence grew, and he changed their whole way of thinking," Telo said. "It's possible. Is that right, Santabe?"

The sky exploded with clouds of birds. Flights of them, of all different species, flying low and fast. All in the same direction—headed behind them. A crow passed by Teresa's ear, cawing in outrage. There for the briefest of moments, then vanishing.

A deer came bounding toward them, then another. Barely changing course enough to detour around them, the animals showed no fear. Smaller animals followed: rabbits and packrats. Some dived into holes as Teresa watched. Others continued to run.

"A fire?" she wondered aloud. She'd heard animals stampeded like this before a fire. But no smoke hung in the air. Her confusion remained . . . and then the reason became clear.

As far as she could see in either direction ahead on the road, spread a line of Northerners with thick-bladed swords. They hacked and slashed at all the scattered vegetation, taking out anything taller than her knee. Five of them worked together to bring a saguaro down in seconds. With over ten arms, the great cactus must have stood for hundreds of years. Birds scattered out of the woodpecker holes near its top as it fell.

A sob caught in Teresa's throat. It was like watching an ancient grandfather being cut down. An affront against all that was good.

A rumble like nothing she'd ever heard shook the ground, vibrating in her chest.

"The army," Telo said. His face had gone gray.

"Saints," Teresa breathed. Too late to run. They'd already been seen. Several of the soldiers clearing the way left their tasks and headed for them. Her hands clutched at her clothing in a vain attempt to find strength. Her knees felt like water. She very much prayed she didn't shame herself and wet her britches. "I hope you know what you're doing, Father."

Santabe gestured. A flood of her language snapped forth, crisp and sharp like orders. The soldiers broke into a run toward them, while one headed back toward the rumbling and the army.

Father Telo dropped his pack in the road. He reached into the pocket of his robe and drew out something, holding it out to the approaching soldiers. He said one word in their language that Teresa couldn't understand and then, "Ordoño."

Shock and surprise leached over their faces, complete and swift as if she watched a play on a stage instead of real life. Their mouths gaped and green eyes ogled.

"What is it?" Teresa tried to make out what the priest held and could only see a wink of gold in the sunlight. Whatever it was, it had the soldiers confused and uncertain.

Santabe spat out another flood of commands, but Telo flourished the object again and repeated the foreign word and "Ordoño."

They seemed to come to some decision, for two of them came to Teresa, removing the knife she wore in plain sight in her belt. A weapon she'd taken from the band of Northerners who had bought her from the bandits. Now she was a prisoner again.

To her relief, they treated Santabe the same way, muttering, and pointing at the chain that linked the priestess to Father Telo. One kicked their pack to the other side of the roadway. They tried to question Father Telo, but the man could only shake his head, unable to understand.

All the while, the black smudge on the horizon that was the army resolved into individual men, coming closer. The rumbling vibration grew louder, making it impossible to talk. The nearest soldier pulled her arms behind her back and pinned them there. Santabe and Telo were treated the same, pulling them together so they stood in a compact huddle.

Teresa stared as the first units of the army reached

them. In another situation it would have been a glorious sight. Men must have fanned out for a mile in either direction. Thousands upon thousands in black-and-yellow uniforms. Some carried black banners, limp with no wind to lift them, to Teresa's disappointment. She would have loved to see what symbols they favored. You could learn much from symbols.

They seemed to be marching grouped in squares of some kind. All had some kind of weapons: swords, spears, knives, in addition to small packs on their backs. She saw some squares with shorter pikes and one section that carried bows and quivers. A few looked her way, light eyes curious. Others walked without a sound or a shift of the eye. Some spoke together as they walked, like firm companions.

Something united one and all, though: a hardness, a determination in their eyes. They had run from a fight they were supposed to win, had been tricked. They had something to prove.

The first ranks went by and more and more. Teresa waited for it to end, but it didn't. It seemed they must be more numerous than the entire population of all the *ciudades-estado* combined. Sometimes one of their wagon houses broke the monotony, creaking and squeaking over the dusty road. Once she saw a square formation of men and women in the white robes of their priests and held her breath until they vanished. She lost count of the white robes at around two hundred.

How were two small people of no importance supposed to stop an army of this size? Teresa pressed her lips together. They had no chance. Even in her own mind, she didn't pretend to be a hero. She was no warrior like Ramiro. No leader like the *Alcalde*. Not even full of faith like Father Telo. With the Northern numbers so overwhelming, what remained of her people would die—as would she.

Oh saints. We need help.

The small, detached part of her brain noted how quickly she turned to the spiritual for salvation when her world came crashing down and scoffed . . . but the rest of her prayed harder.

Her shoulders began to ache from the strain of her arms behind her back. The pressure grew to the sort of pain she couldn't ignore, and she lost focus on the army marching by as she concentrated on her personal misery.

As the noise of the army faded and the last troops passed, she became aware of another group standing with them. An ordinary man in plain brown clothing with the skin and eye coloring of her people was surrounded by a small group of uniformed soldiers. Lord Ordoño at last. Teresa counted his companions at eight; of the soldiers, four of them were older men and two of them were about her age of thirty. She recognized their type, like Captain Gonzalo, these were men who made decisions. The other two in the entourage wore the white robes of priests, one man and one woman.

She tried to twist away from her captor, only to

be yanked back, the pain in her shoulders redoubling. Eyes turned to her for a moment, and she felt every tear in her clothing and snarl in her short hair tenfold. Dried bloodstains from Alvito and others still covered her clothes. She was dirty and tired and no fit representative to meet the elite members of a foreign army.

"My old *Acorraloar* partner returns," Ordoño said, looking at Father Telo. "And my lost lamb and one other." He touched the chain around Telo's waist. "What is this about, Santabe?"

"I brought her back." Father Telo offered the object in his hand.

It proved to be a large earring in the shape of the sun and made of gold. Some of the rays were sharpened to points and others curved. Teresa craned her neck for a better view. It matched the earrings worn by the white-robed pair with Ordoño, no doubt some symbol of their office.

"It is mine!" Santabe shouted. She struggled in her captor's grip, breaking free, then punching him in the throat. The soldier fell, gurgling as he struggled to breathe. She shouted the same foreign word Father Telo had used as three more soldiers jumped on her. She landed a fist on one that would insure a black eye before they subdued her again.

"I thought you might be missing her," Telo said, his sarcasm carrying clearly to everyone.

"That word you spoke," Teresa asked him, curiosity simply too strong, "the one she just said. What is it?"

"Their favorite word," Telo said. "*Blasphemy*. They have so much suspicion of each other that they even doubt the word of one of their high priestesses, especially if she happens to be missing her jewelry of office and her robes."

Ordoño laughed, eyes crinkling as at a good joke. "Ah, priest. You never disappoint. I don't regret saving you, though it looks as though Santabe got a piece," he said, referring to the missing hand. He took the earring, then said to the soldiers, "Have you searched them?"

A fourth soldier patted down Santabe, despite her snarls. Teresa gasped in relief as the man holding her arms released her to check her clothing, running his hands down her legs and inside her boots before heading up to more embarrassing areas, but she hadn't so much as a hairpin. She wiped sweat beading on her forehead.

"Wait! Don't do that!" Telo shouted. Answering cries of surprise came from Father Telo's guards. One had a hand inside the top of the priest's robe. The soldier locked in a spasm, then fell boneless to the sand. The senior officers from Ordoño's entourage jumped in front of him, pushing back their leader even as the priests surged forward.

More pushing and shoving ensued, then a white Diviner lay in the sand. Both priests held their Diviners in their hands. "Blasphemy!" they yelled in their own language, so incensed, veins stood out in their necks. The soldiers holding her pulled their swords.

A sharp point blossomed against Teresa's spine. Her eyes flew open their widest.

This is it.

"Hold!" Ordoño shouted, flinging out his hands, yet somehow looking utterly calm. He spoke in the Northern language, then repeated, "All of you hold."

Teresa thought nothing could halt their deaths, but somehow the plain-faced man brought everything to a stop. The knife lifted from her spine, and she collapsed to her knees in relief.

Ordoño spoke a few more short sentences, and Teresa dearly wished she understood what he said.

The priests still stood with Diviners raised over Telo, but the soldiers from Ordoño's entourage had their swords at the priests' throats. Telo had his eyes closed, mouth moving in a prayer. All hung poised on a knife edge, and Teresa wondered if anyone dared breathe. She certainly didn't.

Oh so slowly, the priests lowered their Diviners and secured them in their belts, and the tension drained from the group. The soldiers sheathed their weapons as well. Teresa drew in a great gulp of air as the female priest took the third Diviner from the sand.

Ordoño gave a nod as if he hadn't just survived some kind of test and issued more unintelligible orders. Santabe scowled blackly.

"What . . . what was that?" Teresa whispered. "What happens to us?"

Ordoño's eyes snapped to her, and she flinched at the power in them. He'd overheard. "How rude of me. I said, bring all three. I have too few entertainments. You're to be locked in a wagon together until we reach Aveston. It'll be interesting to see which of you come out—if any of you do."

The soldier at Teresa's back yanked her along, and a little squeak escaped her mouth as she looked at the hate-filled fire burning in Santabe's eyes. Their situation had gotten no better after all. Then the hardness of determination filled her. Like the Northern soldiers, she had something to prove as well, and it started with living.

CHAPTER 25

Julian let the guards hurry him down the ornate hallways. He'd been summoned once again, making that three such meetings in as many days in the palace of Crueses—each one more tedious than the last. He'd been dragged to another last night for an interminable, two-hour dinner, so he could be told that Ramón was returning to Suseph. A note would have sufficed and spared him the boredom. By the saints, let this be the end to their meetings.

This time, they took him to the smaller, private breakfast room, where *Alcalde* Juan sat behind a table groaning with food. Juan waved a bejeweled hand. "Come sit with me. Eat."

With a murmured apology, Juan's wife got up from her end of the table and left, leaving Juan alone at his meal. The woman was a shadow. Unlike Beatriz, the First Wife of Crueses added little to the city—like the decorations of this room, she was all fluff and little substance. Juan had picked her solely for her wealth, and not her welcoming personality or appearance, relying on a new mistress every year for his affection. Julian had always felt a bit sorry for the woman. Juan paid less attention to her departure than the napkin in his lap.

Julian held his place by the doors as his guard shut them. "I've already eaten." Indeed he had, and at a reasonable hour. Breakfast was best served in the morning hours, and the earlier the better—not nearly noon. By now, Julian had usually been about the work of his *ciudad-estado* for longer than Juan had been awake. He rather doubted Juan had done anything but pull up his lime green hose over his fatty bottom—if he even did that himself.

Petty thoughts.

Since when had the maneuverings of politics upset him and made him judgmental of others? Where was his patience? Three days stuck in a suite of rooms or spent with the most trying of *alcaldes* had him more irritable than a goodwife denied her Winter's Eve party. Or perhaps it was acting the part of a beaten dog that had him so short-tempered? He'd never been good at letting others take the lead, not even in his days as a merchant. And deferring to these two rulers was worst of all. They couldn't be more dissimilar from Julian in their concern for the welfare of this city and the people inside it.

"Is there news?" Julian asked in a more polite tone.

Juan wiped his mouth. "Indeed. Your citizens will be here before nightfall. All our churches and public buildings will be open to them. My residents have been encouraged to offer their homes and take in more. *Alcalde* Ramón will take half at Suseph. If necessary, any surplus can go in stables until better can be arranged."

Julian nodded calmly enough, but a joy burned in his heart at the thought of seeing Beatriz before the evening ended. No doubt that separation added to his irritableness. He could defer his departure to press battle for that pleasure.

"And have you word from Aveston?"

Juan held up a tiny slip of paper. "A bird brought this at sunrise."

Julian ground his teeth as the only servant in the room—Juan's confidential secretary—stepped forward to take the paper and bring it around the table. Saints forbid Juan walk it over himself or allow Julian to fetch it. The supposed importance of the secretary wouldn't let him go faster than a snail's pace.

The message had come at sunrise, and he was just now learning about it. Hours of worry could have been alleviated. Instead, he was forced to wait while Juan had his hair oiled and curled. Julian reminded himself sternly that the last laugh would be his.

The tiny paper held just one short phrase in curly script. *"We will be ready."*

"And you're sure no one else saw this?" Julian asked. "It couldn't have been intercepted by the Northerners?"

Juan held up another slip. "The bird from here went to our relay post outside Aveston. A fresh bird is sent inside the city by our man with the original message attached. Our man saw it go over the wall himself, right over the Northern army. A different bird brought their return."

"That is truly a blessing." If they survived this conflict, Julian would have to acquire some of these miraculous pigeons, even if he had to outbid Crueses for them. Contact with Aveston meant all the difference to his plan. Contact he hadn't been able to manage on his own. "Then I leave as soon as the *pelotónes* of Colina Hermosa can be ready." He turned to go, but a sound from Juan made him pause.

Juan cleared his throat again. "Our bargain is intact? We protect your people and you fight the Northerner army outside Aveston?" He didn't need to say that the people of Colina Hermosa would be his safety net if the Northerners should appear here.

They had asked the same promise of him at each meeting, enjoying putting him in his place and proving how indebted he was to them—the leader of the largest and strongest *ciudad-estado* now with nothing but the clothes on his back.

Well, his city may be gone, but the army and the will remained. Julian kept his face clear of emotion as he answered, only working his left thumb open and closed against his leg, trying to build up its strength. Soon the groveling would be over. "Yes, of course."

"Swear it."

"I swear it."

"Then why this?" Juan held up a broadside, torn at one corner where it had been jerked free from a nail or tack. Satisfaction oozed from his pores. The man had been waiting to produce this. Julian looked closer and saw one of his writings detailing the Northern terms, which Arias had hidden under his uniform and smuggled out of the palace.

"Did you not know we would watch you like a hawk?" Juan continued. "That any attempts to dodge our bargain would void it all? Yet, we found your servant putting these up all over town for the last two days, and passing them out in taverns." He kicked the table, knocking over a water decanter and making the salt jump in the open salt cellar. "You would undermine my authority with my people! You attempt to discount my rule in order to install yourself!"

Julian turned slowly, glancing toward his guards, knowing dismay covered his face. Though he believed his plan to be complete and secure, one never knew when an arrow shot in the dark could backfire and bring down all his work. He wasn't prepared for the charade to end so swiftly.

But he also wasn't prepared to cower for this frivolous man.

"Save your false fury," Julian said. "We both knew I would act when you imprisoned me. That I had your people's better interest in mind—you've seen the Northern terms. Your people deserve to know what they're getting into, too." Too bad none of the broadsheets got through. The people did deserve to know, only now it wouldn't come from him. "But I have no desire to rule your city. Not unless you force me to take it."

When Beatriz arrived with her ability to manipulate rumors, she would do a much better job at converting the people of this city to their cause. He had always planned to leave the task of spreading the Northern plans to her honed skills, but now she'd have to plant the news from the ground up.

He had no doubt at her ability to do just that.

Juan sprang to his feet, his thick neck turning purple. "Guards, take him back to his rooms and confine him there! No need for you to see anyone anymore, Julian. I think we shall send your military to Aveston without you. They don't need you to coordinate or carry out the attack."

The guards drew their swords.

A satisfied smile spread over Juan's face. "You can come out to lure your people inside, then my need for you is finished. Don't try anything else or we'll kill First Wife Beatriz or whoever else you care about."

Fury rose in Julian—so much that he shook with it and couldn't find words. That they would threaten his family—that went beyond all bounds. It wasn't done, not even at the worst of times. Yet, he needed to keep a cool head. Being captured at the obvious act of appealing to the populace had always been his intention. Let your opponent focus on your right hand, when all along what your left did was the true object.

"What are you waiting for?" Juan shouted when he said nothing. "Guards!" When the men didn't stir, Juan whirled on his secretary. "What is going on here? I gave an order!"

The nearer guard looked at Julian for a response. Suddenly Julian had enough of the farce. "They only take orders from me now." Their swords pointed at Juan. "As I said, I don't want your rule or city.

"Only your military."

For an instant, he wanted to have the soldiers of Crueses lock Juan away where no one would ever find *him*. But that would set a bad precedent, and as he said, he hadn't come here to take over the rule of this city. He pulled open the doors to reveal the entire collection of *pelotóne* captains from Crueses. "Keep your fancy palace and ineffectual rule, but your military answers to me. They march with me to Aveston."

The expression on Juan's face caused no little satisfaction. No, the rival *alcalde* had not guessed what Julian's left hand was doing. As expected, his lack of approval with his people had blinded him to his unpopularity with the military. It had been easy enough to convince the captains to ignore their orders and bring their troops to Aveston where the real fighting would take place.

"*Bastardo!* You can't take them," Juan shouted. "You would leave us defenseless!"

"You have your walls and your 'way of life,'" Julian said. "I will leave enough men to defend you, but the Northerners will be busy elsewhere. Think of it as 'insurance,'" he mocked, using the very words employed against him on their first meeting. He was not the one maneuvered into a corner now. "I take your military to insure my people are treated well by you while we are gone. And if you touch a hair on my wife's head, I'll have yours on a plate."

Julian picked up a slice of bread and added a poached egg on top with his fingers and took a bite, as Juan gaped, speechless like a drowning fish.

For a moment in time, Julian's inner landscape held, a firm road rising before him, allowing him to ignore the pits and fissures surrounding him. Then Julian shook off such thoughts—he had less than four days of his time as *alcalde* remaining.

He turned his back on Juan and joined the soldiers of Crueses at the door. "We meet my people and organize my men, then leave tonight."

"Very good, sir," they answered in voices deep and confident, one and all ready to stand with him and show the Northerners the points of their swords.

CHAPTER 26

Ramiro looked down at the house in the valley below him with no little amusement. Apparently, Claire's mother had built their home to look exactly like the place where she was born. Except for the dimensions being bigger, this house had the same low eaves and large porch, the same layout of outbuildings and garden. It was located in a tiny valley as well, built into the hillside, surrounded with climbing landscape to make it snug and hidden. The rising sun showed it was even painted the same colors. It appeared it wasn't her home she wanted to leave behind—only Jorga.

"What are you smirking about?" Jorga demanded from her crouch beside him. They hid behind a screen of bushes and trees, waiting for Bromisto to return. The old woman had insisted on getting down from the horses with them, despite her creaky knees.

"Shh, grandmother," Claire whispered. Her hand

rested on his back to help her balance, and Jorga directed her eyes at it with a glare. "We're supposed to be quiet."

Ramiro's smile widened at seeing Jorga put down. It was salve after the hurt look on Claire's face last night when he'd instructed her to ride with Jorga instead of himself. Already, she sensed him trying to keep her at arm's length. He wanted to explain to her—Saints, he wanted to reach for her—but the bushes rustled behind them, and he spun, sword coming up. The sky had lightened enough to show Bromisto pushing through the thicket.

"I'm not sure," Bromisto said. "The trails are dry here and used a lot. I can't pick up footprints. There was nothing off trail to suggest the pale soldiers have been here."

Ramiro swore, relaxing his grip on the sword; he'd been afraid of that. The paths leading up to the house were wide and well established. Jorga had never needed to hide her living quarters. Northerners could have walked right down the trail and be concealed inside the house—or not. There was no way to tell for sure.

"You three wait here. I'll go down and check. Don't come out until I wave for you."

"Ridiculous," Jorga said. "It's my home. I'll go."

Ramiro lifted his sword, letting the hilt find its natural balance in his hand, confidence flooding back. "None of you have any training in fighting. It could be an ambush."

"I have magic. I'm better equipped to—"

"That's why you're staying here with Claire and Bromisto. I'm the expendable one. Got it?"

"No," Claire said, her small face getting its stubborn expression. "We all go together."

Jorga took her granddaughter's hands and held them. "He's right. We do as he says." Claire squirmed in her grip, but the old woman didn't slacken or let the girl loose. She had steel under her wiry and gnarled muscles.

"I'm good with that," Bromisto said, holding his distance from the women. The boy kept himself so scarce on this trip that Ramiro hardly saw him, or stranger yet, heard him. Ramiro missed the boy's running chatter. He'd expected Bromisto to slip away and not come back, and had given him plenty of opportunity to do just that, but so far, the boy always reappeared.

As *she* always did, Jorga ignored the boy to talk right over him. "Errol. My son's name is Errol. He's . . . different. He doesn't take to strangers."

Ramiro frowned, unsure what she was hinting at. "You mean he's going to bite me. Can't you do that wind speak thing and tell him company is coming?"

"No. He's deaf to magic—all sons are. And I mean he'll probably hide. Errol is not used to people."

"Peachy." He rolled his neck and felt the tendons pop, then touched his medallion of San Martin.

"Wait. Your armor," Claire said as he got to his feet.

He shook his head. "I'll need to move quietly."

"I don't like this," she pleaded, heart in her eyes, even as she tugged harder at her grandmother to free herself. "You need your armor if any of those priests should be there. Their magic will kill you otherwise. Let me come with you."

He touched her chin. "It's a ten-minute hike and a quick look around, I'll be right back." It was a risk to go without his armor, but most likely no one was there, and keeping any chance at surprise seemed more important. To Jorga and Bromisto he said, "Sit on her if you have to," then he hurried before Claire could work loose, or he could change his mind. He'd already told Sancha to stay put, and now she grazed on any grass within reach.

The skin on the back of his neck prickled uneasily. He waited for a premonition or word of warning and got nothing. A fine time for his family's legendary Sight to take a nap—or did it mean he worried for nothing?

He tried to focus on stepping where his feet would make the least sound, but thoughts kept intruding.

Estúpido. You actually said you're expendable. It was to obtain his way, but couldn't he have found another word? There was no need to give Jorga ideas.

He passed with only a rustle through honeysuckle vines that hung from an oak. Normally, the swamp would be big enough to conceal a thousand Northerners and their paths would never overlap to stumble upon them. The odds would be in his favor. But this enemy wasn't merely passing through; they hunted. If it was his decision, he'd move in grids to search a wide area quickly. Meeting up with trouble seemed inevitable, and of all the worst times for it to happen, this would be it.

The deepest cover took him out closest to the barn, so he slipped in there first. The large stall inside looked to be for goats and was empty, hopefully, the animals outside for the day already. Only a few chickens strutted importantly among the straw. Every spotless tool lay on its own peg or hook. Rope was neatly spooled. Nothing was out of place. The straw didn't quite lie on the dirt floor in neat rows, but it came close.

"Jorga," he whispered. It was the tidiest barn he'd ever seen—it hardly even smelled. Beatriz couldn't have installed more order. He peeked behind some barrels in the corner. No boy hiding. Not even a cat, though Ramiro doubted mice would dare enter Jorga's domain. He rifled through some loose straw in the hayloft and the few hay piles, coming up with nothing.

Short checks of the chicken house and another small outbuilding revealed no boy and no sign of Northerners. Ramiro relaxed his grip on his sword and put his dagger down long enough to wipe sweat from his hand. Perhaps the boy had gone out with the goats. He'd search the house then signal the others.

A sweep of the long porch showed nothing but two rocking chairs and a wind chime of flattened scraps of metal above the single step. He crossed the boards and laid a hand on the door. Creepy-crawlies ran up his spine and the warning finally hit. He sprang from the door, reasserting his grip on sword and dagger even as he stepped back.

The door opened. A spindly kid stood inside with a flour sack on his shoulder. Nearly his age but a head shorter, his shockingly bright blue eyes focused somewhere over Ramiro's shoulder. "I'm ready. Hurry."

"Wha—"

The kid pushed past him. "I'm Errol. Hurry. It's coming."

Ramiro followed Errol from the porch. "What's coming?"

"It, of course. Where's my mother?" Errol looked up at the woods leading from the valley, turning in a slow circle in the center of the yard before the house. He stopped, facing right where Ramiro had left the others. "There."

The creepy-crawlies sent a fresh brush of ice down Ramiro's spine. "How did you know that?"

"No time." The kid darted for the barn as a squad of Northerners marched at a half trot over the lip of the valley in plain sight up the wide road. Ten or more in number, they shouted in alarm at catching sight of them. Ramiro shook off his surprise and raced after Errol as the boy darted behind the barn.

Saints. The kid was right?

It wasn't the time to ask questions. He pelted for the relative safety of the trees. The cover would blunt the Northerner advantage of numbers. From the way the Northerners put on a burst of speed, they knew it, too.

Someone behind them shouted, and an arrow whipped past Ramiro's ear.

Mierda. Of course they had bows.

He'd reached the first trees, dodging behind one, only to stumble over Errol crouched on the ground with his hands over his ears. The flour sack containing the saints knew what lay where it had been flung.

"What are you doing? Get up, kid!" He tugged at the boy, but it was like he had grown roots into the ground. Ramiro couldn't budge him. "Get up! We've got to run!"

"Demon!" Errol rocked, moaning.

The first Northerner reached them. Ramiro had no choice but to turn and defend.

Though beardless, the man was taller and heavier, and tried to use his momentum to bowl Ramiro over and finish him. Gomez had had him practice evading just such a maneuver from a larger opponent—usually the sergeant himself. Ramiro stood his ground, parried the blow aimed for his chest, and moved just enough to let the man flow right past him. Spinning, he left his dagger buried to the hilt in the man's back.

"Demon!" Errol shouted again from the ground, head cradled.

"No shit," Ramiro said as the rest of the Northerners rounded the trees.

No white robes. He didn't have time for relief at seeing no priests, however. They'd sent five soldiers after him and left the rest of their number to check the house to be sure this wasn't a diversion. They wore leather armor instead of chainmail, which was quieter and would stop a glancing blow, but not a determined strike like he'd made on the first man. All had swords out except the two with short recurved bows, like the kind used for hunting.

The precepts Salvador pounded into him bound him tighter than chains. *Always see first to Colina Hermosa's civilians . . .* It didn't matter if Ramiro no longer wore the uniform or Errol wasn't actually a citizen, it held him anyway.

With no choice, he stood over the boy, sword in hand. He had no illusions about them ignoring the unarmed person among them if he stepped away to fight them. They'd use the opportunity to skewer Errol.

But he'd not live long enough to see it.

Ramiro set his feet, but it seemed the world suddenly got bigger. The precepts didn't just apply to the people of Colina Hermosa and his brothers in arms. It applied to anyone who needed his help against an unjust opponent. A lesson learned too late.

The two bows raised, wicked sharp arrow tips aimed at his chest. He braced, knowing there was no evading their speed. He stood ready, anyway, with sword in front of him, sideways, and feet apart as Salvador had taught. If he were done, let it be with chin up and eyes open.

No arrow shaft came.

The Northerners said something, their voices easy and relaxed. Someone laughed. A harsh, shaming laugh that grated on his nerves. They tried to goad and humiliate him, thought him a *bisoño*, new to his beard. Ramiro refused to flinch, to show the least reaction. His muscles remained locked, rock solid.

The biggest man nodded and spoke. The foreign words flowed past Ramiro. The bows remained aimed at him, but the big man moved forward, sword spinning in controlled circles in the Northerner's hand—a beautiful ballet with steel. He gestured, inviting Ramiro to begin.

Ramiro tensed further, expecting a trick, even as he moved a pace from Errol and balanced on his toes for better mobility. They were barbarians. Did they seek to honor him with a man's death or have fun at his expense? The man handled his sword in a way that spoke of mastery.

The first strike came so fast he hardly saw it. He couldn't parry. Couldn't dodge. Metal ripped through his sleeve, leaving blood trailing down his bicep. The Northerners laughed at his expense again, but the arrow tips lowered a fraction as they found him less of a threat.

Sweat chilled him from head to toe. He managed to catch the next strike aiming for his neck, but the man twisted and aimed unexpectedly low next, clipping his thigh. This blood ran hotter, this cut deeper. It would soon slow him. Their sword forms were unknown to him. He couldn't wait, in hopes Claire would arrive to use her magic.

He centered himself in front of the unmoved Errol

again and lunged forward in attack. The Northerner jerked back, hazel eyes wide. Not quick enough. A tiny sliver of blood oozed from the Northerner's cheek, just under his left eye. The man touched it in amazement, and the laughter of his fellows cut off, then resumed, aimed as much at him now as at Ramiro.

As the Northern soldier's face sobered, he sprang forward, unleashing a relentless torrent of blows. Ramiro managed to get his sword under the first and the second, but the soldier's size gave him all the advantage he needed. The sheer force beat him down. The third broke the lock of his wrists and broke his guard, punching him to his knees.

"Demon!" Errol shouted again.

The fourth strike that would have clove through Ramiro's head faltered enough at the distraction for Ramiro to reset his sword. Still, the blow skittered off the hilt and smashed his fingers, making them numb. His sword fell.

Something foul and putrid touched the air. It smelled of rot.

The brush clattered, and Claire broke through the trees. Her eyes blazed with determination in her pale little face. Men shouted at her appearance. The arrow aimed at Ramiro flew wide by an inch, letting him feel the breeze of its passing. The second bowman swung around at Claire and loosed.

"No!" Ramiro stumbled to his feet. He glimpsed Jorga by Claire, then his large opponent got between him and them, preventing him from seeing what happened. The man hefted his sword, taking his time as he measured Ramiro for the final blow.

Ramiro staggered backward, uselessly searching the ground for his sword with his left hand. Pain stung his chest.

His head shot up, expecting to find the Northerner finishing him off, but the man was two steps away. A foot-long cut had appeared across Ramiro's chest, slicing through clothing and skin. It stung like all the fires of hell.

"Saints," Ramiro cried out. Another stinging swipe tore a bleeding gash across his hand. The fear he hadn't time to feel flooded over him.

What in all the hells?

No one touched him. No one was close enough.

Had Claire's magic become real? Or was it Jorga's doing? Nothing of steel or metal had been anywhere near. But no, he heard no singing, and all their magic was illusion, only in the victim's head. It couldn't draw blood. He swiped at the red streaks, feeling the wetness, smelling the odor. The pain alone told it was real.

None of the Northern priests were here to work this magic either.

Across from him and suddenly uninterested in their fight, the big Northerner cried out and looked down. An equivalent wound carved across his chest. As Ramiro watched, blood bloomed on the Northerner's hand just as it had on his own.

What the hell?

"Demon," Errol yelled. "It's here!"

A sense of evil overshadowed everything but fear. It bore down like a tangible weight, and Ramiro found himself on his knees. The force of it popped his ears, then clogged them. It drove out all hope, all memory of anything beautiful, just as it had when Claire sang the Northern army into panic and retreat. But that had been *illusion* of evil—not real—and soon gone.

Or so he thought.

Another stinging blow made a whip mark across his forearm, cutting deep and leaving a trail of reddening flesh. All around him men were crying out in terror and pain. The Northerners collapsed, suffering the same nightmare.

"Dal!" someone moaned in a voice of such hopelessness it bled into the soul. A god made real and exacting a terrible revenge, until Ramiro remembered—

Claire!

Was she being preyed upon also?

Ramiro couldn't stand. Pure darkness reached into his heart and tried to pull out his soul. He crawled like a worm in the direction he'd last seen Claire. "Claire! Santiago, aid me." Blood sprayed across his face; this time not his own. Tears stained his cheeks, not from any sorrow. He cried with the effort of going beyond his selfish need to collapse and deny the force pushing him into the grave, to simply keep moving.

This was what Lupaa had encountered in the desert. It had torn the refugees into tiny pieces. For an instant, he revisited the arm hanging from the cactus, the lumps of unidentifiable flesh. It was doing the same to them. But Lupaa had shown him the key to survival. He fumbled for the words Lupaa used.

Claire. He had to reach her.

He opened his eyes to judge the distance, and it was like the evil foulness latched onto him. It stole everything. Family. Honor. Memory. He couldn't picture Beatriz's face. Couldn't remember Salvador's smile. Couldn't recall Julian's wisdom. He cried out as something ripped into him. Cried again as he felt its joy at sucking out his life—his essence.

Ramiro closed his eyes. "San Martin, soldier to soldier, hear me."

The evil lessened enough that he could lift his head, panting with the pain. He dragged his body toward where he'd last seen Claire, around the Northern soldiers. "Santiago, help me. San Martin, spare me." The prayer acted as a shield, sparing him from the violence to his body, though not the punishment of his mind. Over and over, he chanted it as he crawled through things he'd rather not think about and as the screaming rose around him to become something inhuman.

He managed to find his way, taking quick glimpses of his surroundings. He didn't dare stop or the dark pressure would never let him move again. At last he touched Claire, recognizing her by the braid, drawing her into his arms. A risked glimpse showed blood everywhere as if splashed from buckets. The sun shone high above, but here the air was full of shadows, darkened like a fierce and silent storm raged. Jorga lay nearby with an arrow shaft rising from her body.

He sobbed like a child, robbed of strength. He couldn't tell whether Claire breathed. She hung silent and limp in his arms. Cuts and slices bled from skin as ripped as his own. He shook her, but her eyes didn't flutter. The evil pressed down as if sensing his resistance.

"Santiago, help us. San Martin, spare us."

The foul sense turned to innumerable hands touching his skin from all directions, filling him with revulsion. The very air seemed to solidify into a malevolent mist, full of hatred and loathing. It sought to make him lose his lifeline and fall. With all his effort, he fumbled into it, managing to pull Jorga closer. He hadn't the strength to lift her.

It didn't seem possible to feel worse, but there was no way he could locate Errol or discover if Bromisto were near. Failure clawed at him, inviting him to give in and stop fighting.

"Santiago, help us. San Martin, spare us. Let me die. Let it be over."

He cleaved to his litany of prayer even as he buried his face in Claire's neck and clung to her like a lifeline in quicksand.

CHAPTER 27

Julian stood at the open gates of Crueses as the sun rose and watched the column approach that contained all that remained of his people. It spilled across the width of the road and onto the sand beyond, trailing back to vanish in the distance, like a snake's tail. Juan's estimate of their arrival had been off, pushed back until morning, but not even the scouting reports that it would be hours yet could deter Julian. He'd waited all night for them here while Juan sulked at the palace. An aching back and tired eyes and feet made an easy trade-off for the sight of the organized column. A tear stood in Julian's eye to see it outlined against the sun. There could be nothing more beautiful.

A cool breeze touched his face. The sort of breeze that brought the rains and made it possible for Crueses and Suseph to be the grain basket of the *ciudades-estado*. A breeze generated by the mountains east of here and that very seldom reached Colina Hermosa.

The gates he stood beside were not bronze like Colina Hermosa's but sturdy timbers. The wall of Crueses stood a good ten feet shorter, nor was it as wide. It contained no barracks or storage rooms sheltered within the depths of its stone. No staircase led to the top, only plain ladders. But the blocks of stone were thick and the mortar solid and in good repair. Both younger and smaller than Colina Hermosa, Crueses lacked the same strength, but pride ran through its people—as evidenced by so many of them here to receive their homeless kin.

The military had spread the word of their arrival and the people of Crueses had responded. All night Julian had received offers of food and shelter for his citizens. The generosity of their spirit renewed his belief in all that was good and kind, counteracting how *Alcalde* Juan and *Alcalde* Ramón had soured it.

Now, he scanned the front of the column of refugees, checking first the only carriage in sight, but it contained naught but white-headed, elderly passengers. Next his eyes roved to the horses, to see them overloaded with children and babies, many of them waving in joy. Finally, he picked out a tall black mantilla among the people afoot, and saw Beatriz's familiar figure. Only she would wear her full dress of black mourning in this heat.

He'd planned to make a stately walk out to meet them in accordance with his station. Instead, his feet broke into a run. Tears blurred the sight as the mantilla stopped, then, too, darted ahead of the rest of the column.

They met in the middle. Beatriz threw herself into his arms.

"*Mi amor.*" He clasped her tight, and a piece of the world clicked back into place—something he hadn't known was missing made right. He kissed her hair, then her lips when she raised her head. She looked barely touched by the long journey, with only some dust in the folds of her dress and in her hair, and a faint shine of perspiration. Trust Beatriz to be well looked after by a flood of servants. She'd always had an effortless way of inspiring devotion.

"Always and forever," she sighed, then wiped at her eyes and laughed at the same time. "It went well with you?"

"The military of Crueses goes with me. We leave for Aveston within the hour. And you? You look well. You were walking."

Her chin came up. "I have strength."

He nodded, hearing all he needed. Of course, she would walk so the weak and infirm could ride. He put an arm around her as they strolled leisurely toward the slowly moving column.

"Ramiro?" she asked, a note of hope in her voice. "I know your answer, but my heart can't help hoping this once I am wrong and he is here."

"No. As you suspected. He was not. And you have not heard from him?"

"Not a word. He is with the girl." Beatriz touched forehead, heart, liver, and spleen in quick succession, her face suddenly pale. "Let him be well."

"I'm sure he is," Julian said hastily. He prayed it were so and that Ramiro stayed out of this mess and in the swamp where he would be safe. Better there than about to go into battle here. He quickly turned to the present. "The *alcaldes* opposed me as we supposed. I won their military to my side. We managed to make contact inside Aveston. They will be ready to fight with us. Our numbers should be enough."

"Then they do have messenger birds," Beatriz mused, before focusing and tugging his jacket. "You do not need to go. You are no captain and no fighter."

A smile crept across his face. *So predictable.* Her answer was as certain as the sun. "Do you imagine they'll put me in the front wave, *mi amor*? No, I stay well back out of the way. I am there to support, and to coordinate between our military and Crueses'. I am the face both sides know." Before she could speak, he held up his right hand. "This I swear to Santiago: I will do no fighting. Does that satisfy you? I am the glorified figurehead."

Her eyes flashed, though her words were mild, letting him know she was not satisfied inside. "The election is in three days. I did what I could on the journey here, but the people need to see you."

He had no doubt she had done much—much more than he would have bothered to do toward winning votes. The people would not have forgotten Lugo's death or the false note left on his body. They could not be won back by showing himself, nor did he have the heart to try. Other things than the election for *alcalde* were on his mind—like surviving. "They will have to make do with you. That is the better bargain in any case." He kissed her cheek. "They would much rather look at the cactus rose than the thorn."

She bristled, but glowed. Her hand slipped into his, chilly as always, but firm. "You change the subject. What else do I need to know of Crueses?"

"Juan intends to accept the Northern terms if the enemy—when, I should say—when they make it here."

She stopped. "That is insane."

"He plans to use our people as the blood sacrifice."

Now, ferocity overspread her features. The look he'd seen so often when their sons were young and Beatriz believed them shorted or ill-treated. It sent a painful twinge through him as he thought of Salvador, remembering his loss anew, like the first time. Always it was close to his thoughts and yet always seeming a surprise and shock each time he remembered his son's death.

Julian spoke first, cutting short the painful memory. "The people of Crueses do not know the Northern terms. It has been withheld from them."

Ferocity turned to cunning as her features smoothed into her calculating expression. "That can be rectified." Her mantilla bobbed as she nodded.

"I supposed it a cause best left to you."

"You are correct, husband. Leave it to me. I will

change this *ciudad-estado* and have it done before you return."

His love for her soared. No one understood like Beatriz. They were like a matched set of horses in every way—perfect complements of each other. And with one stroke, he'd given his wife something to occupy her and keep her from running after him or trying to hide among the soldiers. This gave her a reason to stay put, far from the danger. He'd have no more of her in the hands of the Northerners. That day had killed him. Aloud, he said, "Leave Juan intact. It is no time to be making such a change."

"I wouldn't think of it. To remove a sitting *alcalde*? It isn't done! As you should know." Like lightning, she changed the subject back to what was really on her mind. "One speech before you go. To drum up the support again. It wouldn't take much to tilt the vote back to you."

"I have more important things to do—like spend the short time I'm allowed with my wife. Let sleeping dogs lie, *mi amor*. It will be as it will be."

She went still against his side as they resumed walking toward their people, obedient to drop the subject, but ready to bring it up again at his first sign of weakening. He'd not heard the last from her on this topic. "Speaking of dogs, I have good news," she said. "When we merged with the second camp, I found Maria and my dogs! Pietro will be so happy to see his daddy again. I left him to amuse the children, but I'll fetch him before you go."

Julian rolled his eyes, making sure she couldn't see. "Lovely. I can't wait." He would rather she grilled him about the vote again. A quick kiss, then he put on his public face, straightening his back, ready to meet the *concejales* and *pelotón* captains among those coming forward to greet them.

A small cheer rose from his people at his arrival, tired faces brightening. It rippled back down the column. He acknowledged it with a raised hand, then turned to the city leaders.

"*Capitáns*, we leave within the hour for Aveston to take on the Northerners with our brothers from Crueses. Please prepare yourselves. *Concejales*, I leave you in charge again."

The captains fairly glowed at his short instructions. They stood taller, bold lights appearing in their eyes. "Hi-ya, *Alcalde*," they answered.

In contrast, the *concejales* couldn't look more shocked. Some sputtered, others were left completely speechless, mouths hanging open.

"You would leave us defenseless?" Antonio sputtered. He'd put aside his butcher's apron but still wore the sturdy work clothes beneath, showing bloodstains from his profession on the sleeves. "We've only just arrived. Let us settle first, Julian."

"There is no time if we are to surprise the Northerners," Julian answered. "I leave the gate and wall guards of both cities for your defense. It should be all you need. This is our chance to strike a real blow against a significant portion of their troops. It may not be decisive, but we have rallied Crueses and Aveston. I had no time to reach Suseph. Perhaps this battle can draw the military of the rest of the *ciudades-estado* to the fight." It could be their only chance to do so. "Win or lose, I would have us go down fighting."

"The council must meet and vote," Osmundo argued. "You cannot just make these decisions and take our troops—"

"But I can." Julian turned his back. "Have you forgotten because I've listened to you and heeded your council that in war the *pelotónes* report directly to me? For three more days, my word is law."

Beatriz squeezed his hand in approval, and Julian allowed a discrete smile. It felt good—to lead again—to pretend he had put doubts aside. To be himself with his old confidence. No, the time for doubts had passed—for the moment at least.

He hurried over more instructions. "Our people will need to be split in half. The weakest and most fragile to stay here; the strongest to walk the extra mile to Suseph. They can't all fit in this city. Is the bishop here?"

"In our carriage," Beatriz said, looking that way.

"The priests can help organize, but you *concejales* must be the brave face to inspire the people." The councilors nodded along. They might not like his plans, or him personally, but they weren't blind to wisdom when they heard it. "Are all the *pelotónes* gathered?"

"We still lack Captain Gonzalo's unit," an officer said. "They are a day behind us."

"We leave without them. They can catch up as they may." Julian turned to Cruesos to lead them inside. The course for good or ill was set—for now—and only the saints could foresee the outcome.

CHAPTER 28

"Santiago, save us! San Martin, spare us!" The screams had seemed to go on forever, long past Ramiro's rational belief that a person could exist in such agony. But it was an eternity after they stopped before the sense of foul taint had retreated, leaving fresh air to tease his skin. Gone was the sense of worthlessness, the hopeless despair. The evil.

A trick to make him let down his guard.

"Santiago, save us." He held tight to his mantra until the trill of birdsong broke the silence. A sound so sweet and so pure, it shocked him into forgetting the prayer he'd repeated for an eternity. Only then did pain rush in to fill the void. Cuts and slashes covered his body. Without looking, he knew the wound across his leg would require stitching—an injury caused by . . . nothing tangible.

Saints.

He shivered and retched, bringing up nothing. A second heave called attention to the dryness in his mouth, his tongue practically cleaving to the roof of his mouth, as if he was on a training exercise and had gone a day without water.

"What . . . what was that?" His mouth reacted slowly like he'd forgotten how to speak other words. When he tried to move, he found his hand clamped around his medallion of San Martin in a grip so tight it hurt to twitch his fingers. The metal cut into his skin. Sweat gone cold and something stickier covered his body, chilling him. His eyelids fluttered, letting in piercing brightness. His whole body responded with agonizing slowness. Lessons from his training took over.

Take stock of the situation.

His eyes focused first on the distance. Trees. Sky. A sun just above the horizon. Somewhere deep his brain suggested sluggishly that not much time had passed. Other than that he found no threats. No enemies. Just pain.

His wounds throbbed—the ones inflicted by the Northern sword no different than the mysterious injuries that had appeared out of thin air. Blood covered every inch of him. Driven into his clothing, his skin, his hair. Some of it was his own, but most belonged to others. He smelled the metallic taste of it every time he breathed. The ground around him was puddled with it . . . and chunks of other . . . things he refused to identify. Things that had been the Northern soldiers.

Claire lay across his lap, her hair matted to her scalp with the blood that covered every inch of her as well. He blinked and fumbled for her, realizing her chest moved in even breaths before his hands responded to his commands. Gashes and lacerations marred her skin, injuries identical to his own: hand, leg—but the blood covering everything made it impossible to tell how deep they went.

He shook her. "Claire. Claire!"

No response.

Jorga lay against his legs in the same condition, with one addition: an arrow stood from her thigh. She, too, breathed, if more shallowly and broken. He could see no signs of Errol, but then he feared to look too closely at the devastation around him.

They needed water and lots of it. Medical supplies. A way to clean their wounds. And most of all came a burning desire to flee, to escape this spot and never come back—if he could stand. Given the rubbery weakness of the rest of him, getting his legs to take his weight seemed doubtful.

He gathered Claire to his chest and held her close, trying to take in the smell of her. But there was only the scent of blood, sickening and fetid. Death.

"Claire!" Her eyelids fluttered.

She mumbled so low he had to lean closer. "I . . . hurt."

Something snapped inside him, allowing panic to flood in.

"Bromisto!" he screamed, hoping against hope

the boy could hear and come to their aid. Most likely the boy was in no better shape than they, or had fled, like back when he'd first encountered the witches. "Bromisto!"

The boy could be dead. How far had that evil reached? Had it gotten to Bromisto, the horses?

Saints . . . "Sancha."

Ramiro put two fingers in his mouth, heedless of the blood covering them, and whistled, loud and shrill.

"A demon" Errol had said. "Dal" had been the Northerners' cries. They hadn't sounded like ones pleading for mercy, but rather had pronounced the name in fear. The feel—the reek—of whatever had happened had been the same as when Claire had sung her song of Dal for the Northern army. Just such a sense of impending doom . . . of malign intent had appeared then, too.

It was not coincidence.

None of that mattered. Not when Claire could be dying.

He scooted Jorga off, then forced his legs to gather under him, ignoring the screaming pain as he lifted with his knees. His body tilted as he tried to stand holding Claire, corrected, and made it upright. He stood swaying, unsure where to go or what to do. That's when he noticed it.

The blood spatters, lumps of flesh, and puddles made a perfect circle in the clearing. It missed the end of the barn, encompassed several trees, and had a clear edge around the ring, as if drawn by a giant finger in the sky. Goosebumps rose over his skin.

"The house," a voice croaked.

Ramiro glanced down to see Jorga's eyes open. The arrow had struck the middle of her thigh, missing the bigger vessels on the inside. "Take her to my house."

"There were more soldiers there." He was in no shape for a fight, couldn't remember where he'd even dropped his sword. Instead, he looked toward the top of the valley and the hill where they'd left Bromisto and their supplies. His legs trembled even considering the idea of going uphill.

The bushes crackled, and he tried to brace himself, but only ended up staggering backward and nearly losing Claire. Branches pushed aside, and Sancha cantered to the edge of the blood-spattered clearing—Bromisto on her back. The boy gripped the reins of the second horse, drawing her along behind despite the mare's obvious reluctance.

As the boy slid down, Ramiro tottered toward them, trying to lay Claire across Sancha in the boy's place. He managed it just before his legs gave out. He groaned and held on to the mare, just breathing and taking in the smell of dusty horseflesh, clean and not coated with blood.

Sancha butted him so she could bring her soft nose to his face, sniffling and nosing at his head, saying quite clearly in the way of horses, "There you are. What nonsense do I have to rescue you from this time?" He put his arms around her neck and just held on.

Bromisto stood at his side, reaching out to touch Ramiro's clothes, then jerking back his hand as if he thought better of it. The reins of Claire's horse were still in his hand, and the animal pulled against them, trying to escape. Bromisto held firm, even as his eyes rounded in astonishment as he took in the carnage, his face pale. "What happened? What is this?" His voice rose as shock turned to panic.

Ramiro had no answer other than to release Sancha. "It's over. Where can we take them? They need a healer."

"The house," Jorga croaked again.

Irritation bloomed at her stubbornness. "I told you—there are soldiers there. We've got to get away before they find us." Again came the urge to flee—to escape before whatever struck them and shredded human flesh returned.

"Nobody's there," Bromisto said eagerly. "When the screaming started, they ran in your direction. I thought the screaming meant the *sirenas* took care of them. Did they do this?"

"No," Ramiro said. "It was... something else." He didn't want to frighten the boy more, and he hadn't a clear idea of what to tell Bromisto if he did speak out. "The extra soldiers must be dead then." Maybe they *should* go to the house. There would be water there, supplies.

"Stay here," he told the boy. He didn't want Bromisto walking in the puddles of blood. He waded back in alone, and made it to Jorga, bending down a little too fast as his knees folded at the last instant. The wound across his thigh blazed, and for a minute, the world spun. When it righted, he got his arms around the old lady. "Hold on to my neck," he instructed. "This is going to hurt both of us."

"Errol," she panted in his ear as he lifted. She felt like a feather compared to Claire, all skin and bones. He tried to avoid the arrow, but brushed it, and she screamed.

"One thing at a time," he managed to gasp. Bromisto helped settle Jorga across the other horse. Despite his clumsiness with the arrow, she remained conscious, even sitting upright. The only concession she made to the agony she must be suffering was to clamp her hands around the arrow as if to hold it stationary.

"Errol." For once, her words sounded more like an entreaty than a command.

"I'll look." He had no hope of success, but Jorga wouldn't stop or calm until he did. Once more, he forged into the puddles of blood, skirting around chunks of flesh, trying not to see, yet unable to avoid it. A glint of metal caught his eye—a button. Metal was about the sole thing that remained identifiable. Even the leather armor had been shredded. The Northerners' weapons lay where they had fallen. Ramiro touched none of it.

Unlike the last time this happened in the desert, the body parts were too small to tell apart. He couldn't even pick out the black-and-yellow of their uniforms—not under all the blood.

As he approached the last spot he'd seen the boy, Jorga kept him under sharp surveillance. Ramiro feared to see something he *did* recognize as his face would surely give it away to Jorga. The boy wouldn't know to petition the saints for their protection. It was only luck Ramiro remembered how Lupaa survived. There was no way Errol could be alive. Nothing moved here. Even carrion birds seemed too frightened to gather.

His toe caught on a protrusion, and he looked down to recognize his sword, lying atop the top of a boot with a square chunk of leg still inside.

He retched, gagging again with the horror. Even the Northerners hadn't deserved that kind of death.

After a deep breath, he steeled himself to reach for the blade. It had done no good here against whatever attacked them, but he couldn't leave it. His parents had gifted it to him before his first ride.

A large shape rose from the ground to his left. His heart seized. Ramiro shouted and jumped, but not before gripping the hilt of his sword securely. He held it before him as he turned.

Errol scrubbed at blood encrusting his face. "Demon."

The kid looked to be uninjured. Despite being in nearly the center of the circle, he had less blood covering him. Most of his front was clean, like the blood couldn't penetrate to him in his hunched position. Ramiro gasped in relief, before lowering the sword and shaking his head. "Can't you say anything else? How are you alive?"

"The Great Goddess shields children and the simpleminded," Jorga said. "So why are we still alive?"

Ramiro's gut tightened, unsure whether to be awed or frightened. "A miracle."

CHAPTER 29

When Claire woke, it felt like she'd come home. A familiar low ceiling and loft structure rose over her head. The building had the same back wall built into a hillside, lacking windows. She wanted to snuggle down in contentment, but she blinked groggily and realized the furniture was darker and heavier. The kitchen, while in the same spot, was arranged differently. Not home, but something similar. They must be inside her grandmother's house.

She sat slumped in a chair covered with a stiff tan fabric and plump stuffing. Unlike her mother's rocking chair, it didn't stir as she sat up. A white cloth bandage circled her hand. Another had been wrapped around her upper leg. The flesh under the wrapping throbbed dully in time with her slow heartbeat. A sharper throbbing came from the side of her head and a careful touch found a large lump. She must have struck it on something. Innumerable small cuts and slices marked her skin in other places. The bandages formed the only clean places on her body. The rest of her seemed to be covered in drying blood.

Blood!

Ugh. She wanted to claw it off her face, her body, with her fingernails, but they were already clogged with the sickening substance. It tightened her skin as it dried, clinging more firmly, like a layer of repulsive mud. As much as she wanted to plunge into a tub of water, somehow, she couldn't drum up the effort to move. It took all her strength simply to lie there. The thought of cleaning off the blood exhausted her. Her head was a mass of fog, unable to think clearly. She felt sucked dry of decisiveness.

The bump on her head. It must be affecting her. How had she gotten it?

She stared at herself, trying to remember.

She'd broken loose from her grandmother and run to Ramiro's rescue to Sing the Hornet Tune. Before she could start, an arrow was aimed at her. Jorga pushed her aside as the arrow flew and . . . it was dark after that.

Yelling interrupted her thoughts, and Claire looked up. Jorga lay stretched across the kitchen table, propped on her elbows. Ramiro and Bromisto stood over her, their backs to her. Bromisto looked a decided shade of green and kept hiding his eyes behind his hand. Ramiro had left his own injuries unattended, except for a white bandage around his thigh in the same spot as her own injury; he limped when he moved farther down the table. An older boy with fair hair crouched under the table with his hands over his ears—it must be Errol. Ramiro and her grandmother were splattered with the same gore that covered her. The only clean parts were their hands. Claire rubbed her eyes in disbelief. An arrow with black feather fletching stood up from her grandmother's leg.

That's where the arrow had gone.

Her grandmother had taken the wound meant for her.

Claire tried to sit up, to speak to them, but she felt so comfortable lying in the chair. It was such an effort to join them. Maybe in a little bit. A tiny part of her knew she should be more worried, but that part could wait just fifteen more minutes.

"Would you hold still?" Ramiro shouted again. "It's not like I know what I'm doing, and you're making it harder! I should be helping Claire, not wrestling with you!"

"I thought men were supposed to know everything," Jorga snapped, jerking and nearly upsetting the bowl of water next to her. "Ow! By the Song, don't move it that way. The other way! My granddaughter just needs rest now. She's in a natural sleep, not unconscious any longer. I told you she'll be fine. Now pay attention! Do I have to do it myself?"

"Be my guest." Ramiro flung up his hands. "I didn't train with Alvito on the healer skills and now I remember why—too many cranky patients who want to be their own healers."

Jorga lay back, letting her head rest against the wooden tabletop. "Leave it. It's too deep to pull out. It needs to be cut free."

"Then it's beyond me," Ramiro said. "I'd be as likely to make you bleed out as save you."

That sent a pang of concern through Claire. She lifted her hand weakly, but let it drop back down—just another few minutes. Then she'd go to them.

"My sister is a healer," Bromisto said, speaking for the first time. "Or she's training to be one. Elo hasn't handled anything like this, but her teacher could do it."

Jorga's face was set with pain, teeth bared in a grimace. "The Women of the Song have healers."

"Are they closer than the swamp village?" Ramiro asked. "Which one can you reach the quickest because your life might depend on it? Not to mention we're going to have to drag you through the swamp to find them. It's not bleeding much now, but the strain of travel will surely do more damage. Unless—can you 'speak' to one of your kind and have them come here?"

She shook her head. "Errol," Jorga called. "Mother needs you." She had to repeat the call three times before the tall boy would come out from under the table. When he did, he held on to her hand like he would never let go.

"What, Momma?" He stared into the kitchen above her shoulder.

"Which direction? To our kind or the man village? Should we try and Speak for help?"

He ducked his head and hunched his shoulders. "I don't want you to die, Momma."

Her breath hitched in with a hiss. "Is it certain?"

He wiggled unhappily as if he were five instead of fifteen. His mouth turned down in a frown and his eyebrows knit in concentration. Claire stared, suddenly more unwilling to break up this strange conversation from interest instead of lack of desire. Dread pulled at her. She sensed an end coming and didn't want to face it.

"Where should I go to survive the arrow?" Jorga asked him.

"The man village."

She sat back again, but limply as if defeated, and idly stroked Errol's hand. "Then that's what we do."

"You take his word?" Ramiro asked. "What *is* Errol?"

Claire wanted the answer to that also. Some of the fogginess in her head was starting to lift—her normal desire to be involved returning. She wanted to know more about Errol, too. Even from her limited observation of him, she found her uncle odd. Not like any of the people she'd ever met.

Jorga sighed and turned to look at Claire, the only one to notice she shammed sleep. Claire realized the words were intended for her. "He's a boy. A very special boy. When Women of the Song have male children, they are different. Deaf to magic, they can see more than others—like parts of the future. They keep us connected to the world and to each other. That's how I knew to go to Rosemund's and wait."

"Seers? Prophets?" Ramiro frowned. "It's like the religious texts are coming to life. So he could know about the Northerners—could confirm that they are a threat to you?"

"If asked the right questions—yes. Errol and the others don't volunteer information, or at least, not often."

"He said 'demon,'" Ramiro said. "What does that mean, Errol?"

The boy released Jorga's hand and darted back under the table, putting his hands back over his ears.

Jorga shook her head. "Likely he doesn't know. And he won't speak to you anyway."

Claire almost pushed herself out of the chair to ask if Errol would speak to her, but held her place. Demon? She had missed something while knocked out. If the lump on her head came from when Jorga thrust her from the arrow, what had caused her other injuries?

"I think we should try," Ramiro insisted. "Ask him."

Jorga's face went flat. "You should attend to your wounds. There's a stream behind the chicken shed. Go clean up. Claire will wake up soon. She can help me in here."

Ramiro glanced in her direction, and Claire quickly shut her eyes before he could see her awake. It might be easier to ask what had happened, but her brain felt muddled. She need more time to think—for the fog to finish clearing.

Ramiro lowered his voice. "Look, we need to figure out what that *thing* was. It can kill without weapons or . . . a body. Kill in large numbers. I felt it when Claire sang at the Northern army—a darkness. Now it's back. Whatever it is, I need to warn my father. My people have to know about this—especially if it's what I think it is."

The sinking dread grew in Claire. She didn't understand it all, but this is what she feared: Ramiro would be compelled to return home. A sob stuck in her throat. He would leave her.

So many times, it had seemed he was on the verge of saying something to her—of taking her hand—of kissing her—of declaring that his feelings matched her own. Heat flooded her at the thought. But every time he retreated. And for the last day, he'd seemed extra distant. He avoided her. She knew his situation weighed on his mind and had been patient. Had given him space, afraid to push and break the friendship they'd built.

Being around Fronilde and hearing her story of how Salvador had courted her, Claire realized she couldn't take the lead. His culture believed a hundred percent this was a male role. To make him comfortable, she could wait. Besides, if she pushed he might remember his people considered her a witch and back away.

Now, the world had done it for her.

"Just like a man!" Jorga was saying. "I have my own people to warn!"

Bromisto backed toward the door as the anger level rose. "Maybe I'll just go find that stream for you."

"Have you forgotten who just pulled you out of there and saved your life," Ramiro snapped at Jorga as if he hadn't heard the boy. He pointed to Errol. "But you go ahead and do what you want! Though your kind already have a warning system. I'm sure they already know the danger. But then, your kind doesn't care about anyone else. You've made it abundantly clear. I'll do what's right. You do what's easy!"

Claire cried out as her wounds stretched when she stood and the pounding in her head shot up in volume. This conflict between them tore her apart. She wanted to love them both. "Stop! Just stop! Every time you go back to this fighting! I can't stand it!" Her hands clenched at her side. Tears threatened and she pushed them back—just. "You're the only family I have. Stop fighting."

She took a deep breath. "You're both right. For shame, Grandmother, it sounds like Ramiro has saved us both—again. He's right that we need to know what's caused this." She held out her bandaged fist. "But Ramiro, we need to warn everyone—not just your people. Grandmother, ask Errol. See if he can tell us more."

Both had the grace to look ashamed of themselves. Ramiro limped over and tried to soothe her and put her back in the chair, but this time, she evaded *him*. She'd sat there too long, listening and letting her injuries make her weak. It was time to be back in the thick of it.

Claire made them tell her what she missed, growing more concerned with each recount of the taint, the evil presence that had taken out a unit of seasoned warriors and almost killed them.

It took much longer to coax Errol out a second time. While Claire tried to help, Ramiro went to the stream to wash up and returned as they were just getting Errol from under the table. Claire had to join Ramiro and Bromisto in being banished to the loft, leaving mother and son alone—or as alone as possible in the small house. Claire crouched under the low roof and tried to settle in to listen next to Ramiro, reaching for him, but he waved the boy to settle between them. She frowned and fingered the lump on her head. Was his snub accidental or was he already retreating? Cold grew in her chest.

As each question came, Errol stared at the floor, shaking his head and twisting his hands together, refusing to say a word.

"It's not working," Jorga said with a huff. "He doesn't know or he's too scared to say. He gets like this. Sometimes it's best to wait for him to be ready. It's all right, Errol. Momma isn't mad at you."

Claire found herself sliding down the loft ladder that had been worn smooth from years of such use. "Let me try." She walked very slowly to the table, holding out her unbandaged hand. "Errol, you're my uncle," she said in a gentle voice. "Have you ever been an uncle before?"

For a second, his eyes flickered over hers, and she had the impression of deep interest. Then his eyes went back to the floor. His hair was lighter than hers, almost white. His eyes had the light blue of a summer morning. A head taller, he acted years younger.

"I've never been a niece before either. You know something hurt me and your momma. We need to know what it was. Can you help?" She held very still, afraid to move and spook him. "Something very bad is out there. Our magic isn't big enough to stop it." Somehow she knew that to be true. "It hurt me. Hurt your momma. We need to know more about it to make sure it stays away. Can you help?"

Eyes still down, Errol took her hand, and Jorga's mouth widened in an O of surprise. Ramiro and Bromisto leaned over the loft rail in a bid to see more. Her uncle led her to the door and pointed. Claire opened it, and he took her onto the porch. The two horses crowded onto the wide area, tied to posts as if Ramiro couldn't bear to leave them in the barn.

Errol pointed to Sancha.

"You like the horses?" Claire asked, puzzled. "You want to go for a ride?"

Ramiro and the smaller boy huddled just inside the doorway, and Jorga lifted herself on her fingertips to see over them from the table.

Errol shook his head and led her closer to Sancha. He pointed again, but this time, he indicated one of the saddlebags. He let go of her hand and moved back against the wall by a window as she fumbled with the straps. Her fingers shook and it wasn't from the head wound. Everyone held their breath. She touched the leather gingerly, like it contained hordes of double-bite spiders.

Slowly, she upended the bag over the boards of the porch. Out tumbled an empty pot that had contained honey. A coil of rope followed with some other supplies. A variety of Ramiro's unworn and half-dirty clothing came from the bottom, bringing with it his scent. The smell wrapped Claire in a bubble of deliciousness that popped when a shirt spilled open and a stick rolled across the porch. She jumped back before it could reach her feet.

The Northern priest's weapon. The one that could kill with a touch. Father Telo had called it a Diviner.

Usually a yellowed white like an old bone or a tooth, it wasn't that color now. Every inch of the Diviner shone the red of fresh blood, lighter than the old stuff drying on her body.

The flesh crawled on the back of her neck. She traded looks with Ramiro and saw the same fear mirrored in his eyes. Though the color of the Diviner was flat and dead, it glowed with a menace she could almost taste. The horses whinnied uneasily and pressed back as far as their restraints allowed.

She didn't care what kind of powerful weapon it was—she just wanted it gone.

"What is it?" Jorga called in an impatient voice.

"This is what drew the attention of the darkness?" Claire asked Errol. "This led it to us?" If so, then they had only to get rid of it to be safe. It could be sunk in quicksand and banished forever. She let out a sigh of relief, but Errol was shaking his head again.

His fingers curled around the storm shutter he stood beside. "Not that. Blood. Blood calls it."

"Not it. Dal," Ramiro whispered. "It has to be."

Claire felt all too aware suddenly of the gruesome crust covering her. Jorga still bled from her arrow wound. Ramiro had neglected most of his injuries to care for theirs. She ignored her pain, but that didn't make it less. Was that enough blood to bring this Dal back?

How much power did it have? Could they stop it again?

Claire backed until the wall of the house hit her spine, and she stood beside her uncle. He made tiny whimpering sounds almost too low to hear and rocked from heel to toe. Claire ignored him.

She might have missed out on the terror that happened a few hours ago, but recalled the hatred that had come during her Song about Dal all too well. The contempt for anything living. The glee and savage joy it expressed at the ability to snuff out a life, and the anger at being unable to accomplish that yet. It seemed Dal had moved past that stage.

Well, she wasn't about to lie down and accept it.

Ramiro threw his old shirt over the blood-colored Diviner as if hiding it solved the problem.

"We need to clean up and leave this place," Claire found herself saying. "We've got people to warn." If they would believe the warning.

She gathered her courage and stepped from the wall. The separation she feared from Ramiro was coming, and there was nothing she could do to stop it. Best to meet it like a Woman of the Song.

CHAPTER 30

The guards escorted Telo and his two companions toward a wagon house with a wooden roof and no windows. The soldiers assigned to pull the vehicle leaned against the yoke tongue when it drew to a halt, apparently eager for any respite. After the guards removed the chain connecting Telo to Santabe, he stood back to let the women enter first as a guard unbolted the door. The bolt clicked again behind him.

Inside, rich earthy scents of root vegetables mingled with the dusty smell of flour. The interior of the wagon was crowded with burlap sacks piled atop one another with barely room to squeeze past them. With the door closed, the only light came through chinks in the walls and ceiling where the planks had been hastily constructed and didn't fit together well. Telo expected they'd made this hurriedly after being forced to leave most of their wagons behind at Colina Hermosa.

The light was enough to show Teresa's round form wedged in a corner, her fists held up before her face in the sort of pose amateurs believed looked threatening. In reality, the rigidness of her stance worked against her. The brawl pits had taught him well enough that one had to stay flexible, not set.

Santabe reflected that perfectly as she stood at the center of the wagon, arms at her sides, and feet shoulder-width apart, every pore depicting readiness.

Lord save me.

He might have been a match for Santabe before he lost his hand, but not now. It couldn't come to a fight if he wanted to live to fulfill the reason he came here. Good thing twelve years of religious life had taught him to put animosity aside, because even with those years of practicing forgiveness, he had difficulty putting aside the feelings that boiled up when he looked at her. She'd taken his hand, felt no remorse for the children she'd killed, and ended more lives than he could count. If anyone deserved to die, it was she. A roaring filled his ears.

With reluctance, he pushed down the burning anger and put aside thoughts of vengeance. He had a larger target than one priestess.

Justice is mine sayeth the Lord, but Telo wouldn't have minded witnessing her comedown.

Instead, he sat on a conveniently low stack of heaping sacks. The dust that rose and the hard bumps under his rear said he'd found turnips. "Put your hands down," he told Teresa, tucking the stump of his arm under his armpit. Stress seemed to make it ache more. "Nobody is attacking anyone."

"She'll kill us." Sweat ran from Teresa's hairline and too much white showed in her eyes. Telo recognized terror when he saw it.

He glanced at Santabe, seeing the cold eyes of a killer. But he believed he guessed right in this instance. "She'll do no such thing for a number of reasons. First, if she planned that, it would already be done—the moment we entered this room." Telo had no doubts on that question. Santabe was nothing if not quick to act.

Shouts rose outside. The wagon lurched into motion, and all three occupants jerked with it. Telo quickly regained his balance as the movement evened out, taking them to Aveston, city of his birth, as part of the largest army ever gathered in the desert. An army that remained intact because he'd failed to act.

"Second, we're inside," Telo continued as if no interruption had occurred outside or within. "All their executions—sacrifices—are done in daylight and outside where Dal can see." The Northerners had once paused in the process of cutting off his hand to let a cloud pass. That had been his first lesson on their way of thinking. When Santabe did nothing but glower at him hatefully, Telo decided he'd gotten that right.

"I doubt their god needs to witness all her killing," Teresa said, but she lowered her fists at last.

"Maybe not," Telo said. "But she wants to make my death lingering and painful, and most of all humiliating. That's not going to happen in here. She's willing to wait, aren't you, Santabe?"

The look she threw him was pure venom.

He pressed on, unwilling to trust his luck. "And lastly, if she kills us in here, maybe it makes her look more innocent, but maybe they take it for guilt. Remove us and she takes away the only witnesses to the blasphemy she may or may not have committed. She can't really risk it."

Santabe growled deep in her throat and then screamed, the sound one of long, drawn-out frustration. An animal caught in a trap and furious about it. "You!" she shouted. "You I will make pay as none other!"

He bowed his head to her in acceptance of her challenge. Here was one who couldn't release hate. So be it. Her stubbornness and animosity matched against his wits and faith. In effect, a reflection of her bloodthirsty god Dal against the Lord's tolerance. Those were odds he would take. His trust had kept him alive this long and brought him where he wanted to be. The big question remained how long would Ordoño keep them locked in here? Telo's plan only worked if he had access to the Northern leader.

"I don't understand what that was all about." Teresa waved at the walls. "Why did they believe you, Father? Why throw all three of us in here? All because of an earring?"

"Suspicion," Telo said. "Their society trusts no one. How could they with death the judgment for every supposed crime? Blood must be spilled. They have to find victims somewhere. How better than calling blasphemy at every turn?"

"But that doesn't answer—"

"The earring is a symbol of high rank. I simply produced Santabe's and the question became did we take it from her or did she remove it herself? I suspect either case produces the same result—in their eyes a betrayal of their god, where all betrayals bring death."

Teresa sat on her own pile of sacks. Santabe bared her teeth at him, but kept silent, eventually sinking down to a resting position as well. In the uneasy silence of an unsettled truce, they sat as the wagon swayed them along, and Telo fretted on what he could say to make Ordoño trust him again. If the Northern leader truly waited to speak to them until they reached Aveston, it might be too late.

The Northerners came for them at nightfall. Lord Ordoño didn't come alone; he brought a handful of guards and three of their priests. As the guards removed them from the wagon, Teresa glanced fearfully at him. Telo touched heart, mind, liver, and spleen, giving her a smile of reassurance, yet inside he felt no such warmth of hope.

The wagon had stopped right on the road in the middle of the army's temporary camp. Overhead, wispy cloud cover shut out the stars.

A guard set down a folding stool for Ordoño, and

the priests arranged themselves into a semicircle at his back. One man and two women, they were the oldest Northerners Telo had seen, each with gray hair and curved backs, a little shrunken from their lost youth. All three wore the sleeveless, white robes of their kinds, completely unadorned and simple, and Diviners hung from their waists. The nearest dropped a bundle wrapped in gold cloth. The sun earring of rank hung from, not one, but both their earlobes. A high rank indeed, Telo guessed. Come not for him, then, but for Santabe.

In proof, Santabe dropped to the ground, placing one knee down and the opposite hand. She bowed her head and remained that way. Telo edged away, putting a small distance from her, and Teresa followed suit, keeping place with him. He gave a brief nod of his head in respect to their age, but he owed no other fealty to the followers of their bloodthirsty god.

"Isn't it true that priests don't lie?" Ordoño asked, making Telo shift his feet, unsure whom the man spoke to. Ordoño wore the plain brown coat and breeches that Telo always saw on him, the sort that would blend in on a market day. Yet, the commanding force in Ordoño's eyes pinned him down. "Father Telo? Your kind speak the truth, even to go so far as insulting old ladies by telling them their hats are ugly . . . unless that old lady should be a rich patron. Then it is permitted to lie. Such is the way of the world."

Telo found his voice. "Some worlds perhaps. I do not see a reason for insulting ladies, no matter the amount of coins in their purses . . . or the ugliness of their hats. But when *Called*, we put honesty above all else. Even I can manage to tell the truth when asked."

Ordoño spoke a word or two to the priests behind him. One answered, then Ordoño said, "They speak our language imperfectly, and I am not much better in theirs, but I believe we understand each other. I ask, then: Why did you come back here? Did Santabe bring you for a reason of her own?"

The calm in the brown eyes facing Telo said Ordoño already knew the answer to that.

A trial, Telo reasoned, complete with judge, jury, and witness. Telo cleared his throat. "I brought her."

The three priests muttered, but Ordoño held up a hand. "For what purpose?"

"To produce a change of heart in your chest, my son."

Ordoño seemed to chew on that for a moment, then indicated Teresa. "And your companion?"

"A student of other cultures from the University of Colina Hermosa. She came to learn."

"Did she? You give me your word on that?"

"I do."

"And has there been a change of heart at the universities? The last I remember, they didn't let peasants inside their doors unless they carry a broom. Or is she not a peasant at all? Intriguing." Ordoño waved his hand as though at a fly. "But enough. That's not why we are here. Put the woman back in the wagon. She can study us another day." He followed that up in their language.

Teresa gave a muffled yip as the guards pressed her back up the steps and inside the wagon, and Telo found sweat beginning to form on the back of his neck. His words had consequences for more than just one.

A female priestess—they looked so alike it was hard to tell them apart—held up an earring Telo assumed belonged to Santabe and let off a flood of words. Santabe answered with an equally unintelligible string, keeping her head down all the while and with more humility in her voice than had ever been there before. The back and forth went on for some time before Ordoño snorted and said, "Enough. We achieve nothing with this. You see, the priests of the Children of Dal have no compunction against lying.

"Father Telo, do you confirm this woman was captured on the battlefield by your people, and stayed under duress?"

"I can confirm she was captured by *our* people and held under duress, yes."

Ordoño didn't rise to the reminder of his origin except to lift an eyebrow. He spoke to the gathering behind him, and without waiting for a reply switched languages and asked, "Can you confirm her earring was removed against her will? Consider your answer carefully."

Ordoño plucked the earring from the female priestess and walked forward with it, depositing it in Telo's hand. Like most things it seemed simple from afar, but up close complexities leaped out. The sun symbol had been created from a single piece of gold. An easy job to beat a piece of metal flat and round, except the sun's rays had also been crafted from that single piece and somehow made to project out as individual arcs. A fine work of art, proving there could be beauty even in things perverted.

Ordoño stood mere inches away. Briefly, Telo considered seizing him now and ending his quest. But six guards surrounded them, not to mention three Diviners that could finish his life in seconds. And he was not the man he was . . .

He looked at his raw stub. Like a toothache, it continued to pain him every second of every day. He was only beginning to learn the things he could no longer perform or the simple tasks made ten times more difficult. He doubted his ability to act quickly enough with one hand.

One hand.

A fact owed to Santabe. And now he held her life in that one hand. A word from him would end this trial, and end it in only one way. He could have his revenge, getting justice for many. After coming with the intention to commit the greatest sin known to mankind, what did a few lesser sins matter? They were only lies.

The stubborn streak that refused to bend rose in his heart.

"I . . . I cannot say. I was not there and did not see it myself." The memory formed clear of the sight of Santabe before she'd murdered Taps. Her hair had been chewed off, her clothing torn and dirty, all done at her own hand, but the earring had been intact. "Yet, I believe it was forcibly removed. I found it among the *Alcalde's* things in his tent." Even as Telo said the words, half of him felt sickened, but the other half soared at standing with his principles.

As the priests muttered among themselves, Ordoño took back the earring and returned to his seat. The smaller female priestess spoke at length, her eyes on Telo.

A bitter little smile crossed Ordoño's face. "I'm bid to tell you, she thanks you for speaking honestly as a representative of your god, and you've grown in their esteem, much as you may care, I'm sure. She wants to know how many days you spent with Santabe."

"Too many," Telo said before recollecting himself. "Tell her more than three, my son."

"And they all wish to know whether Santabe turned her back on Dal during that time or indicated his religion was less than glorious in any way. I'm paraphrasing of course as this is growing rather tedious. We could be here hours more until they are satisfied, but some duties can't be shirked, much as we would like." Ordoño's sharp eyes cut right through Telo. "You could have finished her, and yet you did not. Your enemy lay literally sprawled at your feet. I don't know whether to admire that or laugh in your face."

"'Blessed is the peacemaker,'" Telo quoted. "When you decide, please do tell me." He glanced at the woman near his feet. All the killings she committed from here on out were on him. Had he done the right thing? Speaking the truth could never cancel out additional deaths. His earlier pride at sticking to his principles was now tarnished and dirty. "We both know she is entirely single-minded and could never consider the ground she stands upon may be built on a fault. She is not the type to change when fortune turns the other direction. Tell them that." He thought for a moment, when a revelation hit him.

"In that way she is perhaps to be admired. Torture would never make her recant or forsake what she believes." Telo stood stunned to have found something about Santabe he envied.

"Unlike myself, you mean, who you believe would turn wherever the wind blows."

"I was thinking of myself," Telo said distractedly. "My own weakness."

Santabe shifted enough to look up at him. The hatred in her eyes had not died in the least. It mattered not a jot to her that he had saved her life. She still saw him as nothing but an unbelieving barbarian. Somehow, that constant proved an anchor point upon which Telo clung, remembering his task and why he had come here.

"No," Telo said forcefully. "She never acted contrary to her religion or scorned your Dal."

More words broke from the priests even as Ordoño considered him with open speculation. Santabe climbed to her feet with a smile wider than the cat who ate the canary. Ordoño shrugged. "They didn't understand the half of that, but then they wouldn't.

They did pick out the part important to them and have decided to reinstate our friend. Glorious days indeed," he said sarcastically.

The priests left their spot and encircled Santabe now, touching the palms of their left hands to her forehead as though in benediction.

Of all the people in this camp, Santabe spoke his language the best. She had to have spent considerable time with Ordoño. Despite Ordoño not rescuing her when he had the chance, Telo had considered her a pet project of the Northern leader. Had he been wrong? "You could have ended this with a word and ordered her reinstatement."

"Yes, and they'd have her dead the minute my back was turned. What good is a blunt tool?"

"You used me," Telo said. "You knew I wouldn't throw her to the wolves."

"I thought it fairly certain," Ordoño said. "Santabe isn't the only predictable one. Occasionally, you must work within the system. Now, shhh."

Telo followed Ordoño's gaze and saw the male priest upending the bundle of gold cloth. From out of the middle, he lifted a Diviner colored a frightening red. Santabe gasped as though stunned. Telo couldn't tell whether she were elated or petrified at the strange spectacle.

Ordoño translated as though in a trance, sending chills down Telo's spine. "They say they need all their numbers in the time to come. They found this at the site of a massacre. One of their priests torn to pieces along with twelve of my soldiers. Dal has . . . I'm not sure of the word . . . manifested, maybe? It has happened five hundred years too soon." Ordoño grimaced. "They do get funny ideas in their heads."

The Northern leader stopped translating, a light of speculation in his eye as he began calculating how to use this to his advantage. He obviously saw this as nothing more than another opportunity. Telo was not so sure. He'd never seen Santabe at a loss for words before. The goose bumps covering his skin refused to fade.

CHAPTER 31

Teresa abandoned the chink in the wall of the wagon as the guards brought Father Telo in her direction. They hustled him up the steps and through the door. She stepped back to give them room and held her breath until they left, bolting the door behind them. Telo sank on a pile of sacks, his dark skin flushed and sweaty. He slumped, hand and raw stump covering his face.

"What!" Teresa demanded. "Are they going to kill us?" She could see what went on outside perfectly well, but could hear almost nothing. Had the Northern leader given them a death sentence? She hadn't come all this way to die now. When the priest didn't respond, she shook him, panic driving away her manners. "Father! Are we done?"

Telo raised his head. "Not yet. At least, not that I know of, my child. It was about Santabe, not us. Lord forgive me, I think I just did something horrible. Yet, to do it another way would have been worse. It was a trial and I vindicated her. I told the truth and set that monster back on the world."

Relief coursed through Teresa's veins, followed quickly by compassion. She touched his shoulder. "The Lord forgives all things. You did what you felt was right. Everything happens for a reason, right?" She faltered to a stop, realizing she was babbling meaningless comfort.

"Santabe is just a minor level person in this camp," she said instead. "I think she has little influence or power from what I saw out there. It's not your task to become judge and executioner. Will this bring you closer to Ordoño? That's the true goal."

"Undoubtedly exonerating Santabe was what he wanted," Telo said slowly, his gaze locked on the hand in his lap. "It should make him happy with me."

"He wasn't what I expected," Teresa continued, thinking of the ordinary-looking man. "I thought the leader of such an army would seem more . . . well, mad. Less polite country gentleman and more maniac."

"Ordoño is what he wants people to see." The priest sat up. "He's like a mummer on a stage, showing people a false face. I have no idea what the man inside is actually like."

Teresa sat across from him, the burlap sacks compacting under her weight. "Interesting. Signs of cunning? Or just the nature of a secretive man? Some people are so private about every aspect of themselves. Others couldn't care less if their emotions are on show. The differences in people have always intrigued me. And did you notice the religious leadership didn't defer to him? Before they banished me, they didn't call him by a title, as far as I could tell. Seemed to interact with him on an equal level or perhaps considered themselves above him.

"Though Ordoño didn't defer to them either," she continued, "as say an *alcalde* like Julian Alvarado would have done with our bishop. A fascinating dynamic. I couldn't decide who was in charge." Teresa wound down, sliding into her own thoughts.

Telo looked at her for the first time. "Who was in charge? There can be no doubt. Ordoño manipulated everyone out there, without them even knowing. He walked away with exactly what he wanted. He's worse than a maniac. Saints help us, he's perfectly in control and aware of what he does, and I might be the only one who can stop him. If I can just catch him alone."

"Alone?" Teresa echoed. "Can you not talk to him around others? They wouldn't be able to understand you anyway with the language barrier."

"I'm not here to talk to him. My role *is* executioner. I'm here to kill him."

Teresa sat stunned. "But I thought . . ." What had she thought? Or had she thought on it at all? She'd just assumed he came to talk to Ordoño, remind him of his home and where he came from or something equally asinine. As if real life were a morality tale where the villain would see the side of good and repent. She had been stupid and naïve. The man she had just met was not a one-dimensional character out of a story. He had convinced an entire culture to invade another sovereign country, basically for slaves to satisfy their god. He'd burned her home, destroyed the university, because he *could* and for no other reason than his own selfish desire.

She flung morality out the window and took Father Telo's good hand. "How can I help?"

They had two days to discuss it along with what had happened with the scene outside the wagon, as no one came near them except to bring them food and water. They weren't taken out for necessity trips either, left instead with an embarrassingly, not-private chamber pot. A fact that would have had Teresa in fits, if she weren't so petrified. She fretted more with each passing hour as they drew steadily nearer to Aveston, stopping each night to camp. None of the soldiers spoke their language and wouldn't have answered questions if they did understand them, making it impossible to receive new information.

And the old was disturbing enough.

Teresa couldn't make heads or tails of the story Father Telo told her of the Diviner turning red or Dal manifesting. Her opinion held that none of the religious happenings mattered. It would neither slow nor stop the army, so it shouldn't be a worry, while Telo argued that understanding it might be important. She didn't want to hurt his feelings by saying she found all religions more myth than fact—ancient history that had little to do with the world today, except in the political pull that religious leaders and the churches exerted. But he clearly saw that she didn't buy into his theories, and so they agreed to disagree and let the subject drop—mostly. Every now and then one of them would prod at it like a sore tooth.

If anything, it broke up the monotony of terror.

The wide chinks in the wagon planking allowed them a view of the camp, causing Telo to remark that he didn't remember so much activity when here before. It also revealed that no guards watched their wagon. What would be the point? The flimsy construction would allow them to break free at any time, but with the plan incomplete, they had no reason to go and every reason to stay.

Teresa paced or tried to. They'd piled most of the supply sacks into the corners to give them more space, but the tight quarters restricted her to a few steps. "What if we made a racket? They'd notice us then."

Father Telo just stared at her, a half-finished turnip in his hand. "They'll come in their time, my child. The Lord didn't send me here to let me lack for opportunities."

"What if we have to make our opportunity?" She sighed and peered out a crack. The army had stopped to camp and it wasn't dark yet. Why weren't they more in a hurry? It worried her, just as everything did lately.

A door rattle gave them all the warning they got before four guards entered, making the living quarters unbearably tight. One seized her under the arm, pulling her along. His gesture to follow was more comprehensible than his words.

They were bustled through the camp with Teresa unable to catch more than snatches of it. A noise buzzed in her ears and everything faded to a blur as they passed, terror rising steadily in her breast and blotting all else out. She wasn't ready to die. Yet, for some reason, her brain could find no other reason for their abrupt removal.

The guards stopped them at the end of a long line of her countrymen—or fellow citizens, rather—Teresa saw men, women, and children in the queue of about twenty.

"Father, help us." The woman next to them sobbed, grabbing Father Telo's sleeve. She dropped to her knees in a posture of begging. "Save us."

That's when Teresa saw the front of the line.

A thick carpet, the dimension of a large room, had been unrolled upon the sand. A single table and chair rested in the middle of it. A priest in a white robe stood at the edge, holding a Diviner. He wore no earrings of rank. This was a Northerner she'd never seen before. As Teresa watched, he touched the Diviner to an elderly man with skin burnt almost black from too much time in the sun—most likely a farmer. The man seized, muscles tight, then dropped into the waiting arms of two guards, who dragged his corpse away. The guards behind pushed forward the next person.

A line of execution.

Teresa's heart tried to start out of her chest. She gasped, eyesight closing in to a foot around her, as if by doing so it could shut out the truth. Dimly, she heard Telo speaking, trying to move to the front of the line, and guards pushing him back none too gently, forcing him to keep his place at the back.

The people around her clung to Father Telo, those farther ahead, called out to him. The line shuffled ahead, more and more innocent people going under the Diviner and carried off like empty sacks. Father Telo spoke the words for the dying, his voice rising above the weeping and wailing around them:

> *Oh Lord, be gracious to me;*
> *Oh Lord, have mercy on me;*
> *Forgive my sins;*
> *Santiago, do not abandon me;*
> *Oh Lord, into thy hands I commend my*
> *   spirit.*
> *Santiago, I entrust my soul to thou, do thou*
> *   save it for me.*

Teresa fastened on the numbers between her and the Diviner. Fifteen. Fourteen. Her legs didn't want to bear her up. *Oh Saints*. It couldn't end like this.

Salvador and Gomez. Alvito. All taken. Now her turn. She couldn't bear to watch anymore.

Someone cleared their throat. The sound so simple and calm in the midst of panic. Teresa turned. Ordoño stood, polishing an apple against his brown coat.

"Stop this. Stop this now." Father Telo's face was clenched in anger.

"I could if given a reason." Ordoño held the apple up to the bright sunlight.

"It is the right thing to do," Telo snapped. "For once in your life, do what is right."

"That's not a good enough reason. I only send them to their precious afterlife a bit sooner. They should thank me."

The guards had to restrain Telo as he lunged at the Northern leader. "Stop this sideshow! You've proven you hold our lives in your hands!"

Teresa glanced ahead. Thirteen. A young girl of less than twenty winters was next. This was getting them nowhere. "The army," she stammered. "An army like this succeeds partly from instilling fear, forcing surrender. Let them go so they can help with that. Let the last of these people go and they'll take their terror with them. Spread it to their homes."

"Hmm," Ordoño mused, chewing. "Possibly." The young girl died.

Twelve.

"Do you want cities under your power or burnt out husks like Zapata and Colina Hermosa?" Teresa sobbed. "Fewer of your soldiers would have to die in battle. Let them go!" The words sickened her even as she spoke them. Here she was, giving him clues to make his army more efficient, just to save her skin.

Ordoño snapped his fingers and guards sprang to his side. He handed the nearest his half-eaten apple and waved to the priest up front. The Diviner in the priest's hand went back to his belt. "A decent reason," Ordoño said. "One I gave to Santabe when she ordered this yesterday. I've told my men to release the hostages after we arrive at Aveston and not before. We wouldn't want them carrying news."

At the mention of Santabe, Telo seemed to shrink, drawing inward and closing off. Teresa scrubbed at her face, brushing off tears of relief. She'd saved some of these people. This time at least. "And us?"

"Give me a reason not to let Santabe have you."

"Easy enough," Telo growled. "*Acorraloar*. You brought us here to see this as a lesson. You're selfish enough to save our lives just to have opponents for your game."

"A lesson, tsh—do you take me for a teacher? Though it is interesting to view a person so convinced his way is best. It's like pinning an ant down by one leg and watching it struggle. But even that gets tiresome after a while." Ordoño sighed. "I did leave the pieces as they lay when we were so rudely interrupted. I suppose I could send for you the next time I'm bored."

Teresa watched her countrymen being led off by the guards—some had to be carried due to emotional collapse. "Bored? Is that what this was?"

"You want a lesson?" Ordoño said to them, his eyes cold. He pointed at the prisoners. "Listen and learn. Money can buy only so many spies. Clemency can buy so many more. To the ones who bring me useful information, it can spare their family. I've given them the incentive to help me. Santabe is right: Love makes you all weak."

The wind went out of Teresa. She hadn't saved these people—it had been his plan to let some live all the time.

"And speaking of weak," Ordoño continued. "Your *alcalde* plans to take out the men I left at Aveston. I guessed his next move and left them there on purpose to draw him in. Sadly, your numbers are no match for my full army." He studied the sky. "Thus our early stop today. It wouldn't do to march my army there too soon. I wouldn't want to spoil the old fox's surprise at our appearance."

Teresa had the bad feeling Ordoño was, not three, but a half dozen steps ahead of them.

"We have scouts, too," Telo said. "They will see you coming."

"Ah yes. We caught two of those this morning." Ordoño nodded to where posts were being erected. One already contained a gristly dismembered head—the beard hacked from the cheeks. "They may see us, but they won't live to report us. No. Your ability to pull off a shocking victory is over. I think no witches will come to save you this time."

Father Telo touched heart, forehead, liver, and spleen.

Teresa gagged, as much from the sight as the roiling in her stomach. She had come to study the Northerners and their leader and learn to predict their next move—outthink the enemy. In Ordoño, she had met a master at studying human reaction. He anticipated everything, which meant he must know their reason for being at the camp. She bit back a whimper.

CHAPTER 32

Bromisto jumped lightly from one hillock of grass to another with Errol following more shakily. It appeared to be some kind of game to see who would get wet first. Ramiro could do very well without any more wet. Beyond his soaked feet, the air was already so saturated that wherever the sun reached through the forest canopy, vapor rose through the air like patches of cloud brought to earth. It created an eerie cast to the swamp. Sun and cloud made strange bedfellows—like soldiers and witches.

Errol wobbled dangerously on his latest landing, and Bromisto smothered a laugh behind his hand, keeping up a running commentary of instruction that left Ramiro glad the other boy had to hear it all. They made as interesting a contrast as the sun and clouds: one tall and fair and the other skinny and dark. Head and shoulder shorter, Bromisto had to look up to give

Errol orders, the elder boy hardly able to meet the smaller in the eye. Their five years age difference reminded Ramiro much of him and Salvador, except he couldn't remember Salvador ever letting him play the leader.

Ramiro winced as Errol made another leap and ended on his butt in one of the many puddles of swamp water around them. From ahead where she walked guiding Sancha and the second mare, Claire turned to look at him and share the fun. Her light eyes danced with mirth. It lifted his own heart, and he laughed with her.

Or tried until Jorga heaved another sigh. The old woman rode on the makeshift litter they'd built for her—one end pulled by Sancha while the other dragged on the ground. Ramiro walked beside her to guide it around obstructions and over bumps, trying to spare her as much as possible—most of the time. To be honest, he'd let it hit a few of the smaller bumps purely from exasperation with her waspish tongue.

"When will you switch places?" Jorga demanded with another sigh. She'd crossed her hands across her breast, like she expected to pass at any minute. "I need to spend what time I have left with my granddaughter."

Claire insisted on taking her turn guiding the litter and not always be at the easier job of going ahead to lead the horses. Jorga agreed but would have Claire always at her side ever since their second day when Jorga began insisting she would die soon and needed to impart as much wisdom to Claire as she could before the end.

Ramiro didn't see any sign of Jorga dying, though he acknowledged the trip must be hard on her. But the old woman was too stubborn to die of something like an arrow. In fact, he didn't believe death wanted Jorga either. "I'd rather be walking with your granddaughter, too," he quipped just to shock a reaction from her. She gave over her plaintive whine-face long enough to scowl.

"Impertinent, city man. She's not for you. Women of the Song—"

"Belong to themselves," he finished. "Yes, I know. You've only said it once an hour for two days. If she belongs to herself then perhaps Claire should decide for herself." He had her there, and they both knew it. Interfering between him and Claire meant giving over her principles. Principles won.

That didn't mean she couldn't lecture.

Jorga started to shake her finger at him but grabbed for her leg instead as Ramiro pushed the travois from catching on a stump. They'd wrapped the arrow and all their wounds in many layers of bandage, doing all they could to keep any blood from showing through. Ramiro didn't understand exactly what drew Dal, and Errol would say no more on the subject, but they weren't taking any chances. There was too much they didn't understand. Ramiro couldn't wait to lay this burden on wiser shoulders. His father was better suited to figuring out what was happening and would have the resources. Ramiro ached to set a faster pace, knowing he couldn't until they managed to escort Jorga to the healers.

The thought drew his eyes to Claire again to watch the sway of her braid across her back. He did long to walk beside her, though he didn't know how to say he planned to leave her and go home. It got harder and harder to keep her at a distance between them. His heart just wasn't cooperating.

The whispered laughter of the boys rose as one of them almost fell again. The sound wouldn't carry far—they tried to keep it quiet—and he hadn't the heart to shush them completely, though he should.

"Take care of her for me," Ramiro whispered, but Jorga's sharp ears heard.

"What's that? Leaving are you?" Her features brightened. "Maybe I could live after all."

It was Ramiro's turn to scowl. "Don't say anything to her. I want to tell her." He waited for her reluctant nod before asking, "Have you decided the *witches* need to be part of this?" He didn't see how she could deny it any longer—not after the Northern soldiers had been cut into tiny cubes like meat for the stew. The comparison made him sick, but it was too close to the truth.

"Women of the Song," she corrected. "Perhaps."

"You know we could use your help." Much as it hurt to admit it. "And . . . we will offer you our help in return. I came here with Claire only thinking about what we could gain from you, when I should have been thinking how we could help each other." All along his desires had been nothing but selfish. "We do need to warn everyone we can reach, all the Women of the Song, the people of my cities, Bromisto's clan, even the other cities. I apologize for thinking otherwise. We need a true partnership more than ever. I'd like to be able to give my father some numbers. How many of you are there?"

Jorga's face wrinkled like she'd bitten a tart apple, but she surprised him by answering, "Near on to fifty, spread over a hundred miles and more."

"Hard to pass the word out to so few, so far apart."

She grunted, the closest she would come to agreement. "The Rose Among Thorns happens soon. Most of them will be there. It's the best chance to reach the largest number."

"Your yearly meeting. Where?"

"A clearing, near the center of the swamp. A spot we've used for centuries. I suppose I could go there, if I live long enough." She not-quite touched the arrow standing up from her thigh and cried out as the ends of the poles dropped into a pothole hidden by a puddle of scummy water. "On the other hand, the warning requires a haste I can't accomplish. I will give the directions to my granddaughter. She may be a stranger to them, but they'll believe Errol about the massacre. The problem may lie in my sisters considering the deaths a fluke."

"Then flukes repeat because I encountered what was left of one. Another massacre in the desert by

Colina Hermosa. Errol doesn't seem to think it a fluke." Much as he'd like to dismiss what happened to them, Ramiro had the feeling it would grow worse, not better.

"No." He thought Jorga would let the subject drop and had to strain to hear her. "I fear it's just starting. A partnership, then, for both our survival."

Claire dragged herself into Suero's camp as the sun dropped far behind the trees and the shadows lengthened. Every muscle in her body ached from shoving at and correcting the stretcher for two days. She couldn't even complain about it as Ramiro had offered to spare her the task and she'd been the one to demand her turn. She stood in a half daze as Bromisto came running to meet them with his sister, Elo, and the motherly looking healer woman.

The healer took one look at the arrow and said, "Take her to my shelter."

Claire stood as stationary as one of those odd desert cacti as Ramiro unharnessed the stretcher and pulled it after the healer, leaving Bromisto to take the horses. Silently, Errol tugged at her arm, drawing her to stumble along in their wake, wanting to be with her grandmother, but finding it too hard to think or react, stupefied by exhaustion coupled with worry. She could sleep for a week.

After.

After Jorga was resting comfortably, that is. She

held on to positive outcomes, refusing to consider other conclusions, and thought of her time with her grandmother.

Jorga had lectured her on the Song for the whole trip, trying to pack everything into Claire's head in hours instead of months. Most of it Claire couldn't hold on to and the rest got flushed away by concern when her grandmother became unconscious a few hours ago. Despite their efforts to stop the blood loss, they could only do so much with the arrow still intact. She knew they'd moved as fast as they could. Claire clasped her hands together, pleading it was enough.

She heard Ramiro warning the healers about the dangers of blood and the healer saying something in return, but she couldn't focus.

When she tried to duck into the little mud shelter after Jorga, Elo took her arms and stopped her. "Wait out here. Too many people block the light." Then she was gone.

Wait outside?

Claire blinked, coming alive to notice Errol hunched by the shelter, curled in a ball as he rocked on his heels. Ramiro stood beside her, concern etched across his face.

"Claire, did you hear me?" he repeated. "I asked if you're all right."

She stared at him stupidly. "Tired."

He helped her down onto a blanket by a cook fire, then took a blanket to Errol. The light and heat sent waves of sleepiness across her. She wanted to lie down and pass out. When Ramiro returned, she clamped on to his arm, feeling the muscle beneath and drawing on his strength. "Don't leave me."

She bit her lip. She hadn't meant to ever say that aloud. By the Song, she was no better than a big baby. Next she'd be crying.

As if called, a tear rolled.

He brushed it away. "I'm not going anywhere tonight."

"*Tonight.*" She locked the rest of the tears inside. "But you are going."

His eyes shifted and she took that for yes. "It's all right," she said instantly. "Of course you have to go. I can stand on my own feet." Part of her knew that was all true, the other part curled up like Errol and whimpered. Jorga could be dying. Whether she did or not, it was up to Claire to warn the other Women of the Song, women she'd never met and who likely wouldn't believe her.

"I've been derelict of my duty for too long," he said. His eyes looked over her and into the growing darkness, not seeing her, and not here. "Word has to be spread of our danger. I'll take it one way and you the other."

"You can tell them that the Women of the Song will stand with them." She'd find a way to make that true. "You've impressed my grandmother. She said . . . she said at least if she were to . . . die . . . she felt she left me in good hands."

"She said that?" Ramiro looked entirely skeptical.

"Well, she actually said I could have found worse, but close enough."

He laughed and she relaxed at lifting his spirits, though hers were crushed. "Then you'll leave in the morning?" she asked.

"I hope to be gone before Suero comes back from hunting. I really don't want another run-in with that man."

"Ah." When had she missed that news? She gave herself a mental slap to pay attention from now on and not let tiredness be an excuse.

She closed her eyes for a second and opened them to find Ramiro nearer, her back leaning against his chest as his worry for her brought him closer. His scent filled her, so distracting. Stubble from his beard caught in her hair. She kept her head down, afraid to turn and become lost in the depths of his brown eyes.

He was leaving tomorrow and she might never see him again. Her anger at the injustice of that flared. He might not intend to say anything, but, by the Song, she could.

She slid away and turned, surprising him enough that his arms came up to encircle her. "Fronilde said I should leave this to you, but I can't." Her knees lifted her taller to kiss him, her hands fastening onto his shirt to hold him there.

He didn't resist or turn his head aside as she feared. His lips met hers, just as ready. For an instant all was right. Troubles and fears melted. His hands stroked her hair, and her heart rejoiced.

Then it was over.

He set her aside. Worry for Jorga came pouring back along with fear of the future.

"I just wanted you to know how I feel," she said. "Before you go. Just in case . . ." No more would come out on that subject.

"I want that, too."

"You do?" Astonishment filled her chest with hummingbird flutters.

"I told Jorga so, but . . ."

"But?" she pushed, giving over that he'd talk to her grandmother about this subject, but couldn't speak to her.

"I can't drag you down with me."

That again. She almost blurted out that none of that mattered. Maybe his people would want to arrest him or worse. They could run away from all that. She didn't need to live with his people and neither did he. They'd do just fine on their own. But he could never be happy if his honor was tarnished. It was what made her trust him in the first place. He wouldn't be Ramiro without it.

She seized his shirt again. "Then fix it and come back to me. As long as we understand each other, that's all that matters."

This time his kiss took her by surprise. It was hot and fierce and made her head spin in a most pleasant way, leaving her breathless as it stripped her inhibitions. Now, she held on to him to prop herself up.

"Go tonight. Don't wait for morning," she choked

out when she could speak. "The sooner it's done, the sooner you return. You don't need to worry about me. I can protect myself." That was a lie she hoped he wouldn't catch. "Jorga has been helping me with the Song. I know more about pitch and intent now." Or the theory of it at least.

He leaned close to whisper in her ear, his beard tickling her cheek in a way that sent shivers down her spine. "I knew you could master the magic."

She slapped at his chest to find his eyes laughing at her. "You! No teasing. Now, you owe me a favor. Wear your armor." It might keep him from accidentally bleeding and calling the demon.

"Day and night," he said solemnly. "If it makes you happy. Even in the bath."

"A bath would be a very good decision," she said primly, trying desperately to pretend she wasn't imagining sharing one with him. Her cheeks heated anyway. "I recommend it. Alone," she added quickly.

"Alone, is it?" he shot back with a suggestive smile. "You mean you won't join me. We'll see about that—someday. Right now, your fragile and delicate stink isn't so fragile and delicate. And I don't think your heart is truly in it—not with your grandmother's life in the balance." He leaned in again to kiss her by the ear and whisper, "No goodbyes. I'll find you as soon as I can." The heat in his eyes held a promise. Then he was gone.

Claire clamped down on the sorrow that tried to cut her apart. She wanted to chase after him, bawl for him to take her with him. Her eyes turned with reluctance to focus on the mud shelter where they'd taken Jorga. This time, her place was here. Her mother used to say, "it would be well; given time, all things would be well." She tried hard to believe it enough to make it true.

CHAPTER 33

Telo glanced up as the door to the wagon creaked open and held his breath in anticipation. Ordoño had summoned Telo twice over the last days, always after stopping early and always to play on the *Acorraloar* board they'd started weeks ago. With Santabe watching and Teresa confined to their wagon, Telo had found little opportunity to put his plan into action. Santabe would stop him from killing Ordoño before he even got started. He knew it was foolish to throw his life away when he should wait for a better opening. Yet, each hour he didn't act brought them closer to Aveston, and Ordoño wiping out their small army.

So the last time they had played, Telo had committed little mistakes to make the game end early, all the while hinting how much more challenging it was to place stones in *Acorraloar* with more players. Players who understood the game: not Santabe and the grudging attention she paid to it, but a new player with university experience. Ordoño had both a respect and strange hostility toward anything about the universities. The Northern leader asked questions often about Teresa but failed to summon her, until now.

Telo's prayers were answered. The guard waved them both from their wagon.

"Surely the Lord sent you to my aid," Telo whispered to the heavyset woman as they left their rolling prison behind. More proof that his interpretation of God's wishes was correct. His heart beat at a faster rhythm and his palm grew sweaty. Today, he could prove that letting him live had served a greater purpose. They might have failed to save Colina Hermosa, but he could spare the other *ciudades-estado*.

The huge Northern army would fall apart. With no rider on the wildcat, it would split in a hundred directions.

He wobbled, light-headed, and realized his breathing had gotten too shallow, correcting it with deep, even breaths.

Enigmatic are the ways of the Lord. He glorifies the humble and casts down the mighty, Telo recited to himself. *Even one as insignificant as myself can play a part in his design.*

A calm settled over him. He would do what he must.

Teresa looked a little green, and he took her arm. "Be not troubled, my sister. Do your part and all will fall out as is meant."

"I'll say little and follow your lead. How close are we to Aveston?"

"Less than an hour." Telo considered their location, a little village, now long abandoned. He knew it well from his time as a wandering friar. "This is the perfect place to hide and wait to rush into the battle at the last minute. Our side will be crushed. We have no more time." The soldiers they passed looked like they could be ready for battle in moments. They wore their armor and weapons, waiting on their feet instead of lounging around cooking fires.

Even if *pelotón* scouts found the Northern army hiding here and managed to report, it seemed unlikely their forces could retreat fast enough to escape.

The guards took them to the wagon with the *Acorraloar* board. The roof was of canvas and half of it had been pulled back to allow fresh air to enter, while the remainder shaded the interior.

Ordoño and Santabe already waited inside. "Ah, the guests. Do you like the new board?" Ordoño asked.

Telo stood frozen in the doorway. The small two-player board had been removed and a larger two-foot by three-foot game installed in its place. It stood upon wide legs like sawhorses. In a larger room, it would swivel for ease of play. Instead of plain wooden squares, these were enameled in different colors and the playing area arranged in an organic shape to represent a real map with inlets and peninsulas. Whole squares of tiles along the sides were loose, to be lifted free and replaced in order to give the board a fresh shape. It was a showcase board, meant to be the center of a collection.

Ordoño moved to the side containing orange tiles, hefting his pouch of *Acorraloar* stones in his hand. "Choose your spot."

The guards shut the door, staying outside. Ordoño had tested Telo plenty of times before, and Teresa appeared as no threat with her awkwardness and cumbersome weight. No, Ordoño had no fear his tame dogs would turn and bite.

Telo broke out of his trance and moved to the board.

It represented a map of the *ciudades-estado*. Ordoño had chosen for his base the westernmost land that depicted Aveston. At the northern point of the board, the blue squares stood for the burnt city of Zapata. Telo picked the brown bag of stones that went with Colina Hermosa in the center—the spot where he could stand nearest to Ordoño—while Teresa sat at the bottom of the board, taking Vista Sur and putting her seat closest to where Santabe fidgeted in the corner as a spectator. The priestess was again in her white robe, her hair brushed back and trimmed, wearing, not one, but two sun-shaped earrings. Telo took note of her promotion with unease. It could foretell nothing good. Oddly, she wore two Diviners, red and white, at each hip. The sight made his skin creep.

"Ah," Ordoño said, pointing to the brown squares nearest to his home base. "A bold move to stake out land in the center. An offensive stance. You intend to play aggressively, Father."

"You have guessed my plan," Telo said uneasily. "And you have chosen the city where I was born, so I have taken my adopted city. Maybe this time I can defend it. The heart does call to one, my son. We remember places of our birth with nostalgia." He indicated the board. "Perhaps you have chosen the land of your birth as well. Not all the memories can be bad." The Northern leader expected Telo to try and change his heart. Telo didn't intend to disappoint. It would cover his true plan—and one never knew, it might make a difference.

"Perhaps I have." Ordoño did not rise to the bait. His face remained set on that of a pleasant host as he lay out his stones. "Who can say? Or I merely plan my route of attack from my next sure victory. We passed a monastery today where I got this fine game board. The priests there had excellent taste. Did you know it?"

Telo flinched before he could hide it. "Yes, I recognized it." Telo knew every change and variation possible on this board as well as he knew the road between Colina Hermosa and Aveston. He'd seen the side road that led to it and feared for its fate. He had spent many hours of play on this board there, listening to the elder priests discussing matters spiritual and practical. It touched on numerous pleasant memories, as he'd taken orders there. "What happened to the brothers?"

"Fled like the cowards they are," Santabe spat from her corner.

"It provided such a fine game board that I decided not to burn the place," Ordoño said, looking up. "I can quarter soldiers there when your cities have surrendered. Always reuse unless you must destroy to teach a lesson."

"Very generous," Telo managed, clenching his fist around the half-empty bag of stones. "We also have a saying you've no doubt heard: It's easier for a mule to pass through the eye of a needle than for a covetous man to enter paradise. Greed destroys the soul, my son."

"A good thing I want nothing to do with your paradise." Ordoño placed his last stone. "Shall we play?"

Telo set his last also, fanning them out to take the shape of a wagon wheel with a few stones coordinated near the center of his space and the others radiating outward like spokes. Teresa had set a few of her blue stones in a thin peninsula where they would be protected and arranged her others haphazardly around it. She planned to defend, hoping the others spread themselves too thin.

As the player in control of the least area, Teresa moved a single stone to start, Ordoño followed with two, then Telo played three. Play would be rapid at first, slowing as more and more stones were in motion. Failure to remember how many stones to play forfeited your turn.

Telo fell into the rhythm of play, trying to work up the nerve to make his move. His tongue clove to the roof of his mouth, his skin cold, and he placed his stones with little thought to strategy. He must act; there would be no more chances—

Teresa stepped into the silence, startling him with her abruptness.

"You don't want the cities. That's why you are so quick to burn them." She stared straight at Ordoño. "I've puzzled over it and puzzled over it. Once would have been enough of a warning. Twice could be an accident because of the rout at Colina Hermosa. Then you could have moved to a smaller city. It would have folded, allowing its capture. But you went to Aveston—the last city sure to resist. You *want* to burn them.

"I've seen your kind before. Born so poor their life is swept under a rug," Teresa continued. "Never given a chance. Never allowed to make anything of their life, just one more child raised in poverty—trapped. Except, you are smarter than most. You didn't need to lash out at individuals. You could order the world to your liking and lash out at a whole society."

Santabe rose to her feet, anger twisting her face. "You don't speak so to Lord Ordoño, heretic!"

Telo was stupefied—antagonizing wasn't their plan—but Teresa dabbed at her eyes as if she hadn't heard. "It's sad really," she said. "So much lost. The university made a mistake when it cast you aside. You could have changed our world for the better. You might have done anything. Instead you let hate rule. So much death so a man can take petty revenge."

"I expected the lecture from you," Ordoño said to Telo, "not the scholar. Or a quip at the least."

"You'll excuse me, my son. With thousands of lives at stake, the jest has gone out of my spirit. I know you for a reasoning man. One able to put yourself in another's shoes. You must know revenge is hollow. Soon gained and soon dulled. The wildcat doesn't have to run. You could stop it."

"That I'll allow. But conquering a challenge never dulls, priest. You know it yourself or you wouldn't be here. As we speak, your friends line up for their little battle. I scouted them myself and saw their design. I'll let them think they are winning, then I'll order my men in and destroy them. I've ruined your city and now I'll eliminate your military. It will break the old fox, break all your kind, to see your white knight of a city—so honorable to stand up to us—perish."

Telo sighed. "Then there is no hope for us. I'm sorry for that. All must fall out as foretold."

At the prearranged phrase, Teresa turned and jumped at Santabe, tackling the taller priestess to the floor. "Do it!"

Telo slammed the edge of the table. The locking mechanism had always been weak, easily knocked loose. The *Acorraloar* board spun, bumping the wall of the wagon, but running into Ordoño first, sending him stumbling off balance.

As he'd practiced, Telo had his triple-rope belt off in a flash and wrapped one end around his stump. He threw the other around Ordoño's neck, slipping around behind him. With the stump of his arm, he yanked it taut.

Ordoño fought and bucked against him, struggling to break loose. But Ordoño was an average man in appearance, and that included his strength. Telo had fought brutes and giants. The Northern leader posed no test.

Ordoño sputtered and choked, fighting for air. The belt tightened around the flesh of his neck. A knife fell to the floor as the Northern leader lost his grip on it in pulling it from his clothing. Twisting, Telo kicked it away. Ordoño fumbled first at the ropes and then tried to jab his fingers into Telo's eyes. His face set in a snarl, Telo held him secure and waited.

The drumming of Ordoño's feet grew weaker. His hands dropped to his side. The body went limp, and Telo stumbled to keep his hold.

Shock, surprise, and betrayal shone then dimmed in his victim's eyes, the jaw going slack. Accusation remained.

Horror struck at Telo's heart.

He killed a man. Another human.

So others could live.

Murdered. Took a life. The greatest gift God gave.

What was he thinking in his conceit? The Lord would never command this.

In a flash, he flung off the ropes. The body crashed to the ground. Telo knelt beside it and pushed on Ordoño's chest. In and out. Forcing the air through. The throat was bruised and purplish, but he hadn't broken the neck. "Breathe, damn you!" To stop the enemy in this way couldn't be worth it.

Ordoño's eyes fluttered. One hand rose to his throat.

Telo let out a sigh of relief. He hadn't committed the gravest sin.

Someone shoved him aside. Santabe stood over him, white Diviner in hand. He'd failed, lost his nerve and let his people down. "Take me, Lord," Telo said in a rush.

"The one reasonable thing you tried and you botched it," Santabe growled. "This is how you kill, weak priest."

Telo tried to scramble free, but his back hit the wall. The Diviner came down.

Telo tensed and forced his eyes to remain open. He would go out aware of his end.

But the Diviner touched Ordoño. In an instant, the life that had been returning was wiped clean for good.

"What . . . why . . ." Telo sputtered at Ordoño's lifeless body. He glanced for Teresa and saw her lying on her face, motionless. He waited for his turn, for the killing touch, but it didn't come. "He was your—"

"My lord. My mentor," Santabe sneered. "He was all that and more. He accomplished what no one else could. He picked me out of the masses to elevate. I've sent him to his reward. Spared him the terror to come. He conquered in this life, now he can do so in the next and ensure Dal's favor."

Telo grasped for sense, but the words spun around him. "I don't understand. Is this because he didn't rescue you back at our camp?"

"Bah. I needed no one's help." Santabe returned

the Diviner to her belt. "Dal has manifested. Five hundred years early, thanks to your witch. Armies don't matter anymore. Lord Ordoño was made—what is your word—not needed, obsolete, here. I spared him the pain Dal would have inflicted and sent him ahead of me to the next life to take that world as he took this. He would thank me."

Telo shook his head, but Santabe wasn't looking at him anymore.

"I dreamed of finding a way to convince the Children of Dal to change. Then he came. Like one of your miracles. Don't you see? The Children of Dal kept *Him* from the world and protected your kind for centuries past remembering. Now we are free of that and Dal is free to take the world. It will die in blood and pass to the next stage where we all begin again. To strive to rise to the top. If only I were favored to go with Ordoño, as worthy as he. But is that right? Is Dal done with him here?" She fingered the red Diviner. "Maybe . . ."

Telo couldn't speak. The woman stunned him. She acted as unstable as others accused Ordoño of being.

"Were the sacrifices—executions—to call your god or to hold him at bay?" a weak voice asked. Teresa had sat up, holding her head with one hand.

Santabe snapped out of her thoughts and stepped in Teresa's direction. "She understands. A compromise of both. Years ago, His leadership split, some arguing one way and some the other. We spilled enough blood to keep Dal happy and to create new Diviners."

"So—" Teresa began.

"Enough questions!" Santabe snapped, hands held over the Diviners at her waist. She fingered her second earring and looked at Telo. "I owe this to that one. For that, I let you go, this one time. Don't think it a kindness. You don't deserve to go to your reward. I will tell the guards to take you to the edge of camp. Go and suffer Dal's wrath. Watch this world fall."

She actually went to the door and spoke in their language to a guard, though hiding Ordoño's body with her own. Telo flexed his hand and thrust his aching stump into his armpit. He would live. If Santabe had given her word, she would keep it. His eye slid over the body. His task was accomplished without the blood on his hands. Yet, he'd never felt more wretched in his life. It had all gone horribly wrong.

He used the wall as support to reach his feet. Teresa took his arm and pulled him along. He couldn't begin to guess how the army would react to Santabe. Could she gain control or would they fall apart as he hoped? Somehow, he didn't think she'd even try to command them. She seemed so sure she didn't need to act. What did it mean?

He glanced back. Santabe smiled widely from the doorway, now holding the red Diviner. "Our killing before today was a raindrop in a hurricane to what will come, priest. Remember that and fear. Your kind god will not save you now."

CHAPTER 34

Over the three day march to Aveston, Julian had tried hard not to dwell on how the battle would start—gallant dashes, sneak attacks—he left planning to the experts. A wise choice from a cautious man. All good decisions to the side, he hadn't anticipated both sides forming up into neat ranks while facing off across the large empty field in front of Aveston's walls. There couldn't have been any lead-up more dull, more anticlimactic, than this careful maneuver in full view of the Northerners—both sides showing exactly how their forces would be deployed, able to fully weigh and measure their opponents. From his location with the *pelotón* captains on a knoll behind and separate from the arranged ranks, Julian had the best view of all. As the captains and their lieutenants discussed strategy, and messengers and runners came and went, he was left to be an observer on the crowded hilltop.

Julian expected rushes of emotion. Determination. Bravado. Even fear. Not this cerebral planning, with all the excitement of a safe and controlled game of *Acorraloar*. Yet...

The air fairly crackled with tension. Salvador would call it the feel of a bent bowstring—full of anticipation and possibility—alive and bursting with static energy beneath the surface. Men would die today. Win or lose, and much as they tried to forget the fact, they discerned some would not survive to see the sunset. Nerves and hearts beat with the knowledge they could be among the dead. The goal of the battle aimed to save the whole at the expense of losing the individual. The transience of life made Julian sit taller, clasp the reins of his horse with more awareness, feel every breath, and savor every second.

In this moment of stillness, he felt his own mortality stronger than ever before. On his shoulders rode the knowledge that all the lives lost here today would be by his order. If he let it, that weight would suck the strength from his body and lucidity from his soul. He touched mind, heart, liver, and spleen. A man could only do his best and pray it was enough. However, no internal command to relax could convince his hands not to sweat and his pulse not to throb.

By the saints, he wished it would start so it could be over.

The desire to scream and break the stillness or simply flee built and built in his chest.

As if sensing he and everyone else had reached

their limit of endurance, the cluster of *pelotón* captains broke apart, some jogging their horses back to their units, others remaining on the hill where they could better make adjustments to the battle as it progressed. Captain Muño brought his horse beside Julian, sitting companionably in silence, though surrounded by others. Acquainted for years, since Salvador had raised Muño as an enlisted man from the ranks to be his lieutenant, Julian felt a new intimacy and closeness with him that could only come from the nearness of death. So this is why Salvador had had such devotion to his men.

"It begins soon, sir," Muño said, gesturing to a uniformed man on foot, holding a mass of flags, and struggling to climb a raised wooden platform. "Watch."

Julian couldn't have torn his eyes away if the sky fell on him. As the most junior captain, Muño was almost as much an observer as himself, no doubt assigned as nursery keeper over the one civilian there.

"There is no reason to 'sir' me," Julian said. "The vote must have taken place. I'm likely no longer *alcalde*, just a civilian now."

"That would not be the case if the *pelotónes* were there to vote, *sir*."

"I thank you for that, though not a one of us would change our positions and be at Crueses to keep me in power when we are needed here—least of all I," Julian said unhurriedly, then turned the conversation from the painful subject. The raw stab in his heart told him exactly how much he would miss being their leader. "I didn't anticipate the buildup to the fighting would be such a slow process."

"Slow?" Muño huffed with a short laugh. "This has been quick—it usually takes days—but wait, soon it will move like lightning—and as unpredictably."

"Will it go our way?" Julian asked and then cringed. Such negative talk must be in poor taste, but his companion took it with ease.

"They outnumber us. Their long pikes offset our horses. They have more archers than we expected. It depends on Aveston. Will they join as planned? There's plenty of activity atop their walls. They'll do something, but mayhap too late for us, sir."

Julian grunted. That had been his part to play, and he knew exactly how tempestuous their relationship had always been with their nearest neighbor—sometimes allies and more often adversaries over border disputes and trade differences. A common enemy didn't mean Aveston would act in Colina Hermosa's best interests.

The flagman fidgeted, readjusting his bundle of flags to ready one uppermost. Julian leaned forward and felt a corresponding stir across the leagues of space between them going through the ranks of men.

"There's something I should have said, sir," Muño began, "but never found a good time. Ramiro. Is he off on a mission for you? Are there circumstances I don't know behind his desertion?"

Julian's gaze jerked from the flagman to stare at

his captain, thoughts rushing, then settling as hope flared. "Have you heard some news?"

"That I have not. But if . . . when he returns there must be a trial. Unless you can prove otherwise—if he had a reason to be gone. Secret orders?"

Julian hesitated, the desire to protect and defend strong. Beatriz would not have deliberated—her baby came first. At the same time . . . Would Ramiro's pride thank him for lying? Did false words do his son favors? "He did not have any such orders. But I trust my son's judgment. He left for a good reason."

Muño nodded, looking unhappy. "The men of our unit see Ramiro as their own son. But the law is the law. It will have to go to trial."

Julian was flooded with memories of a young Ramiro tripping underfoot of the men, following after his brother, begging to try their weapons, and the men treating him like an endearing puppy. Tears filled Julian's eyes as he turned back to the flagman. *To think it would come to this . . .*

"I owe your family much," Muño continued. "Born in the slums. Just a sergeant. Invited into your home. Salvador may have raised me, but you all made me. By my honor, I cannot . . . I cannot . . ."

Julian knew of the discrete lessons in reading and writing that had brought Muño up to officer material when Salvador decided this man had to be his lieutenant. He had pulled some strings himself to get Muño in the university to audit courses on warfare and strategy.

"Show favoritism?" Julian supplied. "I understand, Captain. Salvador made a strong choice. My son recognized a leader of men when he saw one. He was a good judge of character. We were happy to help you." Julian clapped him on the shoulder. "I do not expect you to do anything that isn't your duty, nor would Ramiro."

"I thank you again, sir. Serving under your son was a privilege."

From the corner of his eye, Julian caught movement from the remaining captains on the hilltop, and the flagman raised high a brilliant blue flag and let it drop. Beside him, Captain Muño stood in his stirrups. Julian tried to do the same and nearly overbalanced onto his ass. He settled for a half stand in time to see the church's *pelotón* sweep forward in a charge; the long lances that were their claim to fame set and braced against their saddles. By tradition, the opening of any battle went to them.

Scores of arrows flew, some finding a mark and most bouncing from armor. Men and dappled-gray horseflesh crashed against the Northerners and cleaved through like water—until they struck a square formation of Northern pikes braced to meet them. Then the orderly charge dissolved into a chaos of stabbing and falling, blood and death and horses screaming. At the same time, dozens of other units surged forward, the orange and white of Crueses among them. The Northerners reacted in kind, running forward in some spots, staying put in others. It broke down into a huge flow of motion to Julian's untrained eye, which sometimes surged here or there. The flagman continued to give signals that meant nothing to him, putting fresh units in play.

Muño grunted, and Julian resisted the urge to tug at his arm. "It goes well?"

"As expected. Decidedly even."

Julian tried and failed to detect that in the masses of men, striking and counter-striking at each other. To him it looked like a kicked anthill—the neat, straight lines all dissolved. Here, sections of it seemed to move in their direction, while there it went the opposite way, but in most places the tide held ground. A unit of horses swung around and hit one such bulge, knocking it back. At their distance, he couldn't distinguish who fell or the extent of the injuries. There was no smell of blood, no whimpers of the wounded—except for the death shrieks of horses, he could have been watching a game or training exercise.

It felt wrong to be here—safe—when so many perished in his cause. His promise to Beatriz stung and then subsided. She was right. His left arm shook. Even if his hands had their full strength, they were too old for this fight. He contributed in other ways.

His eyes shot to the gates of Aveston and detected nothing changed. They remained shut fast.

"All the reserves are committed," Captain Muño commented.

Julian knew the doom of that. A glance at the flagman showed him with a white flag uppermost in his arms, ready to be displayed. *No. No. No. Not yet!* Julian's fingernails bit into his flesh. The captains would only agree to his plan with a contingency: If Aveston failed to act in time or casualties mounted too high, they would break away and use the speed of their horses to retreat. The thought brought bile to Julian's mouth.

To give up when they were so close.

Common sense said the captains were right. With ninety-five percent of their fighting men here, they couldn't afford a catastrophe. The men of Colina Hermosa must live to fight another day—even if it meant defeat. News of a handful of missing scouts long overdue had jarred the captains, making them even more anxious as they had no word of the main Northern army. Only fast-talking about the timeline had convinced them to commit at all. The military leaders would have little patience.

He stared at the gates along with everyone not directing the battle. As the minutes ticked by, Julian urged them to open with every fiber of his being until sweat beaded on his forehead. *Now! Let it be now!*

And still the men of Colina Hermosa and Crueses fought and died alone.

Minutes inched by to more men dying. Just a little longer. Surely, Aveston would come.

"The white flag," Muño said as the flagman held it high.

"Wait!" Julian cried. He put heels to his horse and bolted to the other captains. "Just a little longer! They will come!"

"It's too la—"

"The gates!" the flagman shouted. Julian spun to see the white flag flutter and fall to the ground, tossed away and replaced again with the bright blue.

The gates of Aveston had cracked, great metal doors ratcheting up into the walls. Legions of horses raced outward to cross the field with manes and tails flowing. Julian shouted until his voice cracked, joining the bellows from a thousand other throats. He whooped with joy, a grin splitting his face, like he hadn't smiled in an age of days. All around him normally upright and dignified captains pounded upon each other's backs, unrestrained.

Aveston had answered the call. They hit the Northern ranks like a summer flood, pushing all before them.

As the Northerners were pressed across the field toward the olive groves, Julian wiped at suddenly blurry eyes. Circumstances had gone wrong for so long, it had seemed as if God abandoned them. To finally have something go right . . .

Julian laughed aloud as Muño seized his hand and tried to shake it out of its socket.

A young messenger tugged at his leg. "Sir! Sir!" He held out a folded paper. "For you, sir!"

The paper with his name uppermost held familiar writing. Julian unfolded it and ripped the paper around the seal in his haste, heart in his throat. *Had something gone wrong?* He should never have let himself celebrate. It was sure to provoke God to send a defeat.

My dear Husband,

I take up my pen to remind you of your promise to avoid any fighting. But I'm sure you are much too wise to hazard any such thing.

Julian shook his head. Beatriz could have been right there before him. He could picture her accusing face set just so as if she were actually present.

I'm afraid you will be much annoyed with me, dear husband. The vote has taken place with most astonishing results. But I must go back.

With half an eye on the turn of the battle—Muño would alert him if anything changed—Julian groaned and shuffled through the pages, before returning to his spot. Beatriz tended to ramble in her letters.

I did as we discussed and most judiciously released into certain channels the exact terms of the Northern surrender that Alcalde Juan had been withholding from his people. Such news quickly made the rounds and, indeed, exceeded my expectations—actually causing a literal firestorm at one point—as a certain inn caught fire and burned to the ground, during some protests. I considered restitution but thought it better to cling to plausible deniability.

Julian rolled his eyes. Her gossip outdid itself apparently.

But certain <u>sources</u> saw through my denials. I mean to say, Alcalde Juan made some rather harsh statements, and might I say, they devolved into quite personal attacks against your wife. He was most venomous and insinuated I was not a <u>lady</u>, nor was my birth legitimate.

"Lady" had been underlined three times. Julian knew exactly which insult must have incensed more.

Others leaped to my defense, and things got heated. There were some <u>threats</u> on my life. My guards insisted on sleeping in my room—most indecent—until Fronilde stepped forward in her usual kind way and offered to keep me company. A gesture most appreciated as she has such a way with Pietro. The poor dear had been most <u>upset</u> for his dear mummy.

"Barking his head off," Julian mumbled. He noted the Northerners continued to give ground as he skipped several paragraph about Pietro's fits.

—well, with the election so close, imagine my astonishment. Not only of all the ladies of Colina Hermosa, but of Crueses as well. They voted as they never had before in all our history. Concejal Antonio said he'd never seen such a sight as the lines of skirts

waiting to cast their ballots. He most graciously gave me all the credit when I'd only put a few <u>suggestions</u> into the right channels. Imagine my delight at the turnout! Isn't it wonderful!

But my dear, very dear, husband, it pains me to say they did not take all my suggestions. It seems the women of Colina Hermosa, and of Crueses—I must give them credit also—made up their own minds. Though I very much hoped their ballots would go to you, it didn't fall out that way at all. I was shocked. Positively <u>SHOCKED</u> at the results! I blame it all on the number of people running for alcalde. It must have confused the ladies, because they cast their ballots— can you believe—(and you must not frown at me so) I must out with it—they saw fit to elect <u>ME</u> as alcalde of Colina Hermosa.

Julian's mouth opened and closed. He checked the words again, but there could be no mistake. Beatriz had underlined "ME" so heavily it tore the paper. He held the letter close and devoured the rest.

Not only that, dear husband. They also elected <u>ME</u> the alcalde of Crueses. (Juan was a most perplexing purple color at the news, so I heard.)

I'm informed, though there is no precedent of a female alcalde, it is <u>perfectly</u> legal. Of course, I immediately begged them to turn it over to you, but it seems that is <u>not</u> legal, and would actually go to other people instead. And the ladies seemed so disappointed *with the idea of my stepping down—they did so very much for me—that I do feel I must keep it, rather than let Juan be alcalde again.*

I will tell it all when next we meet. I pray to our Lord every day that your battle goes <u>well</u>. Until then I remain your loving and <u>loyal</u>,

Beatriz

"It can't be." Julian let the pages flutter to the ground. *Beatriz as* alcalde?

"Is something wrong, sir?" Muño asked, leaning closer. "All is well here. The battle is won. It may not be over yet, but anyone with half an eye can tell. The arrangement of our troops is even keeping any enemy from escaping."

"Astonishing."

"Pardon, sir. It was your plan and certain to succeed with Aveston's cooperation, which we have. Has something gone wrong at home?"

"What? No. Something has gone very, very right. What would you say if I tell you we have a most brilliant—and kissable—new *alcalde*?"

"Sir?"

Julian turned his face up to the waning rays of the rapidly setting afternoon sun and soaked in the warmth. Just a week ago life had seemed hopeless. "I never knew fortune—or God's favor to turn so fast. I just wish my sons could be here to learn their mother is *alcalde*."

A broad grin stretched across his face, only to be tempered by the smell of rotten flesh that blew from the east. Julian's nose scrunched. A chill that cancelled the heat of the day sent a prickle across his skin. Julian sat up as his horse shifted, its feet dancing nervously. Like a ripple, the unease spread throughout the fighting as men of both sides paused and looked at the sky. The joy Julian had felt movements ago evaporated, replaced with a scratching at the base of his spine.

Muño clutched at his elbow. His voice trembled as he asked, "Sir, do you see it?"

A dark cloud of dust or haze hung over the battle, obscuring the men. Had more Northerners arrived? Fear closed over Julian's heart like a fist.

CHAPTER 35

Twisted olive trees gave shelter as Telo slunk toward Aveston. Slunk because a scholar and a friar were hardly trained in evading children, let alone professional scouts. Santabe had given them escort out of the army camp, but that scant safety wouldn't apply if they were caught now. They had no idea what occurred back at the camp—if Ordoño's body had been discovered and the army fell apart—but they'd come too far to die today.

The guard had dumped Telo and Teresa on the opposite side of the camp from Aveston. It had taken several hours to double back around and approach the city, listening all the while for the sounds of battle, and afraid of being overtaken from behind. The sun had sunk low behind the trees, ready to steal the last of the daylight.

"It makes no sense. Why would she kill Ordoño?"

Telo asked, the words spoken aloud more from frustration than any expectation of an answer. He should be drunk with joy at seeing the Northern leader dead—yet all he felt was dread.

Teresa grasped a tree trunk, standing still for a moment. Her breath came in little huffs from the pace he'd set and the uneven ground. "Obviously, we're missing information, but it has to tie in with their religion. Something to do with an afterlife and proving themselves." Teresa sounded scattered. "Their views are so different, but why would she kill him before their army wiped us out? I suspect there's something we don't know. Either that or she's purely mad. Does it matter? The goal was accomplished and we actually got out alive. I never expected that."

Telo had not either. The victory, however, felt hollow. He couldn't believe Santabe insane. She was a sadist, but not mad. What didn't they know? Why did she believe they would all die horribly? He couldn't forget the sight of her standing over Ordoño with the red Diviner in hand. Did it work the same as the other? Why have another color? "I—"

The first gory survivor lurched from the trees and died at their feet. Blood covered him from head to toe so completely it was impossible to tell the color of his uniform. Slices in his flesh crisscrossed his body.

Telo touched heart, mind, liver, and spleen and began the words for the dead, but Teresa pulled on his belt. "Come back and do it later. The battle must be over or we'd have heard some kind of noise. We need to see what happened—if we won. A delay won't matter to this poor soul."

He let Teresa lead him on. With Ordoño in charge there had been a logic to the enemy's movements. Ordoño followed strategy like an *Acorraloar* player. Unfortunately for all their sakes, there would be no guessing at Santabe's reasoning. She might do anything, including return to their homeland—or change her mind and send the army after all. Urgency sped him on. Maybe they could reach *Alcalde* Julian with a warning.

They soon passed other bloody victims in the same condition. Most looked as if they had been crawling from the fight. "Is this what a battle looks like?" he mused aloud. Then the trees ended and they stumbled into a nightmare.

The city of Aveston rose in the distance, less than a mile away. On the flat plain before them, spread a horror show. The battle had taken place near the groves. Bodies lay everywhere, in all positions. Impossibly, armor was rent right through. Flesh fragmented. Red smears of blood covered everything. Horses torn apart or split open—many of them were the precious, dappled-gray *caballos de guerra* that came only from Colina Hermosa. Not a man stood, Northern or Southern. An eerie silence prevailed broken only by a few moans.

Telo stared, sickened.

Where were the victors? Why had no one from the city come to offer help?

"Water," someone pleaded in a broken whisper. Telo glanced down to see a blood-drenched man, clutching a canteen, flat upon his back. Most of his left leg was gone below the knee. Teresa knelt and pulled the water skin from his hand to hold it to the man's lips, but he paid no heed, continuing to plead for a drink even as Teresa poured it over his lips. His eyes glazed as life fled.

Chills chased themselves over Telo's body. "This is not the way a battle looks." He had no experience, but reason said he spoke true. Survivors from the winning side should be checking for wounded. Officers, who had hung well back during the fight, should be handing out orders. The only thing moving was the wind.

Everyone from both sides had been flattened down to the last soul.

"Look," Teresa said, standing and shading her eyes. Two horses crossed the plain from the direction of the city, riders low on their backs.

They had to pick their way through the gore to meet the riders, trying their best to step carefully. In spots, the dead were so packed together they had no choice but to tread on them, scattering clouds of flies. Banners of Colina Hermosa, Aveston, and Crueses matted with blood, clung to broken flagpoles. The stench of death covered everything with a nauseating miasma.

The worst part was walking past the few wounded. With no supplies or medical training, there was no way to help such horrific injuries. At some point, Teresa started retching and couldn't stop, still valiantly keeping pace even while gagging with tears streaming down her round cheeks. Telo held his sleeve over his nose and mouth, feeling guilty for benefiting from that small relief when so many others had suffered or continued to suffer.

"What happened here, Father?" the first rider on a chestnut mare demanded in greeting as soon as they reached shouting distance.

"We were hoping you could tell us." Telo's voice boomed across the field of death, chasing echoes. "We've just arrived. We were prisoners in the main Northern army. They're camped barely an hour's walk. Did we lose?"

The scout held out empty hands, apparently too numb to react to their warning. "We were winning. Every member of our fighting men went to help— even the gate guards. Our men joined the other *pelotónes*. We pushed them back against the trees. Then the orderly lines disappeared. From the walls, we could see a red cloud of haze and naught much else. When it cleared . . . this."

"All dead. We took triple pay to come see up close," the second scout offered as he pulled up. "No one would do it for less. Haunts. Or magic. Maybe them Northerners got their own witches." He kept his horse well back from the nearest dead, eyes too wide on both mount and rider. "No telling if it's over or if it will start up again . . . with us."

No shadow of fear grew in Telo at the scout's apprehension, only a great gaping hole of sorrow and loss. The hole that came from thousands of souls taken too soon, never to finish the course of their lives. Telo stared at the city, trying to find understanding for this disaster. Unlike Colina Hermosa, Aveston didn't favor stucco and whitewash, but gray stone. Their walls gave off no welcome radiance when haloed by the sun sinking behind it. The sinking sun...

A sun god.

"Dal," he said, and then bit his tongue. Santabe had warned against saying the name aloud, though she used the name herself. He glanced at the decapitated corpse of a Northerner at his feet. Next to him, the orange uniform of Crueses, the man split open from collarbone to pelvis. The death-blow injuries seemed random but all the victims bore the same deep slices across faces, torsos, appendages—caused by the same source. Who knew the priestess had meant this could happen? He'd just reasoned out the missing information and it terrified him. This is what was meant by Dal manifesting. Suddenly, Santabe's apathy to use the army made sense. Then he remembered what he knew of Dal. "I believe it is over. Safe until morning at least. Summon your healers. Bring help! Supplies! Hurry!"

"Hi-ya, sir." The second scout wheeled his horses in a gallop back to the city, only too glad to escape.

"He's manifested," Teresa said, also reaching understanding. "This is what she meant. Oh saints." She moaned, shifting her feet among the carnage.

"I've seen this before. Not this exactly, but this sort of wasteful killing, only with animals. A *god* kills for the Northerners."

Telo shook his head. It felt like he'd run full tilt and face-first into a brick wall. Why did the Lord permit this to happen? How were they to defeat a god? A being incomprehensible and all-powerful. It had been bad enough when it was only the Northern army to face. He hung on to the only good news he could find. "It killed their men as well. We should be safe until sunrise," he added as much to reassure himself as the others.

Calm. He had to stay calm.

He picked his way forward until he stood on clean grass by the remaining scout. "You said Aveston sent all their soldiers. How about the other cities?"

"Everything. We counted the *pelotónes*. They brought all but maybe one unit from Colina Hermosa. Everything Crueses had was here, though I didn't see men from Suseph. All the other *ciudades-estado* are tiny by comparison." The man looked stricken. "Are we finished?"

Telo touched mind and heart, but it brought no comfort. All their best leadership, their best fighters would have been here. The *capitáns*. *Alcalde* Julian. Was he here? All dead. Who would lead them now? It was all he could do not to join the scout in panicking. "Only the Lord can say. Where was the command positioned?"

The scout pointed to a small rise, separated by a

short space from the larger battle. Bodies lay atop it. Telo hiked up his robe to hold it out of the gore as he strode back into the killing field. With a shake of his head, he dropped it. Too late. His robe had absorbed blood from the ground like a sponge. Too late, just like all else.

"Wait here," he told the scout and Teresa absently. Teresa had bent over a survivor, offering what comfort she could with no healing supplies or bandages, ripping strips from her poncho.

The sunset. That must be why some survived. The sunset had chased off Dal before he finished the job. But who knew? Maybe he had simply grown bored and gone elsewhere. Could you even assign sex to a god? Telo's mind lurched at straws, grasping at wasteful thoughts that didn't matter.

Nothing moved on the small rise as Telo reached it. Here, there were no Northern uniforms. No one to have caused the devastation he witnessed. These wounds weren't cause by any enemy blade. He must face facts: It *was* the hand of a depraved god. He recognized faces of some of the *capitáns*, like Captain Muño with his curly beard, as well as other officers and enlisted men who must have been runners for sending orders to the field. But he saw no man without a uniform and most wore armor. Surely, *Alcalde* Julian would be here in the midst of the action.

Telo moved among the dead, checking each face. Clouds of flies began to gather for the feast. Broken horses lay everywhere. The only clear ground lay where a stallion had pushed bodies aside in its death agony. Its chest and belly had been split wide open, the skin peeled back as though by a death surgeon.

He surveyed each face, then turned back to try again, not finding the one he sought. How were they to survive without *Alcalde* Julian's wisdom? "Lord, let him not be here."

A small hope rose until he spotted the curl and twist in a horse's body. It lay upon something. Telo ran to it, sinking upon his knees.

The horse had fallen on a man's legs and torso. The animal had acted like a shield, protecting from the god's wrath. No cuts prevented the identification of *Alcalde* Julian. The wise face so many came to for reassurance had gone still.

"Ah, my friend," Telo said sadly. "That it should come to this." He fumbled for Julian's hand and found it warm, not cooling. A thready pulse answered his frantic search. The horse hadn't completely crushed Julian.

"Hurry! Bring your horse!" Telo shouted to the remaining scout. They would need help to shift the dead animal. Life remained. Perhaps all was not lost for their chances.

CHAPTER 36

Ramiro stood in the gray world of fog. A part of him knew his body remained on Sancha, dozing as she took him toward Colina Hermosa, then there was nothing but the fog. It shut out everything but his hand before his face—and Salvador.

His brother didn't stand watching this time. He walked with his back turned toward Ramiro. A tug pulled at Ramiro, dragging him along with his brother. He took a step and almost fell. A fall to end him. Unlike before when the ground in the gray world was made up of sand or wet ground, this time his foot touched nothing.

Nothing. No ground below. It was as though they moved in the clouds.

Yet, he remained in place.

Salvador kept moving and something said his brother would not wait. If Ramiro were to see what brought him here, he must follow. Thank the saints, the fog concealed whatever waited below, covering his body from the waist downward. At least he didn't have to see it. He pushed down the fear to venture another step. Again his foot touched nothing, but this time, he didn't falter. The tug coming from Salvador held him upright.

As was the way in dreams, Ramiro accepted it all without surprise, any oddity seeming perfectly normal. He kept pace behind Salvador, never drawing nearer or farther, always two steps back. Never able to move faster than a steady pace.

To his left, the fog unveiled a transparent window, revealing a type of city he'd never seen before—a city of wood. More wood than existed in the entire swamp. The beams of the outer wall were three times the size of the largest oak tree. The houses were wood—all the buildings—built of thin planks hammered over more wood with no stone or stucco to be seen. Guards in yellow and black stood atop the wall to keep people out, while priests in white robes stood outside, red Diviners at their waist, to keep people in.

The sun rode high in the sky and strange sandy-haired people went about their business. In a public square, a priest waved a hand and soldiers struck off the hands and head of a kneeling supplicant, blood splashing into awaiting bowls. A cut appeared across the priest's face. Then a soldier fell with a slice across his back. All over the city of wood, people cried out as their flesh yielded to invisible thrusts—a massacre that murdered the old, the young, the innocent with the guilty and even the animals. As more blood flowed, the people retreating inside became victims as the killing force moved through walls and windows.

Dal was among the Northerners.

The window in the fog closed over and another opened to Ramiro's right, and still he walked, following Salvador, letting the tug from his brother hold him upward. This window showed Crueses and a child with a scraped knee. The father bending over the child was ripped in half in the blink of an eye. Again, the city fell. The citizens torn apart.

Time and again, windows opened to show Ramiro a sword practice accident in Vista Sur, a healer removing a tumor in Suseph, a woman giving birth, all the small incidents of blood bringing Dal's evil until nothing survived. Bile rose in Ramiro's throat, yet he couldn't look away.

A new window to his left showed a woman with a blond braid lying across her threshold in the swamp as something cut her into tiny chunks—a Woman of the Song. The scene flashed to reveal smoke rising from another bungalow house with a wide porch to lift into a moonlit sky. Dal struck at night now and the whole world fell.

"What am I to do?" Ramiro said. "I'm just one man. Only a soldier."

Salvador stopped. Slowly, he turned until Ramiro could look upon his face. He saw his brother's features, his brother's expression, and the eyes holding love.

Love for every soul alive, every rock, every tree, and every grain of sand. Love enough to span the skies.

"You're not Salvador, are you?" Tears touched his eyes at that realization. He would truly never see his brother again.

For answer, the Being touched Ramiro's forehead. A single word reverberated through Ramiro's soul though the figure never opened his lips. *"Intellect."* A finger traced his heart. *"Courage."* Moved to his liver. *"Compassion."* Then dropped to his spleen. *"Righteousness."*

"I'm not the proper person to show this to," Ramiro tried. Awe dropped him onto his knees to wallow in the fog, while desperation pulled his insides into knots. "Why me? Why bring this to me now and not before it all started and Dal began killing?"

A new window opened, revealing a picture of Ramiro in a tent speaking to his father, a scene from his past, from before he'd left with Claire. His Past Self spoke, "Why bother to go to Crueses? They won't help us. And they don't deserve to share our information. Let *them* suffer as we have. It should be their turn for the way they let us down. If they'd been there . . ." Ramiro squirmed with shame, trying to turn away but the vision held him fast.

"I didn't know about Dal," he protested.

That window closed and another opened in its place. This time there was no sound, just a vision of his Past Self walking away from Suero and the women and children by the swamp lake, leaving them without a warning of the Northerners advancing into the swamp.

A third window opened, revealing him standing over Errol, sword raised but hesitation on his face as he faced a handful of Northerners at Jorga's house. Then his face firmed as his Past Self realized he couldn't leave Errol to die. That snapped shut and opened with Jorga wounded and on her stretcher. "I came here with Claire only thinking about what we could gain from you, when I should have been thinking how we could help each other," his Past Self said. "We do need to warn everyone we can reach, all the Women of the Song, the people of my cities, Bromisto's clan, and the other cities. I apologize for thinking otherwise."

The window closed and the fog covered all again. The Being turned to him and touched his heart for a second time. This time the touch brought no voice echoing in his head. Ramiro's mind spun, trying to take in all he'd been shown. It was a dream that had first helped him decide to journey back to the swamp with Claire. A dream sent with a purpose to lead him. "You wanted me away from my people so I would see others' suffering—to change my mind. It was a lesson? A lesson in compassion." Ramiro struggled with the implications, gripping his medallion. He'd passed some kind of test and now graduated to a new level of interaction in the dreams. "Then I have been found worthy, as you face me now. But why me? I'm no saint."

Two windows snapped open of equal size, side by

side, both featuring his Past Self. The first showed instance after instance of petty behavior, every snub Ramiro had ever given, every time he'd let someone down, every moment of jealousy, selfishness or greed, flipping past lies and cowardice in the blink of an eye. The second window moved equally fast, display moments of standing up for another, compassion, empathy, bravery, and on and on. Both equally disturbing in separate ways.

Ramiro wanted to sink through the clouds that supported him—to turn away and not have to see. To disappear. Anything to make it stop. He waited for the window of good to take precedence—for the other to shrink and give way to his better qualities—for good to tip the scales of balance. Isn't that what he was being shown? That his life had been weighed and found to lean toward the side of virtue.

But the visions kept appearing without diminishing on either side, given equal importance. The Being waited.

"We . . . humans . . . aren't evil or heroic," Ramiro stuttered, thinking it out. "We are a mix of . . . both. My parents. My friends. Claire. The Northerners. All of us. Neither one nor the other. Even the saints?" The windows snapped shut, releasing him to stare at the fog swirling around his knees. Strength returned to his heart with acceptance. He stood, getting off his knees. "But that still doesn't explain," Ramiro protested. "Why would you pick me?"

The fog whirled and he got the impression of vastness, a million, million souls contained within, all working for and against one another. All connected to the Being. "I'm not the only one in which you take interest," Ramiro breathed with absolute certainty. "Not the only one you entrust this to. I'm one of millions. But the others . . . they don't see you."

A single word echoed in his brain. There and gone. *"Dreamer."*

I don't understand. Can't you stop what's happening? Stop Dal?"

Salvador's figure held up his hands, and now they were bound with a wire full of barbs and vines of thorns, cutting into his flesh though no blood flowed. He opened his mouth to reveal no tongue or teeth, just a space without end, endless and vast, black as night, and still it expanded. Tiny stars twinkled inside the Being's mouth along with entire worlds. Terror rose in Ramiro's heart. A person could fall into that space and never touch bottom.

"But I don't know how to fight it!"

Ramiro woke with a start, nearly toppling off Sancha before he clamped on with his thighs. Sweat covered his body, as if he'd run miles in full armor. Awake again, the dull ache of missing Claire snapped back into existence, while a phrase and a promise echoed through his soul. *"You will have help."*

The loss of Salvador mixed with fear, tried to turn his strength to water. Had he just seen God?

The thought was too big for him. He needed a priest—a professor. Even his mother's advice. Someone more learned than himself. He pushed it aside to focus elsewhere.

Dal's insatiable lust for blood would destroy, not just the Northerners, but the witches, the *ciudades-estado* and any other humans or animals across the seas and around the world. Claire's song had somehow released it. And who had come up with the plan and urged her to sing it?

He was responsible.

In his selfish desire to save his home and family, he'd unleashed the beast that would ruin it all. That made him accountable to try and put it back, even if he didn't know how.

Somehow, he doubted the scenes shown to him had already happened. Whatever this Dal was—ghost, spirit, demon, or god—it could not yet go through walls or roam at night. What would be the point if it were too late? On the other hand, he no longer believed his father—his people—needed to be warned. His gut said they knew already. Something else drove him to return, some other burden called. They needed him for some task.

"You will have help."

Though he wanted to vomit from pure fear, the words echoed, becoming something to cling against as a storm of indecision and uncertainty raged. He wouldn't have to do it alone. Sancha nodded her head like she read his thoughts—in reality she was probably just shaking off flies—but the motion reassured.

He stroked her neck, deriving comfort from the

touch. "How about we run a couple of miles, girl?" Ramiro slipped from her back to pelt alongside the mare, his breastplate clinking as they ran. His wounds pulled and ached but the pain felt good. As he eased into full speed, she tossed her head and increased her pace to match his, falling into the shared stride they'd practiced endlessly. Heading back home, though, his heart called to Claire. If he got to have someone at his side through what was to come, he wanted it to be her. That would come in the Lord's time. He would make sure of it.

CHAPTER 37

"You'll go in the morning," Jorga said. "Take Errol to the Rose Among Thorns. Warn them."

"Only if you come with me, Grandmother." The fire crackled next to Claire, holding off the terrors of the night. Even at this late hour, the women of the village moved about on their small chores, catering to the menfolk who sat and did nothing now that the day's hunting was over—in many ways more conservative than Ramiro's city people in how they divided the work. Despite being left alone and separate in the camp, Claire didn't feel isolated. Not with her grandmother at her side. "You can ride my horse. The healer says your wound is mending and shouldn't reopen. We'll go together."

"Using the magic takes strength. Strength I can't

rebuild as quickly as I used to." Jorga tapped her bandaged thigh. "You don't notice the drain because you're young. I haven't the magic to frighten a squirrel, girl."

"Then you'll come to share your company with us. The Women of the Song will want to hear from you, not me."

Jorga glanced over at the sleeping Errol, curled in his blankets, his hair matted down with sleep sweat. "There's another reason. He won't speak to me, but my son is easy to read. He sees my end coming, did as soon as the arrow took me. I'd slow you down."

"Stuff and nonsense," Claire said, trying to speak lightly, though her heart said otherwise.

"Lying to yourself fools no one. A seer reports what will be, not what we wish would be." Her grandmother's strict face softened. "'Course I've had fifteen years to understand the truth of his powers. Errol is new to you." She hesitated. "That city man you're missing will come back for you. Nothing will hold such a man back when he's decided, and he's decided on you. Just remember you don't need him—or me—to be strong."

"I know that. That doesn't mean I want to be apart from either of you. Even Women of the Song are stronger together. Say you'll come with me," Claire wheedled in the tone that always worked on her mother.

"Very well. I'll come with you. But I know you'll

be strong when the times comes. I've told you what you need to know—remember firm intent is the key to using the Song." Jorga reached over to pinch her cheek. "Keep that in your silly brain and you won't go wrong. Confidence grows with time, and at least age can't take that from you."

Claire kept her head down and answered with a nod.

Fingers grasped her chin and lifted her face up. Jorga's sharp eyes bore deep. "You think I can't see what's happening? You refuse to practice and only want to speak about theory. I'm afraid this is your mother's doing. She scared you too much. You need to find your belief, girl."

"It wasn't mother," Claire said hotly, pulling away. "Don't blame her."

"I'm not. The blame lies in *you*—You are the one giving in to fear."

"You weren't there. You didn't call a monster. You didn't feel that evil."

"Maybe I wasn't there, but I've felt it now." Jorga shivered. "You think hiding from the responsibility you feel will cure things?"

Claire turned her eyes to the fire, and her grandmother barked a short laugh. "I'm glad to see you know it, too. Running from it solves nothing. Ask your city man—he knows. Are you less than him?

"Listen to me well, girl. The magic is a tool, like a shovel or an ax. Do you blame the sword for killing, or the hand that held it?" When she received no answer, Jorga pressed, "Use it defensively only if that eases your conscience, but don't reject a tool just because you haven't the stomach for the results it causes. Do you hear me?"

"Aye."

"Then think on it. I know the blood in your veins down to the last speck. You're like me. You don't want fear controlling your life. You need to shape your destiny. That means accepting who you are and making your own decisions. Pull on your strength, girl, and it will surprise you. I believe in you. Now get some sleep."

Claire lay back on her blankets. Her grandmother might have constructed a thick shell of self-reliance that made her prickly as a desert pear, as if she didn't care about anything, but inside the woman was soft. Claire smiled to herself. Jorga cared much more than she wanted anyone to know.

Claire couldn't hold back a yawn.

She pulled the blankets to her chin, trying to soak in a feeling of safety, but Jorga's words had left her unsettled. Instead of letting sleep come or facing her own problems, she could only think about Errol always being right with his visions. Her uncle hadn't said much on the trip through the swamp, but when he wasn't with Bromisto, he'd followed her like a puppy. She'd asked him about stopping the "demon," and had been the only one to hear his answer, given almost as if in a trance:

"No man or woman has that power—only the Blessed."

Then the boy had run off and Claire had thought nothing of it—until now. If everything he predicted came true...

Sleep.

Everything seemed bleaker at night. In the morning, she'd laugh at her fears. After all Jorga was alive and well in spite of Errol's worries. She closed her eyes, but repeating the Goodnight Song didn't help calm her. Piece by piece, she built an image of Ramiro in her head, remembering each detail of him. Gradually tight muscles relaxed and sleep claimed her.

She woke what felt like heartbeats later to the sound of screams and metal clanging.

Claire jerked bolt upright.

Swords crashed together. Fighting!

The fire had died down to a soft glow. She searched frantically out in the camp, but could see nothing. As she tried to climb to her feet, Jorga grabbed her wrist. "Stay here."

Claire shook her off. "You stay here, Grandmother. One of us has to see what's happening."

As she crept from the blankets, a shadow took form. A Northern soldier, then two materialized at the edge of the campfire's glow, dressed in leather. Swords in hand, they came toward her, stepping carefully, free hands up as though trying not to startle her. "Witch," one said.

Claire gasped; they spoke in her language. Her tongue clove to the roof of her mouth and the lump in her throat blocked her voice. She fought for words;

the Hornet Tune tangling with the other Songs Jorga had taught her, leaving a jumbled mess. Fear closed her off. Instead of launching into a Song, any Song, she backed from the fire. If she could draw them from Errol and Jorga . . .

Her grandmother lay perfectly still, feigning sleep. Once out in the center of the camp, the hunters would help. The sounds of fighting had not died down. Suero and the other village men might not like the Women of the Song, but they hated the Northerners who had killed their kin.

As Claire took another step away, hoping to lead them off, Jorga snapped upright and seized the leg of the nearest man. He casually backhanded her off, then thrust with his sword. It passed clear through her grandmother's body to pin her briefly to the ground.

A scream broke from Claire's throat.

The Northerner twisted the blade before withdrawing it.

All thought of escape fled. Her will hardened to iron, intent forming.

The Song burst from her, pitched low as Jorga had taught so that it would only reach her target. She aimed not to frighten or injure. Words mattered less than the inner meaning she hurled into them.

And she intended to kill.

Fear, panic,
Cold hands,
Icy shakes.

Knees buckle,
Strength flees.
The grave waits, darkness.
Loss, Emptiness, Defeat.
Foe's too strong.
Strength fails.
Heart stills.
Pain, Agony, Suffering,
Luck fails and failure comes.
Death reaches.
Unmade.
Nothingness.
Inevitability.

The soldiers seemed to fold inward on themselves. Swords dropped from limp hands before she finished the first few lines. As it ended, they collapsed like empty shells, eyes sightless.

Claire stood trembling from head to toe. A child had once asked if the magic could kill men and she had laughed. Laughed at something ridiculous and ignorant.

Now she knew the magic could kill—if she held the intent.

She'd killed without a touch. No better than the evil god Dal. Or these Northerners. Except . . .

She'd acted to protect and defend. Her magic was self-defense. In service of the weak and helpless. That made her different, didn't it?

The anger left her in a rush, replaced with horror.

She hurried to her grandmother, but her body already grew cold. Errol lay over her weeping. "Momma. Momma."

The sight of his tears brought her own. She clutched her uncle and cried. This was her fault. She'd let the fear keep her from acting. If she'd responded immediately, Jorga would be alive. Her weakness robbed her. Fear tried to take all from her: mother, grandmother, even love.

She brushed away tears, straightening her shoulders. Fear shouldn't win. She didn't care what horror Errol predicted next. Her own dread had taken enough from her life.

Her hesitation had caused enough harm.

Resolve grew and her grandmother's last words returned to her. She pulled on her strength. Even if it meant killing, she'd find a way to prove a prophet could be wrong.

Nothing would stop her from convincing the Women of the Song and bringing them to her side. As her grandmother wished, she'd go to the Rose Among Thorns, and once there, she wouldn't be denied.

Another resolution formed: She'd use her magic. No more would she turn from the Song. Never again would someone die because she couldn't act.

They'd stop the Northerners from harming more people.

Her hands balled into fists.

Someone must know how to kill a god.

ACKNOWLEDGMENTS

Most serious writers learn pretty quickly not to put too much time or thought into a sequel. No matter how much you love your characters and storyline, you never know if a book will sell. Writing time is just too valuable to spend working on something that no one may ever see. So serious writers know that they have to put dreams of sequels aside until the ground is firm beneath them. That's why having the opportunity to follow through with a set of characters and a premise is so very special.

I am indebted to David Pomerico from Harper Voyager for giving me the chance to see where Claire and Ramiro might go. He believed readers want more of Julian, Telo, and let me add Teresa to that mix. I will do my best not to disappoint. Thank you, David, for making this writer's dreams come true.

Thank you also to the friends who helped me

make sure Beatriz didn't veer off and become too silly, or that the story didn't stall somewhere in the middle. Carla Rehse, Angie Sandro, and Joyce Alton kept me grounded with their tough critiques.

For hand holding, I want to thank Laura Heffernan and dozens of other friends for continuing to tell me I'm a good writer on the days when it didn't feel true. May you never suffer writers block.

And my last thanks go to my parents, children, and husband for not letting me sit at a computer and dream all day. You make me take part in real life where all ideas originate.

ABOUT THE AUTHOR

MICHELLE HAUCK lives in the bustling metropolis of northern Indiana with her hubby and two kids in college. Besides working with special needs children by day, she writes all sorts of fantasy, giving her imagination free range. A bookworm, she passes up the darker vices in favor of chocolate and looks for any excuse to reward herself. She is the author of the YA epic fantasy *Kindar's Cure*, as well as the short story "Frost and Fog," which is included in anthology *Summer's Double Edge*.

Find her on twitter under @Michelle4Laughs or her blog Michelle4Laughs: It's in the details http://www.michelle4laughs.blogspot.com/.

Discover great authors, exclusive offers, and more at hc.com.